A Magical Christmas

PATRICIA THAYER
MEREDITH WEBBER
LYNNE MARSHALL

MILLS BOON

9 39666403

Published in Great Britain 2014
by Mills & Boon, an imprint of Harlequin (UK) Limited,
Eton House, 18-24 Paradise Road, Richmond, Surrey, TW9 1SR

A MAGICAL CHRISTMAS © 2014 Harlequin Books S.A.

Daddy by Christmas, Greek Doctor: One Magical Christmas and *The Christmas Baby Bump* were first published in Great Britain by Harlequin (UK) Limited.

Daddy by Christmas © 2010 Patricia Thayer
Greek Doctor: One Magical Christmas © 2009 Meredith Webber
The Christmas Baby Bump © 2010 Janet Maarschalk

ISBN: 978-0-263-91209-8
eBook ISBN: 978-1-472-04504-1

05-1114

Harlequin (UK) Limited's policy is to use papers that are natural, renewable and recyclable products and made from wood grown in sustainable forests. The logging and manufacturing processes conform to the legal environmental regulations of the country of origin.

Printed and bound in Spain
by CPI, Barcelona

DADDY BY CHRISTMAS

BY
PATRICIA THAYER

Originally born and raised in Muncie, Indiana, **Patricia Thayer** is the second of eight children. She attended Ball State University, and soon afterwards headed West. Over the years she's made frequent visits back to the Midwest, trying to keep up with her growing family.

Patricia has called Orange County, California, home for many years. She not only enjoys the warm climate, but also the company and support of other published authors in the local writers' organisation. For the past eighteen years she has had the unwavering support and encouragement of her critique group. It's a sisterhood like no other.

When not working on a story, you might find her travelling the United States and Europe, taking in the scenery and doing story research while thoroughly enjoying herself, accompanied by Steve, her husband for over thirty-five years. Together they have three grown sons and four grandsons. As she calls them, her own true-life heroes. On rare days off from writing, you might catch her at Disneyland, spoiling those grandkids rotten! She also volunteers for the Grandparent Autism Network.

Patricia has written for over twenty years and has authored over thirty-six books for Mills & Boon. She has been nominated for both the National Readers' Choice Award and the prestigious RITA®. Her book *Nothing Short of a Miracle* won an *RT Book Reviews* Reviewers' Choice award.

A long-time member of Romance Writers of America, she has served as President and held many other board positions for her local chapter in Orange County. She's a firm believer in giving back.

Check her website at www.patriciathayer.com for upcoming books.

To my own little heroes,
Harrison, Griffin, Connor and Finley.
You're the light of life.

CHAPTER ONE

SHE hated relying on a man.

Mia Saunders glanced around the filled-to-capacity community room at the Mountain View Apartments complex. It was already decorated for Thanksgiving and the tenants were hopeful that they would still be living here at the end of November.

At one of the many card tables were Emma and Charlie Lowery. They'd lived here for over twenty years. So had the Nordbergs, along with Second World War veteran and widower, Ralph Parkinson. They'd all come here for the same reason—affordable rent gave seniors on fixed incomes some independence.

At the age of twenty-nine, Mia was an exception, one of the few, younger tenants who lived in the aging apartment complex.

"You've got to help us, Mia!"

She turned to tiny, gray-haired Nola Madison standing beside her. She was a widow who had lived in the complex since her husband's death ten years ago. With social security and a small pension, Nola could survive living alone here without burdening her children.

"Nola, I'm going to try, but I'm not sure how much I can do."

"You're a lawyer," Nola said, her soft hazel eyes seeming larger behind her bifocals.

"Not yet. I've only just started law school." That had been put on hold this past semester and she had no idea when she could start up again.

"But you will talk to the owner for us when he gets here."

"*If* he gets here," Mia added. So far that hadn't happened. They'd tried a half-dozen times to have a meeting with the man to discuss the fifty-year-old apartment complex's crumbling condition. No improvements had been done in years.

"It seems the new owner has been avoiding us."

"Well, he has good reason. He doesn't want to fix things any more than the last owner." Joe Carson, another of the elderly tenants, spoke up behind her. That got the crowd going.

Mia waved her hand and they quieted down. "This isn't getting us anywhere. In all fairness…" She glanced down at the paper. "Mr. Jarrett McKane only took possession of this property a few months ago."

"McKane," Nola repeated. "I wonder if he's any relation to the teacher at the high school, Kira McKane. My granddaughter, Hannah, talks about her all the time."

Joe stepped forward. "I don't care who he's related to, he has to take care of our demands."

Joe's wife, Sylvia, gasped. "What if he evicts us?"

That started more grumbles around the crowded room.

Mia eyed the tenants she'd gotten to know since coming to Winchester Ridge when her brother, Reverend Bradley Saunders, took over as pastor of the First Community Church a half mile away. She'd found a one-bedroom apartment in the affordable complex about three years ago when Brad and his wife, Karen, decided to make the small Colorado ranching community a permanent home. It was a perfect place for raising a family.

All Mia's life, it had been her brother who'd been there for her. Brad had never given up on his little sister, even when she gave up on herself. Over the years, he'd pulled her back from some pretty dark places, and let her know that she was important and loved. When their parents disowned her, Brad stood by her and helped her get her act together and get into college.

She'd do anything for him. Sadness washed over Mia, knowing she would never get the chance again.

Sam Parker hurried into the room and called out, "One of those fancy SUVs just pulled up. A shiny black one."

Those standing scurried to find a seat as if they'd been caught doing something wrong. Mia didn't rush much these days, but she felt the excitement and nervousness as she took a chair at the head table, and then turned her attention toward the door.

Nothing had prepared her for this man.

Jarrett McKane walked into the room as if he owned it. That was because he did. He was well over six feet, and his sheepskin jacket made him look ever bigger as his broad shoulders nearly filled the doorway. There was a brooding look in his ebony eyes that made him look intimidating.

It didn't work on her.

She was Preston Saunders's daughter. No one could intimidate like the CEO of a Fortune 500 company. Though there was no doubt that Jarrett McKane could give good old Preston a run for the title. Intimidator.

She released a breath and put on a smile. "Mr. McKane. It's good of you to come."

Jarrett turned toward her, his eyes showing some surprise and interest, and he returned a smile, showing off a row of straight white teeth. Oh boy. He was going to try to charm her.

"Ms. Saunders?"

"That would be me."

He walked to the table, pulling off his leather gloves then he held out his hand. "It's a pleasure to meet you, Ms. Saunders. I must say I've enjoyed your colorful letters."

She tried not to react as his large hand engulfed hers. *Get down to business,* she told herself and withdrew her hand.

"Well, they seem to have worked. You're here." She motioned to the chair across from her. "Please have a seat and we can begin."

Jarrett McKane didn't like this woman having the upper hand. Well, it wasn't going to last long. He eyed the pretty, long-haired brunette. Even tied back into a ponytail, those curls seemed to have a mind of their own. Her eyes caught his attention right off, a dark, smoky blue. She looked to be in her mid-twenties. He hated trying to guess women's ages, but he knew she was old enough.

He slipped off his jacket and she watched with interest. He liked that. Maybe this would be easier than he thought.

Mia Saunders glanced down at the paper in front of her. "As I stated in my letters, Mr. McKane, there are several apartments that need your immediate attention. The bathrooms in several of the units aren't working properly, and many of the heaters aren't functioning at all. They're outdated and possibly dangerous." She looked up. "The conditions here are becoming unlivable, Mr. McKane." She slid the list across the table to him. "We need you to fix these items immediately."

Jarrett read over the itemized page. He already knew it

would cost him a fortune. "And the previous owner should have taken care of these problems."

"Since you are the current owner, Mr. McKane, it's your responsibility now."

He glared at her.

She ignored it. "I'm sure you bought this property at a reduced price, and a good businessman would know the condition of the place. And since you are the owner now, we're asking that you please address these problems."

Jarrett glanced around at the group. He hadn't expected to find this when he arrived, especially not mainly senior citizens. He pushed away any sentimentality. "I can't fix these problems."

"Can't or won't?" she retorted.

"I don't see how that matters."

"It does to us, Mr. McKane."

"Okay, for one thing, I haven't received any rent payment since I took over the property."

"And you won't until we see some good faith from you. Some of these people don't have hot water or heat. Winter is here."

"Then relocating you all is the only answer." He stood. "Because in a few months, I'll be tearing the place down."

The group gasped, but Mia Saunders still looked calm and controlled as she said, "I don't think so, Mr. McKane."

Jarrett was surprised by her assertiveness. He wasn't used to that, especially not from a woman. No that wasn't true, his sister-in-law, Kira, gave him "what for" all the time.

Ms. Saunders held up another piece of paper. "We all have leases giving us six months to relocate. When you bought the building, your lawyer should have told you about it. Unless you didn't use an attorney."

Dammit, he didn't have an answer to that.

"And you still have to honor our leases."

He shook his head. "Can't do it. I want to start demolition by the first of the new year. And I'm sure the town council will go along with me since this is the site for a new computer-chip plant. It's estimated to bring over a hundred jobs to this town." He saw the panicked looks on the tenant's faces and added, "And I'll help anyone who wants to be relocated, but I can't let you stay here for six months." Finished, he headed toward the door.

"You might not have a choice," Mia called to him.

He turned around, perversely enjoying the exchange. He liked the fire in her pretty eyes, the set of her jaw. He wondered if he could find a way to sway her loyalty. A little dinner and maybe some romancing might help his cause. "I don't think you can win this fight, Ms. Saunders. But I'm willing to discuss it with you, another time."

She rose from her chair and that was when he noticed her rounded belly. Pregnant? Damn, she's pregnant.

Mia Saunders seemed to enjoy the surprise. "You can count on it, when we see you in court."

Thirty minutes later, Jarrett was still thinking about the attractive Mia Saunders as he drove his Range Rover down the highway. He shook his head. What the hell was he doing fantasizing about a pregnant woman? A woman carrying another man's baby.

He turned off onto the road leading toward the McKane ranch. After selling off his part of the family cattle ranch, he hadn't called in here much to start with. He and his half brother, Trace, hadn't gotten along while they were growing up, but the past few years that had slowly begun to change.

Maybe he was getting soft. Of course, his brother's wife, Kira, had a lot to do with it.

Now, he was an uncle and he was crazy about his niece, Jenna. She could ask him to walk over hot coals, and he'd do it, smiling. At three years old, the toddler had his number.

He parked around the back of the house. They hadn't always been a happy family: he recalled just a while back when Trace and Kira were barely surviving a crumbling marriage. Kira's problems getting pregnant had put a strain on them that had nearly ended their five-year relationship. Then a miracle had happened, and now they had Jenna.

Climbing the back steps to the century-old ranch house, Jarrett's attention turned to another pregnant woman, Mia Saunders. It was true what they said about expectant mothers, they did have a glow about them. And unless he had been mistaken, she'd directed that rosy glow toward him.

He knocked on the door and walked in. "Everyone decent?" He peered into the kitchen, knowing he'd be welcome. That hadn't always been true. There was a time he'd tried everything to one-up his younger brother. In their youth, he had wanted nothing to do with the ranch, or with the half brother who'd gotten all the attention. So, after their father died, Jarrett had accepted his share in dollars.

It had taken them years to work out their differences. And with the help of Kira and a sweet little girl named Jenna they'd worked through a lot of their problems, mainly just trying to be brothers.

Kira stood at the stove. "We have a three-year-old. There isn't any time to get indecent." His sister-in-law smiled as she came to him and gave him a kiss on the cheek. "Hi, Jarrett. It's good to see you."

"Hi, sis," he said, returning the hug. He'd used to have

trouble with her being so demonstrative, but she said they were family, and that was how family acted.

Jarrett heard a squeal and little Jenna came charging into the room.

"Unca Jay. Unca Jay," the girl called.

Jarrett caught her up in his arms, swung her around, kissing her cheeks and blowing raspberries. "How's my Jenna girl today?"

The child's tiny mouth formed a pout. "Mommy put me in time-out. I was sad."

Kira arrived on the scene, brushing back her long blond hair. "Tell Uncle Jarrett what you did."

"I got into Mommy's makeup."

Suddenly, Jarrett could see the faint remnants of lipstick on her mouth. "Uh-oh."

"I just want to be pretty, like Mommy." She turned those big brown eyes on him. "Are you mad at me, too?"

"Never." He kissed her. "But you're already pretty, you don't need makeup." He glanced at Kira. "But remember you don't like anyone getting into your stuff, so you shouldn't get into other people's things."

"'Kay." She looked at her mom. "Can I play now? I promise to be good."

Kira nodded, and they watched the child run out of the room. She turned to Jarrett. "Thanks for backing me up."

He nodded. "I don't know how you ever punish her. It would tear me up."

"It part of being a parent."

"That's a job I don't want."

Kira smiled. "You just haven't found the right woman."

He arched an eyebrow. "I've found a lot of women and I like it that way. There's safety in numbers." He winked at her. "Among other things."

She shook her head. "Like I said, you haven't found the right woman."

"But I found mine."

They both looked toward the door to see Trace. His brother went straight to his wife and kissed her. Jarrett hated the envy that engulfed him. To his surprise, his thoughts turned to Mia Saunders again. Well, damn.

"Hi, bro," Jarrett greeted him. "How's the cattle business?"

"If you came out here more, you'd know for yourself."

"If I came out here more, you'd put me to work. You know how I feel about ranching. I'm doing just fine the way things are."

"I take it you're still trying to get by on your looks and your wit. So what brings you out here?"

Jarrett shrugged. "Do I need a reason?"

Trace hugged his wife close. "Of course not. Stay for supper."

Jarrett smiled. "Don't mind if I do." Whatever had happened during their childhood didn't seem to mean much anymore. It had taken years, but Jarrett had finally realized that Trace wasn't competing with him. After they'd found natural gas on McKane land a few years ago, they'd worked together and ensured a prosperous future for them all.

They also found they could be friends.

Kira went to check on Jenna while Trace poured two mugs of coffee. He handed one to Jarrett and the brothers sat down at the large farm kitchen table.

"So, I hear you bought the old apartment buildings on Maple."

Jarrett frowned. He'd been trying to keep the project quiet. "Where did you hear that?"

"It's a small town. There aren't many secrets."

Kira returned. "We heard it at church last Sunday. One

of your tenants, her brother used to be our pastor. Reverend Brad Saunders." She shook her head. "It was such a tragedy about their deaths."

"I don't go to church. What happened to them?"

"A few months ago Brad and his wife, Karen, went on a missionary trip and their small plane crashed in Mexico. Poor Mia."

"What about her husband?

Kira raised an eyebrow. "Mia doesn't have a husband."

Interest sparked in Jarrett, catching him off guard. "Surely the guy responsible for the baby will step up."

Kira exchanged a glance with Trace. "There is no guy to step up. It's not Mia's baby."

CHAPTER TWO

JARRETT stared at his sister-in-law. "Okay, it's been a few years since Biology 101, but I would remember something like this."

"Mia is a surrogate," she explained. "Or maybe I should say she was."

"There's definitely still a baby," he added, recalling the generous curve of her stomach.

"But no parents."

"So what's the story?"

Kira gave her husband a quick glance. "It wasn't exactly public knowledge, but Mia is carrying her brother and sister-in-law's baby."

"The hell you say!"

Suddenly Jenna came running into the kitchen. "Unca Jay, you said a bad word."

Jarrett ignored Trace's disapproving stare. "I'm sorry, sweetie," he told her. "I'll try to be better."

"You got to give me a nickel for the jar." The child held out her tiny hand and smiled. "Pay me."

The little thief. With a smile he dug into his pocket. "Here's a quarter."

"Jenna, go wash up for supper," her mother said.

"Okay, Mommy." She smiled and went and hugged Trace. "Hi, Daddy."

While father and daughter exchanged pleasantries Jarrett tried to wrap his head around this news.

Once the child left, Jarrett turned back to Kira. "Was Mia Saunders going to give the reverend and his wife her baby?"

Kira shook her head. "No, she's been carrying Brad and Karen's baby all along. Surely you've heard of a fertilized embryo being implanted in another woman and she carries the baby when the biological mother can't. In this case, Mia was doing this for her brother and his wife."

Kira got up from the table, went to the oven and checked the roast, then she returned to the table. "But now everything has changed with Brad and Karen's death. Mia will not only be giving birth to her niece or nephew in about six weeks, but now she'll be raising the baby, too."

In the past, Jarrett had always run as far as possible from romantic entanglements. He didn't do relationships beyond a few months, no matter how beautiful or intriguing the woman. It would mean he'd have to put his feelings on the line, to be vulnerable—something he'd avoided since he'd been a kid when his mother had died. Still grieving, he'd soon learned that his father's new wife didn't want to deal with someone else's kid.

He'd concluded a long time ago he wasn't cut out to be a family man.

Yet, this woman caused him to pause. Why was he even giving her a second thought?

A woman with a baby?

He recalled the scene from earlier that day in the community room filled with all those elderly tenants and how Mia Saunders had led the pack. Those amazing blue eyes had dared him to challenge her demands. She'd tried to act tough, but he could see her nervousness.

"Does she have any other family?"

Kira shook her head. "From what I heard there was only her brother. Since her brother was a pastor, Brad and Karen didn't exactly have a fat bank account. Mia had been going to law school, but she had to drop out after the accident. I know she does Web design because she works from home, which is important now with the baby coming. The church is helping as much as possible."

And he was about to throw her out of her home. "When is the kid due?"

"Would you believe Christmas day?" Kira smiled. "I feel that's a good omen. I believe there's a miracle out there for her."

Jarrett hoped it happened before the New Year.

"They have the best food around," Jarrett told Neil Fulton the next afternoon at lunch. "Prime Cut's Barbecue is outstanding. It's all local beef, too. Some of it comes from my brother's ranch."

The fifty-five-year-old business executive looked as if he'd spent a lot of time behind a desk. His skin was pale and his hair thinning. "You own part of that, too?"

"No, I got out of ranching a long time ago." Jarrett hadn't liked all the hard work or a father who drove him to do more than a kid should have to do. For what? To wait out another drought, low cattle prices or a freezing winter without going bankrupt. And you're still poor. He liked the finer things in life, and he'd found a way to get them.

"But my brother is good at what he does. I guarantee you'll love the beef."

"Maybe another time, I usually eat a lighter lunch." Neil looked over his half-glasses at Jarrett. "My wife insists on it."

Jarrett would do everything he could to move this deal along. With the slow economy, he needed to make sure this sale didn't fall through. If only he could find a place for the Mountain View tenants, life would be perfect.

"Why not have the best of both worlds?" he said. "If you lived around here, you could enjoy hearty meals, because there's plenty of hiking and skiing around to keep you in shape. And there's a great gym where you can work out."

Neil smiled. "You've kept in shape well enough since you left football. How do you do it?"

Jarrett couldn't believe people still remembered his college career. But he'd use it if it helped seal the deal with Fulton Industries.

"I have a home gym," he explained. You and your wife will have to come by and I'll show you. It's Robin, isn't it?"

Fulton nodded, then returned to scanning the menu.

"I also want to show you both some houses in the area. There are several estates with horse property. Riding is another great way to keep in shape."

Neil raised a hand. "First, I need to put all my energy into building this plant. Robin will stay in Chicago until we can get things moving along. From past experience, once my wife gets going on a new house, she'll throw herself into decorating it."

"Well, when that happens I'll have one of my top agents help her find the perfect house."

Neil frowned. "You don't know Robin. She's hard to please."

Jarrett bet he could handle her. "Then I'll work with her personally."

Neil laughed. "You may live to regret that offer."

Before Jarrett could respond, a young man approached the table. "Excuse me, sir, are you Jarrett McKane?"

"Yes, I am."

The guy pulled out a manila envelope from inside

his jacket. "This is for you." He smiled. "You've been served."

Jarrett felt his face heat with anger. Then he glanced across the restaurant as the man stopped at a table. He sat down beside a dark-haired woman. Mia Saunders.

"Is there a problem, Jarrett?" Neil asked.

"No. Just a minor disagreement with a client."

Mia raised a hand and waved.

"This doesn't have anything to do with our project, does it?"

Jarrett nodded at Mia. "Like I said it's a minor problem. Nothing I can't handle."

The following morning, Mia drove to her doctor's appointment in Grand Junction, about forty miles away. The roads were clear so far, and she only hoped that northwest Colorado's winter weather would hold off for another month.

Since she was in her last trimester, she had to travel there regularly. Not a problem; she liked her doctor, Lauren Drake. In her forties, the attractive fertility specialist had been there for her from the beginning of the surrogacy. She'd also supported Mia through Brad and Karen's horrible accident and death.

"How have you been feeling?"

"Great," Mia said. "Except the baby is pretty active. He or she is kicking all the time."

The attractive blonde was tall and slender and happily married to her college sweetheart. Mia should hate her for her perfect life, but Lauren was too nice to hate. She had become a good friend. And Mia needed as many friends as she could get.

"I know the pregnancy is going well, but I'm worried about you, Mia. Your life has been turned upside down in the past few months. And now, you aren't even sure about a place to live."

"So what else is new?" Sadness crept in. She missed her brother desperately. He'd been her rock for most of her life. Even with Brad's help, it had taken her years to get her act together. Now, she felt on the verge of falling apart. What kind of mother would that make her? Not a good one.

"I know you've had to deal with a lot," the doctor said. "You only planned to be the aunt to this baby. Now, you're going to be the mother, unless you've changed your mind on that."

Mia shook her head. Well before Brad and Karen had moved ahead with the surrogacy, everyone had agreed that if something ever happened to them, Mia would raise the child. Yet, no one had ever imagined the loss of both parents even before the baby arrived.

"It's a big responsibility, Mia. Even when there's a father in the picture."

Mia added, "A single mother with no money and no apparent means of income isn't the best candidate."

"Don't say that."

Mia hadn't hidden anything from the doctor before the procedure began. Dr. Drake knew about everything in her past.

"There are agencies around to help, too."

Mia shook her head. She had some money set aside. And Brad and Karen had some left-over insurance money. "I just want a job."

"I'd prefer you didn't take any more on your plate right now."

Mia fought her panic. "Is there something wrong?"

Lauren shook her head. "Just watching your blood pressure. It's a little high, but no worries right now." She quickly changed the subject. "Have you picked out any names?"

"No, I haven't thought about it." She had some personal things of Karen's, a baby book that might give her a clue and a letter from her sister-in-law that Mia wasn't supposed to open until the birth of the baby.

"Well, do it. And stop trying to take on everyone's problems. Think about yourself for a change. You won't get the chance after the baby comes."

Mia knew she couldn't walk away from her neighbors. Not now. They'd been so good to her. "We're just trying to stay in our homes for a little while longer. We're going to court next week, and we're hoping the judge will rule in our favor."

Having a place to live was her main concern right now. She couldn't be homeless again. Not with a baby.

A week later, Jarrett walked into the courtroom. What he didn't expect to see were several of the tenants there, too. Of course, leading the pack was Mia Saunders.

She looked professional in her dark skirt and a long wine-colored sweater draped over her rounded stomach. Her rich brown hair was pulled back from her oval face and clipped at the base of her neck. She didn't wear makeup. She didn't try to highlight her already striking blue eyes or her rosy-hued lips. She did nothing to enhance her good looks. She didn't need to.

He wasn't interested in her anyway. She had issues he didn't want to deal with. Yet it seemed he would be dealing with her whether he liked it or not. He hoped today would end any and all future meetings.

That was why he'd brought his lawyer. Matthew Holliston wasn't only his attorney but a longtime friend from high school. And he was damn good at his job.

Although, when Matt had heard that Judge Barbara Gillard was going to hear the case, he'd been worried. She had a reputation as a tough judge, and something else went against Jarrett. Years ago, he had dated Judge Gillard's sister, Amy, in high school. It hadn't ended well, so Matt had suggested that he make a generous offer to the building tenants. They had written up something to appease the judge and, they hoped, the tenants.

"Good morning, Ms. Saunders," Jarrett said.

She nodded. "Mr. McKane."

He was quickly drawn into her sparkling gaze and lost the ability to say more. That was when Matt stepped in and guided him to his seat.

The court deputy soon called their case. "The Mountain View tenants versus Jarrett McKane Properties."

"Here, your honor," Matt acknowledged. He and Jarrett went to the front of the courtroom.

"We're also here, your honor." Mia Saunders walked up with two elderly people.

Everyone waited in silence as Judge Gillard glanced over the case papers in front of her. There were also pictures and estimates for several repairs. The judge's gaze turned to Jarrett. "How can you expect your tenants to live like this?"

Jarrett started to speak, but Matt stepped in. "Your honor, as you read in our deposition, my client only purchased the property three months ago."

The judge just looked at him, then said, "I assume, Mr. McKane, you did a walk-through of the property before purchasing it so you had to know the conditions. And if that wasn't enough, Ms. Saunders contacted you several times. So you should have, at least, begun to make some of the repairs."

"Your honor," Matt tried again. "It would be a waste of time and money. Mr. McKane will be demolishing the building so a factory can be built there—a computer-chip plant that will bring several new jobs into the area."

"Your honor," Mia Saunders interrupted. "The tenants had to sign a lease agreement when they moved in. It states that if the property is ever sold they have six months to relocate." She flashed a cold stare at Jarrett, then went on. "Even with the change of ownership, until each tenant is contacted about their eviction, they still have five months and three weeks to stay in their apartments."

Matt fought back. "Your honor, isn't six months a little excessive? A thirty-day notice is a standard agreement now."

The judge looked at the lease in her hand. "Well, this agreement *is* from 1968." She glanced over her glasses. "But no one thought to change it." She held up the photos. "I'm more concerned that many of these apartments aren't suitable to live in."

Nola stepped forward and introduced herself. "Your honor, I'm Nola Madison, one of the longtime tenants. May I speak?"

The judge nodded. "Yes, Mrs. Madison, you may."

The tiny woman made her way to the front. "Many of us have lived at Mountain View Apartments for a long time. It's our home, and like all of us, it's getting old. With a little work and some minor repairs, we can live comfortably for the winter. Please don't ask us to leave yet."

"You know that in six months you will have to move anyway," the judge told her.

Nola glanced around to her group of friends and neighbors. "Next week is Thanksgiving, your honor. For years a lot of us have spent it together. Christmas, too. If this is our last year, I really would like to be with my friends. My family. And we need the time to find affordable places to live and to save the extra money to move. So staying until March would be helpful."

Seeing the judge blink several times, Jarrett knew he was in big trouble.

"Your honor," Matt tried again. "This is not a good situation, but there is an important business deal pending here. A factory is to be built on this site. A factory that will bring jobs into our community."

The judge straightened. "From which your client will benefit nicely, I'm sure. While these people will lose their homes." She glared daggers toward Jarrett. "Mr. McKane, you knew the conditions of the lease, and you also knew the deplorable condition of the building when you made the purchase."

He didn't agree or disagree. "What I had planned was to help the tenants relocate," he replied.

The judge wasn't buying it. "Seems to me if you'd been sincere you would have answered their letters three months ago," she observed. "Now you're throwing them out of their homes as though nothing matters as long as you make a profit. Well, it's not always about profit, Mr. McKane. My ruling is that you make the necessary repairs to bring the building up to code. I'll waive the fine as long as you begin immediately."

Jarrett bit the inside of his mouth. "Yes, your honor."

"Don't think that's all there is, Mr. McKane. You're to make all repairs so the place is livable." Judge Gillard paused and looked at Mia Saunders. "Is there a vacant apartment?"

Mia nodded. "Yes, your honor, but the apartment is unlivable."

The judge nodded. "Good. What's the number?"

"Two-oh-three-B."

"Jarrett McKane, I order you to move into apartment

203B at Mountain View complex until all repairs are completed. No eviction until March first. Although, I do want to see you back here after the holidays to learn about your progress." She hit the gavel on the block. The sound echoed around the courtroom. "Court adjourned."

"Judge, this is highly irregular," Matt called, but she had already exited the courtroom.

That left Jarrett thinking about everything he was about to lose. No, he couldn't lose this. He'd fix this, like he'd fixed everything all his life. He'd figure out a way to get what he wanted. He always did.

The next day, Jarrett and Matt parked in front of the Mountain View Apartments. "You can't bend any of the rules, Jarrett," Matt told him. "You have to sleep here every night, eat here and even work here. You can only go to your home to get more clothes and food, that's all, or the judge could toss you in jail. You know she means business when she instructed me to escort you here personally."

"Dammit, Matt, you'd better get me out of this mess. If Fulton finds out, he'll walk away from the deal."

"Well, unless he'll wait until April, you're in big trouble. The only alternative you have is talking them into moving out."

Jarrett was frustrated. Thanks to Mia Saunders, he had to figure out something. But honestly there weren't many options since housing was limited in Winchester Ridge.

He looked toward the yellow-and-brown structure with the peeling paint and sagging rain gutters. It seemed even worse with winter-bare trees, but the grass was cut and the hedges trimmed.

"In its day, the place was probably a showcase," Matt observed.

"Well, it's not 1960," he told his friend. "And I'm only

going to do the minimum that needs to be done. It's a waste of time and money."

Jarrett looked out the Mercedes' windshield to see someone coming toward them. It was the older woman, Mrs. Madison. He pressed the button so the window went down.

"Hello, Mr. McKane." She slowly made her way to the car. "I'm not sure if you remember me, I'm Nola Madison."

He got out of the car. "Were you checking up to see if I was coming?"

She smiled despite his rudeness. "As a matter of fact, we were watching for you, but only to warn you about what to expect in your apartment." She shook her head. "It was once the manager's, but he didn't take very good care of it. We tried the best we could to clean it up." She held out a key dangling from a heart keychain. "But I'm afraid it needs more work than any of our places."

Feeling like a heel, Jarrett took the key from her, and pulled his jacket together against the cold. "You shouldn't be out in this weather, Mrs. Madison."

"Please, call me Nola. Let's go inside, but it isn't much warmer."

Jarrett grabbed his duffel bag from the back of the car, asked Matt to have his car brought over from the office, and followed the woman up the walk. They went into a bare lobby. He'd seen this area before and knew how bad it looked, but it hadn't mattered to him, since it was tagged for demolition. He headed for the elevators to find signs that read, Out of Order.

On the walk-through of the property he hadn't noticed that. "There is no elevator?"

She shook her head. "Not in the last year."

Jarrett recalled that day in the community room—two of

the tenants were in wheelchairs. "How do the handicapped get upstairs?"

She led him to the wrought-iron staircase and they started the climb. "Oh, we found two tenants who were willing to move upstairs, and Joe and Sylvia's son, Ryan, built ramps for both Margie and Harold. Now they can get in and out or their apartments. It's important to be independent."

"Who exchanged apartments?"

"Well, Mia was one who moved upstairs, and when her brother, Reverend Brad, was alive he used to help us with a lot of repairs. Many of his congregation did, too."

"Where was the owner? Some of these repairs are required by law."

She shook her head. "He threatened to double our rent if we kept complaining. So we started fixing things ourselves." They made it to the second floor. "But some things we can't fix. We need an expert."

Once again he was confronted with dingy walls and worn carpet. They passed a few doors, then she stopped in front of his apartment. He paused. Hell, he was afraid to go inside.

Suddenly the door across the hall opened and Mia Saunders stepped out. She actually smiled at him and he felt a strange tightness in his chest. "Moving in, Mr. McKane?"

She was dressed in a long blue sweater that went to midthigh, with a pair of black leggings covering those long legs. He looked back at her face. "Seems I am. Looks like we're going to be neighbors."

"Isn't that nice," Nola said, then glanced at her watch. "Oh, my, I just remembered I have a doctor's appointment. I don't know where my head is today. Mia, could you show Mr. McKane around?"

Mia frowned. "Do you need a ride, Nola?"

"No, thank you, dear, my daughter is coming by." With a wave, the older woman walked off.

Mia didn't like Nola's not-so-subtle disappearing act. Why did anyone need to show Jarrett McKane around?

She walked to the apartment entrance. "Brace yourself." She swung open the door, reached in and flicked on the lights, then motioned for him to go inside first. He frowned and stepped into the main room. She heard his curse and couldn't help but smile as she followed him in.

The apartment walls needed paint, but not before numerous holes in the plaster were patched. Under the slipcovers that Nola and her welcoming committee had recently put on, the furniture was thrift-store rejects.

"Joe cleaned the carpet, or what's left of it. It's probably the original. At least the place doesn't smell as if someone died in here anymore."

Without comment, he continued down the hall and peered into the bath. Again another curse.

She called after him. "It might not look very good, but I can guarantee you Nola and Sylvia cleaned it within an inch of its life. And there are fresh towels. And they made up the bed for you, too." Then she murmured to herself, "Why they're being so nice to you, I have no idea."

The good-looking Jarrett McKane came out and stood in front of her. His dark hair had been cut and styled recently. His clothes were top-of-the-line, too. Everything about him rang out success and power. So why was she even noticing him?

Hormones, she concluded. It was just late-pregnancy hormones. She'd learned a long time ago to stay away from men like him.

"Why did they do all this?" he finally asked.

Jarrett McKane was standing too close, but she refused to step back. She refused to let him intimidate her.

"It's their way of being neighborly," she told him. "It's the same with everyone here. Over the years, they've all become a family. Some are alone. Some have family that didn't have time for them so they take care of each other."

"Or it's their way to get me to not tear the place down."

She smiled, not wanting him to see her anger. "It's just some towels and linens and a few home-cooked meals. But yes, they feel it's worth a try. Enjoy your stay." She turned and started to leave when he called her name.

When she turned around, he gave her a sexy grin. "Did you do anything to sway me, Ms. Saunders?"

Her heart began to pound in her chest. "There might be a plate of oatmeal raisin cookies on the kitchen counter."

"I'm looking forward to seeing how far you'll go to persuade me."

Mia arched her aching back, causing her stomach to be front and center. "I'm afraid cookies are as far as I'm willing to go."

CHAPTER THREE

MIA couldn't get out of there fast enough.

She stepped inside her apartment and closed the door. She didn't want Jarrett McKane in her life, or in her space. And he was suddenly in both.

A long time ago, she'd learned about men who thrived on control. Her father was one of those. It had taken her years to get out from under his reign and finally to be free of him.

She walked across her cozy living area. A secondhand sofa and chair faced the small television. A triangular rug hid a lot of the worn carpet underneath. A small table off the galley kitchen was used for eating and for working on her computer.

Her laptop was the only thing of value that she had and the only means she had these days of make a living. Despite her privileged upbringing, she'd never been materialistic. Maybe that was the reason it had been so easy to walk away, or in her case, run away.

To Preston and Abigail Saunders their daughter had always been a problem, a disappointment from the start. An overweight child, Mia had morphed into a rebellious teenager. She had never fitted into her Boston society family. So, once she was of age, she'd just disappeared from their lives.

Even Brad had eventually bucked their father's plans for him. Instead, her older brother had became an ordained minister and had ended up disowned, too.

Now she'd lost her only family. She caressed her stomach, feeling the gentle movement of the baby. At least she'd have a part of Brad and Karen and she vowed to love and protect this child. So she wasn't about to let her parents know where she was. Or let them find this baby.

Mia sat down in the chair, still in awe of the life she carried inside her. Onetime wild child, Margaret Iris Ashley Saunders was going to have a baby. She blew out a breath. She was going to be a mother and D-day was approaching soon. There were so many things she had to get done before Christmas.

She closed her eyes. For months, she'd had to push aside all the feelings she was having for this baby. A mother's feelings. The only thing that had saved her was knowing this child would always be in her life. Brad and Karen would have been the perfect parents and she could be the favorite aunt who spoiled the child.

Now, Mia had to step up and be a parent to this baby. She wasn't sure she was cut out to do it.

That afternoon, with the help of his office staff, Jarrett had made several phone calls. He'd finally found someone to start on the repairs. A local furnace repairman was to come out. He'd also contacted the handyman who serviced some of his other properties to help out with some of the minor fixes.

Flipping his phone shut, he decided to wait downstairs and get out of his depressing apartment for a while. In the hall, the door across from his opened and Mia walked out carrying a large trash bag. She stiffened the second she saw him.

He smiled. "Hello, Mia."

She nodded stiffly. "Mr. McKane."

She was dressed in her standard black pants and over-size blouse, but with an added long sweater for warmth.

"I don't see why we can't be on a first-name basis since we're going to be neighbors."

"You're the man who's evicting us. Why would I get friendly with the enemy?"

He took the bag from her. "It doesn't seem to bother the others." He gave her a sideways glance. "Someone must have really have done a number on you."

She glanced away. "Now you're a psychiatrist?"

"No, just observant."

"Well, observe somewhere else. Thanks to you, I have a lot on my mind."

He wasn't crazy about having to move her in her condition. "I'm not your enemy, Mia. I'm trying to find all of you places to live."

"We can't afford most of the other places."

Was that his fault? "The rent here is well below average for this area. Even if I kept the place and did all the repairs, I'd have to raise the rent."

"Well, you can't yet. Some of us are barely getting any heat or hot water."

"I'm taking care of that."

"I can't tell you how many times we heard that from the last owner."

"The last owner hadn't been court-ordered," Jarrett said. He slowed his pace so she could keep up. He knew little or nothing about pregnant women. Only that Kira had had a rough time with her pregnancy and had had to stay in bed the last few months.

"That's where I'm going now," he continued, "to meet with a furnace guy."

She stopped. "You mean we could have some heat today?"

He shrugged. "I'm paying him extra to start right away."

They continued their way down the stairs to the main lobby. "I would like to ask a favor," he said.

She paused with a glare.

He hid a smile as he raised a hand. "Good Lord, woman, do you mistrust everyone? I only want you to help get everyone together so we see who has the worst problems and fix them first."

"Then come to the community room. It's where a lot of the tenants hang out because it has a working heater."

They stepped outside into the frigid weather. He first tossed the sack into the Dumpster, and then they continued on to the center.

"I hear your baby is due on Christmas day."

She gave him a sideways glance. "Who told you that?"

"My sister-in-law, Kira McKane. You both go to the same church."

She seemed relieved. "How does she feel about you tossing us out of here?"

"I haven't tossed out anyone, and according to the judge, I won't be able to until the spring." Not with Barbara Gillard watching him anyway. If only he could come up with a way to convince everyone to leave a few months earlier.

His only other chance was to get Fulton to hold off on the takeover date. They couldn't begin construction until the ground thawed. But he wouldn't get his money either.

He'd put a lot into this project, buying up the surrounding land, including this place. He had too much to lose.

And it would cost him even more every day Mountain View Apartments stayed open. And now he was being held prisoner here.

While Jarrett went to the community room, Mia knocked on Joe's door and asked him and Sylvia to gather the other tenants and bring them to the community room.

Sending the others on ahead, Mia then went to Nola's place and they walked over together. "We need to make sure you have enough heat, Mia," Nola said. "For you and the baby."

They went through the door of the community room to see a dozen or so tenants already there. "I'm fine for now," Mia answered. Her apartment wasn't too bad. "I wouldn't mind a new faucet for the sink, though. It came off last week."

"You should have told Joe."

"I wasn't going to complain when there are apartments with bigger problems."

Nola gave her a tender look. "You and the baby are a priority."

Mia smiled. Everyone here had rallied around her like overprotective grandparents since they'd heard the tragic news. "He's not even here yet."

"It's a boy?" Joe said, walking over to them.

"I don't know," she insisted. "So you haven't won the baby pool yet."

The older man grinned. "It's a boy all right. He's going to be born at 12:05 on the twenty-fifth of December."

Mia looked up to see Jarrett walk in, followed by a middle-aged man with Nichols Heating and Air printed across his shirt pocket.

"Good, most of you are here," Jarrett began. "This is Harry Nichols. He's here to look at the heating units."

Several of the tenants were already on their feet to greet the repairman. Once the niceties were over, the tenants commandeered Harry and went to start the work.

With everyone gone, Jarrett walked over to where Mia sat at the table. "That seemed to please them."

She studied her new landlord. He was sure proud of himself. "Why not? It's been a while since they've had reliable heat. You'll probably be rewarded with some more baked goods."

Jarrett took a seat next to her, filling the space with his large frame. She inhaled a faint scent of his aftershave.

"I had no idea the extent of the last owner's neglect. I thought it was mostly cosmetic. Now, I'm paying a lot for the repairs."

Mia eyed his expensive clothes, leather jacket and cowboy boots. She'd seen his top-of-the-line Range Rover parked out front. "I doubt you'll starve, Mr. McKane. Besides, this isn't your only property in town."

He arched an eyebrow. "The last I heard, it's not against the law to make a living."

"No. Not unless the properties have been neglected like this one."

He looked at her with those dark, piercing eyes. "In the first place, I wasn't the one who allowed this property to fall apart. Secondly, most of my other holdings are commercial buildings. I've spent a lot of money renovating run-down properties. You can't ask for top rent without a quality product."

Why couldn't he do the same here? "Have you ever considered putting money into this place? You have a whole other section that's vacant. That's twenty-four units that are empty." She shrugged. "Like you said yourself, this town doesn't have enough rental properties. With some remodeling you could sell them as townhomes."

He studied her for a while. "Sounds like you've put some thought into this."

"When we heard that the owner was selling, the tenants tried to buy the complex themselves. They didn't have enough money, or the expertise to do the repairs."

"I doubt if anyone can keep up with the repairs of this old place. No one would want to sink the time and effort into it, without knowing if they could recoup their money. The real estate market has been unpredictable."

He sounded like her father. "Does it always have to be about money?"

He arched an eyebrow. "It does or I go broke."

She'd been both, and she was definitely happier like this. "I can't believe you'd lose everything. You still have family and a home. You might lose a little money, but you'll survive. A lot of these people won't. They can't afford to move and pay double the rent elsewhere."

He frowned. "What are you going to do when the lease is up?"

She blinked, fighting her anger. "Is your conscience suddenly bothering you about evicting a single mother?"

He straightened. "I'm not happy about evicting anyone. But I don't have a choice. This deal has been in the works for months."

"Like I said, it's all about the almighty dollar."

"What about the jobs this factory will create for the town? The economy isn't that great to turn this opportunity away."

"Does a factory have to be built on land that drives people from their homes?"

"I will find them other places to live. I'm not that cruel—I won't put seniors and single mothers out on the street."

"Well, you can stop worrying about me. I don't want your charity."

"Fine. Let's see where your stubbornness gets you."

"I've been able to take care of myself so far."

"Then feel free to continue." He stood and started to leave.

She tried not to let him see her fear. She raised her chin. "I will."

Suddenly she felt her stomach tighten and she automatically covered it with her hands.

He must have seen it, too. "Are you okay?"

She nodded as she moved her hand over her belly and rubbed it, but it didn't help. Then her back began to hurt, too. She tried to shift in the chair, but it didn't help.

"Mia, what's wrong?" Jarrett asked.

She shook her head. "Nothing."

He knelt down beside her chair. "The hell it's nothing."

She shook her head, looking around the empty room. There wasn't anyone else there.

His expression softened. "Mia, let me help you."

A sharp pain grabbed her around the middle. "Oh, no," she gasped and then looked at him. "I think the baby's coming."

Fifteen minutes later Jarrett pulled up at the emergency-room doors. He threw the car into Park, got out and ran around to the passenger side. He jerked open the door. Mia was taking slow measured breaths. Not good.

"Hang on, we're almost there."

She couldn't hide her worried look. "It's too early for me to go into labor. I can't lose this baby, Jarrett."

"And you won't," he promised. He had no idea what was going on, or even if the doctors could stop the contractions. "Let's get you inside and find some help." He slid his arms around her shoulders and under her legs, then lifted her into his arms.

"I'm too heavy," she said.

"Are you kidding?" He smiled, taking long strides across the parking lot. "During roundup, I used to have to hoist calves a lot heavier than you."

"You used to work on your brother's ranch?"

"Back when I played cowboy, it was our dad's place. That was a long time ago."

She studied him. "I can see you as a rancher."

His mouth twitched. "There's the big difference, darlin'. I never did," he drawled as he carried her through the automatic doors.

On the drive over, Mia had phoned her doctor and been told to go to the nearest emergency room, then she'd given Nola a quick call so her friends wouldn't worry if they noticed she was gone.

Winchester Ridge Medical Center was the closest. Once inside, they were met by a nurse who led them into an exam room. Jarrett set Mia down on the bed and stepped back out of the way. Nurses immediately took her blood pressure, asking questions about due dates and the timing of the contractions. All the while, she kept looking at him.

Jarrett tried to give her some reassurance, but he didn't know what to say.

"Excuse me," a nurse said, getting his attention. "Are you the father?"

He shook his head, but hesitated with the answer. "No." Mia didn't have any family.

"Then you'll have to leave while we examine her."

"I'll be right outside," he told Mia. "Just holler if you need me."

Jarrett stepped back behind the curtain and found a row of chairs against the wall. That was as far as he was going.

For the next few hours, Jarrett watched medical personal go in and out of Mia's cubicle.

But no one told him a thing.

Finally they moved her down the hall to a room so they could keep monitoring her. Recalling the frightened look on her face, he knew he couldn't leave her alone. So he followed her and camped outside her room.

He glanced up from the newspaper someone else had left and saw Nola.

He stood as the older woman walked toward him. "Mr. McKane." She gripped his hand with both of hers. "How is Mia?"

"I don't know any more than what I told you when I phoned. And the doctor won't tell me anything because I'm not a relative."

Nola nodded. "I know, I fibbed and said I was her grand-mother so I could come back here."

He walked Nola to the sofa and sat down. "How did you get here?"

"One of the parishioners from the church," she said. "Joe can't drive at night, and Ralph doesn't have his li-cense any more." She shook her head. "Mia always takes us places we need to go." The older woman blinked. "Oh, Mr. McKane, what if something is wrong with the baby?" Those watery hazel eyes turned to him. "She wants this baby so much."

He already knew that. He'd never felt so helpless and he hated that. "Nola, the doctors here are good and her specialist is here, too. So try not to worry." He put on a smile. "And will you do me another favor? Please call me Jarrett."

She beamed at him.

He'd broken one of his cardinal rules. Not to get personally involved when it came to business. A week ago if someone told him he'd be sitting here worried about a pregnant woman and a couple of dozen retirees, he'd have told them they were crazy.

An attractive blond woman in a white coat came down the hall toward them. "Are you waiting to hear about Mia Saunders?"

They both stood. "Yes, we are," Jarrett said. "I'm Jarrett McKane, I brought Mia in. This is Nola Madison, her… grandmother. How is she?"

The doctor smiled. "Nice to meet you both. I'm Lauren Drake, Mia's doctor. She's fine for now. We managed to stop the contractions, but I want her to stay overnight as a precaution."

"What about the baby?" Nola asked.

"The fetus is thirty-four weeks, so if Mia does go into labor, she could deliver a healthy baby. Of course the longer she carries it, the better."

"Well, we'll do everything we can to make sure of that," Nola said.

The doctor nodded. "I'm glad, because when she goes home, I want her to stay in bed for the next few weeks. She needs to avoid all stress and just rest."

No stress, Jarrett thought. *Great.* He'd dumped a truckload on her. "Is that what caused the contractions?"

"We all have to agree that a lot has happened to Mia in the past few months," the doctor echoed. "Losing her brother and sister-in-law was traumatic for her."

Nola spoke up. "We've all been trying to help her through it."

Dr. Drake nodded. "I hope that can continue, because she's going to need someone to be around more, or at least within shouting distance to check on her."

"We can be there as much as she needs us," Nola said and turned to him. "Right, Jarrett?"

Great, he was the last person Mia wanted around. "Of course. I live across the hall. I guess I could keep an eye on her."

Thanks to the medication, Mia was feeling groggy. She didn't like that. For years, she'd avoided any and all drugs. But if it kept the baby safe, she'd do whatever it took.

Closing her eyes, she wondered how she was going to manage over the next few weeks. She had deadlines to make, and she needed the money.

Stop! Worrying wasn't good for the baby. She rubbed her stomach, knowing how close she'd come to delivering early. She wasn't ready for the baby. She didn't even have any diapers and very few clothes. The baby bed wasn't set up, either. She sighed. How was she going to do everything? How could she do everything and be a good mother, too? A tear slid down her cheek.

She thought back to her childhood. She'd always messed up. How many times had her father told her that? She couldn't please him no matter how hard she tried. He'd been too busy for her, but the one way she got his attention was being bad. Until he finally gave up on her altogether. No she couldn't let Brad down. She was going to be a good mother to his baby.

Mia glanced toward the door and saw Nola and Jarrett standing there. She quickly wiped away any more tears and put on a smile.

"Hi."

Nola rushed in. "Oh, sweetheart," she cried. "How are you?" Nola hugged her.

Mia relished the feeling, the love and compassion. "I'm doing better now."

The older woman pulled back. "We were so worried about you."

Mia looked at Jarrett. "I didn't want you to worry."

Nola frowned. "Of course we'd worry. You are special to us. We love you." She fussed with the blanket, smoothing out the wrinkles. "And we're going to take good care of you. Aren't we, Jarrett?"

"Looks that way," he said, feeling awkward standing in the room.

"I can't impose on either of you."

"You're not imposing on any of us. We're happy to do it. You need someone around to help you. Jarrett and I volunteered." She clutched her hands together. "Oh, I need to go and call the others. I'll be right back."

"Here, use my phone," Jarrett said, handing it over to her. They both watched the woman walk out of the room.

Jarrett turned back to Mia. "So how do you really feel?"

"Scared, but good."

"You need to stop that. Your doctor said you need to relax and avoid stress."

"Did you tell her that you lived across the hall?"

He fought a smile, but lost. "Yes. Did you tell her that you and your friends brought me there?"

She met Jarrett's gaze. Her heart sped up and the monitor showed it. "So, I guess we're stuck with each other for a while."

CHAPTER FOUR

THE next day, Mia arrived home the same way she'd left. In Jarrett's car. He pulled into a parking spot at the front of the building. There were two heating-and-air-conditioning-repair trucks there, along with several uniformed workers.

"Looks like we'll have heat soon," she said.

Jarrett turned off the engine and glanced out the windshield. "It's just in time. There's a snowstorm coming in tonight." He looked at her. "Soon you'll be tucked into your warm bed. But be warned, Nola is heading a welcome-home committee."

"Oh, I don't want them to go to any trouble."

"I doubt they think you're any trouble. Too bad she and her group don't run this town. A lot more would get done." He climbed out of the SUV and walked around to her side.

He pulled open the door and the cold air hit her. She shivered as she tried to climb out, but he wouldn't let her.

"Remember what the doctor said? Bed rest."

"I will as soon as I get to my apartment."

"No, as soon as I get you to your apartment." He scooped her up into his arms.

"Please, you can't carry me all the way upstairs."

"Of course not. Once I get you inside, Joe's going to take over."

She made a face at him. "Very funny."

Mia refused to admit she liked being taken care of by a big, strong man whose mere presence made her aware she was a woman. The way he smelled, his rock-solid chest and arms. She bit back a groan. Hormones. It was all just hormones.

She had to think of Jarrett McKane as the man who would be kicking them all out of their homes in a few months. Nothing more.

Sylvia held open the door to the building so they could come in. "Welcome home, Mia."

She got more greetings from a group of tenants waiting in the lobby.

"Thank you everyone. It's good to be home."

"Okay, let's get you upstairs." Jarrett continued to the stairway to her apartment.

Nola was waiting there and motioned him toward the bedroom. "Bring her in here."

"No, I can stay out here on the sofa for now."

Jarrett stopped, then said, "Doctor's orders are to put you to bed." He continued through the short hallway and into her room.

Mia blinked as they entered the bedroom. It didn't look like the same room she'd left yesterday. The dingy walls had been painted a soft buttery yellow. The furniture was rearranged and her bed was adorned with a pastel-patterned quilt.

She turned around and saw the white baby bed that had been Brad and Karen's last purchase for the baby assembled. It was decorated with yellow-and-green sheets and an animal mobile hung overhead.

Tears flooded her eyes. "Oh, my."

"Do you like it?" Nola asked. We were going to give you the quilt for Christmas but since you're going to be spending so much time in bed now, we decided not to wait." The older woman pulled back the covers so Jarrett could set her down on the snowy-white sheets.

"Oh, it's beautiful." She examined the intricate work. "How could you get all this done? I've only been gone overnight."

Nola exchanged a look with Jarrett. "We knew we had to. The scare yesterday made us realize that you've been working so hard for us, you put off getting ready for the baby." She helped Mia take off her shoes and put her feet under the blanket. "So we hope this helps you to stop worrying so much." She stood back. "And when you've rested I'll show you all the baby clothes we've collected."

Nola walked to a small white dresser. "Joe found this for you. He sanded and painted it last week and Jarrett helped bring it up. Sylvia and I washed all the baby things and put them inside. If you don't like how we arranged them, you can change it."

"I'm sure it will be perfect." Mia clasped her hands together. "I don't know what to say."

"You don't have to say anything." The older woman came to the bed and hugged her. "Just take care of yourself. We love you, Mia. You're like family."

"I love you all, too."

She'd tried for a lot of years not to get too close to people, except for Brad. Starting with her parents. Whenever she'd let people in, they'd ended up hurting her. She looked across the room at Jarrett standing in the doorway. She definitely had to keep this man away.

"Tell everyone thank you."

"I will," Nola assured her. "Now, you rest and don't worry about lunch. Sylvia will be here to fix you something."

"She doesn't have to do that."

Nola raised her hand. "She wants to. We all want to help." The older woman went out the door, followed by Jarrett. Mia called him back. "Mr. McKane, could I speak to you a moment?"

Frowning, he came toward the bed as Nola left. "Suddenly I'm Mr. McKane again."

"I appreciate everything you've done for me. It's better if we don't become too friendly…given the situation."

He studied her for a moment. "The situation you are referring to is that you've already gotten to stay here until the spring." He shrugged. "But, hey, I won't bother you again."

He turned and walked out. The soft click of the front door let her know she was truly alone. She told herself it was better this way. She couldn't get any more involved with a man like Jarrett McKane. Not that she had to worry that he'd ever give her a second look.

She rubbed her stomach. All she needed to focus on right now was her baby.

Jarrett kept hearing a ringing sound. He blinked his eyes as he reached for his cell phone on the bedside table.

"Hello," he murmured, running a hand over his face. It was still dark outside.

"Oh, I'm sorry, did I wake you?"

It was Mia. He sat up. "Mia? Is there a problem?"

"No. No. I shouldn't have bothered you."

"Wait, Mia. Tell me what's wrong. Is it the baby?"

"No, the baby's fine. I just need a favor, but I'll call back later."

"I'll be right over." He hung up, grabbed a pair of jeans and put them on along with a sweatshirt. He grabbed his keys and phone and headed across the hall. He let himself into her apartment with his master key and hurried to the bedroom.

Mia was sitting on the bed, dressed in a thermal long-sleeved shirt that hugged her rounded belly and a pair of flannel pajama bottoms. Somehow she managed to look somewhere between wholesome and far too good at this time in the morning.

Was it morning? "What's the problem?"

She looked embarrassed. "I'm so sorry I woke you."

"Well, since you have, tell me what you need."

"Could you pull out the table and see if my cable is plugged in? I didn't want to move the table by myself."

"You're on the computer at this hour?"

She shrugged. "I slept so much during the day, I'm wide-awake. So I thought I'd get some work done."

Jarrett went to the bedside table and pulled it out. Seeing the loose battery cable, he knelt down and pushed it back into the outlet. "It's fixed." He moved the table back and stood next to the bed. "You're really not supposed to be working."

"I'm bored. Besides, if I don't work, I don't eat or pay my rent."

The computer screen lit up and he asked, "What are you working on?"

She kept her focus on the screen. "A Web site for a Denver-based company."

He glanced at the home-page logo. "Are you going back to law school?"

As she clicked the mouse and another program opened, she didn't show any surprise that he knew her history. "Not for a while, but I hope I can go back someday. It won't be easy with a baby."

"I'm sure everyone here would love to help you."

"We won't be living here…together," she said.

When she looked up at him with her scrubbed-clean face, large sapphire eyes and her hair in a ponytail, she looked fifteen. "How old are you?"

Mia blinked at his question. "Don't you know you're not supposed to ask a woman her age?"

He shrugged. "You look like jailbait."

"I'm twenty-nine. How old are you?"

"Thirty-seven."

She studied him for a few seconds. "You look it."

Frowning, he combed his fingers through his hair. "What's that supposed to mean?"

"What did you mean when you called me jailbait?"

"I meant it as a compliment. You look young for your age."

"Thank you." She sobered. "Are you really going to try and find us all a place to live?"

"I'm not sure I can find everyone a place, but I'll see what I can do." Was he crazy? Where would he find affordable apartments for them all? He moved away from the bed. "Man, I'd kill for a cup of coffee."

"Sorry, I'm off caffeine for a while," she told him. "But I'd fight you for a jelly donut."

"I guess that's one of those crazy cravings, huh? Well, I'd better go." He walked out, thinking a donut didn't sound so bad.

He retrieved his car keys and a jacket from his apartment and headed down to his car. The ground was covered in a dusting of snow. He climbed into his vehicle, missing the warm garage back at his house. Pushing aside his discomfort, he started the engine and the heater. He was on a quest for one hungry pregnant woman.

In every town there always seemed to be a twenty-four-hour donut and coffee shop and Winchester Ridge was no exception. He picked out a couple of dozen assorted donuts along with a large coffee and an orange juice.

He returned to the apartment building just as dawn was breaking. Funny, this wasn't how he usually spent early mornings. He'd never shared breakfast with an expectant mother, either. With his offerings in hand, he returned to Mia's apartment and gave a loud knock before he walked in.

"It's me, Ms. Saunders. I've got something for you." After hearing Mia's greeting he walked into the bedroom.

She was still working on the computer. "I thought you went back to bed."

"Not after you talked about donuts." He raised the box. "Freshly made." He opened the large box and the aroma filled the room.

Mia groaned. "Oh, my God." She put the laptop aside and reached for one. He pulled back.

"I thought you were going to fight me for one."

She looked confused.

"Of course, if we were on a first-name basis, I'd happily share. Especially if someone had been willing to get up before dawn and help out a neighbor."

Mia was embarrassed by her actions. Yesterday after Jarrett had left, Nola had returned and told her how he'd stayed at the hospital and called everyone with any news. She was even more ashamed when she learned that he'd bought the paint for her bedroom.

"It does seem to be one-sided, doesn't it? I apologize. You have helped me so much. I don't know how I would have made it to the hospital without you."

"Did I say I minded helping you? I just don't want to keep being treated like the enemy here. I can't change things that happened in the past."

"I know. I'm sorry, Jarrett."

He smiled. "What did you say?"

She sighed. He wasn't going to make this easy. "Would you be my friend, Jarrett?"

"You just want my donuts."

She nodded. "And you'd be wise not to get between a pregnant woman and those donuts."

He put the box down and her mouth watered as she eyed the selections. "There are so many to choose from." She rubbed her stomach, feeling the baby kicking her.

He sat at the end of the bed. "Are you all right?" he asked as he nodded to her stomach.

"Yeah, he's just active and hungry."

"Does he move around like that all the time?"

"Well, the baby's bigger now, so I feel it more."

He handed her juice. "Here's something to wash down your donut."

"Thank you." She motioned to the box. "Aren't you going to have one, too?"

"Sure, but ladies first."

"Wise choice." She couldn't help but smile as she bit into the jelly-filled treat. "Mmm, it's so good."

"You might not be able to have caffeine, but you're definitely getting a sugar rush."

Mia watched Jarrett finish off a glazed donut in record time. He looked good even with his finger-combed hair and wrinkled clothes. There were just some men who couldn't look bad. He was one of them.

"I should let you rest." He stood, but his gaze never left hers. "Is there anything you need me to do before I go?"

She hesitated to ask him anything else.

"Come on, Mia. What is it?"

"I can wait for Nola."

"What for?"

"I need to take a shower, but the doctor said someone

should be close by." She waved her hand. "Don't worry about it, Nola's coming in a few hours."

He swallowed. "How close by?"

"Just in the apartment. In case something happens there'll be someone to help me."

He stood there for what seemed like forever, and then he said, "Sure, what are friends for?"

Once Jarrett heard the shower go on, he took out his cell phone and began to check his messages. He had to get some things done today. One was to stop by the office for a few hours and check in with his agents.

Over the last couple of days, between the repairs here and keeping watch on one pregnant lady, he'd neglected his other business.

He was surprised at the next message. It was from Carrie Johnston. He smiled. The pretty blonde from Glenwood Springs he'd met at the real estate conference in Denver last summer had left him another suggestive message. She wanted to see him.

Jarrett should feel a little more excited. During their time together, the two had definitely set off sparks. So why wasn't he more interested in her invitation?

When it came to women, he'd always loved having variety in his life. So why suddenly did it seem too much trouble to make the effort? Maybe thirty-seven was too old to keep playing games.

He thought about what Mia had said, *You look it.*

He wasn't *that* old. Wasn't he considered in his prime? Okay, so most men were married by now, like his younger brother. Trace had found Kira years ago. And it had been love at first sight.

Jarrett didn't believe in that. He wasn't sure he believed in love at all.

Suddenly the bathroom door opened and Mia stepped out. She was dressed in her black stretch pants and a soft-pink sweater. Her dark hair lay against her shoulders in waves. Those big blue eyes looked at him and it became difficult to breathe. Damn. What was wrong with him? This woman came with far too many complications.

"Well, since you're finished, I'll go."

"Of course." She sat down on the sofa. "I appreciate you helping me. Thank you, Jarrett."

"Just do what the doctor told you and stay in bed. He pulled out his wallet and handed her his business card. "If you need anything."

She nodded.

"I mean it. Don't be stubborn about asking for help." He found he wanted to be the one she called.

The snow had been coming down like a holiday greeting card, but by the next afternoon, Mia was getting cabin fever.

She had watched every television talk show and finished up her work on the computer, even cried over an old movie. Neighbors stopped by with offers of help. Even parishioners from her brother's church had called her. She'd taken naps off and on for the past two days and she was still exhausted and totally bored. And no Jarrett.

"You know next week is Thanksgiving." Nola's voice broke through her reverie. "And we have a problem. The oven in the community room is broken."

"You can use mine. It's a little tricky on the temperature, but we could adjust it. It's small though. Don't we usually cook three or four turkeys?"

The older woman nodded. "Remember last year we fed those people from the mission? There were nearly fifty here."

Mia thought back to last year. She'd had family then. Brad and Karen had just begun to research surrogacy as an alternative for a baby. And by Christmas, Mia had volunteered to carry her brother and his wife's child. They all were so happy, and then in a flash she had lost them both.

Tears flooded Mia's eyes and she quickly brushed them away. She looked at Nola. "I'm sorry."

Her friend sat down beside her. "There's no reason to be sorry, dear. We all miss Brad and Karen. They were wonderful people, but they left you a child. A child you get to love and raise as your own. What a special gift."

"I do know. And I love this baby, but I'm scared. What if I can't be a good mother?"

"I have no doubt you'll be a wonderful mother. You know why? Because you're a wonderful person and this little boy or girl will be blessed to have you."

"Oh, Nola. I hope you're right."

"I am. You know what else? We're all going to be around to help you."

She cleared her throat. "I'm so glad because I'm going to need you."

Nola patted her hand. "Well, count on me. Now that that is settled, where are we going to find a big enough oven to cook our Thanksgiving Day turkeys? The ones at the church are already being used, and ours barely work. Too bad Jarrett couldn't replace the one in the community center."

"I'm not going to do that," a familiar voice said, "But I may have another solution."

Jarrett hadn't meant to eavesdrop, but he'd wanted to check on Mia and had found the door partly open.

"I overheard. You're having trouble finding working ovens."

Nodding, Nola stood. "We always feed a large group on Thanksgiving. And this might be the last one that we're all together." Her eyes brightened with tears. "You said you might have a solution."

"I have two large ovens at my house."

Nola immediately smiled. "You do?"

Jarrett stole a glance at Mia. She didn't look impressed by his offer. "Yes. When I built the house I was told it would be a good selling feature. They're like new." He shrugged. "You're welcome to them."

"Oh, my, that's the answer to our prayer." The older woman paused. "There's one condition. You have to come to our Thanksgiving celebration."

In the past Jarrett been happier to stay at home and watch football. He had gone by his brother's house last year for dessert, only because little Jenna had asked him to. He had a weakness for pretty young women. He glanced at Mia. Maybe is it was time to count some blessings. "I'd be honored to come by."

CHAPTER FIVE

HE had to be crazy to have suggested cooking Thanksgiving dinner here.

Jarrett stood back and watched as half a dozen women scurried around his kitchen. He'd told himself earlier that he wasn't going to hang around, but they'd showed up at dawn, ready and eager to begin the baking and cooking.

He had to admit that the place was filled with wonderful aromas. The one disappointment was that Mia wasn't there. It was crazy of him even to think about her at all. She was pregnant, and her life was going in one direction while he needed only to think about one thing—the computer-chip-factory project. And getting out of the jail of his crummy apartment.

Nola walked over to him. "You have a wonderful kitchen, Jarrett. Every modern convenience a woman could ever want. Seems such a waste that you don't have someone to share this with."

Jarrett smiled, but ignored her comment. "I'm glad you like it."

"Just so you know, we'll clean up everything. You won't even know we were here."

"I'm not worried. I have a cleaning service."

"Well, just the same. The place will be spotless when we leave."

Just then his phone rang. He grabbed the extension in the office. It was his brother. "Hi, Trace. Happy Thanksgiving."

"Same to you," Trace echoed. "I've been given orders to call you and see if you changed your mind about coming to dinner today."

Kira couldn't stand for him to be alone. "I appreciate the invitation, bro, but I seem to have a place to go. A few of the tenants have asked me to share the meal with them."

There was a long silence. "You better be careful, no telling what they might put in your food."

"Very funny. I do have a few friends. Besides, the tenants and I are getting along fine."

"Well, that's good."

He didn't want to talk about any apartment troubles. "I take it Kira is fixing dinner today."

"It'll be just us since Jody and Nathan have gone to be with Ben at the army base."

Jarrett remembered Kira's student who'd gotten pregnant in high school. Jody had had the child and Ben had joined the military, but he'd stayed in touch. The couple had gotten married this past summer.

Suddenly the doorbell rang. "I've got to go, Trace. Tell everyone happy Thanksgiving."

After replacing the phone, Jarrett walked across the great room and into the entry. He pulled open the door to find Mia and several other people standing on his porch.

He frowned. "What are you doing out of bed?"

"I'm allowed out now. Some," she added stubbornly. "I just have to stay off my feet as much as possible."

He took her by the arm and led her to the sofa, followed by the other dozen or so tenants. "Why did you come here? We're going to bring the food back to the community room." He folded his arms. "You aren't supposed to do anything."

She nodded. I know, but there's a problem at the community room. It's flooded."

Jarrett cursed. He didn't need another thing that he had to pay for. "How bad?"

Joe spoke up. "I shut off the main valve, but there's about an inch of water on the floor."

Jarrett murmured some choice words as he turned back to Mia.

She suddenly looked unsure. "We didn't know what to do, so we came here."

Nola walked into the room. "Mia, what's wrong? Is it the baby?"

"No, I'm fine, but the community room is flooded." Mia looked back at Jarrett. "We have no place to have our dinner."

Every eye turned toward him. He had no choice. "Well, since everyone is here, I guess it'll be at my house."

Cheers filled the room, then everyone scattered to do their chores. He pulled out his phone and punched in the McKane Ranch number, wondering how he'd gotten into this situation. He glanced at Mia Saunders, those big blue eyes staring back at him. A sudden stirring in his gut told him he was headed for disaster if he wasn't careful. Hell, he'd never been careful in his life.

His brother answered the phone.

"Hey, Trace. Why don't you load up Kira and Jenna and come here? It seems I'm having Thanksgiving at my house."

Two hours later, Mia was still sitting on the large sofa in Jarrett's great room. Although it wasn't her taste, the place was decorated well. A lot of chrome-and-glass tables and black leather furniture filled the room. The most beautiful feature was the huge wall of windows and the French door that led to the deck and the wooded area at the back of the house. Although the trees were bare and a dusting of snow covered the ground, she could picture it in the spring with green trees and wildflowers along the hillside.

She turned toward the open-concept kitchen, looking over the breakfast bar to see rows of espresso-colored cabinets, and marble counter tops. The commercial-size stainless-steel appliances looked as though they were getting a rare workout today.

The dining room was on the other side, the long table already set up for the meal, along with several card tables scattered around to accommodate all the people coming today. Mia didn't even want to count them. All she knew was that her brother and sister-in-law wouldn't be at any table. These people were her family now. She rubbed her stomach. Hers and her baby's.

"Are you okay?"

She glanced up to see Jarrett standing beside the sofa. "I'm fine. Really. Thank you for having us today."

"There wasn't a choice, and you know it."

"It's still very generous that you let us use your home."

He shrugged. "I also get a home-cooked meal."

"You have family. And I bet you could get someone to cook for you pretty easily."

His dark gaze held hers. "I'm pretty selective in choosing my friends." His mouth crooked upward in a sexy smile. "Also who cooks for me."

"Well, you've got some pretty good cooks in your kitchen right now."

"I'm glad about that, because I'm getting hungry just smelling all the wonderful aromas." He sat down across from her. "If your cookies are any indication, I'd say you know your way around a kitchen, too."

The man was too handsome and, when he wanted to be, charming. She scooted to the edge of the sofa. "Could you direct me to the bathroom, please?"

"Of course." He helped her up, but didn't release his hold on her arm. They were walking toward the hall when the doorbell rang.

She looked at him. "I thought everyone was here."

Jarrett pulled open the door to a young couple with a little girl. She recognized them from church.

"Happy Thanksgiving, Unca Jay," the girl cried as she ran inside.

He scooped her into his arms. "Happy Thanksgiving to you too, Jenna. I'm glad you could come today. Welcome, Kira, Trace."

They all exchanged greetings.

Jenna kept her hold on her uncle. "Mama said it must be a really special day because we never get invited to your house. She's really happy because family should be together."

"Jenna," her mother warned.

"Well, you did say that," the child acknowledged, then looked at Mia. "Who's this lady, Unca Jay?"

"Hi, I'm Mia."

Jarrett set her down. "I'm Jenna, and I'm almost four years old. But my daddy says I'm really thirty." The child caught sight of Mia's rounded stomach. "Are you going to have a baby?"

"Jenna." Kira sent another warning glance to her daughter, and then looked at Mia. "Hi, Mia. It's good to see you again."

Trace removed his cowboy hat and nodded. "Hello, Mia."

"Nice to see you, too. I hope you don't mind that we took over Jarrett's house."

The pretty blonde smiled and glanced up at her husband. Love radiated between them just as Mia had seen between her brother and his wife.

"We think it's wonderful," Kira said. "I'm just wondering how you did it."

"I believe a judge did it, along with several of the tenants."

They all looked toward the living room and saw the numerous people. "Welcome to Mountain View Apartment's Thanksgiving Day celebration." Mia turned to Kira. "If you'll excuse me, I need to find a restroom."

Jarrett watched Mia walk down the hall. He wanted to go after her. Why? She was capable of finding the bathroom.

"How is she doing?"

Jarrett looked at his sister-in-law. "She should be off her feet. So would you watch her?"

"Sure. If you and Trace unload the car. I brought a few things for dinner, too. I'll take Jenna to the kitchen and see if they need any help."

"Just ask for Nola."

"I know Nola Madison. I see her at church nearly every week."

"Okay. You'll probably know a few of the others, too."

Once the group of seniors spotted Jenna, they began to fuss over her. His niece couldn't get enough of the attention.

"So tell me about you and Mia Saunders," Trace said.

Jarrett turned around. "There's nothing to tell. She had a scare with her pregnancy and I had to take her to the hospital. The doctor ordered bed rest. She was allowed to come here, but she needs to stay off her feet."

He glanced down the hall. "And if she doesn't come out soon, I'm going in to get her."

Trace arched an eyebrow. "So when did you become her protector?"

Jarrett turned to his younger half brother. Trace stared back at him.

"She doesn't have anyone else," Jarrett reminded him. "Remember, she lost her brother a few months back."

Trace nodded. "Yeah, Reverend Brad was a good man," he said, studying Jarrett. "I just never knew my brother to care much about anything that wasn't about the almighty dollar. You must be getting soft in your old age."

"Hey, I'm not that old." He didn't want to discuss his age or his relationship with Mia. They were neighbors. Temporary neighbors. "But don't go thinking I've bought into the family scene."

"Never say never, bro," Trace challenged. "I've seen you with Jenna. You wouldn't be a bad dad."

Jarrett froze. He didn't want to be a dad at all. His own father had been lousy at the job. "Look, as soon as I make the repairs to the complex, I'm out of there. And I won't be looking back."

On returning from the bathroom, Mia discovered that everyone was taking a seat at the tables. She glanced around for to find one last vacant chair. Next to Jarrett.

Smiling, he stood and pulled out her chair. "Looks like you're next to me."

She caught Nola smiling from across the table. Little Jenna was on the other side of Jarrett and Trace and Kira sat beside her. "I'm just happy we have a place to eat. Thank you, Jarrett, for having us here."

Nola and Margaret stood and went into the kitchen and soon returned, each woman carrying a platter with a large turkey. The group made approving sounds as the birds were placed on the table alongside sweet potatoes, green-bean casseroles, stuffing, gravy and other side dishes too numerous to count.

Nola stood beside the table. "Before we all dig in, we should give thanks for this wonderful day." She turned to Jarrett.

Mia watched as he nudged his brother and said something to him. Trace nodded. "Everyone, take hands and let's bow our heads."

Jarrett reached for Mia's hand. His large palm nearly engulfed hers. She was surprised by the roughness of his fingers, but also by the warmth he generated.

"Dear Lord," Trace began. "We thank you for all the blessings you've given us this past year. There have been some rough times, but sometimes that brings out the best in people. And today, we see that special bond as friends gather together as a family.

"We also ask for your blessing for those who aren't here with us." Trace paused. Mia thought about Brad and Karen. She felt Jarrett squeeze her hand. "We also ask a special blessing for Mia's baby.

"We ask you to bless this food in your name. Amen."

"Amens" echoed around the room.

Mia kept her head lowered, thinking of her brother and his wife. How much she missed them. Brad had always been there to guide her, to spout optimism whenever she wanted to give up. Now, she had to go on without him.

She opened her eyes to see that she was still holding hands with Jarrett. She turned to him to catch him watching her.

"Are you okay?" he asked.

"I'm fine." She pulled her hand away. "I wish people would stop asking me that."

"Then eat a good meal today, and we'll get you home to bed."

His deep voice caused her to shiver. "I can get myself to bed, thank you," she said in a quiet voice.

"Well, one thing is for sure, you're not climbing the steps."

Since when did he become the boss of her? "I wouldn't have to if you'd fix the elevator."

He glared. "That will be Monday. I can't get anyone out before then."

She heard his name called and they both looked up at Nola.

"Jarrett and Trace, would you do the honor of slicing the turkeys?"

The brothers stood, went to opposite ends of the table and began to carve. The side dishes were passed around and Mia put small helpings onto her plate. With Jarrett gone, she dished up food for him, too.

"Are you Unca Jay's girlfriend?" Jenna McKane asked from across her uncle's empty seat.

Mia smiled. "No. We're neighbors in his apartment building in town."

The little girl frowned and turned to her mother. "Mommy, what's an apartment?"

"It's a big building with a lot of houses inside. It's like where Aunt Michele lives."

"Oh." The child turned back to Mia's stomach. "Are you going to have a baby soon?"

"Yes, I am, in just a few weeks."

Jenna grinned. "I have a big brother, Jack. He's old and he doesn't live with us. So my mommy and daddy are trying to have a brother or sister for me."

"Jenna McKane," Kira said, giving her daughter a stern look. "You don't have to talk so much. Now, eat."

Kira looked at Mia. "I'm sorry. Trace and I forget how much she hears."

Mia smiled as the platter of turkey was passed to her. She nodded toward the child eating mashed potatoes. "She's adorable."

Kira looked at her daughter lovingly. "She's our miracle baby. And a very welcome surprise." She looked at Mia. "If you ever need anything, Mia, please don't hesitate to ask. All of us in the church want very much to help."

Mia was touched. "Thank you, Kira. Everyone has been so generous already. I think I'll be fine if I can find a place to live by spring."

Before Kira could say any more, Jarrett arrived back in his seat. For the next twenty minutes everyone concentrated on the delicious food and friendly conversation. Finally the men leaned back groaning at the amount of food they'd consumed.

"There's pie, too," Nola announced as she stood and took several empty plates. She looked at Jarrett. "Jarrett, would you mind helping me with the coffeemaker? I'm not sure on the measurements."

With a nod, he stood. "Sure." He grinned. "If I get first choice of pie."

Nola smiled, too. "You think because you're good-looking, you can charm me into anything, don't you?"

"Hey, I do what I can to get an advantage." He put his arm around her shoulders. "Is it working?"

Mia never heard the answer as they walked off together.

"He's a flirt, but he's a good man."

Mia turned to Kira, but didn't know how to answer that. Was Kira trying to sell her brother-in-law's better qualities to her?

"I wouldn't have said that a few years ago," Kira went

on. "But something in him has changed. And he and Trace are working on being brothers."

She turned and looked at Mia. "I know you're not happy about having to leave your apartment, but I might be able to help with that. We have a guest house at the ranch. It's small, but it has two bedrooms. A friend had been living there during college, and now she's gone to be with her husband in the army."

"Oh, Kira." Mia didn't want to get too excited. "What about Trace? I bet you haven't even asked him."

"Haven't asked me what?" her husband turned toward her.

"About Mia coming to live in the cottage."

He raised an eyebrow as if to think about it. "That's a great idea. The house is sitting empty." He shrugged. "You're welcome to live there as long as you need."

Mia was getting excited. "What is the rent?"

"There isn't any rent."

"No, I would expect to pay something."

Trace glanced at his wife. "I think we owe your brother a bigger debt. He helped us through some rough spots a few years ago. I think Brad would want us to help you and the baby."

"Can I come over to see the baby?" Jenna asked. "I'll be really quiet."

"If I decide to move there, of course, you can." She looked at Kira. "Maybe I could even babysit you so your parents could go out."

A big smile split Trace's face. "That's a deal I'll take."

"What's a deal?" Jarrett sat down next to Mia.

Trace was still smiling. "Mia is coming to live in the guest house at the ranch."

"The hell she is."

* * *

The entire room went silent at his outburst.

"Unca Jay, you said a bad word," Jenna piped in.

Jarrett reached into his pocket, pulled out change and set it on the table for his misstep. "Here, sweetie." Then he turned to Mia. "You can't move all the way out there. Not in the winter."

She glanced around nervously. "I don't want to talk about this now," she said as she pushed away from the table. "Excuse me." She stood and walked out.

Jarrett went after her. He caught up with her right before she got to the bathroom door. She would have disappeared, but someone was using the facility.

"Mia," he called.

"Go away."

"That's not likely." He gripped her by the arm and escorted her down the hall.

"What are you doing?"

"Taking you to a bathroom."

"I don't have to go. I just needed to get away from you and your crazy idea that you can tell me what to do."

He wasn't listening as he took her by the hand, led her to the master suite and opened the door to the large room. He pulled her inside and shut the door.

"Stop this," she demanded. "And stop telling me what to do. You can't boss me around."

He glared at her. "Someone needs to take you in hand. You can't move all the way out to the ranch. If we get a snowstorm—and the possibility is strong that we will—you might not make it to the hospital when the time comes."

"I can take care of myself. And why does it matter to you, anyway? You are my landlord, Mr. McKane, not my keeper."

"Dammit, stop calling me that. It's Jarrett." He leaned closer as her eyes widened. "Say *Jarrett*."

"Jarrett…"

His gaze moved to her full lips. Suddenly, he ached to know how they would feel against his and how she would taste. He couldn't resist and slowly lowered his mouth to hers. He took a gentle bite, then another. Each one a little sweeter than the last.

Her eyes widened, her breathing grew labored.

Finally, he closed his mouth over hers and wasn't disappointed. With a groan, he wrapped his arms around her and drew her closer. She made a whimpering sound and her arms move to around his neck as he deepened the kiss.

Jarrett pressed her back against the door, feeling her body against his, then suddenly something kicked against his stomach. The baby. He broke off the kiss with a gasp, suddenly remembering the situation.

Mia's shocked gaze searched his. "Why did you do that?"

"Hell if I know." He hated that he was so drawn to her. She was a complication he didn't need, but he couldn't seem to stay away from her.

Her hand went to her stomach protectively. Was she having a contraction?

He picked her up in his arms and carried her across the room.

"What are you doing?" she demanded.

"Taking you where you should have been in the first place. To bed."

CHAPTER SIX

MIA was fuming as Jarrett walked out the door, leaving her alone on the bed. His bed. What she hated the most was that she didn't have much say in the matter.

All her life, she'd had to do what she'd been told. Go to the best schools, make the best grades, be the perfect daughter. It had taken years, and although she'd made many bad turns she'd finally gained her independence. She wasn't about to give it up now. Not even for a man.

She glanced around Jarrett's bedroom. Large, dark furniture dominated the spacious room, including the king-size bed with the carved headboard. The walls were a taupe-gray and the floors a wide-planked dark wood. Two honey-colored leather chairs sat in front of huge French doors that led out to a deck and the wooded area beyond. It was definitely a man's room, which reminded her she shouldn't be in here.

Mia's thoughts turned back to Jarrett McKane. What had possessed her to let him kiss her? She shut her eyes reliving the feel of his mouth against hers, his strong arms around her. What she hadn't expected was the way she had reacted to him.

Of course, she would react to the man—any man for that matter. How long had it been since she'd been in a relationship? She couldn't even remember that far back. Not that she was eager to start one now. There hadn't been any time for a man. Then Mr. Hotshot McKane had stormed into her life, with his good looks and his take-charge attitude. No, she didn't need him in her life.

She started to get up when she felt the mild contraction and covered her midsection with her hand.

"Oh, please, no."

After several slow, relaxing breaths she eased back against the pillows and shut her eyes. Why had she come here today? Okay, she'd wanted to come to the party. And Dr. Drake had said she could be out for a few hours if she was careful and didn't overdo things.

Mia caressed her stomach, feeling the tension slowly ease from her body.

There was a soft knock and the door opened and Jarrett came in carrying a tray with a slice of pie. He stopped at the side of the bed, frowning. "You okay?"

"I'm fine," she fibbed. "I'm just resting."

He continued to stare at her. "You don't look fine."

She closed her eyes again. "Then don't look at me."

He sat the plate on the nightstand. "Are you having contractions?"

She opened her eyes. "Just a little one."

Jarrett pulled out his wallet from his back pocket and took out a business card. He grabbed the phone off the table.

"What are you doing?" she asked.

"Calling your doctor."

"You can't, it's Thanksgiving."

"Then we go to the emergency room." He paused. "Your choice."

* * *

Jarrett had worried this might happen if Mia left the apartment. They were lucky that Dr. Drake was on call today, and it only took her minutes to return his call.

The doctor talked with Mia, who didn't look happy when she handed the phone back to Jarrett.

"Yes, Doctor?" he said.

"I instructed Mia not to get out of bed for anything except to use the bathroom, and I want her in my office first thing in the morning. Could you bring her in?"

"We'll be there when your doors open." He ended the call and hung up. "Looks like you'll be staying here tonight."

He watched her eyes widen. "I can't stay here. It's not fair to you."

"Hey, I haven't been staying here anyway."

"But this is your room, your bed."

Smiling, he glanced around at the large space. "I guess we'll have to share."

She glared. "You need to get a life, McKane."

"I have a life, thank you, or at least I did before I moved into the Mountain View Apartments."

There was another soft knock on the door and Kira peered in. "Is everything okay?" she asked.

"It's under control now. Mia's had some contractions. Her doctor wants her to stay in bed and come in tomorrow."

Mia sat up. "I tried to tell Jarrett that I'll be able to rest better in my own apartment."

Kira stood at the end of the bed. "I know this is difficult, Mia, but you really need to stay put. In the last months when I was pregnant with Jenna, I couldn't even sit up to eat."

"See," Jarrett said. "And she delivered a healthy baby. So you stay."

Suddenly two more people appeared at the door, Nola and Sylvia, looking concerned.

"Please don't worry," Mia said. "I'm fine. But I guess I have to stay put for tonight."

Nola came closer and patted her hand. "We're not worried. Jarrett will take care of you." She looked down at the tray of food. "You need to eat."

Jarrett backed out of the room, leaving the women to pamper Mia. He couldn't help but wonder if he was the cause of her problem.

He rubbed his hand over his face. He had no business near her, let alone kissing her.

What happened to keeping your distance, McKane? The woman is pregnant, for Christ's sake.

He looked up to see Trace coming down the hall. "Is everything okay?"

Hell, would the cavalry be coming next? "Mia had a few contractions, but she's resting now."

"That's good." Trace studied him. "You seem to have inherited a lot more than just an apartment building. Need any help?"

Jarrett wasn't surprised at his brother's offer. For years the kid had tried to get close to him, but Jarrett had always rebuffed him. It made him ashamed of his past actions.

"Thanks, but I'm handling it."

Trace smiled. "I never thought I'd see the day my brother entertained a group of senior citizens in his house and had a pregnant woman in his bed."

Jarrett started to argue, but he had no words.

Trace grinned. "Be careful, bro, you're getting soft, or else, Mia Saunders is doing something no other woman ever has."

Jarrett sighed. "I don't want to hear this." He walked out into the great room, seeing the rest of his guests waiting for some news. He hoped he could convince them everything would be okay. First he had to convince himself.

Darkness surrounded her, but Mia knew she wasn't alone. The small room was filled with loud music, a lot of voices trying to be heard. She could smell cigarette smoke. Someone was smoking.

No! It was bad for the baby. She tried to stand, but someone pulled her back down.

"You can't leave, honey," a man with a slurred voice said. "The party's only getting started. Here have another drink." He put a glass in front of her face and she nearly gagged on the stale smell of beer.

"No! Let me go." She managed to break his hold, and get out the door. The night's cold air caused her to shiver as she looked around, but she couldn't recognize anything. She had no idea where she was, but knew she had to get home. But she had no home.

"Margaret!"

She turned and saw her father. She gasped and tried to run, but her legs were too heavy to move fast and Preston Saunders grabbed her arm.

"You can't get away from me," he threatened.

"Let me go," she cried. "I don't want you."

"I don't want you either, but my grandchild is a different matter. If you think I'll let you raise this baby you'd better think again. It's a Saunders."

"No, it's my baby. It's mine! It's mine!" she cried.

"Mia! Mia! Wake up."

She felt another touch. This time it was different. Gentler. Soothing. She opened her eyes and saw Jarrett leaning over her. With a gasp she went into his arms and held on. Tight.

Jarrett felt her trembling. His arms circled her back and

pulled her close and he felt her breasts pressed against his bare chest. The awareness shook him, but he worked to ease her fears.

"Ssh, you were having a bad dream. It's okay, Mia." He felt her tears against his shoulder. "I'm here."

She shivered again and then pulled back but refused to look at him. "I'm sorry."

With the moonlight coming through the French doors, he could see she wasn't all right.

"Bad dream, huh? You want to tell me about it?"

She shook her head, but didn't let go of his hand. "It's just one of those where someone is chasing you."

"Anyone you know?"

She shrugged. "Just someone from a long time ago."

That had him wondering about a lot of things. "A bad-news ex-boyfriend?"

She didn't answer for a long time. He suddenly became aware she was wearing one of his T-shirts, and he was only in a pair of sweatpants, all cozy together on his bed.

"I don't want to talk about it."

He nodded. "Do you want me to get you anything?"

She shook her head. "No, thank you."

"Should I leave?"

She finally looked at him. "Would you mind staying? For a little while?"

He had to hide his surprise. He didn't cuddle with women, not unless it led to something. He was about say, "Not a good idea," but instead he answered, "Not a problem." He changed position, propping himself against the headboard and pulled her back into his arms. "This okay?"

She nodded and then lay back down, her head against her pillow next to him. She blinked up at him with those trusting eyes.

Okay, this wasn't going to work. "Try and get some sleep."

"I don't want to start dreaming again."

He covered her hand with his. "I'm here, Mia. No one will hurt you or your baby as long as I'm around."

Somehow she'd managed to get to him, and he'd just taken on the job of her protector. It was crazy, but he didn't mind one bit.

Mia snuggled deeper into the warmth, enjoying the comfort of the soft bed. She smiled, feeling the strong arms that were wrapped around her back, holding her close.

Slowly, memories of last night began drifting back to her. The nightmare. Her father.

She opened her eyes and was greeted by bright sunlight coming through the French doors. What was more disturbing was the feeling of the bare skin against her cheek. She raised her head to see she was in bed with Jarrett McKane.

Oh, God. What was he still doing here?

She studied the sleeping man who was making soft snoring sounds. He suddenly turned toward her, reaching for her, pulling her against him.

Oh no. His chest was hard and doing incredible things to her out-of-whack libido. But she had a more desperate urge right now. She had to use the bathroom, and quick.

Careful not to disturb him, Mia managed to untangle herself, slide to the side of the bed and escape into the connecting bath.

A few minutes later she returned to find Jarrett awake and leaning against the headboard. His chest was gloriously naked, exposing every defined muscle under his bronzed skin.

"Morning," he murmured, raking fingers through his hair. "We seem to make a habit of this."

She had to put a stop to it. "Well, as soon as I get back to my apartment I won't be bothering you anymore."

Frowning, he got up and came around to her. "First thing, you need to get back into bed," he told her, giving her a little nudge to climb in. Once she complied, he continued, "Secondly, I wasn't complaining, just stating a fact."

Jarrett hadn't had much time for female companionship the past few months. Lately it had all been about business, until Mia Saunders and her group of merry followers had appeared in his life. They might be a costly headache, but he'd found he liked the diversion.

He sat on the edge of the bed. His gaze moved over her soft brunette curls and met her pretty blue eyes. Damn, he could get used to this. "Any more dreams?" He could still hear her frightened cries.

She shook her head. "I slept fine. Thank you."

He smiled and finally coaxed one from her. *Damn, she's pretty,* he thought, suddenly realizing his body was noticing, too.

"Okay, I better get breakfast started." He stood. "Will you eat eggs, or do I need to go on a jelly-donut run?"

Two hours later, Mia sat in the exam room with Doctor Drake, with Jarrett sitting just outside.

After the exam, the doctor pulled off her gloves. "You're doing fine."

"What does *fine* mean?" Mia asked as she sat up.

"You're effaced fifty percent."

"Oh, God. Am I going into labor?"

She shook her head. "You aren't dilated yet. And you haven't had any more contractions, right?"

"Not since last night."

There was a knock on the door and a technician came in pushing a machine.

"I want to do an ultrasound as a precaution," the doctor explained.

"So you are worried?" Mia asked.

"A little concerned. This baby coming early is a very real possibility." She raised a calming hand. "You're thirty-six weeks, Mia. All I want to do is check the baby's weight."

There was a knock on the door. "Yes?" the doctor called.

Jarrett poked his head in. "Is everything okay?"

The doctor glanced at Mia. "You want him in here?"

Mia looked at Jarrett and found herself nodding. "You can stay if you want," she told him.

He looked surprised but walked right toward her as she lay back on the table. Although covered with a paper sheet, she realized that she'd be exposing her belly for Jarrett to see.

Dr. Drake nodded toward the opposite side of the exam table for Jarrett to stand, then she began to apply the clear gel on her stomach.

Mia sucked in a breath.

Jarrett took her hand. "You okay?"

She nodded. "The cream is cold."

The doctor went to the machine and made some adjustments, then began to move the probe over her stomach.

Jarrett had no idea what he was doing here. Then he saw Mia's fear, and knew he couldn't leave her. He eyed the machine, watching the grainy picture, and then suddenly it came into focus. He saw a head first, then a small body.

"Well, I'll be damned," he murmured, seeing the incredible image. "That's a baby."

"What did you think it was?" the doctor chided.

Jarrett was embarrassed. "The way she's craved jelly donuts, I wasn't sure."

The doctor laughed. "Since your weight's okay, I'll tell you to indulge, a little. After the baby comes, you'll be on a stricter diet while you're breast-feeding." The doctor glanced at Mia, then back at the screen. "The baby's in position. So that's one less thing to worry about. This is a 3D machine so let's get a better look at this little one." The picture became a lot clearer and a tiny face appeared.

"Oh, my gosh," Mia cried and gripped Jarrett's hand tighter. "It's crazy but he looks like Brad's baby pictures." Tears formed in her eyes and a sob came out. "I'm sorry."

The doctor patted her arm. "It's understandable. Are you ready to know the sex?"

Mia looked at Jarrett. He shrugged, trying to handle his own emotions. "I say it's a boy."

Mia gave a slight nod and the doctor scanned in for a closer look. He saw all the proof he needed. "Well, hello, BJ."

Mia gave him a questioning look.

"I take it you're naming this little guy after your brother," he said. "Bradley Junior."

During the ride home from Grand Junction, Mia had zoned out, not noticing much of the trip until Jarrett stopped in front of the apartment building.

"We're home," he said, but didn't move to get out of the car. "Mia, are you all right?"

No! she wanted to scream. She hadn't been okay since the day her brother had died. She looked at Jarrett, seeing his concern. "Seeing the baby today made it seem so real." Her voice grew softer, more hoarse. "A boy. How can I raise a boy?" Tears filled her eyes, but she couldn't cry any more. "A boy needs a father. Brad should be here."

He reached across the console and took her hand. Even with the heater going, her hands were still cold. "Hey, this kid's got the next best thing. You."

She wasn't the best. "You don't know that. I've done things, made bad choices."

"I can't believe that, or your brother wouldn't have chosen you to carry this baby."

"But not to raise his son." She sighed. "Besides, I've always had Brad to help me, to guide me in life. Now, I'm on my own. What if I make mistakes again?"

He frowned. "Everyone makes mistakes, Mia, but you can't just give up."

Jarrett had never been the optimistic type, but he was a good salesman. "Don't forget, you have friends to help you. Is there any other family around?"

Mia shook her head. "No. There's no one else." She wiped her eyes. "God, I hate this. I never cry."

"I hear it's normal," he consoled her, hating that he kept getting more and more involved in her life. Not to mention the lives of the other tenants, too.

Once he got off house arrest and they all found other places to live, this time would just be a fleeting memory. They wouldn't be his problem then. They'd move on, and he'd move on. But could he? He thought back to being beside Mia and seeing her baby on the ultrasound.

Damn. He needed to get this apartment building in shape and get the hell out of here. "We'd better get inside and out of the cold so you can rest."

She grumbled. "That's all I've been doing."

"From what Kira tells me you won't get much sleep after the baby comes, so enjoy it now." He started to climb out of the car when she stopped him with a soft touch on his arm.

She nodded in agreement. "Thank you," she said softly. "Thank you for being there with me today."

He caught her pretty blue eyes still glistening with tears and something tightened in his chest. Dear Lord. He was in big trouble.

CHAPTER SEVEN

BY the next week, Jarrett had accomplished several things. He'd finally gotten one of the elevators repaired and a plumber had replaced the rusted pipes in the community room. Somehow, he'd even been talked into helping put up some Christmas decorations. Joe convinced him that since this would be Mia's baby's first Christmas, they should celebrate it.

The major thing he'd wanted to do was keep his distance from Mia. He'd gotten too involved with the expectant mother.

Thanks to Nola, Jarrett knew how Mia was doing, whether he wanted to or not. By afternoon, he'd seen several women going into his neighbor's apartment carrying presents for a baby shower.

Kira and Jenna stopped by his place afterward to see him and tell him all about the gifts Mia had gotten for the baby. His niece also had several things to say about the condition of his temporary home. None were good.

"Unca Jay, I like your other house better."

"I still have my other house, sweetie. I'll move back there soon."

She smiled, then looked thoughtful. "But you have to take care of Mia until she has her baby. Promise you will."

What was going on? "Okay, I promise as long as I live here I'll watch out for Mia and the baby."

That seemed to satisfy the three-year-old and she smiled. "Then you can come see her at the ranch. She's going to move in with the new baby." She turned to her mother and was practically jumping up and down. "I can't wait. I get to hold the baby, too."

Jarrett looked at his sister-in-law. "So, it's definite?"

Kira nodded. "I'm pretty sure I have her convinced it's best for her and the child."

"Isn't that neat, Unca Jay, she's gonna be in our family? It's almost going to be our baby, too."

"That's great," he said.

The girl's eyes lit up more. "Maybe if you ask, Mia will share her baby with you, too."

Jarrett looked at Kira for help, hoping she didn't read anything more into his relationship with his neighbor. "Where does she get this stuff?"

Kira only smiled. "Sounds like a pretty good idea to me."

The next day Jarrett drove to his office, McKane Properties, and started two of his staff working on finding affordable apartments for some of the tenants. He needed to get this over and done with.

He needed everyone to move on, but if Mia and the baby moved out to the ranch, he'd still see her. Would that be so bad? With Kira and Trace looking out for her, at least he wouldn't worry about her so much.

That way he could go back to business as usual and a life without Mia in it. He turned his thoughts to the day at the doctor's office and seeing the ultrasound. He'd had no business sharing that with her. Just as he'd had no business kissing her Thanksgiving Day.

He had to stay away.

There were other things he needed to think about, like the Fulton plant project. It had been a big cause of his loss of sleep. He'd been working on some changes, changes to the factory site that might help everyone.

For him to survive financially, Jarrett knew he had to finalize this deal, or he might be living in the Mountain View Apartments permanently.

A few days later Jarrett was awakened in the middle of the night by his ringing phone. He grabbed it off the bedside table.

"Hello," he groaned.

"Jarrett," a familiar voice said. "I'm sorry to bother you, but could you come over?"

"Sure." He hung up, got out of bed, pulled on jeans and shirt along with boots. He crossed the hall, but before he could knock she opened the door.

At 3:00 a.m. in the morning, she looked fresh and dressed for the day. Her dark hair lay in waves around her shoulders and she even had on makeup. "I take it the call wasn't for a donut run?" he joked.

"I need you to take me to the hospital. My water broke."

He froze, then his heart began to race. "You're in labor?"

She nodded. "I've only had some light contractions, but Doctor Drake said I need to come in now."

"Of course." He pointed to his apartment. "Let me grab my car keys." He rushed back, slipped on a coat and hurried back to find her waiting with a small bag.

"I hated to ask you, but Nola's daughter is sick and she's helping with the grandkids," Mia apologized.

He took her by the arm and they slowly made their way

to the elevator. "I'm glad you asked me, I don't want Nola to drive at night." He gave her the once-over. "You okay?"

She smiled. "Outside of being a little scared, I feel pretty good."

"I think it's normal to feel scared."

They rode down one floor and the doors opened. "Thank you for helping me out, Jarrett. I know this isn't in your landlord duties."

"Hey, I told you it's not a problem." They stepped off the elevator and walked outside. "Is there anyone you want me to call?"

Mia shook her head. "Nola was supposed to be my coach, but I can't take her away from her grandkids."

"Is there a backup?"

She stopped and looked at him pleadingly. "You?"

"You're kidding?"

"Do you think I like asking you again?"

"I didn't say I mind doing it, I just don't know what to do." He wasn't making any sense.

"Join the club. This is my first time, too," she began, then suddenly groaned.

He saw the pain etched across her face, but it was her fingernails digging into his arm that told him what was happening. Labor had begun.

"Looks like you're getting an early Christmas present."

Thirty minutes and five labor pains later, Jarrett pulled up at the emergency-room door. An attendant brought out a wheelchair, and Mia took the seat. Then Jarrett drove off and she was wheeled inside to get admitted.

After minimal paperwork, she was taken up to the maternity floor and into a labor/delivery room. Once dressed in a gown and in bed, she was hooked to monitors to watch her progress.

"Looks like you lose the bet for a Christmas-day baby."

Mia looked up as Dr. Drake walked in and nodded to the other doctor leaving. "December fifteenth seems like a fine birthday to me."

"How are you doing?" Lauren asked, checking the monitor.

No sooner were the words out than Mia felt a contraction begin to build.

"Breathe," the doctor instructed her as she came to the bedside. "It's almost over. There. Take a cleansing breath."

Mia sighed and lay back against the pillow. "That was stronger than the others."

"They're going to get even stronger before the baby comes. Don't worry, the anesthesiologist should be here soon with your epidural." The doctor glanced around. "Do you have someone here with you?"

"Will I do?"

They both turned to find Jarrett standing in the doorway. He hadn't gone back home.

"Jarrett, you don't have to stay. This could take all night."

He came in anyway. "I called Kira and she's on her way. So how about I be a stand-in until she arrives?"

"Kira's coming all the way here?"

"I didn't ask her to, she just said she's coming to help you."

Mia had to blink back tears. She wasn't going to be alone. She managed a nod at Jarrett. "Thank you."

"I know my limitations. My only experience is birthing calves." He shook his head. "And that was a long time ago."

"I'd like to see you all decked out in Western gear, cowboy hat, chaps." Mia found herself saying, feeling oddly relaxed in between pains.

"Hey, I didn't look bad." She knew he was nervous about his role as coach and trying to distract her. "I had a few girls following me around when I did some rodeos. Calf-roping was my event. I was known for my quick hands."

Mia couldn't hide her smile. "I bet you were," she said as another contraction grabbed her. "Ooh…"

The doctor looked at Jarrett. "Do your job, coach," she told him.

Jarrett took Mia's hand as Lauren instructed him on what to do.

Over the next hour, Mia's contractions grew more frequent and more intense. It helped if she focused on Jarrett's encouraging words and gentle touch, even his humor. She did her breathing, and he wiped her brow.

After another series of strong contractions had eased, she noticed him watching her. She had to be a mess. Her hair was matted down and she was sweating as though she'd run a mile.

His dark eyes locked on hers. "You're amazing. And you haven't even complained once." He spooned her some ice chips that soothed her throat. "You're going to make a great mother."

"You're not doing so bad yourself. A great stand-in coach." She started to say more when the door opened and the anesthesiologist walked in.

It didn't take the doctor long to work his magic, and soon Mia was relaxed and feeling no discomfort, just pressure from the contractions.

Jarrett stood beside the bed. "Is it better now?"

Smiling, she nodded. "Isn't medication wonderful?"

He laughed. "I'd still have to be knocked out to go through what you're doing."

Over the next hour things began to move a lot faster. Mia's contractions started coming faster and harder, and they were different. She felt more pressure, lower.

Dr. Drake came in and checked the monitor. "Could you step outside a minute, Jarrett?"

He squeezed Mia's hand. "I'll be right back," he promised as he walked out.

The doctor checked her. "You're close, Mia," she told her. "It won't be long now."

"Really?" She glanced at the clock. She'd only been here a few hours.

Lauren smiled. "Sometimes it happens like this, short labor is rare with the first baby."

Mia's thoughts turned to Brad and Karen and sadness swamped her. They should have been here.

Outside the room, a nurse handed Jarrett some paper scrubs. "But I'm not her coach. My sister-in-law is supposed to be here."

The nurse frowned. "Well, if someone plans to be with her, they'd better get inside because she's ready to go."

Jarrett paused momentarily. He didn't want to leave Mia to do this alone. She hadn't complained, but there wasn't anyone else here. He quickly slipped on the scrubs and walked back into the room.

"If you want me to leave, I won't be offended. Just say the word."

Before Mia could speak a contraction seized her and she grabbed his hand. Things happened quickly after that. The doctor instructed him to stand behind Mia. He continued to coax her through each contraction, and held his breath with each push. When she became exhausted, he made her focus.

The next thing Jarrett knew he was witnessing a miracle as Mia's son made his noisy entrance into the world.

"Here's your son, Mia." Doctor Drake held the baby up for inspection.

Jarrett found he was counting fingers and toes and other male body parts. He swallowed hard. "Well, I don't think you're going to have any trouble hearing this guy."

He looked down to see Mia's tears. "He's so beautiful, don't you think?" she asked.

"Well, he runs a close second to Jenna, so yeah, he's a good-looking kid."

A nurse took the baby, carried him to a table and began to clean him up. "He's seven pounds and ten ounces and twenty-one inches long," she announced.

Mia gave him a tired smile. "Jarrett, thank you."

He leaned closer to her. "Hey, you did all the work," he said, brushing back her damp hair. He suddenly felt the urge to kiss her. To signify this special moment.

"Yeah, I did, didn't I?" She looked sleepy. "I hate to ask, but would you call Nola? Let her know that I'm okay?"

Jarrett expected she wanted some privacy. He nodded and left. Outside the room he saw Kira hurrying toward him.

"Sorry I'm late." She studied his face and smiled. "I take it the baby's arrived."

He could only nod, feeling his emotions rushing to the surface. "Yeah, it's a boy. Mia and the baby are fine."

She nodded. "And it looks like you did a good job as a stand-in."

He didn't even bother to deny it. "I couldn't leave her."

Kira took his hand. "Be careful, Jarrett. People might mistake you for a good guy," she teased.

"I don't think I have to worry about that." He turned away, wondering when he could see the baby again. "Mia will probably want to see you." He stripped off his cap. "I need a cup of coffee." He started to walk away, but stopped. "Tell Mia I'll be back in a little while."

His sister-in-law studied him for a long time, then said, "Don't look now, brother-in-law, your feelings are showing. It's about time."

Thirty-six hours later, Mia was nearly ready for the trip back home. She and her baby had been checked out, deemed healthy and could be discharged from the hospital.

There was one thing left. She had to put a name on her son's birth certificate. During the night, she'd taken out the letter her brother and sister-in-law had left for her, not to be read until after the birth of their baby.

Mia sat up late to read it and let the tears fall—for the parents who would never know their son, and for the baby who wouldn't have the chance to know them, either.

She opened the envelope.

Dear Mia,

Words can never express the joy and love we feel for you at this moment—the moment we learned that you were pregnant.

Joy and love not only for your unselfish act, not only for giving up a year of your life, but for carrying our child. For that Karen and I will be eternally grateful.

We don't care if this baby is a boy or a girl. But like all mothers, Karen has chosen names for the child. Bradley Preston for a boy or Sarah Margaret for a girl.

Our son or daughter will know what a special person you are. To make sure of that, you will always be a big part of his or her life. Karen and I would like you to be the godmother to little Brad Jr. or Sarah.

If, God forbid, anything should ever happen to either of us, we want you to be the child's guardian. After all, you carried this little miracle in your womb and in your heart for nine months. So who better? Our only other wish is that you find the happiness you truly deserve.

Love always, Brad and Karen.

Mia had sobbed most of the night after that, then the baby was brought to her to be fed. The second she held him in her arms, she knew that she loved him. Yes, BJ was her heart. And he was her son now.

Two hours later, Jarrett parked outside the apartment building and Mia glanced back at the baby. She still had trouble thinking of herself as a mother.

It didn't take long for a welcoming party to open the door and wave. "Looks like everyone is anxious to see the new resident," Jarrett announced.

That made Mia smile. "BJ's going to have many surrogate grandparents, that's for sure."

"Let's get him inside before they start the inspection," Jarrett said.

He climbed out and came around to the passenger side. He opened the back door and unfastened the baby carrier from its base. "Come on, fella. You've got people to meet."

He raised the carrier's hood and used a blanket to protect the baby from the cold, then lifted him out of the car.

Mia was waiting and took his offered arm as they made their way up the shoveled walk to the door and went in.

"Welcome home, Mia," Nola called along with several other tenants as they walked inside.

"Thank you. It's good to be back."

She glanced around the large entry to see it had been decorated for the holidays. A large tree sat in the center of the area and lights and garlands had been strung along the wrought-iron stairway.

She went to one of the grouping of sofas and Jarrett placed the baby down on one of the now slip-covered sofas. Mia pulled back the blanket and everyone gasped.

"Oh, he's perfect," Nola cooed and glanced at Mia. "And so handsome, like your brother. What's his name?"

Mia swallowed. "Bradley Preston Saunders, Junior. That's the name Brad and Karen chose. I'm going to call him BJ."

Nola smiled. "It's perfect."

She felt Jarrett's presence behind her. It seemed so natural for him to be there. Too natural.

"I think these two need some rest," Jarrett told everyone.

Normally, Mia wouldn't like him making decisions for her, but she was tired. "Maybe you can come up later."

"Of course, but you need to rest now," Nola added. "If you need someone to watch this little guy, I'm available."

Jarrett picked up the carrier and placed a hand on her elbow as they made their way to the elevator. She was glad she didn't have to climb the stairs. They stepped into the small paneled compartment. He punched the second floor button and the doors closed.

"This is nice," she said.

He frowned. "What, the elevator?"

She nodded. "You have to remember it's been a while since we've been able to ride upstairs."

The doors opened and Jarrett motioned for her to step out first. "Well, only one's working," he said. "The other has multiple problems. I'm going to have to mortgage my home just to fix it."

"You're kidding?"

He suddenly grinned and her heart tripped.

"Almost. These old parts aren't easy to find. But all I need to do is make sure it runs for the next few months."

They reached her apartment and she unlocked the door. Once inside, she tried to take the baby, but Jarrett had already walked into the other room. Her bedroom.

She went after him, knowing it would be best to end this…dependency. She had to do this on her own. No distractions. And Jarrett McKane was definitely a distraction.

"I can handle it from here." Besides she wanted time with her son. Alone.

He set the carrier on the bed and stepped away. "I just didn't want you to lift anything yet." He shrugged. "You just got out of the hospital."

"The baby isn't heavy. Besides, I need to get used to carrying him." She worked to unfasten the straps and he began to stir, then made a little whimpering sound. She lifted him into her arms, feeling the tiny body root against her shoulder. If Jarrett would just leave.

Even though they had shared the birth, she had to draw a line at having an audience while breast-feeding.

"Not a problem."

"I'm sure you have plenty to do. And I need to feed him."

He looked embarrassed as he quickly glanced at his

watch. "Sure, I have a meeting anyway." He started out and stopped. "If you need anything…"

"I know, you're across the hall," she echoed, knowing how easy it would be to depend on him. To care more and more for this man. But she had to stand on her own and raise her son. "Jarrett, I could never begin to thank you for everything you've done."

"Hey, what good are landlords if they can't step in as labor coaches?" He glanced at the baby. "Be good to your mom, hot rod." He turned and walked out.

Mia heard the door shut and it sounded so final. But it had to be. She couldn't get involved with Jarrett McKane.

She laid BJ down on the changing table. Startled, the baby blinked open his eyes and looked at her. Something stirred in her chest as his rich blue gaze stared back at her.

"Hey, little guy," she whispered, almost afraid he would start crying. Instead, he stilled at the sound of her voice. Her throat tightened. "Welcome home, son." She swallowed, knowing there could be only one man in her life.

"Looks like it's just you and me now."

CHAPTER EIGHT

A FEW nights later, Jarrett got off the elevator on the second floor after a friendly poker game with Joe and friends in the community room.

Friendly, hah. They were card sharks. All of 'em. They had set him up, and by the time Jarrett had figured it out, it had cost him nearly a hundred bucks. Nothing to do but cut his losses and go home.

Fighting a smile at how the old guys had tricked him, he unlocked his apartment door. Before he got inside he paused, hearing a sound coming from across the hall. A baby crying. BJ. He checked his watch. It was after midnight. He waited a few minutes, but the crying didn't stop. Concerned, he went to Mia's door, and the sound got louder and angrier.

"Mia." He knocked, and after a few seconds the door opened.

A tired and anxious-looking Mia stood on the other side. Dressed for bed, she had on a robe, but by the looks of her, she hadn't gotten much sleep.

"Is everything okay?"

She didn't answer, instead she handed him the baby wrapped in a blanket. "Here, you make him stop. I've tried everything."

He quickly grabbed the bundle, then she turned and walked across the living room.

Jarrett looked down at the red-faced infant with his tiny fists clenched, waving in the air. "Whoa, there, little guy." He closed the door and followed after the mother. "It can't be that bad."

The answer was another loud wail. Not good.

He looked at Mia. "Did you feed him?"

She sent him a threatening look. "Of course I fed him. And I diapered him, bathed him, burped him, but he won't stop crying." Tears filled her eyes, her lower lip trembled. "I'm lousy at this."

"Stop it. You're just new at it."

He readjusted the squirming baby in his arms. Hell, he didn't know what he was doing either. He raised the baby to his shoulder and began rubbing his back. The baby stiffened, but Jarrett didn't stop.

"Has he been eating good?"

Mia nodded, but looked concerned. "Maybe he's not getting enough. I feed him every two hours."

"Maybe he's got an air bubble," Jarrett said.

He went to the sofa and sat down, laying the screaming baby across his legs. He remembered seeing Kira doing this with Jenna. After a few minutes a burp came from the little guy and the loud crying turned to a few whimpers and then, finally, silence. He kept patting the baby's back until he fell asleep.

He smiled at Mia who still looked close to tears. "Hey, BJ is fine now."

She didn't look convinced.

He lifted the baby into his arms and caught the clean sent of soap as the tiny bundle move against his shoulder, then finally settled down again. Protectiveness stirred in him as he carried the infant into the bedroom.

There was a night-light on over the crib, and he placed BJ down on his back. He made room as Mia adjusted the baby's position and covered him with a blanket. The kid stirred but didn't make another sound. The silence was golden.

They stepped away from the baby's bed. "He's so exhausted, he should sleep for a while," Jarrett said encouragingly.

"Thanks to you," Mia said, then added, "I couldn't even figure out it was gas."

Jarrett took her by the arm and led her across to the queen-size bed. They sat down side by side.

"So now you'll know," he said, seeing the dark circles around her pretty blue eyes. He brushed back wayward strands of hair that had escaped her ponytail. His heart pounded at the surge of desire that shot through him. He needed to leave, but he already knew nothing could draw him away from her.

"Call Kira. She had trouble with Jenna, too. That's how I knew what to do. And the next time you'll know, too."

She swiped at the last of her tears. "You're lucky to have family."

He glanced away. "Trace and Kira didn't always think so." He'd made so many mistakes with his brother.

"You and your brother haven't always been close?" she asked.

"Try never," he admitted. "It was mostly my fault."

"You two look pretty close now."

"Sometimes damage can't be fixed. But thanks to Kira, we've been working on it."

She watched him, waiting for more. "You're half brothers?"

He nodded. "Different mothers. I lost mine at six." He

shrugged. "My dad remarried, and his wife had a baby, Trace."

"Was she a good stepmother?"

"Alice? She didn't have much time for me, so I don't know much about her mothering skills. My dad just dealt with the ranch business, and that included taking me along." He glanced away. "I hated it. I can still smell the stink of the cattle, the burning hide of the steers during branding. And it's damn hard work, for damn little money. And as soon as I could, I got out. Straight into college."

She smiled. "Bet they were proud of you."

"Yeah, sure.

"Brad was my cheering squad. My best friend. Whether I wanted him to be or not." She glanced away. "All I gave him was trouble."

"I can't believe that. I bet you were a good kid."

She shook her head. "I was resentful, headstrong, but mostly stupid. An overweight girl who did anything to fit in. I turned out to be a big disappointment to a lot of people." She released a breath. "So I ran with a crowd that accepted me."

Jarrett could only nod, but he wanted to know so much more about Mia. What had hurt her so much she couldn't talk about it?

"Sometimes we can't see what's right in front of us." He began. "I took out resentment for my father on Trace. And it was well over thirty years before I figured out he wasn't my enemy. We're still working on it."

She brightened. "I bet little Jenna helps."

He tried not to smile but failed. "Okay, the little squirt has my number. But look at her. She's too cute to tell her no." *So are you,* he nearly confessed, trying to fight the attraction he felt.

"I agree. You are so lucky to have them."

"I'm realizing that." He eyed her closely. "When was the last time you slept?"

She shrugged. "I nap when BJ does."

He breathed a curse. "It's not enough, Mia. You haven't even been out of the hospital a week." Had it been that long since he'd seen her? Since he'd been purposely avoiding her? He'd worked late at the office, staying away to finish the repairs. Anything not to get any more entangled in her life. Trace was the family guy, not him.

Tonight, he realized how much he'd missed her. His gaze went from those brilliant blue eyes to her full mouth. God, he had to be crazy, but he couldn't stop himself as his head lowered to hers.

"Jarrett…"

"I like the way you say my name, Mia. A lot." He reached for her, pulling her to him until his mouth closed over hers. She released a sigh as her fingers gripped his arms and she leaned into him.

Only the sound of their breathing filled the room as his mouth moved over hers in a slow, sensual, drugging kiss, taking as much as she was willing to give. And he wanted it all.

Hungry. He was hungry for her. His tongue slid past her parted lips and tasted her, but it wasn't enough. He never could get enough of her.

He broke off the kiss and they both drew in needed air. He knew he had to stop, it was too soon for her.

Yet, it was already too late for him.

Mia stirred in the warm bed. It felt so good as she pressed deeper into her pillow. Sleep. She loved just lying in bed. Soon her thoughts turned to last night and Jarrett. The kiss. Smiling, she opened her eyes to the morning light coming through the window, then reality hit her, as she registered her tender breasts.

"BJ," she whispered, throwing back the covers to get out of bed. The crib was empty. Her heart pounded in her chest and she raced out to the other room. That was when she heard a familiar voice in the kitchen. Nola.

She stood in the doorway. "You are getting to be such a big boy," the older woman cooed at the baby in the plastic tub. BJ's tiny arms waved in the air as he enjoyed his bath.

Nola glanced at her. "Well, good morning."

"Good morning, Nola." She brushed her hair back. "What are you doing here? And why didn't you wake me to feed him?"

"He slept most of the night until five o'clock, which is when Jarrett called me and asked about using the bottle of breast milk in the refrigerator. I instructed him on how to heat it and he fed BJ. That was an hour ago, when I came up to relieve him. So I decided to steal some time with this guy while you got some more sleep." She grinned down at the baby, who was cooing. "BJ and I are getting to know each other."

Mia glanced around the empty apartment. When she'd dozed off last night Jarrett was still here. She suddenly recalled several things from their evening together. The things she'd told him about herself. Things she hadn't told anyone.

"If you're looking for Jarrett, he had a meeting to go to. He said he'd be back later today. I hope in time for our Christmas party."

"Who said I was looking for Jarrett?" She hated that she was so easy to read. "Why did he call you instead of waking me?"

"Because we're both worried about you." She nodded

for Mia to hand her the towel. She lifted the baby out of the water and Mia wrapped her son in the hooded terry cloth. "New mothers can get burnt out."

Mia hugged BJ to her. "I need to be able to take care of my son."

"You are a good mother, Mia," Nola assured her. "You're also doing this alone. But you have what's most important, a good heart and a lot of love for this little boy."

Together they walked into the bedroom and dressed BJ in one of his new outfits with a shirt that said, Chick Magnet.

Before Mia could pick him up, Nola did. "You need to eat something first. And I figure you have just enough time for some breakfast and a shower before this guy wants his mommy's attention."

She smiled. How lucky she was to have friends. "Thanks, Nola. I don't know what I'd do without you."

"We owe you a lot, too. We'd all be homeless without your help."

"We'll all be homeless soon anyway. So I didn't help that much."

The older woman pushed her bifocals back in place. "It's not over yet. I have faith in our handsome landlord. I also see the way he looks at you, Mia." She smiled. "And you should have seen him with BJ this morning. He's a natural."

Mia tried not to think about Jarrett McKane. He wasn't the man for her. He was the kind who only thought about the financial bottom line. Business before family. It was all about profit. The money. "He's counting the days until we're all out of here."

Nola watched her. "Yeah, that's the reason he had us all out to his house for Thanksgiving. And helped Joe paint your apartment. And stayed with you at the hospital during the birth of this little one." She glanced down at the baby, but quickly looked back at Mia. "Jarrett has a few rough edges, but that just makes him interesting." She lowered her voice. "And sexy."

Mia felt heat rise to her face. He had always been the one who'd showed up to help her. She recalled the way he made her feel when he kissed her last night. She hadn't wanted him to stop. That was a problem. If she got involved in a relationship with a man, she had to think about BJ, too. They were a package deal.

Worse yet, could she share all her secrets about her past? Even the lies she'd told to protect herself. What happened when Jarrett discovered who she really was?

Just a little before noon, Jarrett walked into the restaurant for his meeting. He hoped his lack of sleep last night wouldn't hinder him from convincing Fulton of his new plans. If he kept thinking about Mia and their kiss, it would. Or the fact that he'd left a beautiful woman's bed and gone into the other room to sleep on the sofa. That had been a first for him. There had been a lot of firsts with Mia, including being a babysitter for her son.

When Nola had relieved him from his duties early this morning, he'd had time to shower at his apartment and then go to the office where he'd finished up the presentation for today.

Over the past week or so, he'd been working on new plans for the Fulton factory. He hoped he'd come up with some changes to the construction that would be beneficial to everyone.

And save this deal for him.

If this new idea didn't go over with the CEO, he could lose a lot more than just a sale. Business ventures like this just didn't come down the road every day. It could take years for him to unload this property.

He walked across the restaurant behind the hostess to find Neil at the table by the window. The man didn't look happy, but Jarrett was hopeful he could convince him to make a few concessions.

"Neil, glad you could make it on such short notice."

They shook hands then sat down. "I hope you have some good news. I'd like to finalize this before I fly out tonight."

Jarrett released a quiet breath to calm his nervousness. *Don't let them see you sweat,* his college football coach had always told him. "Then let's get to it," he suggested.

The waitress came by and took their order.

"Now, tell me what's so important." Neil checked his watch. "I have to get on a plane and be back in Chicago tonight for a Christmas party. Robin will kill me if I'm late, especially since we're hosting it."

"It's what I want to show you." Jarrett pulled out the sketches for the plant site. "As you know, I have two apartment buildings located on the property." He took a breath and rushed on. "Because of airtight lease agreements, the remaining tenants aren't moving out until March."

Fulton frowned. "I thought you said you had it handled, that the building would be demolished by the end of January so we could break ground by early spring." Fulton was visibly irritated. "You assured me there wouldn't be a problem."

"Well, a judge stepped in and said otherwise." Jarrett raised a hand. "So I have another idea that might work even better."

Jarrett opened the folder and presented a sketch of the factory structure. "There's enough land to move the location of the new factory to the back of the property, and put the parking lot in front, leaving the existing apartment buildings."

"And why would I want to do that?" Fulton asked.

"Well, there's a couple of reasons," Jarrett began. "For one thing, it's a better location, a little further from town. So it won't be a traffic nightmare at rush hour."

"It would also cost more for extra materials for laying the utilities," Neil argued.

Jarrett pushed on, hoping his idea would work. "But if you use one of the existing apartment buildings for your corporate offices, you'll save on construction costs."

Neil's brow wrinkled in thought. "You can't be suggesting I use those dilapidated buildings?"

"Use *one* of the buildings," Jarrett corrected. "Why not? They're solidly built. They might have been neglected, but a remodel is a hell of a lot more cost-efficient than brand-new construction, even if you gut it entirely. You'd be recycling and it's better for the environment. And best of all, the building is already vacant. You could start the inside remodel after the holidays. No delay waiting for the ground to thaw."

Jarrett pulled out another drawing. "I had a structural engineer check out the building. It has the fifties retro look, but that can be changed, too. The main thing is it's large enough to house the plant's executive offices. Overall, you'll save money on this project. The shareholders will have to be happy about that."

Fulton didn't say anything for a while as he went over the new plans, then he looked at Jarrett. "There's no way you can remove the tenants?"

Jarrett shook his head. "I can't and won't. The majority are seniors on fixed income and two are disabled. I promised them they could stay until the spring." Then he said something that he never thought he would. "If possible, I'd like them to stay in their apartments for good."

Fulton leaned back in his chair. "You know that there are other locations the board of directors are looking at for this project, don't you?"

Jarrett's gut tightened as he nodded, seeing everything he'd worked for going down the drain. "Yes, I do. But you know this is the best location."

Fulton arched an eyebrow. "These people mean this much to you?"

Jarrett sat back. He hadn't thought about it until now, but these people been more accepting of him than his own father had. Truth was, they were starting to matter to him. Too much. He thought of Mia and BJ.

He eyed Neil Fulton's expectant look and shrugged. "Hey, I'm just trying to stay out of jail."

Later that evening, when Jarrett returned to the apartment building, he was exhausted. Fulton wouldn't give him an answer, but he had promised to talk it over with the board. Jarrett couldn't ask for any more.

He walked up the sidewalk toward the double doors. If Fulton went along with the new plan it meant Jarrett would keep the apartment building open. Of course, he'd have to put more money into the place, starting with paint. A lot of paint.

He shook his head. It was too soon to get excited. In these economic times nothing was a sure thing.

So Jarrett was in limbo. He thought about last night. Mia Saunders had stormed into his life and begun messing up his perfect plans. He'd liked things his way. Most of his life he'd been able to get what he wanted, until everything started to change, thanks to a blue-eyed do-gooder and her merry band of followers.

Hell, he'd never been a follower, and now look at him. Even worse, he was anxious to see her.

He pulled open the entry door and walked in, surprised to hear the sound of singing. A group of about two dozen tenants stood around an upright piano singing Christmas carols.

Standing back, he watched the people he'd come to know over the past few weeks sharing the joy of the holiday. This was hard for him. He couldn't remember when Christmas had been a happy time. Not since he was a small boy.

Then he spotted Mia across the room and felt a familiar stirring in his gut. She looked pretty, dressed in a blue sweater and her usual black stretch pants. Her dark hair was pulled back and adorned with a red ribbon. Smiling, she waved at him.

Maybe it would be a happy holiday after all.

CHAPTER NINE

MIA caught sight of Jarrett when he walked into the open lobby. It was hard not to notice the man. In a charcoal business suit with a crisp white shirt and a striped tie, covered by a dark trench coat, he looked more Wall Street than small-town Colorado.

"That's one good-looking man."

Mia glanced at Nola who was holding BJ. "Both the McKane men are handsome."

Her friend smiled. "But you're only interested in the older brother." She nudged Mia. "Now, go talk to him before someone else lays claim to your man."

She glared. "He's not mine."

"And he won't be if you keep ignoring him."

Nola gave her another gentle push, sending her off in Jarrett's direction.

Mia hadn't seen much of him, so there hadn't been a chance to invite him to the impromptu party. She couldn't blame him for keeping his distance. He was probably tired of taking care of her.

Besides, why would a man like Jarrett McKane be interested in her? Why would he want to take on a woman with a baby? Yet he'd done so many things for her. He'd been there when she'd needed him the most. How could she not care about a man like that?

Mia discreetly moved around the back of the crowd as Nola watched over BJ. Heart pounding in her ears, she walked up behind him. "You're expected to sing along," she managed to say.

Jarrett turned around to face her. Immediately, she caught the sadness in his eyes before he could mask it. "Everyone will be sorry if I do. My voice is so bad I don't even sing in the shower."

"I can't imagine you doing anything badly." Great. She was acting like an infatuated teenager, and she had never been any good at flirting.

"You'd be surprised at all the things I've messed up." His dark gaze held hers. "Did you get enough sleep last night?"

"Yes, thanks to you," she said, wondering if he'd thought about their kiss. Her gaze went to his mouth, then she quickly glanced away. "And thank you for not bringing up my meltdown."

Jarrett couldn't stop looking at Mia. Blue was definitely her color, bringing out the richness of her eyes.

"What meltdown?" he said, trying hard to focus on what she was saying. "You were just exhausted from lack of sleep and worried about your baby."

He couldn't help but remember how, during the night, he'd kept going in to watch her sleep. How strange was that? "I hope you got enough rest."

She nodded. "Plenty. And you're a good neighbor for coming to my rescue."

He tensed. Neighbor? *What neighbor kisses you like I did?* "That's me, just the full-service landlord," he said, trying to keep the sarcasm out of his voice. He started to leave, but she put her hand on his arm.

"Jarrett, what I meant was you went beyond helping me." Her eyes searched his face. "I've asked far too much of you. BJ and I weren't part of the deal when you were ordered to move in here."

"Did you hear me complain?"

She shook her head. "You should. I feel like I've taken advantage."

"Like I said, I haven't minded."

"And I'm grateful for everything—"

Grasping her hand on his arm, Jarrett leaned forward. The memory of last night's kiss had him aching for another. "I didn't do it for your gratitude, Mia."

He watched her swallow quickly, but before she could speak, the singing stopped and someone called to him.

"Unca Jay! Unca Jay!" Jenna came running toward him. "You're here."

He swung the child up in his arms. She had on a pretty sweater with snowflakes and dark pants.

"I have to go to work," he told her. "What are you doing here?"

"It's a Christmas party, silly. We got invited to come and sing." Her big blue eyes rounded. "You know what else?"

He played along. "No, what else?"

"It's only two more days 'til Christmas, and Mommy and Daddy asked everybody to come to our house for Christmas dinner. Even Mia and her new baby, BJ. And I got to hold him."

Jarrett looked across the room and saw his brother and Kira walking toward them. "How nice."

He got a hug from Kira and a handshake from Trace. "So, the festivities are at your house?"

Trace nodded. "Same as every year, but with Jody and Nathan gone, Kira's a little lonely. So why not have a big crowd?"

Jarrett looked at his sister-in-law.

"I love to cook," Kira said. "Besides, Nola and the others are bringing food, too. It's not much different than the group we had at your house on Thanksgiving."

"And now we have baby BJ," Jenna added as she patted her own chest and looked at Jarrett. "Unca Jay, did you know that BJ drinks milk from Mia's breasts?"

"Jenna…" her mother said with a warning look.

Everyone bit back a chuckle while Jarrett exchanged a look with Mia that felt far too intimate. Oh, yeah, he knew that.

His niece drew his attention back to her. "Look, Unca Jay." She pointed up to the sprig of greenery hanging overhead in the doorway. "Mistletoe."

Great. "It sure is." He leaned forward and placed a noisy kiss on the girl's cheek.

That wasn't the end of it; Jenna wiggled to be put down. "Now, you gotta kiss Mia."

Jarrett looked at a blushing Mia. "Sure." He leaned forward and placed a chaste kiss on her cheek. Their eyes met as he pulled back.

"No, not like that," Jenna insisted. "Like Mommy and Daddy do it. Put your arms around her and you have to touch lips for a long time."

Jarrett eyed his brother as Trace shrugged, trying not to smile. He got no help as he turned back to Mia. Without giving her a chance to protest, he reached for her and pulled her into his arms. His gaze locked onto her mesmerizing eyes, and, once his mouth closed over hers, everything and everyone else in the room faded away. It was all Mia and how she made him feel. How she tasted, how her scent drifted around him, how he was barely keeping himself in control.

Finally cheers broke out, and he tore his mouth away. "Did I do it okay?" he asked his niece.

A smiling Jenna nodded her head. He turned back to the woman in his arms. "Suddenly, I'm getting into the Christmas spirit."

Mia glanced at her kitchen clock and debated whether to attend the services tonight. For the first time in ten years, it wouldn't be Reverend Bradley Saunders standing at the pulpit delivering her Christmas Eve sermon. The last three years he'd been the pastor here in Winchester Ridge.

Mia had only been nineteen when Bradley had rescued her from self-destruction and got her on the road to recovery. From then on she'd sat in the front pew, grateful she had the love of family, and a future.

She glanced down at her son in the carrier. BJ would have the same; she would make sure of that.

"It's just us now, kid." She smiled as BJ, dressed in his dark-green holiday outfit, reacted to her voice with a cooing sound. "I might be new at this mother stuff, but no one could love you more." She wished she could give him a traditional family. Every kid deserved a mother and a father.

"I guess we'd better get going, or we'll be late."

She checked her own Christmas outfit, her standard black stretch pants and a long red sweater she'd found in a drawer.

After putting on her coat and BJ's cap and tucking a blanket around him, she picked up the carrier and walked out. She glanced across the hall to Jarrett's apartment.

As much as she tried not to, she'd thought about Jarrett a lot over the last few days. Okay, so it had been from the day he'd moved in. Not that she'd wanted him in her life; he'd just sort of barged into it.

At first, she'd even tried to compare Jarrett to her father, but she quickly realized they were nothing alike. Preston

Saunders would never open his home to a bunch of strangers for Thanksgiving dinner. Nor would he give up his time to help paint a room for her baby son, or even stay and play coach as she gave birth.

Mia touched her lips thinking about the shared kisses. Even though Jarrett had been goaded into the one under the mistletoe, he hadn't acted as if he minded at all. Yet he hadn't exactly shown up at her door the past thirty-six hours wanting to continue what had been started either.

Suddenly the elevator doors opened and Jarrett got off. He immediately smiled. "Hello, Mia."

"Jarrett," she said, trying to act casual. He looked too good in his jeans and sweater with a sheepskin jacket hanging open and his cowboy hat cocked just a little. "Merry Christmas."

He raised his arm to check his watch and she noticed the big shopping bags. "Is it that time already?" He eyed her closely. "I guess I'd better finish up my wrapping." He glanced at BJ. "Where are you two headed?"

"To the Christmas service at the church."

His smile faded. "Give me a second and I'll drive you."

"Jarrett, no. I can't let you do that. I can drive myself. We're not going that far."

"There's a lot of snow still on the roads, and your tires aren't in that great a shape."

He was right, but she hadn't had a chance to replace them. "It's only a few miles."

"And you have precious cargo." He nodded at her son and pulled out his keys. "Then at least take my SUV. It's four-wheel drive."

He was letting her drive his car? She looked at him, telling herself not to read anything into it. It was for her ten-day-old son. She decided to test him.

"Okay, I'll let you drive us, but only if you stay for the service."

He frowned. "You're kidding, right?"

She shook her head.

"It's been a long time since I've been inside a church."

"It's not going to crumble down around you. C'mon, you can handle it. You're a big strong guy," she challenged him.

He hesitated and finally relented. "Okay, just let me drop these presents off in the apartment."

She hadn't really thought he'd come, but suddenly she was glad she didn't have to face this night alone. Nor did she mind spending Christmas Eve with this man.

Nearly two hours later, Jarrett stood in the back of the church, watching as the parishioners fussed over BJ. Mia was enjoying showing off her son. She'd put up a brave front, but he knew it had been hard for her to come back here without her brother, her family.

He glanced around the ornate stone building with the stained-glass windows and high ceilings. He remembered another church across town where his stepmother had insisted they go to services weekly. And the Sunday school teacher who swore that a young Jarrett's bad attitude would send him straight to hell.

That hadn't been a good time in Jarrett's life. His mother had died suddenly when he was barely six, and within a few months his father had another wife. The following year his baby brother, Trace, had been born. And the struggle between the McKane brothers had begun. The father he'd so badly needed after the loss of his mother, turned away and found another family. Jarrett had been told he had to carry more weight and help out. Suddenly there wasn't any time to be a kid, or time to be with the father he'd needed so desperately.

He quickly pushed aside the bad memories. Tomorrow was Christmas, and, thanks to Kira, he and Trace were finally working on liking each other.

Family wasn't the only thing that gave him trouble; he was still hoping to hear from Fulton.

He'd closed the office early today, but Neil had his cell phone number. If the land deal crashed, *no one* would have a happy holiday. He might even end up being a permanent resident in the Mountain View Apartments.

He glanced across at Mia. Not that he would mind being her neighbor. If he was honest, he was happy that he got to spend time with her tonight. He tried to tell himself it was only because he felt protective of the new mother. But he was attracted to her, big-time. As much as he'd tried to stay away, she kept drawing him back into her life. He sure as hell wasn't putting up much resistance, either.

Mia walked over to him. "I'm sorry I kept you waiting. Everyone wanted to see BJ."

"Well he's a cute kid, and you should be a proud mama. It's okay if you want to stay."

She shook her head as she pulled the carrier hood up and covered the baby. "I really need to feed BJ. Could we go home?"

"Sounds good." He took the carrier from her and escorted her through the doors. Once outside they were greeted by a strong wind and snow flurries. He pulled Mia close against his side, trying to shield her from the biting cold.

At the SUV, he helped Mia get in and quickly latched BJ's safety seat in the back, then he climbed in the driver's seat and started the engine.

Glancing out the window, he waited for the cab to warm up. "I was afraid of this."

She was shivering. "I'm sorry. I didn't think the weather would turn bad. It's supposed to be clear tomorrow."

Her coat wasn't heavy enough to keep her warm. He flipped the heater on high and took a blanket from the back seat to drape over her legs. "We're lucky it's not a big storm, just the tail end of it. But I'll feel better when we're back at the apartment."

Jarrett pulled out of the parking lot cautiously. He glanced at the baby in the back seat; he was starting to fuss.

"Hang on, BJ. We'll be home soon."

Jarrett turned off the main street onto a back road, thinking he could shave off some time. First mistake—the road was deserted. Secondly, it hadn't been cleared of snow. Even with four-wheel drive, traction was nonexistent.

"Sorry, this was a bad idea. I'll turn back."

BJ began to cry louder.

Jarrett found a wide spot in the road and slowed more as he began to turn the wheel. He cursed when the back of the vehicle began to slide. "Hang on," he called to Mia. He gripped the wheel tighter, turning into the slide, but he couldn't gain control. When he got the car stopped they were off the side of the road.

Jarrett cursed under his breath and BJ let out a wail. Shifting into Reverse, he backed up, but nothing happened. He tried going forward again, but the only thing he got was the spinning of the tires as the car slipped sideways, deeper into the snowbank. Although angry with himself, he remained calm. "I'll go see if I can dig us out."

"Be careful," Mia called over the screams of the baby.

Placing his hat on his head, Jarrett got out and made it through the ankle-high snow to the back of the car. He opened the hatch and took out a shovel. He began digging, but soon discovered it was useless. He made his way back to the driver's side and climbed in. Pulling off his gloves, he took out his phone. "We need a tow truck." He punched in his roadside assistance. By the time he hung up, he wasn't happy. "She put us at the top of the list because of the baby, but it still could be an hour."

"Long as we're warm, it's okay," she said. "Do you have enough gas?"

"Yeah, a full tank."

"Good. I need to feed BJ. I'll go in the back."

"No, stay up here, it's warmer." He flipped on the interior light, leaned into the back seat and managed to unfasten the crying baby's straps.

"Come on, little guy, settle down," he coaxed. "You'll have your mama in a minute." He lifted the small bundle and handed him to Mia who had already removed her coat, leaving it draped over her shoulders.

She looked at him and paused. "Would you mind turning off the light?"

"Oh, sure." Of course she didn't want an audience.

In the dark, he could see her tug up her sweater. All at once there was silence. Jarrett looked over at Mia as she leaned over the child at her breast, stroking him.

His chest tightened at the scene. Finally turning away, he concentrated on the snow blowing across the front window, but he could still hear Mia's soft voice as she talked to her son. Leaning back against the headrest, he closed his eyes and tried not to think about how much he wanted to wrap his arms around both of them and protect them. Yeah, he'd done a great job of that so far.

Restless, he sat up. "Life is pretty simple to him, food and Mama." He looked at her as she moved the baby to her shoulder and began to pat his back.

"Sometimes it scares me that I have someone who's so dependent on me," she admitted.

"You're a natural at this."

She paused. "How can you say that when you've seen me at my worst?"

BJ gave a burp and she lowered him to her other breast. This time Jarrett didn't turn away from the silhouette of mother and son. He'd never seen anything so beautiful. Leaning across the console, he reached out and touched the baby's head. "I've only seen a mother who loves her child." His chest tightened at the sight.

Their gazes met in the dark car. "I do love him. At first I was so frightened, but he's become my life. I know technically he's my nephew, but—"

Jarrett placed his finger against her mouth to stop her words. "In every way that counts, Mia, he's your son. You carried him in your womb, now you nourish him from your body." His fingers moved and grazed her breasts. "It's beautiful to watch you with him."

"Oh, Jarrett."

At the husky sound of her voice, he shifted closer. He felt her breath against his cheek.

Suddenly a bright light shone through the windshield, illuminating the front seat. He drew his hand away, but continued to hold her gaze.

"It seems we've been rescued," he said, knowing he wasn't so sure about his heart.

CHAPTER TEN

IT was after eleven o'clock by the time the tow truck pulled Jarrett's SUV out of the snowdrift and they'd driven back to the apartment. The night had been long, but still Mia didn't want their time together to end.

Jarrett walked her to her apartment door. "I'm sorry about tonight. I never should have taken that back road." He glanced at BJ in the carrier. "I would never do anything to endanger either one of you."

"Of course I know that. You didn't cause the bad weather, Jarrett."

He watched her a moment, then he finally said. "I probably should let you get some sleep."

She put her hand on his arm when he started to step back. "Won't you come in for some coffee?" Did she sound desperate? "I have something for you."

He looked surprised. "Okay, but let me grab something from my place first. I'll be back in a few minutes."

With a nod, Mia went into the apartment, leaving the door unlocked. She quickly dressed her son in his sleeper and put him in the crib, knowing in just a few hours he'd be awake and hungry. She checked her makeup and went back into the living area, quickly picked up several baby items scattered around and tossed them into her bedroom.

She'd finished plugging in the lights on her tabletop

Christmas tree when there was a soft knock. She tugged on her sweater and brushed back her hair before answering the door.

"Oh, my," she gasped as Jarrett walked in carrying several presents. "What did you do?"

He set the packages down on the table. "I took Jenna shopping yesterday and she convinced me that BJ had to have all these things." He raised an eyebrow. "You should have seen what I talked her out of."

Mia eyed the boxes, but picked up the stuffed bear. "He isn't even sitting up yet."

"Then put some away for his birthday." He smiled and her heart tripped.

She glanced toward the present under her tree. Before she lost her nerve, she grabbed the tissue-wrapped gift and handed it to him. "This is for you."

He looked touched. "Mia, I didn't expect anything."

She shrugged as if it were nothing. "It's probably silly."

He tore through the paper and uncovered the charcoal-gray scarf she'd knitted. As he examined it she wondered if he could see the mistakes.

He stared at her, his brown eyes tender. "Did you make this?"

She managed a nod. "Nola taught me while I was on bed rest. I'm not very good."

She didn't get to finish as he leaned forward and placed a sweet kiss on her mouth. Chaste or not, she felt dizzy.

"Thank you. I've never received anything so nice."

Jarrett had trouble holding it together. He hadn't enjoyed the holidays for a long time. His mother's death only days before Christmas had left a little boy devastated with grief.

"You're welcome," she said, her voice hoarse.

He finally stepped back and draped the scarf around his neck before he lost all control. "I have something for you."

"Did Jenna pick it out, too?"

"No, I did." He pulled a small jewelry box from the bag. "So I can't blame her if you don't like it."

She blinked seeing the store name on the box. "Oh, Jarrett, you shouldn't have done this."

He smiled at her. "You haven't even seen it. Maybe you won't like it."

She gave him a stern look. "Of course I will." She opened the box to see a sterling-silver chain with a round charm engraved with BJ's name and his date of birth.

She glanced at him. "I was wrong, I don't like it. I love it. Oh, Jarrett. It's perfect. You couldn't have gotten me anything I wanted more."

He released a breath. He'd bought women gifts before. Why did he care so much about this one? "I'm glad."

She took it out of the box. "Will you help me put it on?" She gave him the necklace and turned around. Moving aside her rich brown hair, she exposed her long slender neck to him. Somehow, he managed to fasten the clasp, but she was too tempting not to lean down and place a kiss against her exposed skin.

He felt her shiver, but she didn't move. He slid his hands around her waist, pulling her against him. He whispered her name and after a few seconds, he turned her in his arms. "This isn't a good idea. In fact it's crazy. You just had a baby, and I shouldn't be thinking…"

"Oh, Jarrett." She shook her head. "I don't see how… I'm having enough trouble trying to handle my life. You've seen me at the worst times, and you have to be tired of rescuing me."

"Maybe I like rescuing you." He didn't let her go. He

had no business wanting her. He was all wrong for her. But all he wanted was to be with her.

"I want to be self-reliant."

"We all like to be. But there are some things that are fun to do with someone else, someone special."

He dipped his head and captured her mouth. His arms circled her and he pulled her close as he deepened the kiss, tasting the addicting sweetness that was only Mia.

With the last of his control, he broke off the kiss, and pressed his forehead against hers. "You're big trouble, lady."

Before she could say anything, the clock chimed. Midnight.

"Merry Christmas, Mia."

Even though the air was brisk, the day promised to be bright and sunny. A perfect Colorado Christmas, Mia thought as she fingered the charm on her necklace.

She glanced across the SUV at Jarrett. Christmas Eve had already been wonderful and this morning had started out close to perfect, too. Jarrett had showed up with a box of jelly donuts and they'd shared breakfast together. Just the three of them.

It could give a girl ideas. Ideas she had no business thinking when she should only be thinking about her son.

Although the man was definitely making this holiday memorable, especially when he'd insisted on taking her and BJ out to the ranch today. Were they a couple? No. She shook away that crazy thought.

"We're here."

Jarrett's voice drew her attention as he turned off the main highway and drove under an arch announcing the McKane Ranch.

Mia felt the excitement as a large two-story house came into view. She smiled at the snowman in the front yard, then her attention went to the wraparound porch and the dark shutters that framed the numerous windows.

Jarrett bypassed the driveway and went around the house. "We're pretty informal here," he said. "I don't think the front door has been opened in years. Everyone has always used the back door."

That would never be allowed in her parents' home. The service entrance was only for the hired help. "Sounds like my kind of place. I bet you had fun growing up here."

His smiled faded. "Ranching is a lot of work. One of the reasons I left and went away to college."

He parked next to Joe and Sylvia's car at the small porch that overlooked the barn and corral. "So now the place belongs to Trace."

He turned off the engine. "After our parents died, I was happy to sell him my half."

She smiled. "You can still come back whenever you want, and the best part is seeing your family."

There was a long pause, then he said, "There was a long time when I wasn't exactly welcome. But a few years ago, Trace and I became partners in a natural gas lease. The money helps him keep the ranch and not worry about having to run cattle. And I can invest in business ventures. Anyway, then Jenna came along, and somehow I ended up calling by more and we sorted some things out."

Mia was surprised by Jarrett's admission. "Well, I'm glad you and your family have reconciled your differences."

He nodded and turned toward the house. "Oh, look, here comes the welcoming committee."

Kira and Trace stepped onto the porch. "Welcome and Merry Christmas."

Mia got out and the cold breeze brushed against her cheeks. "Merry Christmas," she called back.

Trace came down the shoveled steps and greeted his brother first, then walked around the car to her. "Welcome, Mia."

"Thank you for inviting us. Your place is beautiful."

"We think so." He glanced at his brother. "There's plenty of time before dinner so you can leave BJ with us while Jarrett shows you around." He pointed toward a group of bare trees. "The cottage is just over there, if you're still interested in seeing it."

Mia turned around to see a small white structure about fifty yards from the house. "Oh, yes. I'd love to."

Jarrett got BJ from the back seat while Mia handed a large poinsettia plant to Trace.

When Jarrett's brother started to protest, citing the no-gift clause, she quickly said, "It's from BJ."

With a smile, she retrieved a salad and a pie and carried them into a huge country kitchen with maple cabinets and granite countertops filled with food. Several mouthwatering aromas surrounded her, making her hungry.

Nola and Sylvia were already there helping Kira with the meal. "Just put those things down, if you can find a spot for them."

Kira beamed as she came up to Jarrett and gave him a kiss on the cheek, and then looked down at the carrier. "I'd love to get my hands on this little guy, if I could."

"Sure," Mia told her. "He loves being held."

It took only seconds before Kira had BJ in her arms. "Now you two run off and see the cottage. We can handle things here."

Jarrett came up beside Mia. "They seem to be trying to get rid of us."

"Not at all, but I would love to have this little guy around more." Kira smiled down at the baby and cooed, "Oh, yes I would."

"Let's go." Jarrett escorted Mia out the door and across the yard, but she was distracted by the horses roaming around in the corral.

"Oh, what beautiful animals."

Jarrett changed direction as they detoured to the corral fence. "Trace has been doing some horse-breeding the past few years. This guy is Thunder Road." When he whistled, the horse trotted over as Jarrett climbed up on the fence railing so he could pet the spirited animal. "Hey, Roady." He rubbed the horse's face and neck briskly, then glanced at Mia. "This guy was sired by Midnight Thunder, a champion cutting horse."

"He's beautiful." She could see how much Jarrett loved animals. "He seems to like you, too."

"He knows me. I come out here sometimes."

There was so much about this man she didn't know, that he kept hidden. She glanced around. "I still can't see how you'd want to give this place up. I love the peace and quiet."

He shrugged and released the horse and they watched him run off. "When I was younger, I called it boredom. I wanted excitement and fun." He looked toward the horses. "After my mother died, my father and I didn't get along much."

Mia understood that. "He's gone now?"

"Yeah. When his wife died, he wasn't much for living alone."

"What about your mother?"

He continued to stare toward the corral. "She's been gone since I was a kid."

"I'm sorry, Jarrett. How old were you?"

"Six."

"Oh, God, you were just a child."

He turned toward her. She could see the pain before he quickly masked it. "I grew up fast."

"What about your stepmother?" She wanted him to tell her that she'd been a caring and loving woman. "Did she help you through that time?"

"I don't remember much." He shifted. "She was just there, and soon, so was Trace."

"At least you had a brother to share things with."

"Yeah, right. I did everything possible to let him know how much I hated him."

Jarrett stepped up to the small cottage porch and turned to see if Mia needed help. Damn, he hated that he'd spilled his guts to her. He'd never told anyone about his childhood. Why her?

He inserted the key into the lock. "I know Trace and his foreman, Cal, redid the entire inside."

"The outside is well-maintained, too," she said, coming up beside him. "I can't wait to see the rest."

He swung open the front door, and they stepped into a living room that had a small sofa and two chairs. An area rug covered part of the shiny hardwood floors.

"Oh, this is nice."

He gestured with his hand to go on, and she walked into a galley-style kitchen. All the stained-wood cabinets were new, as were the egg-shell-colored solid-surface counter-tops. The white appliances gleamed. Jarrett had no doubt Kira had been out here cleaning.

"This is so nice. There's even a table and chairs." Mia walked through to a small sunroom that looked toward the open pastures. "This would be a perfect work area. Plenty of light and space for a desk and computer."

She beamed as she walked ahead of him and down the

hall. She stuck her head into the bathroom that also had a stackable washer and dryer. "Okay, I've died and gone to heaven." She went on to check out the two bedrooms. When she came out she looked about to burst.

Her dark hair was bouncing against her shoulders. And he noticed how slim she was becoming, and how long her legs were. Yet, it was her eyes, those blue eyes of hers that made his gut tighten in need.

"This is three times as big as my apartment," she said, bringing him back to the present.

"And thirty miles out of town." But closer to his house. "In the winter that could be a difficult drive."

"But I know I can afford this place," she insisted. "Obviously, if I stay here, I plan to pay rent to Kira and Trace."

He studied the stubborn woman in front of him. She was beautiful and no doubt capable of doing anything she set her mind to.

"Okay, but you have to let me take you to look for a dependable car. That sedan of yours is in bad shape."

Her eyes widened. "I can't afford a new car."

"Not new, but at least an upgrade from what you're driving now. I can get you a good deal, one with decent tires."

She smiled slowly. "You're a fraud, Jarrett McKane. You try to get everyone to think you're this ruthless business-man with no heart, but you're a nice guy."

He stood straighter. "If you think I've gone soft because I'm fixing the apartments up, think again. I have a good reason for doing it. The judge ordered me to."

Her look told him she wasn't buying it.

"Ah, hell. At least while you're living there I can keep an eye on you."

"You're not responsible for me, Jarrett," she told him

sternly. "I can take care of myself, and have for a lot of years."

"I know that." He couldn't help wondering about other men in her life. "What if I just want to help you?" He tested her. "Say if I want to come around to see if you and BJ need anything? I mean, I do visit my brother and sister-in-law out here."

"And Jenna," Mia added.

"And Jenna," he repeated, watching the light play off her hair. Her skin looked so soft.

Her eyes met his. "Aren't you going to be too busy with the new factory project to bother with us?"

He shrugged. "That's not a done deal, yet. I'm still going over things with Fulton Industries."

"It's because of the tenants, isn't it?"

"Things could work out better." He didn't want to tell her his idea to keep the apartment building. "Hey, what's the worst that can happen? The deal goes south and I get to live in the hellhole apartment 203 forever."

"Well, BJ and I would be your neighbors."

He stepped closer. "I thought you were moving in here?"

"Not if the apartment is still available. I like paying my own way. Would you raise the rent on us?"

He smiled at her. "Maybe we can work out a special deal."

An hour later, with BJ asleep in his carrier in the living room, the Christmas dinner could start.

In the McKanes' dining room, there were two long tables dressed with red and green tablecloths and holiday china. A row of delicious food dishes crowded the sideboard, not to mention the overflow waiting in the kitchen, along with a dozen pies and assorted desserts.

Mia carried her heaping plate to the table to find a seat. It was no surprise Jarrett had saved one next to him.

"This is the best Christmas ever." Jenna climbed into a booster seat next to her uncle. "And you know what else, Unca Jay?"

The youngster didn't wait for prompting. "I'm glad you bringed BJ and Mia. And that you aren't mad at Daddy anymore."

Mia caught the exchange between the two brothers who sat across from each other.

"Yeah, well it's Christmas," Jarrett said. "Everyone should get along."

"It's a time for peace and goodwill," Joe added. "And we should think about those who aren't here with us today."

"Like Jody and Nathan," Jenna said. "And Ben, 'cause he's protecting our country."

"That he is," Nola said. "We need to pray for all servicemen who are away from their families, too. And to keep them safe."

Everyone bowed their heads as Trace led them in the blessing. Mia was surprised when Jarrett took her hand in his. It was warm and reassuring. She was glad that she had someone to share this day with.

"Now, let's eat," Jarrett announced after the prayer. And it began. Lively conversation and good food.

"Mia, how did you like the cottage?"

She looked across the table at Kira. "Oh, I love it. It's beautiful and so roomy."

Kira exchanged a look with her husband. "Does that mean you plan to move in?"

"If you still want us, I'd love to move out here."

A big smile spread across Kira's face. "That's wonderful." She looked at her brother-in-law. "And it's not so inconvenient living out here. We have good neighbors. How far away is your place, Jarrett? Five miles?"

Jarrett's fork paused on its way to his mouth. "Something like that."

His sister-in-law was grinning now. "See, there's a McKane around if you need one, and also we have Cal here, too."

The foreman looked up from the other end of the table and nodded. "It would be nice to have another little one around the place."

Trace stood up. "Speaking of little ones." He glanced down at his wife and exchanged a look that showed everyone in the room how much they loved one another. "We have some news, and we thought that this would be a perfect day to share it. Kira and I are expecting our second child next summer."

Jarrett watched as the room erupted in cheers and congratulations. He suddenly felt the old jealousy creeping in. Why would he be jealous of a baby? He'd never wanted a family.

He turned to Mia, who was watching him.

"Isn't that wonderful news?"

"Yeah, it is." He glanced at his brother. "Hey, Trace. Congratulations."

Jenna finally got into the act. "Am I going to have a baby sister? I asked for a sister."

Everyone laughed.

"We don't know if it's a girl or boy, yet," Kira told her daughter. "But I know you'll be happy with either."

Before Jenna could speak, the sound of BJ's crying drew everyone's attention.

"Someone's hungry. Excuse me," Mia said as she left the table.

Jarrett wanted to go with her, but he had no right to

share this time with her and her son. He saw Kira direct her upstairs to a bedroom.

Again he was on the outside looking in, where he'd been for so many years. He didn't want to be there anymore.

Mia sat in the rocking chair in the McKane nursery. Once the room had been Jenna's, but the toddler had been moved to another bedroom and a big girl's bed. How convenient that Trace and Kira already had a beautiful room for their next baby.

She smiled down at her son, and her heart nearly burst with love. She could no longer see her life without this child. He was everything to her, and she would do everything she could to give him a good life. She'd find a way to finish law school and make a home for him. She ran her hand over his head. "I promise you this, BJ, I'll be the best mom I can."

Her thoughts turned to Jarrett. Would he be a part of their lives? Would he come around once she moved out here? Once the apartment building was demolished, he'd be so involved in the factory project she doubted there would be time for her.

Mia fingered the chain around her neck. She was a realist, and couldn't lie to herself. Jarrett wasn't the type of man who took on a woman with a baby. Yet, she recalled him telling her about his mother's death, and his stepmother's neglect. She thought back to her own youth. Seemed they weren't so different after all.

BJ stiffened and began to fuss. "I think you need a burp." She brought him to her shoulder and began to pat his back gently. BJ cried louder. "Sshh, honey. Relax." She continued the rubbing, but it wasn't working.

There was a knock on the door and Jarrett peered in. "Sounds like someone isn't happy."

Mia was both confused and relieved as Jarrett walked in. "You want to try?"

He took the infant from her. He placed her son against his large chest and began to walk and pat. After about thirty seconds, the crying stopped when a burp erupted from the infant.

Jarrett smiled at her. "Looks like I still have the touch."

"Then I'll give you BJ's feeding schedule and you can come by and do the honors."

She didn't hide her smile at his surprised look.

"You know I will if you need me," he said sincerely.

"Don't, Jarrett. I can't keep relying on you to help me." Even if she wanted nothing more than to have him around all the time. "BJ is my responsibility."

He came closer, but wouldn't relinquish the baby. "Why, Mia? Why do you think you have to do this all by yourself?"

She glanced away from those velvet-brown eyes. "It's safer that way, Jarrett. And no one gets hurt."

He touched her chin and turned her back to him. "Who hurt you, Mia? What man broke your heart?"

She stiffened and shook her head. "It's not important. It was a long time ago."

"It's important to me. You're important to me, Mia."

She wanted so much to believe him, but she wasn't good when it came to trust. "Oh, Jarrett. I don't know what to say."

He stepped in closer. "Good. I'd rather do this." Even with BJ against his shoulder, he leaned down to capture her mouth and quickly had her heart racing and her body stirring, wanting more.

He broke off as BJ began to complain. "Maybe we can

talk more about this later." He gave her another peck and straightened up just as Kira walked in.

"I hate to disturb you both, but there's someone here to see you, Mia."

"Who?"

"He says he's your father."

CHAPTER ELEVEN

Mia had been dreading this day for ten years. Why did he have to find her? Why now? She saw the confused look on Jarrett's face, not surprising as she'd told everyone she had no family.

As far as she was concerned, since Brad's death, there hadn't been anyone. Putting a sleeping BJ in the crib, she finally looked at Jarrett. "Please, don't say anything about the baby."

He stared at her a moment, but his expression didn't give anything away. "I'll follow your lead."

They walked out and down the stairs, grateful that Kira had put the unexpected guest in the living room, away from everyone. She glanced at Jarrett. "I need to talk to him alone."

He nodded. "I'll be close by."

With a sigh, she walked into the room. Preston Elliot Saunders stood in front of the massive stone fireplace. Since his back was to her, she took the opportunity to study him. Still tall and trim, his once thick dark hair was now nearly white and there was a slight slump to his shoulders. He turned slightly and she could see he wore a dark wool coat over a business suit.

Had she ever seen him when he hadn't been in a suit? As a child she'd only seen him when she needed to be disciplined. She'd been the daughter who couldn't seem do anything right, so that had been a lot.

Preston finally turned around and she saw that the last decade had added lines to his face. She hoped to see some emotion from him, but, once again, she was disappointed.

She fought off all the old fears and insecurities and stepped fully into the room. "You wanted to see me?"

He frowned. "After all this time that's all you have to say to me?"

"Ten years ago I was a disgrace to the family and was destroying my life. You disowned me and sent me away. So excuse my surprise when you show up here now. There must be a reason." She knew exactly the reason. Somehow he'd learned about her baby.

"No matter what happened between us, you should have had the decency and compassion to tell me about Bradley's death. Your mother and I were heartbroken when we learned about it recently."

Mia noted he didn't mention his daughter-in-law's death. Not only had Preston and Abigail disapproved of their son's chosen profession, they had made their disdain at his choice of a wife perfectly clear. Karen hadn't come from the right family. "It's been years since you disowned us, so why would I think you wanted to know about Brad's death?"

Her father looked sad. "For God sake's, Margaret, we're family."

"Since when? We weren't a family. A family man comes home. You were never there, and when you were, all you did was criticize."

Preston straightened. "You know perfectly well why I did what I did. You were out of control. An embarrassment to yourself and everyone else. We tried to warn Bradley."

Mia tried to hide her surprise. Her brother had contacted their father? "Did you expect him to send me away, or have me locked up in a place where I lived like a prisoner?" She shivered in memory. "Like you had?" She spread her arms. "I've gone to college, and I can support myself. Well take a good look, I'm perfectly fine. Have been for years. So now that you've checked on me, you can go home with a clear conscience." She turned to leave, praying this would be the end.

"Not so fast, Margaret. There's some unfinished business to do with my grandson."

Mia swung around as a fierce protectiveness took over. "He's not your grandchild. You didn't want to be a part of my life or Brad's because we refused to do what you wanted. So you have no claim on this baby."

Preston Saunders frowned. "You're wrong, Margaret. My family has always come first, which is why I'm here." He glared at her. "You can't possibly think you can give Bradley's son the life I can. I've seen where you live. You have nothing to offer him. The boy would be much better off with your mother and me."

"That's not true. Besides I can give him love, which is more than you and Mother ever did. Brad and Karen wanted me to raise their child if something happened to them."

Her father's gaze moved over her. "I don't want my grandchild living in that slum apartment."

"Not that it's any of your business, but I'll be moving soon into a two-bedroom house. I have income and I'll be going back to law school. I can support BJ. And that's all that you need to know."

He studied her for a long moment. "I know more than you might think. And I don't want you moving in with this Jarrett McKane."

She was shaking. "My personal life is none of your business."

Her father stood his ground. "You're wrong. I've asked around. Your ex-football player may have had minimal success during his college career, and even in this small town, but things can change quickly."

Mia hated that this man could still get to her. And he was planning to use her friendship with Jarrett. "What is that supposed to mean?"

He shrugged. "These are hard times, and business deals can easily fall apart. Just recently I was discussing this with Neil Fulton. What a coincidence that his wife, Robin, and your mother were sorority sisters." A smug look appeared across his face. "From what Neil tells me, it's still up in the air about where their new factory is going to be built."

Mia felt sick to her stomach. "This has nothing to do with Jarrett. It's between you and me."

"Then all you have to do is give me what I want."

Jarrett stood in the hallway. If Mia had let everyone think that her parents were dead, there had to be a reason, and he couldn't wait to hear it.

"Is there a problem?" Trace asked coming up to him.

"Not sure." Jarrett had no idea what was going on. "But I plan to find out." When he heard Mia tell her father goodbye, he went into action. He walked into the living room.

"Is everything okay?" He went over to Mia, slipping a possessive arm around her back.

She looked surprised to see him. "Yes. My father was just leaving."

The man didn't move, just turned his attention toward Jarrett. "I'm Margaret's father, Preston Saunders." He held out a hand.

Jarrett shook it. "Jarrett McKane. You should have let us know you were coming to town."

"This was a sudden trip for me." Saunders glanced back at his daughter. "Mia and I have been estranged for…a while."

Jarrett felt Mia stiffen. "It's been years," she insisted. "You disowned me and Brad, and you have no right to this child."

Saunders seemed surprised by his daughter's backbone. "We're still family. And this child is a Saunders which is the very reason I'm here. To help you." He glared at her. "Margaret, you can't possibly think you can give the child the kind of life he deserves." He shook his head. "You and the boy would be much better at home with your mother and me."

Mia was still trembling, even after her father left. Once the front door closed, she wanted to disappear. Instead, she hurried up the stairs to check on BJ. Anything to keep from having to face Jarrett. To have to explain. But he wasn't letting her get away, and followed her.

"Mia," he called to her.

She stopped in the upstairs hall, but didn't turn around. "I can't talk about this right now."

She started for the nursery, but he took her by the arm and led her into a guest bedroom. After the door closed, he pulled her into his arms.

She didn't resist. Shutting her eyes, she let herself revel in the secure sound of his beating heart, his warmth. She fought the tears, but lost as a sob escaped and she began to cry. She cried for the years that her parents weren't there for her. For herself because she couldn't be the daughter they wanted her to be. For the relationship she wanted with this man that now was lost too.

The only thing that mattered now was BJ.

She pulled back and wiped her eyes. "I'm sorry."

"How long since you've seen your father?" Jarrett asked as he pulled out a handkerchief and handed it to her.

"Ten years. It was a few days before my nineteenth birthday." Wiping her eyes, she raised her head. She might as well tell him everything.

"I'd just gotten released from the rehab clinic he'd had me committed to. I was excited because he came to bring me home. Instead, he handed me five thousand dollars and said he'd paid a year's rent on an apartment in Atlanta, Georgia. He felt it would be better for everyone if I didn't return to Boston."

Mia moved across the room toward the bed. She needed space. "Funny thing was, the pills I'd become addicted to were ones prescribed by a doctor my parents insisted I see to help me lose weight."

Jarrett walked over to her. "I can't believe you were ever overweight."

"I had crooked teeth, too."

His finger touched her chin and made her look at him. "And incredible blue eyes, and hair the color of rich coffee," he told her as his gaze moved over her face. "I could go on and on."

She swallowed hard. "No one has ever said that to me."

"Maybe you never gave them a chance."

She shrugged. "I've been kind of busy lately. But Jarrett, as a teenager, I gave my father plenty of reasons not to trust me."

"Didn't we all." He smiled. "I was no angel, either. That doesn't mean you aren't a good mother now."

She gasped. "BJ." She started to leave, but he pulled her back.

"He's sleeping," Jarrett said. "You know that kid's got a strong pair of lungs, so we'll hear him when he wakes up." He paused a moment then said, "Back to you. How did you end up in Colorado?"

"I used the money my father gave me and flew to Denver. Brad was a junior pastor there. He and Karen had just gotten married, yet they opened their arms and took me in. He probably told our parents, but I think Preston was just happy I was out of his life."

"Seems that Brad wanted you," Jarrett acknowledged.

She nodded. "At first I gave him a lot of trouble. But he got me to finish high school, then college. For the first time, I felt good about myself." She felt a surge of panic. "I owe it to Brad and Karen to raise their son with love and compassion for other people. I'll do anything to keep my parents from taking BJ."

He reached for her. "It won't happen. I won't let it."

No! She couldn't let her father destroy Jarrett, too. She shook her head. "No, Jarrett, you have to stay out of this."

"Mia, listen to me. You're going to need some help."

The last thing Mia wanted was for this to go to court. She was doubtful she could win against the power of the Saunderses' money. She shook her head. "I can't let my father scare me off. I have to prove to him I can handle things on my own." She pushed past him and out the door.

More importantly, she had to get Jarrett McKane out of her life. It was the only way she could protect him.

This had been Jarrett's best Christmas in years until the unwelcome guest showed up. Although dessert was being served, he knew that for Mia the celebration was over. Using the excuse that BJ was fussy, he drove her back to town.

Mia's silence continued as they walked into the apartment building. Jarrett tugged on the glass door, hearing the scrape of metal before it gave way and opened. Inside, Jarrett glanced around the large lobby. Even with the elaborate holiday decorations, the place was still a dump.

It needed a lot of work, especially if he was going to rent to more tenants. Whether Fulton finalized the factory deal or not, he should get a contractor out here to look over the building.

Saunders must have come here first. How else would he know that Mia was at the ranch? What if he'd taken pictures? If he was going to fight for custody, would he show them to a judge?

Damn. He needed to get Mia out of here and moved into the cottage. Honestly, he wanted her at his house, but Ms. Independence would never go for that.

At the apartment door, Mia unlocked it and they went inside. She carried the baby into the bedroom.

"I'll bring up the rest of the things," he called to her.

Jarrett hurried back outside in the cold. He opened the back of his SUV and grabbed the box of leftover food and presents. That was when he noticed the car at the end of the car park. With the help of the overhead security light, he saw the shadow of a man leaning against a dark vehicle.

He didn't like a stranger hanging around. He thought about the older tenants, then Jarrett thought about earlier today and couldn't help but wonder if Saunders had something to do with it. Had he hired someone to watch the place? Would he go that far? The man he'd met today didn't seem like the type who gave up easily.

Jarrett carried the box back inside the lobby. He took out his cell phone and called the sheriff's office, asking his old friend from high school, Danny Haskins, to come by and check out the situation. He wasn't going to make it easy for Saunders.

Call made, Jarrett returned to Mia's apartment. When she came out of the bedroom, she didn't hide her surprise that he was there.

"Jarrett, I didn't realize you were still here."

He put the box on the table. "I brought up the rest of the things from the car."

"Oh, I'll put them away, you don't have to stay."

He was discouraged by her rejection. "Look, Mia, I saw a stranger hanging around the parking lot." He took off his hat and coat. "I'm having it checked out, so I'm not leaving here until it's cleared up. Could be your father is having someone watch you."

She looked panicked, but quickly covered it. "I have a good lock on the door. He's not getting in here."

"I want to help you."

She shook her head. "I don't want you involved in this."

He went to her. "I'm already involved, Mia."

"No, Jarrett. You can't keep rescuing me."

Before he could answer there was a knock on the door. Jarrett checked the peephole, then pulled open the door. "Hi, Danny."

The sheriff removed his hat and stepped inside the apartment. "Hey, McKane."

"Thanks for stopping by, Danny."

"Not a problem." He looked at Mia and nodded. "Hello, ma'am."

"Mia, this is Sheriff Danny Haskins. Danny, this is Mia Saunders."

"Nice to meet you, Ms. Saunders. I'm sorry to have to bother you on Christmas."

"It wasn't necessary for Jarrett to call you."

"It's my job to protect our citizens." Danny turned to Jarrett. "There was a dark sedan leaving when I pulled in, but I got the license plate. It's a rental." He pulled out a small notebook. "The name of the customer is Jake Collins of Collins Investigation. He's a P.I. out of Denver and he's been here over a week."

Haskins turned to Mia. "Jarrett told me that your father, Preston Saunders, came to Winchester Ridge after no contact with you for years."

Mia nodded. "He has a P.I. watching me to see if I make any mistakes," she said to Jarrett. "He'll use anything he can against me."

Jarrett saw not only her fear, but the sadness. Damn Saunders. "We're not going to let him," he assured her.

He walked Danny out the door. "Thanks, friend. Is there any way you could keep an eye out for this car? I'll bet my next deal that Saunders is trying to find something against his daughter so he can get custody of his grandson and it's my guess he'll do anything to get him."

"Since he isn't breaking the law, I can't do much, but I'll alert my deputies to keep an eye out. I'll also have them patrol this area." His friend smiled. "I take it you have more than a passing interest in that very attractive brunette."

"Yes, I do. So don't get any ideas."

Smiling, Danny raised a hand. "Enough said, friend. You always had all the luck when it came to the ladies. I'll let you know if I find anything."

Jarrett said goodbye, then went back inside to find Mia in the kitchen putting away leftovers.

He walked up behind her. "I don't want you to be alone tonight. I don't trust Saunders."

She closed her eyes a moment. "My father just wants me to know that he's there, that he's a threat if I don't do what he wants. I can handle this on my own."

"Like you did in the past," he said, regretting the harsh words. "Why are you being so stubborn?"

She stiffened. "Because if you stay it will only infuriate him. Believe me, you're not the type of man Preston Saunders wants his daughter to associate with. You're not successful enough, not from the right family or the right school."

"So a poor country boy isn't good enough for a Saunders?"

She glared at him. "That's correct. It's strictly eastern blueblood."

Jarrett hadn't done too badly for himself, but suddenly he felt like the kid with dirt under his fingernails.

"I'm that poor little rich girl," she told him. "I'll do whatever it takes to keep my son. So please, I need you to leave… And I mean for good."

Mia woke up the next morning, fed BJ and tried to eat but her stomach couldn't handle food. She hadn't gotten much sleep last night, either. All she kept seeing was the look on Jarrett's face.

How could she have said those things to him? The hurt she'd caused nearly killed her, but she couldn't let him get mixed up in her fight. He would lose everything.

So many things rested on her playing nice with her father. Even if she was miserable and lost the man she loved.

There was a knock on the door. She didn't open it until she heard Nola's voice.

"I was worried about you," the older woman said.

"Why? I'm just tired from the long day yesterday."

Nola watched her. "Your father showing up out of the blue might have had a lot to do with it, too."

She nodded. "I'm sorry I never told you about my parents."

Nola shook her head. "We all figured if you didn't want to talk about them you had your reasons."

Tears welled in Mia's eyes. "My father's threatening to take BJ."

Nola took hold of her hand. "He can't do that, you're a good mother. All of us can attest to that."

"But Preston Saunders has money and a legal team on his payroll that I can't compete with. He's a successful businessman, and I'm a law student who can barely make ends meet."

"What about Jarrett? He could help you."

She shook her head. "I can't let him get involved in this. You have no idea what my father could do to him. He'd destroy him without a backward glance. No, this is my fight. And I told him so last night."

Nola nodded. "That explains the man's grumpiness when I greeted him this morning. A bear, he was."

"It's better this way, Nola. He has to stay away from me."

"Why don't you let Jarrett decide if you're worth it or not? He's a big boy. He'd probably go a few rounds with your father and still be standing afterward."

"No. This is my fight. All my life, I've let everyone else do things for me. First my parents, even Brad. Jarrett has already done too much."

"I know you can fight this. You're a strong woman who handled the tragedy of her brother's death with grace and strength. You've fought hard to get into law school. And don't you forget all the times you helped us. I remember a feisty gal who took our landlord to court so we could stay in our homes."

And fell in love with him, Mia thought. "I was only helping out my neighbors."

Nola took Mia's hands in hers. "Did you forget the most unselfish gift of all? You carried your brother's and his wife's baby."

She smiled. "Oh, Nola, that wasn't a sacrifice, that was pure joy for me. BJ is a miracle."

Nola agreed. "And no one could love him more. BJ belongs with you. What's most important, it was your brother's wish. He trusted you enough to raise his child. That should say it all. So somehow we've got to make sure that little boy stays with his mother. That's you. Nothing will ever change that."

CHAPTER TWELVE

THE next morning, Jarrett got out of bed in a bad mood. He left the apartment early so as not to run into Mia, then went in to the office, hoping to get some work done. Not possible. He couldn't clear his head of the stubborn woman.

"Ah, hell." He stood up from his desk and went to the large window looking out over the snow-covered ground. The Rocky Mountains off in the distance were magnificent against the blue sky. The view did nothing to improve his lousy mood.

How was Mia doing today? Dammit! She couldn't cave in to her father's demands. She had to stand her ground, everything would be all right. He needed to be there.…

"Hey, you busy?"

Jarrett glanced over his shoulder and saw Trace peering into the office. "If I said yes, would you go away?"

He walked in. "Sorry, big brother. Your bad attitude doesn't scare me anymore. What happened with Mia yesterday?"

It had taken a lot of years, but he finally realized that Trace and Kira wanted to be the family he'd longed for. "Nothing happened. She sent me packing last night when I offered to help her. So I don't know and I'm not sure I care."

His younger brother placed his hat on the chair and

joined him at the window. "Now, that's a lie. And your way of helping is about as subtle as a bulldozer."

Jarrett glared, but Trace didn't budge. "Thanks a lot."

"I know you mean well, but it's true," Trace told him. "So what's going on with Mia's father?"

"We're pretty sure that Saunders has had a P.I. watching her this past week. He came straight out and told Mia he wants to take BJ away from her."

"What kind of a man would do that to his daughter?"

"You don't want to hear my answer to that. Besides, I told you I'm not involved in this anymore. Mia doesn't need or want my help."

"Poor Jarrett." Trace shook his head. "Ain't getting any lovin' these days."

"It isn't that way with Mia." Damn, if he didn't want it to be though. "She's a new mother."

"And a very attractive woman."

Jarrett studied his brother. "I thought you only had eyes for Kira."

"Kira has my eyes, plus my heart and soul and my fidelity. But that doesn't mean I don't notice a pretty woman. I'm not dead yet. As I remember, a while back you had eyes for my wife, too."

That seemed so long ago. Now he couldn't think of Kira as anything else but a loving sister. "Bite your tongue. She's the mother of my favorite little girl."

"I think you just found the right woman for you."

Jarrett couldn't deny it, nor could he confirm it. Mia was different from anyone he'd known.

He glanced at Trace.

"What?"

"I want to ask you something, but you'll probably think it's stupid."

"Just ask me."

"How did you know that you loved Kira?"

His brother acted surprised by the question, then he turned serious. "Honestly, I can't remember a time I didn't love her, even when our marriage was falling apart."

Trace raised his hand. "Here are a few of the symptoms if you have doubts. When Mia looks at you, you get tightness in your chest, like you can't breathe in enough air. Your heart rate isn't ever normal when she's around. And when she smiles at you." He shook his head. "It's like everything is right in the world."

Jarrett groaned. "Damn!"

There were voices in the outer office, and then his secretary, Marge, came in followed closely by Nola Madison and Joe Carson.

"Sorry, Jarrett," his secretary apologized. "I told them you were busy, but they said it's important they see you."

"It's okay, Margie." He had no idea why they would come here.

As Marge left, Nola hurried across the office. "Hello, Trace." Then she turned to him. "Jarrett, this is important. It's about Mia."

He saw the worried look on the older couple's faces. "Did something happen to her? To BJ?" He came around the desk. "Is her father causing trouble again?"

Nola looked at Joe, then turned back to him. Her large glasses made her eyes look huge. "No, she's fine for now. I would tell you, but I promised Mia I wouldn't say anything."

Jarrett frowned. "Am I supposed to guess?"

Nola shook her head. "No. I did tell Joe and Sylvia, but Sylvia is at the apartment watching BJ so Joe drove me here. He didn't promise Mia anything, so he came along to talk to you."

"Talk about what?"

Joe took over. "Mia's considering moving home with her father, so she'll be guaranteed to be a part of the boy's life."

"What? She can't do that." Jarrett started for the closet and pulled out his jacket. "How is she expected to have a life of her own? And what about BJ? We all know what Mia and Brad thought about their father's parenting skills. No, it isn't gonna happen."

Trace stopped Jarrett at the door. "Hold on there, bro. I think you need a plan before you go rushing in and playing hero."

"My plan is to stop him."

"Bulldozer," Trace reminded his brother.

"What if I tell her how I feel?"

Trace didn't look happy. "Okay. So you're ready to take the next step? The big question is, what are you going to offer her?"

Jarrett swallowed the dryness in his throat. It had been all he'd thought about it. He'd never felt about anyone the way he did about Mia. "I care about her. But you know everything is pending on this Fulton deal. I could be broke in a month."

Nola nodded. "Does that really matter? We all know the way you feel about her."

"Yeah," Joe agreed. "That was some kiss under the mistletoe."

"Thanks."

Nola pushed her way to the front. "But is it enough to commit to her?"

"Stop pushing the guy," Joe said. "He can't think."

"He doesn't have time to think about it," Nola argued. "Besides, how long does it take to know you love someone? If it's for real, you know it." The older woman turned back to Jarrett. "You know she's leaving town because of you?"

His chest tightened. "I don't want her to leave."

Joe spoke up again. "Mia's only leaving to save the factory project. Seems Mr. Saunders knows Neil Fulton and he's threatened to ruin you if she doesn't play his game."

Jarrett looked at Trace for help.

"Okay, maybe it's time we help out a little," his brother said.

Jarrett had never let anyone get this close. He thought of Mia's pretty blue eyes, her smile. Somehow she'd gotten through all his barriers. Now, nothing mattered if he couldn't be with her.

Jarrett looked at the group. "You know, this means I could be living in the apartment from now on."

Joe smiled. "Hey, Mountain View is a great place."

"Just make sure you tell that to the judge when I go back to court."

The next day, Mia walked into the hotel lobby. With each step, she had to fight the urge to turn and run. Run so far that no one would find her or BJ. She detested being here. Even as a child she'd hated that awful feeling that came when she was summoned by her father.

Nothing had changed. She was still sick to her stomach. Of course she was older and hopefully wiser. Bound and determined to stand up to the man, she had a list of rules for if she did return to Boston.

First and most important, she would never give up custody of her son. BJ would be a Saunders, but she would be his mother. So, needless to say, there were a lot of things to be ironed out before she committed to anything. She had to protect her son and herself.

She would never trust Preston Saunders. That had been

the reason she left BJ with Sylvia. He wasn't getting his hands on her grandson, yet. Suddenly she was sad, thinking about leaving this town and all her friends. They'd been like family to her and BJ.

And then there was Jarrett.

She swallowed the ache in the back of her throat. She'd never wanted to hurt him, or herself, but by leaving she'd manage to do both. She knew Preston Saunders well enough to worry that he would destroy Jarrett's factory project. Perhaps even the man himself.

She also had to think about the people in town who needed those jobs created by the project. Not just in the building of the factory, but finished, it would employ a lot of workers.

She went to the desk clerk. "Preston Saunders, please."

The young man looked the name up on the computer screen. "Mr. Saunders is in one of our small conference rooms." He gave her directions.

Mia walked along the carpeted hallway and found the room. The door was ajar and she heard her father's voice. She peered in and saw that he was on his cell phone, looking out the window.

He didn't see her. "I told you it will all be taken care of by the end of the month. Yes, the money transfer will be there by the thirty-first." He nodded. "You have my word."

Mia was only half listening, but she wondered if her father could have money troubles. It wasn't a good time for a lot of businesses. She knew little about the family finances, except that both her parents came from money.

Her mother's wealth came from Ashley Oil and Textiles. Her father's from banking. Their marriage had been more of a merger than a love match.

Since she and Brad had been disinherited, she didn't concern herself with any of that. She only cared about BJ. And she would do anything to keep him. Even sell her soul.

Preston ended his call and turned around to see her. "Eavesdropping isn't polite, Margaret."

She walked up to the table. "You're the one who set up this meeting. Besides, you're the one who's been sneaking around. I don't think I want to stay if you're going to be condescending."

She started to leave and he called her back. With hesitation, she turned around and waited.

"Maybe we both got off on the wrong foot," he said.

"That's what you call destroying my life?"

"I want to be a part of my grandson's life. Is that so awful?"

"You keep saying that." She paused. "What about Mother? Is she here with you?"

He shook his head. "No, your mother stayed home. She didn't want to get her hopes up if this didn't work out."

Mia had realized a long time ago that Abigail was just what Preston wanted her to be. A society wife. She did charity events, but raising her children was just too difficult for her. Nannies had always taken care of her and Brad. Mia was afraid that would happen with BJ. She couldn't let history repeat itself. She reached inside her purse, took out an envelope and handed to her father.

"What's this?"

"The list of conditions you have to agree to if you want me to return to Boston."

"You're in no position to demand anything."

She straightened her back. "If you don't want a court battle, Father, we need to come to terms. I will never hand over my son to you. I'm BJ's mother and that isn't going to change." She still needed to work out the legal adoption agreement. "So we're working on my terms. You've got twenty-four hours to give me an answer."

She swung around and marched out, praying he wouldn't stop her. She'd crumble for sure. But just thinking of BJ gave her strength. He was all she had. She'd lost everyone else, she couldn't lose him, too.

Later that day, Trace and Jarrett were at the office doing research on Preston Saunders. Thanks to his Internet whiz, Margie, they'd been able to learn a lot about the Saunders family, including the fact that Saunders Investments was a Fortune 500 company.

"How much to do you want to bet Mia is a shareholder?" Jarrett glanced at Trace. "I wouldn't put it past Preston to have another reason besides his grandson for showing up here. Could it have something to do with money? Mia's money?"

"Wait, this is all speculation," Trace said.

"You didn't talk to this man—I did," Jarrett assured him. "By Mia's own admission, he's been a lousy father. And on Christmas, he made no bones about trying to use his authority over his daughter by showing up and trying to regain that control and take his grandson. There's got to be a reason why he's here." He stood. "And I'm going to find out what it is."

"Where are you headed?"

"To see Mia. Whether she likes it or not."

That evening, Mia was still shaken from the visit with her father. Of course, this time she'd done a lot of the talking, but he'd definitely had enough to say.

She looked down and watched the baby at her breast and

smiled. She began to calm down. No way did she want to relay her anxiety to BJ.

She knew Preston would be upset with her demands. She'd insisted she have her own apartment, refusing to live in the large house she was raised in. She refused to let her father control her life again. But as long as she had BJ, life would be good.

She heard a knock on the apartment door. "Come in, Nola, it's unlocked," she called from the bedroom.

When she looked up, she saw Jarrett standing in the doorway of her bedroom.

"It's not Nola," he told her.

She tried to cover herself, but BJ was having none of it. He began to fuss. She raised him to her shoulder and quickly made an adjustment to rearrange her blouse.

"Jarrett, I'm busy right now. So if you'll—"

He walked toward the bed. "Leave?" he finished for her. "I will, but first we need to talk, Mia. And we need to be honest."

Mia stared at the man. He looked so good she felt a stirring that made her ache. "We've said everything already."

"No, we haven't." He sat down on the bed. "Look, Mia, I know why you're doing this. It's because of what your father threatened to do to me."

She couldn't answer him. "Who told you that? Did my father say something to you?"

He shook his head. "I wish he had, because I'd have let him know that he couldn't scare me off."

She rubbed the baby's back as he squirmed in her arms. "That's not it. I decided that I need my family around me. It'll be good for BJ."

He leaned closer. "You have family here, too." Those

dark eyes held hers. "You deserve a good life, Mia. I don't believe you'll have that if Preston is running the show."

"I just want to keep my son."

BJ let out a cry.

"Seems the little guy isn't happy," Jarrett said and reached for the baby. "Let me."

Before Mia could stop him, he'd lifted the infant off her shoulder, but Jarrett's focus was still on Mia. She quickly pulled her blouse together, covering her exposed breast.

He put the baby against his shoulder and began to pat his back. He spoke in a soothing voice and, after a burp, the baby calmed down. He returned him to Mia's outstretched arms.

"He should be able to finish his supper now."

Jarrett's gaze held hers and she couldn't look away, nor did she want to. They'd shared so many things in the past few months. He'd been a part of BJ's life from the beginning. She opened her blouse, moved her son to her other breast, and he began to nurse again.

Jarrett drew an audible breath. "I don't think I've ever seen anything so beautiful."

She looked at him, feeling tears building in her eyes. "Please, don't do this. It's hard enough…"

He placed a finger against her lips. "It's going to be okay, Mia. I promise you." He leaned down and brushed his mouth against hers. She sucked in a breath and he came back for more. The slow, lingering kiss wasn't enough, but she couldn't take any more.

With a shuddering sigh he pulled back. "I don't want to let you go."

She swallowed hard. "Oh, Jarrett, there's not a choice."

"There's always a choice, Mia," Jarrett told her and stepped back, away from temptation. "Now, to return to why I stopped by— I believe your father's sudden appearance has to do with money, your money and your brother's money."

She looked confused. "We don't have any money."

"You're listed as a stockholder in the family business."

"No, he took the money away from us when we left home."

"Your father doesn't run Ashley Oil and Textiles. Your maternal grandfather, Clyde Ashley, began that family business. Did you know your grandfather?"

She shook her head. "Not really, I was five when he died."

"It's only speculation, I'm going to bet Clyde had made provisions for his grandchildren in his will. Did you or Brad ever get any money from him?"

"We never wanted anything from the family."

"I understand, but you're entitled to it, Mia. More importantly, you could use it for BJ and his future. And if your brother had his trust coming, it would definitely go to his son."

Mia's eyes rounded as things started falling into place. "That's why Preston wants BJ?"

As if the baby heard his name, he paused and looked up at his mother. She smoothed her hand over his head, and coaxed him back to her breast.

Jarrett glanced away a moment to gather his thoughts away from Mia. How incredibly beautiful she looked with her child. "Have you noticed any correspondence concerning insurance policies, or where your brother's financial records might be?"

"I've already collected Brad's insurance. Every other piece of paperwork that my brother had I put in a file box." She raised BJ to her shoulder and began to pat his back.

"It's in the hall closet." This time, BJ burped like a pro. She got up and carried the infant to the crib. Buttoning her blouse, she went to the hall and retrieved the box.

She carried it to the coffee table in the living room. "I put everything in here after the accident. If it didn't need to be paid, I didn't really look at it."

"You had enough to deal with." He arched an eyebrow. "Do you mind if I have a look now?"

Mia shook her head. She would do anything that might stop her father.

She watched as Jarrett shuffled through the file for a few minutes, then he extracted an envelope and took out the letter. He scanned it. "Bingo. I think I found it."

Jarrett handed the paper to her. The letterhead was that of a law firm, Knott, Lewis and Johnston. It was from James Knott, addressed to Brad and dated a year earlier.

The lawyer said that he was the executor of Clyde Ashley's estate. Since Bradley had reached his thirty-fifth birthday he was now entitled to his inheritance. No amount was given. Just to contact him as soon as possible, and a phone number.

Mia was in shock. "Why hadn't Bradley gone to claim his money?"

Jarrett shrugged. "Maybe he didn't have a chance."

Mia thought back. "He turned thirty-five not long before his and Karen's trip to Mexico. Maybe he was going to contact the lawyer when he returned home."

"And he never got the chance," Jarrett finished. "Maybe the lawyer contacted your father and that sent Preston searching and he found out about his son's death. And since no one has kept it a secret that BJ is Brad's child, your father learned about a grandson."

That didn't stop Mia's worry. "So now he's going to try

and have me proved an unfit mother to get the money. He doesn't have enough?"

"And we can't let him have it. This money will secure BJ's future."

"Not if he proves I'm a bad mother."

"Hey, where's that feisty woman who came after me? Mia, you're a great mother. Besides, you've got the most important thing on your side—your brother wanted you to raise his son. So much so, he put it in writing."

CHAPTER THIRTEEN

LATER that afternoon Jarrett paced his office. Mia was on her way to the hotel to see her father, while Fulton was on his way here to discuss his board of directors' decision about the factory project.

Hell. He didn't want to think about business right now.

What he wanted was Mia as far away from Preston Saunders as possible. That wasn't going to happen today. He'd wanted to go with her, but she'd insisted that she needed to confront the man by herself. Her only concession had been to let Nola go to help watch BJ.

Still Jarrett didn't trust Saunders. He wouldn't put it past him to kidnap them both and drag them back to Connecticut.

"The hell with this." He headed for the door just as Neil Fulton walked into the outer office.

"Hey, Jarrett. How was your holiday?"

"It was busy. And yours?"

Neil seemed to be in a good mood. "The same. I didn't know if I could get away early. I'm glad we could get together on such short notice."

"About that, Neil. An emergency has come up and I need to leave."

The man frowned. "I'm sorry. Can I help?"

Jarrett wasn't planning to mention Saunders but what did he have to lose? He didn't care about the project unless he had Mia. "Maybe you can. I hear you're a friend of Preston Saunders, but the guy's a real bastard."

"Whoa, whoa." Neil raised a hand. "Who told you we were friends? I've only met him a few times at fundraisers."

Jarrett was puzzled. "Aren't your wives sorority sisters?"

He nodded. "They went to the same eastern college, but that doesn't mean they're friends. There's no connection between us, I haven't seen the man in probably five years." Neil frowned. "Rumor has it he's lost a bundle on sub-prime mortgage loans."

Jarrett cursed, and filled Fulton in on the details of what had been going on since Saunders came to town. "He said he'd talked to you about putting a halt to the factory project."

Neil shook his head. "Even if Saunders and I were friends, I would never let personal issues interfere with my business decisions. It never works out. Although I do listen to my wife, and she's definitely a fan of yours. She likes a man with integrity. You didn't toss your tenants out on the street, even though it could mean losing this deal."

"Yeah, even I have a heart."

"That's not always a bad thing. It actually helped you win this deal. Several of the board members are inclined to agree with my Robin." Neil smiled. "She's looking forward to meeting you."

Jarrett blinked. "Meeting me? You've decided to build the factory here?"

Neil nodded. "You were right, your location is the best and there's plenty of room to expand. And as long as the business offices are going into your retro apartment build-ing, Robin wants to help decorate them."

Jarrett knew he was grinning like a fool. "I'll have it put into the contract. Could we talk about this later?" He slipped on his coat. "I need to let someone know I want to be a part of her future. And boot a certain someone else out of town."

"Would you like some backup? I wouldn't mind helping bring Saunders down."

"It could get nasty."

Neil straightened. "I can hold my own. I want to see you get the girl, too."

"Not as much as I do."

Mia pushed BJ's stroller into the hotel. She hadn't wanted to come back here again, but she didn't want her father anywhere near her apartment.

All she wanted was to finish this for good. She wanted Preston out of her life. More importantly, out of her son's life.

No matter what it cost financially.

"Mia, I wish you would think about this for a few days," Nola said as she walked alongside her. "I don't trust the man. You shouldn't, either. Maybe you should call Jarrett."

Two months ago she hadn't even known Jarrett McKane. And now she was hopelessly in love with the guy. She thought about all the things he'd done for her, for BJ. How he'd been there for her when she'd really needed him. He'd coached her through her son's birth. When she was ex-hausted, he walked the floor with BJ so she could sleep.

"Nola, I can't let Jarrett suffer at my father's hand. This is my problem. I should've stood up to my father years ago, but this is going to end today." She couldn't let Jarrett lose everything because of her. Not for her past sins.

That was the reason she'd just give Preston what he wanted. Money. Then he would leave town, and she and BJ could have a peaceful, loving life.

"I know Jarrett doesn't mind helping you." The older woman walked next to the stroller. "You have to know he cares about you and BJ."

"Yes, he's been a good friend." She wanted more.

"Friend?" The older woman gave her a sideways glance. "I think you'd better open your eyes and see how that man looks at you. Even you can't be that blind."

No, she wasn't blind. "Okay, I've seen him watching me." They continued along the hall to the small conference room. "But Jarrett McKane watches a lot of women."

"All men look—until they find the right one. You're Jarrett's right one, Mia. Don't let your father spoil your chance at happiness. Jarrett is a good man." Nola smiled. "He reminds me a lot of Reverend Brad," she rushed on. "Maybe Jarrett has a slightly rougher side, and he curses a little too much, but he has the same good heart."

Mia stopped. "I know all this Nola. It's one of the reasons I'm doing this."

Her friend pursed her lips and shook her head.

"I don't need the money. What Jarrett's doing for this town by creating jobs is much more important. I can work. I plan to finish school and make a good life for BJ. I won't ever let my father hurt the people I care about."

Mia released a breath, and pushed the stroller through the conference-room door to see her father standing by the window. Dressed in his tailored gray suit, he took his time to come to greet her.

"Margaret."

She gripped the stroller handle tighter. "Hello, Father."

He nodded and turned to Nola. "We haven't had the pleasure."

"Nola Madison, Mr. Saunders. I'm a *very* good friend of Mia's."

Mia watched her father look down at the stroller, studying the sleeping child, but he didn't comment on his grandson. "Maybe we should get started."

"Yes," Mia agreed. "We have a lot to cover before you leave town."

At the front desk, Jarrett and Neil got directions to the conference room and headed across the lobby. Their pace picked up when he saw Nola with BJ in the stroller.

"Oh, Jarrett," she cried. "I'm so glad you're here."

"Of course I'm here. Nola, this is Neil Fulton. Neil, Nola Madison. He's going to help us."

The two exchanged pleasantries, then Jarrett nodded toward the door. "Is Mia inside?"

"Yes, she's with her father. I'm worried, Jarrett, she's trying to protect everyone but herself." The baby started to fuss, and Nola rocked the stroller. "See, even BJ's upset."

Jarrett directed Nola to a lounge area a short distance away, and promised her everything would turn out okay. Then he partially opened the conference-room door to hear what was going on. He saw the father and daughter across the small room, their backs to him.

"You can't have BJ," Mia insisted. "And I'm not returning to Boston with you, either."

"You're making a big mistake, Margaret. I hate to go to court and spill all the family secrets, but you know I will. I have to protect my grandson."

"And I have to protect my son from you. Come on, we're

alone, you can admit you only want BJ because of Bradley's trust fund."

Saunders tried to act wounded and failed. "How could you accuse me of something like that? Besides, you should know that any money would stay in trust for Bradley's son. I couldn't get my hands on it."

"As the child's guardian, you'd have access to the account. It must be a sizable amount for you to come all this way."

"I can't touch it. Your grandfather made the trust airtight." He studied her. "You, on the other hand…you have something I want."

After all this time, she'd thought she was immune to his ability to hurt her. She wasn't. "What is that?"

"Your grandfather Ashley was very generous to you in his will. Not only with a trust fund, but with company stock. You can't touch the money until you're thirty-five or married. But there is the question of the stock."

"You want my Ashley Oil stock?"

"I've earned it. I've been voting your shares for years."

"How? You shouldn't have had access once I turned twenty-one."

He smiled. "You don't remember signing power of attorney over to me? When you got out of rehab?"

She hated to think about that time of her life. She did remember her signature had been her ticket out. All she had to do was give Preston Saunders what he wanted, and she'd get her freedom. "So what else could you want?"

"Your grandfather was overprotective. I only had a temporary power of attorney and it's expired."

After all these years, her father had only tracked her down to get money from her. "Why don't I just hold out my arm and you can take all my blood, too."

"Don't act so dramatic. For years, your mother and I had to explain away your indiscretions."

She wasn't going to let him bring her down. "I was your daughter," she stressed, then calmed down. "You never once accepted me for who I was. When I had a problem, you were never there for me.

"You had the Saunders name and money, more advantages than a lot of kids. So it was expected you'd do well. Bradley Junior will have to do the same."

"No, you won't do the same thing to my son."

Preston glared at her. "He's not your son, Margaret. He's your nephew. And he needs to be raised as a Saunders."

"Never," she insisted. BJ was hers. She'd already started legal procedures.

Jarrett watched Mia stand tough. Yet, Preston wasn't relenting, either. "I changed my mind on one of the conditions of our new agreement. Along with your stock, I want to see my grandson periodically. Say, four times a year. And I'll need the stock signed over immediately."

She shook her head. "That's not our deal. You get the money. You walk away."

"You're not dictating to me. Secrets could leak out. There's a certain factory project that hangs in the balance."

Jarrett couldn't stand back any longer. He glanced at Neil as he swung open the door and walked into the room.

Preston Saunders was the first to notice him. "So you brought your cowboy along to save you."

Mia turned around. He could see her shock and some relief. "Jarrett. What are you doing here?"

He came up to her. "I thought you might need some support."

"I don't want you involved in this. I can handle it."

He leaned closer and whispered, "Woman, as far as I'm

concerned, you could handle anything. But if you think I'm going to stand by and let this guy hurt you, you'd better think again." He gave her a quick kiss, then placed his arm around her shoulders and faced the problem.

"Your words are touching, Mr. McKane," her father said, "but this doesn't concern you."

"I think it does, Mr. Saunders. I don't like that you've threatened Mia."

"As I said, this doesn't concern you." He looked at Mia. "Does it, Margaret?"

She looked at Jarrett. "He's right. This isn't good for the factory project."

"You think I care about the project more than you?" He smiled. "I can't tell you how much it means to me that you're willing to sacrifice your future for me. But there's no need."

He turned to Preston. "Okay, Saunders, here's how it's going to be. You're going to leave town *today*. Mia is going to stay here, finish law school and raise her son. Oh, and if I'm lucky, I get to be a part of their lives."

"Well, you're going to have to live off her money, because your future is looking bleak at the moment. You're about to lose everything."

"I think you're wrong about that, Saunders."

Everyone turned toward the door as Neil Fulton walked in. He went to stand beside Jarrett and Mia.

"Neil," her father stammered. "It's good to see you again."

"I don't think so, Saunders. First thing, I don't like you tossing my name around as if we're friends." He glared at Preston. "Secondly, Jarrett McKane and my company just agreed on a rather lucrative property deal. Nothing you say is going to change a thing." He took a step closer to Preston. "So I suggest you do what Jarrett asked, because

I also heard you threaten your daughter. And believe me, you don't want to mess with me."

Her father looked at Mia. "Margaret, are you going to allow this?"

Mia knew he wouldn't stop trying to control her. "Yes." She fought tears that it had to come to this. "Please don't contact me again."

If Preston was surprised, he hid it. "Your mother is going to be so disappointed."

"Please tell Mother that she's more than welcome to visit her grandson."

Preston Saunders started for the door, but stopped and looked back at her. "I wouldn't act so smug if I were you, Margaret, not with your past. There's a lot of things that could come out I'm sure you'd like to keep buried." He nodded to Jarrett. "I'm sure your friends would be interested to know their sweet Mia isn't so innocent." He turned and walked out the door.

Mia felt the heat climb to her face and those dark years came rushing back, threatening to consume her, take away everything she'd made good in her life.

"Mia, are you okay?"

She nodded and put on a smile.

Neil looked at Jarrett. "I think I'll leave you two alone to talk." He turned to Mia. "It's a pleasure to meet you, Mia. I hope we get a chance to talk later." With a nod, Neil Fulton walked out, leaving her with Jarrett.

She looked at him, saw his questioning look, then burst into tears and ran out of the room, too.

Two hours later, Mia was back at her apartment. She fed BJ, and, after putting him down to nap, she dragged her suitcase from the closet and began to pack.

Okay, she was a coward. But when it came to a protecting

her son, she'd do anything, go anywhere. She wasn't sure if her father would bring her past out in court. Would he even take her to court?

Mia sank to the sofa. After all these years, all the things she'd accomplished, she'd turned her life around, and still her past had caught up with her. And she couldn't trust anyone to love her if they found out the truth about her.

She brushed away a tear. "Brad, I wish you were here to help me."

She stood and looked around. There wasn't much worth taking with her, except the baby things. She needed some boxes and went to the stairwell to get some. She found two. As she returned to her apartment, Trace McKane got off the elevator. She couldn't avoid him.

He smiled. "Hey, Mia. Have you seen Jarrett?"

She shook her head. "Not since earlier."

Trace played with his cowboy hat in his hands. "I hear you talked with your father. I hope that went well."

"He's leaving town, and I hope it's the end of it." She motioned to her apartment. "I'd better get inside to BJ."

He glanced at the boxes as he walked with her. "So you're getting ready to move out to the cottage? Maybe I can take some things out today."

She couldn't make eye contact as she backed up to her apartment door. "Look, Trace, I appreciate you and Kira offering us a place to live, but I've decided to move back to Denver for school."

Before Trace could say anything, the sound of BJ's cry distracted them. She hurried inside and got her son back to sleep, then returned to the living room. Trace was waiting.

"I know it isn't any of my business, but are you leaving because of my brother?"

She shook her head. "No, it's me. I feel it's for the best."

He watched her. "I'm not buying it. I know you have feelings for Jarrett, and the guy's crazy about you. What's the real reason?"

She couldn't deny it. She was totally in love with Jarrett. "I don't think it will work out. My father will probably try and cause more trouble." She glanced away. "There are things in my past." She shook her head. "A time in my life when I didn't care much about myself. I did things I'm not proud of."

"All of us have those times. Jarrett and I have a lot of bad history. We really haven't been brothers until the last few years." He studied her. "And Kira and I had our share of rough times, too. It took her years to tell me she'd had a baby when she was fifteen. She gave him up."

Mia remembered Jenna saying she had an older brother. "That must have been hard for her."

He nodded. "I was married to her and she never told me. When I finally found out, of course I was hurt. Not over what she did at fifteen and alone, but because she didn't trust me enough to tell me. We almost split up over it."

She couldn't imagine Trace and Kira not together. "I just have so much baggage. I can't keep dumping it on Jarrett."

Trace smiled. "Do you see the man complaining? He's crazy about you and BJ. Besides, Jarrett isn't an angel, either. There's plenty of women around town that will attest to that."

She wasn't sure what to say, then suddenly she blurted out. "I love him too much to hurt him."

He turned serious. "A few years ago, I would have told

you to walk away from Jarrett, that you were too good for him. But he's changed. Give him a chance to prove that he's the man you need."

By about five that night, Jarrett wasn't sure what he was doing. Things hadn't turned out as he'd planned. He'd charged in to help, but in the end he didn't get the girl.

He knew that talking with her father had taken its toll on Mia. But he also thought that she'd rush into his arms when it was over. Instead, she'd run out the door, right out of his life.

He'd tried calling her several times, but she didn't answer. How could he tell her how he felt in a phone message?

After Mia's rejection, he'd spent the day with Neil going over the changes in the project. That was the reason he'd called this meeting of the tenants. They were going to be a big part of this and he wanted to make sure everyone agreed to his proposal.

He'd hoped to see Mia when he walked into the community room, but she wasn't there. As he made his way to the front, the room grew quiet and everyone turned to him.

"Good evening, everyone." He glanced around, realizing how many of the tenants he'd gotten to know these past months. He'd shared meals and holidays with these people.

"I know you've all wondered why I called this meeting. Well, as of a few hours ago, I finalized and signed the contracts for the new factory to be built. So the construction is scheduled to start in the early spring." The tenants exchanged glances, but didn't say anything. "Since we last gathered, there have been some changes to the plans. Neil Fulton has agreed to build further back on the property. I feel this is a better solution for all of us."

"You mean for you," someone said.

"Just hear me out." He took a breath. "First of all, when I say the factory will be relocated on the back of the property that means the apartment buildings won't be torn down. Instead, the vacant building will be used to house Fulton's corporate offices, and this building will be remodeled and left as Mountain View Apartments."

Jarrett raised his hand to quiet the suddenly noisy group. "Of course, there's going to be a lot of construction noise during the remodeling. So I'm going to compensate you all with lower rents for the next six months."

Joe stood. "Wait, we don't have to move out by March?"

"No. Unless you want to. But it's a better investment for me to keep the building open. We're in an era of recycling, so I want to bring these apartments back to their original state by painting and repairing the structure. The kitchens and baths will be updated, of course, with new appliances and fixtures. So what I need to know is, how do you feel about continuing to live here?"

Cheers went up in the room.

Joe got out of his chair again. "How much more will it cost us in rent?"

"Since you all lived here at the worst time, you shouldn't have to pay any extra once things improve. So there won't be any increase in rent for any of the tenants living here now."

"We'll need to get it writing," a familiar voice called out from the back of the room.

Heart pounding, Jarrett looked toward the doorway. Mia was standing there behind BJ's stroller. She looked tired, but as beautiful as usual.

"I can do that," he offered. "Anything else you need?"

Mia didn't take her eyes off Jarrett as she moved along

the side of the tables. She had so many things she needed to say to him. Maybe this wasn't the place, but she had to see him. She had to give this one last chance. For both of them.

"A good handyman on the premises," she went on. "Someone who can take care of emergencies." Nola came over, took the stroller as Mia continued to the front of the room. She stopped in front of Jarrett. "Someone we can count on."

He studied her for a moment and nodded. "Do you think you'll need someone just during the day or around the clock?"

Those dark eyes locked on hers, and she wondered if he could read her mind, her heart. She could barely speak. "Oh, definitely around the clock. Do you know of anyone?"

"Yeah, I've got just the guy for the job." He took a step forward and she could feel everyone in the room hanging on their words.

"Does he like children?"

Jarrett didn't even blink. "He loves children." Then he smiled. "And pets." He inched closer. "Does this suit you, Ms. Saunders?"

She could only manage a nod.

"Maybe we should go somewhere and discuss this further."

"Just kiss her," someone yelled.

A smile appeared across Jarrett's face. "I'm also good at taking directions."

His head lowered to hers and he captured her mouth. This time whistles and cheers erupted. He kept it light, but he told her everything she needed to know. They might just have a chance.

CHAPTER FOURTEEN

JARRETT wasn't exactly crazy about having an audience when he was trying to talk to Mia. That was the reason he'd hurried her and BJ out of there and into his SUV.

He ended up taking Mia to his house. Guaranteed privacy. He pulled in to his long driveway, opened the garage and drove in. Once the door shut behind the car, he reached for her hand.

"We need to talk without being interrupted." He brushed his lips across hers, then got out, took BJ out of the back and they walked inside through the kitchen.

He looked down at the sleeping baby. "How soon before he needs to be fed?"

"We have a few hours."

"Good." He took her into the living room, only the outside light on the patio illuminating the space. Setting the baby's carrier down on the rug at one end of the sofa, he turned on the gas fireplace and some soft music.

"I haven't been home much lately," he told her. "I don't have much to offer you."

"I don't want anything."

He moved to turn on a lamp.

"Please leave it off," she asked. "It's nice like this. It's peaceful and the view is incredible."

With a nod, he took her hand and they sat down on the

sofa. For a long time, they stared out the French doors watching the wintry scene. The snow on the ground lightened the area, illuminating the rows of bare trees that dotted the landscape.

He began. "Tell me I haven't messed up everything by coming after you today."

Mia squeezed his hand, trying to relay how she felt. She couldn't look at him. Her father had nearly destroyed a lot of people and maybe the future of the town. "No. I'm just sorry you got caught in this mess."

"I don't care about your past, Mia. Meeting your father explained a lot to me. I came to the hotel to support you. When Nola told me the truth about what your father had threatened, I couldn't stand by and let him blackmail you."

"It's only money," she insisted. "I don't care about that. It's BJ I care about. I just didn't want my son raised the way Brad and I were. In a house without love."

"You should have told your father to take a hike. My failure on the project would have saved the apartments."

"I couldn't do that. You've worked too hard on bringing the factory to town. I didn't want my father to destroy you." She took another risk and confessed, "I care about you."

He reached for her, and she didn't resist as he turned her in his arms so she was facing him. He pressed her head against his chest and she could feel the rapid beating of his heart.

"And I care about you," he informed her. Not just you, but BJ, too." He touched her face, tilting her head back so she had to look at him.

"I more than care, Mia. I love you."

Her breathing caught as her throat tightened with emotions. She couldn't speak.

"Crazy, huh?" He placed a soft kiss on her forehead,

then on one eyelid, then the other. "I don't know how or when it happened, I'm thinking the second I saw you." He continued kissing his way down her cheek. "All I know is I couldn't seem to stay away. I used every excuse I could to see you." He placed a kiss against her ear and she shivered, resting her hand against his solid chest, trying to resist. "Then all those precious moments—when we shared the ultrasound of the baby, BJ's birth."

Every word he spoke made her yearn for more. She wanted everything from this man. "I'm glad you were there with me, too."

He ran his mouth over her jaw. "All I know is that when I thought you were leaving, I couldn't let you go."

She gasped. "Oh, Jarrett," she breathed, her body responding to his touch.

He raised his head. "Hey, I'm pouring out my heart here and that's all you have to say."

Tears filled her eyes. "I love you, too."

"You don't sound happy about it." He sat her up, stood and walked to the French door. "Maybe I've read the wrong signals here."

She hated seeing his hurt, but she wasn't sure she could handle his rejection. She went to him. "You might change your mind when you learn about the things I've done."

"We've all done things. So you were hooked on prescription drugs, you already told me that. It's not a problem now, is it?"

She shook her head. "I didn't tell you all of it. There was more."

He waited for her to speak.

"I ran with a wild crowd in high school. You know how bored rich kids go out partying? We drank so to forget our rotten lives. A joke, huh?"

"Not after meeting Preston."

Here was the hard part for her. "I had a drinking problem, Jarrett. My father was right, he helped me get out of several messes. The worst was one night when I left a party so drunk I ran my car into a tree. I wasn't hurt, but my passenger was."

"How bad was he hurt?"

"Thank God, it was nothing permanent, but he was in the hospital for a while. My father rescued me, paid off his family and the local police. Otherwise I might have gone to jail and have a police record, not be working on becoming a lawyer."

"How old were you?"

"Seventeen."

"I was nineteen when I was stopped for drinking and driving. And because I was the local football star, I got off, too." He took a step closer to her. "We were kids, Mia. We were given a second chance. What happened after that?"

"Even that scare didn't stop me. That's when my father put me into rehab and I finally got sober."

"How long?"

"It's been ten years." She released a breath. "I can't drink alcohol, Jarrett."

"Do you feel the need to?"

"I haven't for a while, maybe when Brad died, and then when my father came to town…" She stopped. "I need to go back to meetings. It's been a while."

The last thing Jarrett had expected was to hear Mia say she was an alcoholic. His chest tightened as he tried to imagine what she had gone through. Her brother had been her only support. Now he wanted to be. "If you'd like, I'll go with you."

She blinked and a tear fell. "Why, Jarrett?"

"I've been trying to tell you, Mia Saunders. I love you.

But for some crazy reason, you think you don't deserve that. I guess I'm just going to have to prove it to you."

Jarrett lowered his head and captured her mouth. He swiftly deepened the kiss, drinking in her sweetness that made him so hungry for more. He ran his hands over her body, folding his palm over her lush breast. She moaned and moved against him.

He broke off the kiss on a ragged breath. "Nothing matters but this. Not your past nor mine. It's how I feel when you're close to me. How wonderful it's going to be when we finally make love. I love you, Mia."

She touched his jaw. "I love you too."

He smiled against her mouth. "Now those are the words that get my attention. And I never get tired of hearing them." He kissed her again, and again, until he was desperate for her. "I want you, Mia."

She drew a needed breath. "I want to make love with you, too, Jarrett, but I can't—"

"I know it's too soon." He leaned his forehead against her and groaned. "It's killing me, but I can wait."

She laid her head against his chest. "I may die before then," she added, enjoying him touching her.

"Then we'd better get married fast."

Jarrett felt her tense and she pulled back. "You want to get married?"

He swallowed. "Did I forget to mention that?"

She nodded.

"I guess I should be more direct." Of course, he hadn't exactly been prepared for this moment. He didn't even have a ring. Then he remembered his mother's.

"Just give me a second." He gave her a quick kiss and hurried off down the hall to his bedroom. He opened the top drawer of his dresser, digging through some things until he found the keepsake box he had since he'd been a kid.

Inside was a ring, a small sapphire circled in tiny diamonds. It had belonged to his mother and she gave it to him before she died.

It probably wasn't worth much by today's standards. But it meant a lot to him. He returned and saw Mia standing by the French doors.

He came up behind her and hugged her. "Are you planning your escape?"

She shook her head. "I love it here. It must be wonderful to live out here."

He hadn't realized how wonderful until he'd seen it through her eyes. "I saved five acres before I sold the rest of my share of the ranch to Trace. So neighbors aren't too close."

"I'm glad, and if we have neighbors, it's your family."

He turned her toward him. "Do you want to live out here, Mia?"

She rose up on her toes and kissed him. "Anywhere you are, Jarrett McKane."

That was all he needed. He went down on his knee. "I love you, Mia Saunders. You'd make me so happy if you'll agree to be my wife."

"Yes, oh, Jarrett, yes. I'll marry you."

He stood and took the ring out of his pocket. "It belonged to my mother," he told her as he slipped it on her finger. It was too big. "We can get you something else."

"No, all I want is to have this sized, then it'll be perfect."

He kissed her, sweetly and tenderly. "I have one more request. I'd like to adopt BJ. I don't want to replace his real father, but it's important that we're a true family. I don't want him ever to feel left out, or that he doesn't belong."

"I think Brad would like that." She kissed him. "You're a good man, Jarrett. How lucky BJ and I are to have you."

"I think we make a great team," he said, knowing they were getting what they all wanted—to be a family.

Mia began to look around. "Just think how wonderful this house will look decorated for the holidays."

Jarrett drew her back into his arms. "As long as there is plenty of mistletoe, I'll be happy."

EPILOGUE

It was January.

A new year, a new beginning, but not before he closed one last chapter of his life. Today Jarrett returned to court and Judge Gillard. He hoped it was for the last time. He glanced at his soon-to-be bride next to him. In three days, she would be his wife, and soon after that, he hoped BJ would be his son.

"It's going to be okay," she whispered. "The judge will be happy with the way things turned out."

He thought so too, but he loved having her positive reinforcement.

Suddenly the court was called to order by the deputy, and Judge Gillard walked up behind the bench and sat in her chair. She glanced over her first file, then looked at Jarrett.

"Case number 4731," the deputy began, "Mountain View Apartment tenants vs. Jarrett McKane."

"Here, your honor," Jarrett said.

"We're here, too, your honor," Mia said and glanced back at Nola, Joe and Sylvia who'd come today, too. Trace and Kira were there too, holding BJ. Sometimes, Jarrett found it hard to believe they were rooting him on.

"Your honor," Mia began. "We'd like to drop the charges against Mr. McKane."

The judge looked over her glasses at Mia. "It's too late for that. I gave Mr. McKane a job to do, and for his sake, I hope it's been completed."

"It has been, your honor," Jarrett said. "I have the sign-off from code enforcement, saying everything was completed as asked."

The judge glanced over the sheet, then looked at Mia. "Are the tenants happy with the results?"

Mia smiled. "Very much so. Right now, Mr. McKane is in the process of remodeling the property."

The judge frowned as she turned to Jarrett. "I thought the building was going to be torn down."

"There's been a change," he told her. "With a slight modification to the building plans, the apartments are no longer interfering with the factory construction. So I've decided to keep it as an investment."

Judge Gillard leaned back in her chair and studied him for a moment. Then she turned to Mia. "Is everyone happy about the situation?"

Nola stood up. "May I speak, your honor?"

"It's Mrs. Madison, isn't it?," the judge asked, then, at Nola's nod, she waved her up to the front. "Please, tell us how you feel."

Nola came up next to Jarrett. "It's been wonderful. We're all getting new apartments and Jarrett isn't even going to raise our rent. We're getting a new neighbor, too. Fulton Industries is opening their business office in the other building, and Mr. Fulton said that maybe some of us can work there part-time." She smiled. "This is all thanks to Jarrett McKane, your honor. He gave us a home when no one else cared. Now he's our friend and he's going to marry Mia and be a father to her baby."

The judge looked overwhelmed. "Well, that's more information than I needed," she said. "But I'm glad it all has worked out for everyone."

She looked at Jarrett. "When is the wedding?"

"Excuse me?"

"The wedding?"

Jarrett caught Mia's attention. "This Saturday at the First Community Church, one o'clock. The reception afterward is in the Mountain View's community room. You're welcome to come, your honor. You did play a big part in getting us together."

She gave him a half smile. "Glad I could help. I might surprise you and show up. I wouldn't mind checking out an apartment for my mother. I like how everyone at Mountain View watches out for each other."

"We do," Jarrett assured her. "And there's a full-time handyman and around-the-clock security on the premises. We'll have some vacancies in another month. Joe and Sylvia Carson are going to be the managers."

Joe stood and waved to the judge.

"I'll have to look into it," she said and glanced over the paper again. "Well, it looks like everything is in order."

Barbara Gillard eyed the couple. "I wish all my cases ended like this. Congratulations," she said and smiled. "I guess there's nothing more to say. "Case dismissed."

The following Saturday evening, Mia sat beside Jarrett in the SUV as they left the wedding reception that had been filled with friends and family. Now they drove toward their home. She couldn't believe it, just a few hours ago they'd got married.

"Have I told you how beautiful you looked today?"

"Yes, but I like hearing it."

"You look beautiful." He kissed her.

She still wore the strapless, ivory satin tea-length dress,

with a fitted bodice covered in tiny crystals. Her bare shoulders were covered with a short matching jacket. Her new sister-in-law had taken her shopping in Denver.

She felt beautiful, too. "Yes, but I like hearing it."

He raised her hand and kissed it. "Then I'll have to say it more often."

Her husband looked incredible in his black Western-cut tuxedo. "You look mighty handsome, yourself. I saw a few women eyeing you too."

"The only woman I care about is you." He took his eyes off the highway and glanced at her. "I'm going to show you how much you mean to me tonight."

She took a shuddering breath. They'd decided to delay any honeymoon, not wanting to leave BJ. But Nola and Sylvia were going to watch BJ for this night, giving her and Jarrett time to be alone. Even though she'd gotten the all clear from Dr. Drake last week, they'd decided to wait until they were married to make love.

He went up the drive, then into the garage and pressed the button to shut out the rest of the world.

Silently, Jarrett got out of the car and walked around. Hell, he was as nervous as a teenager. He'd been wanting Mia so much the past few months, and now he wanted this night to be perfect.

He opened her door and surprised her by scooping her into his arms and carrying her into the house. He didn't stop until they were inside the dimly lit great room. He stood her in front of the French doors, but didn't let go, just leaned down and kissed her.

A kiss that soon had them breathless when he eased his mouth away.

"I love you, Mia. I can't seem to tell you enough how much I want you, tonight, and every night to come."

"I love you, too, Jarrett." She couldn't believe everything they'd gone through to get here.

How Jarrett stepped in to help her with her father. She had decided to sign over part of the company stock, but to her mother. Whatever Abigail wanted to do with it was her business. Maybe it would give her mother the courage to stand up to her husband. Even to rebuild a relationship with her daughter.

"Any regrets that I rushed you?" he asked.

"No. Have you?"

He shook his head. "Not me, but I didn't give you much chance. I've known from the beginning you were special."

"I was attracted to you, but I blamed it on hormones."

He cupped her face and kissed her again. "Oh, yeah, mine are definitely working overtime. But there's one last thing I want to give you." He went to the desk and returned with a piece of paper. "I've contacted my lawyer, Matt Holliston. I introduced you to him earlier today."

"And I remember him from when we took you to court."

Jarrett nodded. "Well, I've asked him to start proceedings to adopt BJ."

Tears welled in her eyes. She found it hard to speak.

"If you think it's too soon—"

She touched her finger to his lips. "I can't see any reason not to give my son—our son a loving father as soon as possible."

Jarrett seemed to be the one at a loss. She loved the man who'd trusted her enough to reveal the bad memories of his childhood. Despite all that, or maybe because of it, he was going to make a wonderful father for BJ.

"I love the little guy, Mia, and I love you. I can never tell you how much."

She raised up and kissed him. "Then show me."

There wasn't any hesitation as he swung her up into his arms again and headed down the hall. Mia knew that with Jarrett she didn't need to run away anymore. She had him to ground her. They'd found what they needed in each other's arms.

They were home.

GREEK DOCTOR:
ONE MAGICAL
CHRISTMAS

BY
MEREDITH WEBBER

Meredith Webber says of herself, "Some ten years ago, I read an article which suggested that Mills & Boon were looking for new medical authors. I had one of those 'I can do that' moments, and gave it a try. What began as a challenge has become an obsession—though I do temper the 'butt on seat' career of writing with dirty but healthy outdoor pursuits, fossicking through the Australian Outback in search of gold or opals. Having had some success in all of these endeavours, I now consider I've found the perfect lifestyle."

PROLOGUE

'So I don't know what to do!'

Mak stared at his only sister in disbelief.

Never in his life had he heard this strong-willed, deter-mined, driven woman admit such a thing.

'Have you talked to her?'

Helen shook her head.

'I've written, I've sent emails, and heard nothing in reply. I can hardly just go out there and land on her doorstep. What if she shut the door in my face? Besides, it's impossible for me to get away. Since Dad's death I've been running the business and trying to keep Mum going—you know how she is—the two deaths coming so close together, it's as if she's given up living. Look at Christmas—her Christmas produc-tions rivalled the Oscar presentations. Feast and family, that was her mantra. This year she's doing nothing and when I suggested I do it, she just shrugged.'

Mak was still puzzled. Yes, Helen was busy and, yes, his mother did seem to have understandably lost her zest for life, but did that add up to so much consternation? Wouldn't time—?

'There's also the cousins,' Helen muttered.

Ah!

He waited for Helen to explain, knowing she would, eventually.

It came with a sigh.

'The cousins are doing their best to take control of the business and if we lose control of Hellenic, Mum will have to watch all Dad built up go into other hands. She'll feel as if his whole life was for nothing.'

While Helen paced the office at the top of Hellenic Enterprises city headquarters, Mak considered what he'd just learned. With his father's blessing, he'd gone into medicine rather than following the parental footsteps into engineering, but as well as Helen, half a dozen of his cousins, children of his father's sisters, had entered the family firm.

And held shares in it!

He frowned, realising that, although still part of the company, he knew less and less of what went on within it these days, his studies and work leaving him little time to read the company reports. And his father's unexpected death had left him with a lot of problems to sort out, as he was the executor of his father's personal estate.

'*Can* they take over? I mean, do they have the power to do that—the majority of shares between them? And what would it mean if they did?'

'They can if they get that woman to vote with them in the extraordinary general meeting they've called for January, and the way they are talking they already have her vote in the bag.'

'You know this for certain?' Mak asked, aware of the bias Helen felt against 'that woman'.

'I'm pretty sure and equally sure money has changed hands. Con was out there just last week, ostensibly to check on the experimental power plant but he's never been interested in geothermal power before.' Helen hesitated before adding, 'And there was a rather large item in his expenses, listed as a donation.'

Mak felt himself frowning.

'Did you ask him about it?'

'How could I?' Helen muttered. 'I shouldn't have seen the information—not until the next board meeting when we all table our expenses.'

'You were spying on him?' Mak couldn't hide his disbelief.

'I was not—it was just that Marge, Dad's old secretary, alerted me to it as she typed up the agenda.'

Which was the same as spying, Mak considered, but that wasn't the issue right now.

'Maybe Con really was checking on the power plant, and the donation was just that. After all, he'd hardly bribe the woman with the firm's money.'

'Well, he wouldn't use his own,' Helen snapped. 'You don't know Con like I do—he's changed since he married for the third time. I reckon his wife keeps her hands on the purse strings. He's as tight as a—as a you know what.'

Mak considered his easygoing cousin and wondered if the third wife might not be on to something—keeping control of Con's spending. Was she also behind the push to take over the company? It didn't seem like something Con, or any of the cousins, would instigate…

'This is all supposition, Helen. Let's give Con the benefit of the doubt for the moment. And in any case, why are you worried about a takeover? You'd still be part of the company, probably still CEO, as I can't see any of them wanting that job.'

'I wouldn't stay,' Helen said, her face pale and her lips tight. 'I know how they think and the way they see the future. Heaven knows, we've argued it often enough in board meetings. If they take over it will be the end of Dad's dream to produce clean power, for one thing. They see that as someone else's job or something for the future. Anything experimental is expensive, and there's no certainty of a return. The cousins want profits that are guaranteed and they want them now which would mean taking the firm in a different direction, looking more towards structural engineering than Dad ever did, and probably merging with a bigger firm.'

Mak understood what she was saying but his mind had snagged on the earlier conversation—at the thought of money changing hands, and Con's third wife, and manipulative women in general. The juxtaposition had prodded another thought in his mind—a very unwelcome one.

Theo had been shameless in his pursuit of women, casually promiscuous, but he had always been careful, assuring Mak that he always took precautions—that he wasn't totally irresponsible.

So had this pregnancy been planned—not by Theo but by the woman in question? Had she seen an opportunity to either trap Theo into marriage, or to benefit in some other way?

She'd benefit all right if the cousins gave—or had already given—her money for her votes, benefit at the expense of Helen and his mother, at the expense of his father's dreams and at the expense of their small family unit, which had always been so tight.

Mak felt anger stir at the thought of a deliberate pregnancy, having been caught up in similar circumstances himself, years ago. Although no one, he was sure, could be as devious as Rosalie had been! However, to be fair, the 'money changing hands' scenario was only supposition on Helen's part. As far as he knew, this woman hadn't made any move to ingratiate herself with the family—in fact, the opposite was true, which brought another problem in its train. Mak's Greek genetic heritage was strongly aligned to family values—family made you what you were, and children needed family.

She had a name, of course, the woman, but it was never mentioned in the family—particularly not in Helen's hearing. Any more than Theo's reputation as a ladies' man was discussed in Helen's hearing. To his sister, her only child had been perfect in every way—handsome, clever, loyal, a loving son and an obedient grandson, following the family tradition by studying engineering—the designated successor to his grandfather, the designated heir to the massive conglomerate of businesses that made up Hellenic Enterprises.

But Theo was dead, killed in a motor vehicle accident that had also taken the lives of three of his friends. Four young people tragically dead because of speed and alcohol, and Mak, who as a top emergency room doctor saw far too many young lives wasted this way, had felt more fury than grief when first he'd heard the news. Grief for his nephew, and his sister's suffering, had come, but the fury had returned when Mak had learned that Theo had been irresponsible enough to leave behind an unborn child.

A child who would be family…

'What stage are you at with the exploration teams out there?' he asked Helen, as an idea that filled him with horror started to form, unwanted, in his head.

'We've found hot rocks close to the surface and although the exploration teams will remain out there, we've sent more men in to build the experimental power plant. Now it's nothing more than pipes and pumps but once we're satisfied that the rocks are suitable for our needs, we'll go ahead with a proper set-up.'

'So, you've the first crews, and more men for the power plant and the likelihood that even more men will be going out there shortly. And if a power plant goes ahead, some of those men will be there permanently so families would be joining them. I'd think you must be putting pressure on a lot of the town's resources but in particular the medical services if there's only one doctor in town.'

Helen nodded, but it was a vague reaction, and Mak could almost see the cloud of grief that still enveloped her.

'Helen?' he prompted, but gently this time.

She nodded again.

'We are,' she said, visibly pulling herself together. 'In fact, Theo suggested the company fund another medical practitioner, if only for the duration of the exploration, but he might have had an ulterior motive—that woman might have been prompting him. The company could certainly afford it but how do we find out if that's what the town really needs?'

Mak knew how they could find out because there was already a raging argument going on his head. Go out and check on things for himself? No way, he was on study leave, it was midsummer, the temperature would be up in the stratosphere, he had his thesis to complete. On the other hand, the family was important to him and right now it appeared to be falling apart. Helen, on whom he had always relied to keep things running smoothly, was struggling—physically as well as emotionally, he suspected. His mother—well, if ever anyone needed some new interest in her life, it was her and surely a great-grandchild could supply that interest…

He'd have to think about it.

There was no time to think about it.

'I don't know what to do,' Helen said, taking the conversation back to where it had started, but now her voice was a feathery whisper, filled with pain and loss. 'I've lost my son and now I'll never know my grandchild.'

'I'll sort it out,' he heard himself say. 'I'll go tomorrow and that will give me the whole weekend to sort out somewhere to stay and introduce myself to Dr Singh.'

CHAPTER ONE

HEADLIGHTS coming up the drive lit up the room, rousing Neena from the comfortable doze she was enjoying in front of the television. Not a patient—at this time of the night, getting on for midnight, patients would go straight to the hospital.

Unless there was an emergency out at the exploration site! No, they'd have phoned her, not driven in.

She eased herself off the couch, aware these days of the subtle redistribution of her body weight. Tugging her T-shirt down to hide the neat bump of Baby Singh, she made her way to the front door, opening it in time to see a tall, dark-haired man taking the steps two at a time, coming closer and closer to her, looming larger and larger.

A tall, dark-haired stranger.

'Can I help you?' she asked, checking him out automatically in the light shed by the motion sensors above the door. No visible blood, no limp, no favouring of one or other limb, and gorgeous, just gorgeous—tall, black-haired, chiselled features…

Chiselled features?

Had pregnancy finally turned her brain to mush?

And he hadn't answered her enquiry. He'd simply reached the top of the steps and stopped, his dark gaze, eyes too shadowed to reveal colour, seemingly fastened on her face.

She was beautiful!

Mak had no idea why this should come as such a surprise to him. After all, Theo had hardly been noted for bedding women who weren't. Had he, Mak, been thinking maybe Theo had been desperate, out here in the middle of nowhere, and settled for someone available rather than stunning? Was that why he was standing here like a great lummox, staring at the straight, slim figure in shorts and T-shirt—staring at a face of almost luminous beauty?

Except that her left cheek was reddened down one side, as if she'd been sleeping against something hard.

Maybe it was the heat, pressing against him like a warm blanket, that was affecting his brain.

'Are you ill? Injured?'

Her voice was soft, and concerned, not about the arrival of a stranger on her doorstep at getting on to midnight but about the state of his health.

'No, but you *are* Dr Singh?'

'Yes, and you are?'

He had to get past his surprise at seeing her—had to stop staring at clear olive skin and sloe-shaped dark eyes, framed by lashes long enough to seem false; at a neat pointed chin below lips as red as dark rose petals, the velvety red-black roses his mother grew.

'Mak Stavrou!' Right, he was back in control again, and had managed to remember his name, but she was still looking puzzled.

'Mak Stavrou,' she repeated, and it was as if no one had ever said his name before, so softly did the syllables fall from her lips.

She was a witch. She had to be. Witches had long black hair that gleamed blue in the veranda light. Witches would be able to handle this heat without showing the slightest sign of wilting.

He wiped sweat off his own brow and felt the dampness of it in his hair.

'The company doctor—you must have received an email.'

The still functioning part of his brain managed to produce this piece of information, while the straying neurones were still looking around for a black cat or a broomstick parked haphazardly in the corner of the veranda.

'Company doctor?' she said, shaking her head in a puzzled manner so the long strands of hair that he now saw had escaped from a plait that hung, schoolgirl fashion, down her back, swayed around her face.

'Check your emails—there'll be something there.'

'Check your emails?' she repeated, the red lips widening into a smile. 'Out here we have to take into account the vagaries of the internet, which seem to deem that at least one day in four nothing works. The big mistake most people, me included, made was thinking wireless would be more reliable than dial-up. At least with dial-up we all had phone lines we could use.'

Neena paused then added, 'Are you really a doctor?'

It was an absurd conversation to be having with a stranger in the middle of the night, and totally inhospitable to have left him standing on her top step, but there was something about the man—his size maybe?—that intimidated her, and she had the weirdest feeling that the best thing she could do was to send him away.

Far away!

Immediately!

'And what company? Oh, dear, excuse me. The exploratory drilling company, of course. They're staying on. I'd heard that. And they've sent a doctor?'

It still didn't make a lot of sense and she knew she was probably frowning at the man. She tried again.

'But shouldn't you be reporting to the site office—not that it would be open at this hour. Who sent you here?'

He shrugged impossibly broad shoulders and pushed damp twists of black hair off his forehead.

'*Nothing* is open at this hour. Believe me, I've tried to find somewhere. A motel, a pub, a garage—even the police station has a sign on the door telling people what number to phone in an emergency. And it's not as if it's that late—I mean, it's after eleven, but for the pub to be shut on a Friday night! Finally an old man walking a dog told me this was the doctor's house and I should try here.'

'It's the rock eisteddfod,' Neena explained, then realised from the look of blank incomprehension on his face that it wasn't an explanation he understood.

'The Australia-wide high-school competition—singing and dancing. Our high school was in the final in Sydney last week. In fact, they came second, and as most of the parents and supporters weren't able to travel to Sydney for the final, the school decided to put it on again here—but of course Wymaralong is too small to have a big enough hall, so it's on tonight down the road in Baranock.'

Disbelief spread across the man's face.

'Baranock's two hundred kilometres away—hardly down the road.'

She had to smile.

'Two hundred kilometres is nothing. Some of the families with kids in the performance live another hundred kilometres out of town so it's a six hundred kilometre round trip, but they're willing to do it to encourage their children to participate in things like this.'

'*You're* not there!' Mak pointed out, totally unnecessarily, but the smile had disturbed something in his gut, making him feel distinctly uncomfortable. Or maybe it was the heat. He hoped it was the heat.

Whatever it was, his comment served to make her smile more widely, lending her face a radiance that shone even in the dim lighting of the front veranda.

'Someone had to mind the shop and take in stray doctors. So, if you can show me some identification, I *will* take you in, and tomorrow we can sort out somewhere for you to stay.'

'Did I hear you say you're taking in a stranger?'

A rasping voice from just inside the darkened doorway of the old house made Mak look up from the task of riffling through his wallet in search of some ID.

'Haven't you learnt your lesson, girl?'

The girl in question had turned towards the doorway, where a small, nuggety man was now visible.

'I knew you were here to protect me, Ned,' she said. 'Come out and meet the new doctor.'

'New doctors let people know they're coming and they don't arrive in the middle of the night,' the small man said, moving out of the doorway so Mak could see him in the light on the veranda. A tanned, bald head, facial skin as wrinkled as a walnut, pale blue eyes fanned with deep lines from squinting into the sun, now studying Mak with deep suspicion.

'I've explained to Dr Singh there should have been an email, and I wasted an hour trying to find some accommodation in town. Here, my hospital ID from St Christopher's in Brisbane— I'm on study leave at the moment—and my driver's licence, medical registration card and somewhere in my luggage, a letter from Hellenic Enterprises, outlining my contract with them.'

The woman reached out a slim hand to take the offered IDs, but it was Ned who asked the question.

'Which is?'

A demand, aggressive enough for Mak, exhausted after an

eleven-hour drive made even more tortuous by having to change a flat tyre, to snap.

'None of your business, but if you must know, I was about to explain to Dr Singh that the company has asked me to work with her to evaluate the needs of the community as far as medical practitioners and support staff are concerned. The company realises having their crews and now some families of the crews here is putting an extra strain on the town's medical resources and the powers that be at Hellenic are willing to fund another doctor and possibly another trained nursing sister, should that be advisable.'

'Realising it a bit late,' Ned growled. 'Those lads have been out there a full year.'

'But more are coming, Ned, and we *will* need to expand the medical service.' The woman spoke gently but firmly to the old man then turned to Mak. 'We're hardly showing you the famed country hospitality, putting you through the third degree out here on the steps. Come inside. You're right about there being no one in town tonight, but even if there had been, there are no rooms to be had at the pub or in either of the motels.'

She paused and grinned at him. 'Kind of significant, isn't it—coming on to Christmas and no room at the inn? But in Wymaralong it's been like that all year. The crews from the exploration teams and the travellers that service the machinery have taken every spare bed in town. You can stay here tonight, and tomorrow Ned can phone around to see if someone would be willing to take you in as a boarder.'

'Which you are obviously not,' Mak said, following her across the veranda and into a wide and blessedly cool hallway, rooms opening off it on both sides.

She turned, and fine dark eyebrows rose while the skin on her forehead wrinkled into a tiny frown.

'Obviously not what?'

'Willing to take me in as a boarder.'

'No, she's not!' Ned snapped, following behind Mak, right on his heels, ready, no doubt, to brain him with an umbrella from the stand inside the door if he made a wrong move.

The woman's lips moved but if it was a smile, it was a wry one.

'You can have a bed for the night,' she repeated. 'Tomorrow we'll talk.'

Then she waved her hand to the left, ushering Mak into a big living room, comfortably furnished with padded cane chairs, their upholstery faded but looking homely rather than shabby. Low bookshelves lined one wall, and an old upright piano stood in a corner, its top holding a clutter of framed photographs, while set in front of every chair was a solid footrest, as if the room had been furnished with comfort as its primary concern.

And the air in here, too, was cool, although Mak couldn't hear the hum of an air-conditioner.

'Have a seat,' his hostess offered. 'Have you eaten anything recently? Ned could make you toast, or an omelette, or there's some leftover meatloaf. Dr Stavrou might like that in a sandwich, Ned. And tea or coffee, or perhaps a cold drink.'

Mak looked from the woman to Ned, who was still watching Mak, like a guard dog that hadn't let down its guard for one instant.

'A cup of tea and some toast would be great and the meatloaf sounds inviting, but you don't have to wait on me. If you lead me to the kitchen and show me where things are, I could help myself.'

'Not in my kitchen, you can't. Not while I'm here,' Ned growled—guard dog again—before disappearing further down the hall.

Now her visitor was sitting in her living room, Neena stopped staring at him and recalled her manners.

'I'm Neena Singh,' she said, introducing herself as if there was nothing strange in this near-midnight meeting, although suspicion was now stirring in her tired brain. She recalled something the man had said earlier. 'If you're on study leave, why are you here? Surely you're not studying the problems of isolated medical practitioners.'

'No, but it's not that far off my course. I'm finishing a master's degree, and my area of interest is in improving the medical aid offered by the first response team in emergency situations. I imagine in emergency situations out here you're the first response—you and the ambos. In major situations the flying doctor comes in, but you'd be first response.'

She couldn't argue, thinking of the number of times she'd arrived at the scene of a motor vehicle or farm accident and wished for more hands, more skilled help, more equipment and even better skills herself. Anything to keep the victims alive until they could be properly stabilised and treated.

'Do you work in the emergency field?'

The stranger nodded.

'ER at St Christopher's.'

'And the company plan is what? For you to work with me to gauge the workload in town or will you work solely with the work crew out on the site?'

'Not much point in working out on site when I need to find out how the additional population—now the men are here permanently they'll have family joining them—affects the medical services of the town,' he said, looking up at her so she saw his eyes weren't the dark brown she'd expected but a greenish hazel—unusual eyes and in some way uncannily familiar.

Like Theo's?

Futile but familiar anger tightened her shoulder-blades, and the suspicion she'd felt earlier strengthened. She tried to shrug off the anger *and* the suspicion. The man's name was Greek, so maybe there was a part of Greece where people had dark hazel eyes…

He was still talking—explaining something—but she'd lost the thread of the conversation, wanting only to escape his presence—to get out of the room and shake herself free of tormenting memories.

And to think rationally and clearly about the implications of the man's arrival in town!

'I'm sorry,' she said. 'I should have offered earlier. You might want to use the bathroom, freshen up. It's across the passage, turn left then first door on the right.'

Getting rid of him, if only for a short time, would be nearly as good as escaping herself, but he didn't move.

'Thanks, but I did avail myself of the facilities at the service station. The rest rooms weren't locked—they even had a shower in there, so I took advantage of that as well.'

'Most outback service stations provide showers—for the truckies,' Neena said, imparting the information like a tour guide. If escaping the man's presence wasn't possible, then neutral—tour-guide—conversation was the next best thing. Later she could think about personal issues. 'This is sheep and cattle country and the animals are trucked to market, plus, of course, all our consumer goods have to be trucked in.'

'And products for the farmers—stuff like fencing wire,' Mak offered helpfully, wondering why the woman was so ill at ease in her own home. Or did she know who he was? That he was family? Unlikely Theo would have mentioned him. 'I have an Uncle Mak who disapproves of me' was hardly the kind of conversation that would lure a woman into bed.

'Yes, it did sound pathetic, didn't it?' Neena said, a slight smile playing at the corners of her lips. 'But I'd lost track of the conversation. I was dozing in front of the TV when you arrived and my mind was still half-asleep. I gather you want to work with me, and as far as I'm concerned, that's fantastic because I can learn from you. You've no idea how often I wish I had more skills in first response stuff. Oh, I get by, but there are so many new ideas that it's hard to keep up.'

Mak wished they'd kept talking about trucking. Neena's honest admission that she hadn't been listening to his conversation, followed by such an enthusiastic acceptance of his presence made him feel tainted and uneasy—unclean, really, for all he'd showered. And when she'd smiled—well, almost smiled—his gut had tightened uncomfortably, but he was fairly sure he could put that aside as a normal reaction to such a beautiful woman. It was the deception bothering him the most, but he could hardly announce now that he was really here to suss her out.

'I've made you toasted sandwiches with the meatloaf.'

Ned marched in, bearing a tray which he set down on a small table beside Mak's chair. 'And there's a pot of tea, but don't you go thinking you can have a cup, Miss Neena. You're sleeping bad enough as it is. I'll make you a warm milk if you want something.'

Mak smiled as Neena hid a grimace.

'No, thank you, Ned. I drank some milk earlier, as you very well know, and how can I have a cup of tea when you've only put out one cup?'

'You'd drink it from the pot if you got desperate enough,' Ned muttered as he made his way out of the room, pausing in the doorway to add, 'I've put clean sheets on the bed in the back room.'

A quick frown flitted across Neena's smooth brow.

'Does the back room have rats and cockroaches or is it just

as far away from your room as it can possibly be?' Mak asked, and won another smile from his hostess.

'It's certainly not the best spare room in the house,' she admitted. 'And Ned does get over-protective. But I don't *think* there are rats or cockroaches.'

'Even if there were, I doubt it would worry me,' Mak said. 'It's a long drive and I'm tired enough to sleep on a barbed-wire fence. In fact, if it's okay with you, I might take my tray through and have the snack there. That way we can both get to bed.'

She turned away but not before he saw a blush rise in her cheeks. Surely not because he'd mentioned both of them getting to bed—it was hardly suggestive, the way he'd said it…

'Through here,' she was saying, and, tray in hand, he followed her, noting the bathroom she'd talked about earlier on the right then another two doors before they reached the end of the passage and the back room.

'Oh, dear,' she murmured as she opened the door and looked in, then turned back and ran her gaze over him from head to toe. 'I'd forgotten about the bed in here. You'll never fit.'

And over her shoulder Mak saw what she meant for Ned had put sheets onto a rather small—perhaps child size—single bed, and even from the doorway, Mak could feel the heat emanating from the room.

'I heard him say he'd sleep on a barbed-wire fence,' the gravelly voice reminded them, and looking through a French door on the other side of the room, Mak saw Ned standing on the veranda.

On guard?

'Well, he can't sleep here. Honestly, Ned, sometimes I wonder if your main aim in life is to frustrate me. Come this way,' Neena added to Mak. 'There's a double bed that should take your height, if you sleep crossways, in the next bedroom, and that bedroom has an air vent as well. I'll get some sheets.'

She opened another door.

'I'll have it made up by the time you get your gear out of the car, and as far as I'm concerned you're welcome to stay here. This *is* the doctor's house after all.'

She was doing it to get her own back on Ned, Mak realised that immediately. He also realised it would give him an ideal opportunity to really get to know her!

So why did he feel uneasy?

Because of the deceit? Or because on first impression this woman was nothing like the manipulative gold-digger he'd envisioned?

'You don't have to put me up.' It was a token protest, brought on by the uneasiness, but she waved it away.

'Of course I don't, but sometimes I get very tired of being bossed around by every single person in this town. Sometimes I'd like to be allowed to make my own decisions. Now, get your things—you know where the bathroom is. I'll put some fresh towels in there.'

She whirled away, opening a cupboard near the back room, pulling out sheets and towels.

'Leave the sheets on the bed, I'll make it up,' Mak told her, and she silenced him with a glare.

'Don't you start,' she warned, marching back down the hall, slipping past him into the bedroom.

Mak set the tray down and left her to it, wondering just why the town would be so protective of her. Okay, so it was hard to get doctors to serve in country towns and the further outback you went the harder it became, but...

Maybe it was her pregnancy.

The phone was ringing as he re-entered the house, silenced when Neena must have answered it. He heard her say, 'I'll be right there,' and the click of a receiver being returned to its cradle.

'Bed's made,' she said, passing him in the passage. 'Towels in the bathroom.'

And she kept walking.

Dumping his bag, Mak followed her.

'You're going out on a call,' he said as his long strides caught up.

She nodded but her pace didn't slacken as she crossed the veranda and ran lightly down the steps—running when being back out in the hot night air immediately sapped his energy.

'I'll come with you,' he said, determined to get used to whatever the climate threw at him. 'It's what I'm here for, to see how you work.'

'You've been driving all day and you're tired,' she said, opening the door of a big four-wheel-drive that stood just off the main circular driveway. Then she turned to look at him. 'But it's probably your kind of thing and I could certainly use some help. An accident at the drilling site. The ambulance was out of town but it's on its way.'

Mak didn't answer, instead striding around the car and climbing in the passenger side, relieved to find she'd already started the engine and had the air-con roaring.

'Motor vehicle?' he asked, and as Neena reversed the car competently onto the drive, she shook her head.

'I don't know how much you know about it, but if you're employed by Hellenic Enterprises presumably you know they've gone past the initial exploratory drilling stage and are setting up an experimental geo-thermal power station. Basically they pump water down into the bowels of the earth onto shattered hot rocks, and the heat of the rocks turns the water to steam, which comes up through different pipes and is harnessed and used to make electricity.'

Her explanation had holes in it but as a basic description of a scientific process it wasn't too bad.

'And what's happened?'

'A seam on a pipe burst and steam escaped. Two men badly burned, others less seriously.'

'Steam burns—bad business,' Mak said, wishing he had the facilities of St Christopher's burns unit here.

'The flying doctor's on the way. We stabilise them as best we can and they'll fly them to somewhere with a burns unit.'

'So, it's a first response situation,' he said, turning to look at her. She was studying the road ahead, concentrating on the thin strip of bitumen, so all he could see was a clean, perfect profile—high forehead, straight nose, the flare of lips, the delicately pointed chin.

'Exactly,' she said. 'Most of our emergencies are. We stabilise people and send them on—some, if they're locals, come back so we know about the eventual outcome but many of them, travellers passing through, are never seen again.'

'Most emergency medicine is like that—I rarely see anything of the patients I treat once they've left the ER. Rarely hear how they've fared, for that matter.'

'And does that bother you?'

She glanced his way and he sensed she was really interested in his reply, an interest that intrigued him.

'Why do you ask?'

She smiled.

'I suppose because I know most of my patients so well. The local ones are part of my life and I'm part of theirs so we work together to get the best outcomes for them. I can't imagine a scenario where I don't know what happens next.'

The words rang true, and Mak wondered if a woman who could be so involved in her patients' lives could also be the manipulative female he suspected she was.

Of course she could be. All human beings were multi-faceted.

'I suppose part of the fascination of medicine is that it offers so many different opportunities in its practice,' he said, although the way she'd spoken made him wonder about what *had* happened to some of the patients he'd treated. Just a few who'd made a big impression on him, or those who had been tricky cases…

'Anyway, I'm glad you're here for this job,' she continued. 'You probably have far more experience with burns than I do.'

Her gratitude made his gut squirm and her frank admission about her capabilities didn't fit with the picture he'd built up in his mind. Served him right for pre-judging?

He turned his mind from the puzzle this beautiful woman presented to the task ahead of them.

'Were the pipes in an enclosed space?'

She glanced his way again.

'I haven't been out there for a couple of weeks so I don't know what's been going on, but originally all the piping was exposed—right out in the open.'

Another glance then her attention switched back to the road. 'You're thinking inhalation injuries? Even outside, if they were close to the pipe when the accident happened…'

She paused, frowning as she thought, then asked, 'Would obvious facial burns always be indicative of inhalation injuries?'

She had a quick mind, something he usually admired—and enjoyed—in a woman, but in this woman?

'Yes, it should give us an indication. If there are signs of facial involvement—maybe even if there aren't—we should intubate them. If there's internal tissue damage that causes swelling—'

'Intubating later might be impossible,' Neena finished for him, happy to be talking medicine, although distinctly unhappy about this man's sudden intrusion into her life.

Was he simply who he said he was—someone sent by the company to assess the strain the additional population was putting on medical services? Or had Theo's mother, the coldly formal Helen Cassimatis of the emails and letters, sent him?

He was quiet now. Maybe, like her, he didn't want to get too far ahead of himself before he saw the patients.

She risked a glance at him, pleased he was looking out the window into the darkness through which they passed.

A very good-looking man, but...

Greek name, Greek company...

Not that Neena hadn't expected it. Theo's complaints about his stifling family, while probably exaggerated, had suggested nothing less, and she'd doubted Theo's mother wouldn't do something to follow up the outrageous offers she'd made!

First there'd been an offer of financial help, followed closely by the suggestion that Neena move to the city so she could have the best medical attention. Then a letter just to let Neena know 'the family' had accommodation she could have rent-free in Brisbane so she wouldn't have to work.

And all so 'the family' could get their hands on Neena's child! The same 'family' that had produced Theo—charming, intelligent, handsome and smart, and so cosseted and spoiled, so used to getting his own way, he'd taken Neena's panicky, and admittedly last-minute no as a tease and had forced her.

The squelchy feeling in her stomach wasn't as bad as it used to be, but she still couldn't think of that night without feeling a slight nausea. She breathed deeply, in and out, and concentrated on the road ahead.

They'd left the silent, deserted town well behind them and she pushed the memories equally far away.

The road was dead straight, a single-lane strip of bitumen that in daylight stretched to the horizon. Now, at night, a cluster of lights marked the site of the geo-thermal experimental station.

'Is there an airstrip at the site?' Mak asked. 'Can the flying doctors land there?'

Neena shook her head.

'At first it was just a couple of exploratory crews out here, drilling down to work out how far they needed to go to get to the hot rocks. When they found them closer to the surface than they'd expected…'

She stopped and turned briefly towards him.

'I suppose you know the rocks can be anything from two to ten kilometres beneath the surface of the earth and apparently when you're drilling and pumping water and steam every metre makes a difference?'

'I know a bit about the process—I'm interested in all alternate power sources and geo-thermal in Australia makes a lot of sense. But you're saying that for exploratory purposes there was no need for an airstrip? Because the crews moved around?'

She nodded and Mak saw the frown he'd glimpsed earlier pucker her brow.

'And now?'

Glancing his way again, she shrugged.

'I think they should have a strip. The land's as flat as a table top so it wouldn't cost much to 'doze one, and although I wouldn't for the world wish accidents on any of the workers, they do happen and in cases like this we could airlift the injured men straight out rather than having to bring them into town and then airlift them. Every time they're moved, we put them more at risk of infection.'

'Well, now the company is bringing in more men to build their experimental power plant, maybe they will put in a strip.'

The lights were getting closer—and brighter—glowing in the blackness of the night.

'If it's not already planned, you could put it in your suggestions,' Neena told him, concentrating on how useful this stranger could be rather than the weird sensations he was causing in her intestines.

Or wondering whether the real reason he was here was to take her baby from her—to absorb her child—into the conglomerate that was 'the family'.

Theo's family.

'Suggestions?' he said, sounding so vague, anger surged inside her.

'*Isn't* that the job you were sent for?'

The words grated from her throat as she pulled up outside the camp office, noticing in her rear-vision mirror the flashing lights of the ambulance approaching in the distance. Slipping out of the vehicle, she grabbed her bag from the back seat and hurried into the well-lit but warm cabin.

'We covered them with clean sheets like you said, turned off the air-con and gave them a small dose of morphine,' an anxious-looking man told them as they walked in. He was hovering between two desks on which the injured men had been laid. 'We've a stretcher in the medical room but the light's better in here.'

Neena had set her bag down on the floor and opened it. Mak knelt beside her, silently congratulating her forethought. Burns victims lost heat rapidly, and with shock a likely side-effect of the trauma, they needed to be kept warm.

'One each?' he suggested as she handed him a suction device and an endotracheal tube.

'Suction, intubate then fluid.' She was muttering more to herself than to Mak.

'Large-bore catheters in both arms,' he said.

Although her confirming nod and quiet 'We need to allow good fluid access' told him she was thinking along the same lines as he was.

The ambulance attendants arrived as they worked, took in the situation at a glance and opened up the big bag they were carrying.

'We've a burns kit with treated gauze. Want us to cover the wounds?'

To cover or not to cover? It was a question that had tormented Neena in the burns cases she'd handled previously. She turned to Mak, knowing he'd have more experience.

'You're flying them out to a specialist unit,' he said, 'but you've two transfers before they leave here and another when they get to the city—opportunities each time for contamination. Let's cover.' He was competently siting a large-bore catheter in his patient's arm as he spoke. 'You've Ringer's in your bag?'

Neena nodded, concentrating on getting the catheter sited in her own patient's arm.

'That's the plane,' one of the ambos said, as a roaring overhead shook the shed that served as an office at the work site. 'They said they'd buzz us as they came in.'

'Okay, let's move them,' Neena suggested, as she attached tubing and a bag of fluid to the second catheter on her patient, adjusted the flow, then grabbed a transfer form to complete before the injured men left the site, noting down exactly what treatment they'd been given. 'You guys take them straight to the airfield. Dr Stavrou and I will see the other injured men.'

'Dr Stavrou?' one of the ambos queried, as the other helped Mak lift his patient onto a stretcher.

'Mak Stavrou, meet Pete and Paul, two of our crew of four local ambos,' Neena said, then she stood aside as Pete and Paul lifted her patient.

'He your replacement while you take maternity leave?' Paul asked, wheeling the patient towards the door.

Neena shook her head.

'I'll explain some other time, but for now, would you leave your burns kit here? I'll bring it back to town.'

Time enough for the townsfolk to learn why Mak Stavrou was here. And for him to learn the town's reaction! Not everyone was happy with the exploration crews, or the experimental power plant, but he'd find that out soon enough.

And *no one* in the town would be happy if they knew the suspicions she had about his visit! This was a town that protected its own, and Neena was definitely its own.

She hid a sigh bred from the frustration she often felt over this protective attitude, but they meant well, her town's people...

'Let's go see the others who were hurt,' she said to Mak, who was talking to the foreman.

'They're in the mess cabin, I'll take you over,' the foreman said, as Mak lifted the burns bag from her grasp, his fingers brushing hers in the exchange. 'They're not badly hurt,' the man continued, while Neena trailed behind the two men, telling herself she couldn't possibly have felt a reaction when the stranger's skin had brushed hers.

She was worried about the injured men, and uptight because she'd had this Mak Stavrou foisted on her. The twinge had been nothing more than tension.

'Some of the steam was still leaking from the pipes when they went over to drag their mates away but I'd say they're only superficial burns,' the foreman explained.

They *were* superficial burns, soon treated and dressed.

'Leave the dressings in place until Monday then come into town and we'll check the wounds and dress them again if necessary,' Mak told the three men.

They all agreed and thanked him, while Neena smiled to herself. In this case, Mak *was* the person with the most experience, but as far as these rough outback labourers were concerned, it was as natural to them as breathing to consider the male of the species as the main authority—the chief!

'Best if you're a boy,' she muttered, patting the bump as she made her way back to her vehicle. 'Life's a lot easier for men.'

CHAPTER TWO

BEST if you're a boy?

The phrase he'd heard Neena mutter hung in Mak's head as they drove away from the exploration site, but the weariness of the long drive out to Wymaralong was claiming him and he couldn't think clearly about the implication of the words.

'Do you not know the sex of your baby? I thought with regular scans most people found out quite early.'

Neena didn't take her eyes off the road, simply shaking her head by way of reply.

'I didn't want to know,' she said, and before she could explain the vehicle struck something and jolted to a stop, slewed across the road, airbags inflating so the world turned white.

'What the—!'

The muttered oath told him his companion was conscious and as he fought his way out of the airbag he heard her door open.

'Are you all right?' she asked. 'Can you move your legs and arms? Coming on to dawn, I don't drive fast because I'm always wary of 'roos. I don't think we hit whatever it is hard enough for major injury but your side took the impact and the front wing is crumpled. Are your feet free?'

Mak wiggled his feet and moved his limbs. There was less foot room than there'd been earlier, but his feet weren't trapped.

'I'm conscious and feeling no pain so I assume I'm okay and, yes, my feet are free. What did we hit? I didn't see anything ahead of us and there certainly wasn't anything on the road as we came out.'

'It's a camel, I just looked. I'd heard there was a mob of them out here, but hadn't believed it. They're usually further west, around Alice and over in the Western Australia deserts. By the look of things it was already dead—maybe the ambulance hit it a glancing blow on its way back to town. The damage is on your side so I doubt your door will open. Here's a knife, can you cut your way free of the airbag? I'll phone a tow truck.'

He felt the knife press into his palm then heard her move away, speaking quietly, no doubt phoning for help, but when he made his way out of the vehicle she wasn't on the phone. The headlights, still working on the driver's side, illuminated a macabre scene, the slight woman kneeling by the big animal, talking not to it but to a young calf that stood making bleating noises at its mother, no doubt waiting for her to get up.

'She had this calf—the poor wee thing. See the cord—it's not very old.'

The pain in the woman's voice pierced Mak's heart and he heard his own voice saying, 'Don't worry, we'll look after it.'

We?

He was here for a month and what did he know about raising camels? Raising anything? Okay, so he'd thought he'd be a father—once upon a time—and he'd liked the idea, but his marital experience still rankled. It wasn't something he was likely to repeat.

'I'd like to get a rope around his neck,' Neena said.

Mak smiled to himself, feeling the words were a great segue to his thoughts, then he realised she was trying to hold the struggling baby camel.

Struggling baby camel? The animal was kicking its ridiculously long legs and the woman holding it was pregnant.

'Let go,' Mak ordered. Guessing she was about to argue, he added, 'If it kicks the baby, you'll be sorry.' He lifted it out of the way, standing up with it and wondering what to do next.

He supposed it was fate that the tow truck should arrive at that moment so he was illuminated by its headlights, standing in the middle of the road, a baby camel in his arms.

'You guys been having fun?' The tow-truck driver got out of his cab and surveyed the scene. 'Not your baby, is it, Neena?'

'It is now,' Neena told him, standing up and moving across to where the driver was examining the calf. 'We'd better put him in the back of my vehicle and get him out when we get to town. Can you drag the mother's body off the road a bit before you hitch up to my car, Nick? Oh, sorry, Nick, this is Mak—Mak, Nick.'

'New doctor in town, I heard,' Nick said as he offered his hand to Mak.

'Word gets around,' Mak said, shaking hands with the man, although it did puzzle him just how this had happened in the early hours of a Saturday morning, especially as the town had been deserted when he'd arrived.

He didn't puzzle over it long, putting the calf into the back of the vehicle then helping Nick wrap a chain around the dead camel and walking in front of the tow truck as it pulled the animal off the road and into bushes well off the track. Next, Neena's vehicle, with its badly damaged bull bar and left wheel arch, was attached for towing, and Neena, who had settled the calf in the back of her big four-wheel-drive, talking to it all the time, was persuaded to leave it for the drive back to town.

'Birds like ducks and geese attach themselves to humans if they don't have a mother—do you think camels might do the same?' she asked as she climbed into the tow vehicle, moving across the bench seat to make room for Mak in there as well.

'Patterning, don't they call it?' Nick said, and Mak's world became a dream again. Crammed into the cab of a tow truck as a brilliant dawn coloured the eastern sky, the smell of diesel fuel filling the air, and a slim, pregnant, beautiful woman squashed beside him, chatting on about the patterning habits of birds, stirring heat in his body again...

He'd put it down to tiredness and ignore it, that's what he'd do, but, exhausted as he was, the night was not over. As Nick pulled up outside the big old house and Mak wearily alighted, his hostess was already making plans.

'My office is the first room on the left, the computer's on the desk,' she said to Mak. 'Could you hop on the internet and see what you can find out about camel milk? The little one will need a drink. And Nick, if you wouldn't mind carrying it out to the stables. A rubber glove, that would do for a teat do you think, until I can get something sent out?'

'It's no use arguing,' Nick said to Mak, as Neena made her way to the back of her vehicle to release the calf. 'Once she's got a bee in her bonnet about something, there's no stopping her. I'd better catch up or she'll lift the damn thing out herself.'

Nick hurried after her while Mak wearily climbed the front steps. They felt as high as Everest, but as tiredness cramped his legs he had to wonder just how tired a pregnant woman must be feeling. Not that he intended using her office for the internet search on camel milk.

Was he really about to do that?

Yes, he was, but he'd use his laptop—that's if wireless worked out here. One day in four, she'd said—was that when it did work or it didn't?

He sighed, too tired and confused to think about such irrelevancies. Though wasn't the constitution of camel milk an irrelevance?

Not in Neena Singh's opinion!

He ate the sandwich as he searched the 'net, and even drank a cold cup of tea, making notes at the same time.

'Camel milk is lower in fat and lactose than cow's milk and higher in iron, potassium and Vitamin C,' he reported, after finding his way around the back of the house to what had obviously been stables at some time and entering the one that was brightly lit from within.

Neena, seated on the stable floor with the calf's head in her lap, looked up at him and smiled, although he was so far beyond smiles he wondered how she'd managed it.

'That's great. We can work out some kind of formula but to begin I've given him some newborn infant formula I had out here from when we were looking after an injured foal. There's no vet in town, you see, and the stables aren't used most of the time. Someone told me about rubber gloves and he seems to have taken to it because he drank quite a lot before he went to sleep.'

She held up a two-litre soft-drink bottle to which she'd attached a rubber glove, the fingers tied off so the thumb formed a soft teat.

Mak shook his head, although was feeding a camel calf through a rubber glove any more unbelievable than the rest of the occurrences of the night?

'You should be in bed yourself,' he said, knowing if he didn't lie down soon he'd probably fall down but not wanting to portray such weakness in front of this apparently inexhaustible woman.

'I'll go soon. You go—have a shower and leave your clothes in a heap on the bathroom floor. Ned will take care of them for you. Grab something to eat in the kitchen if you're hungry. You won't sleep otherwise.'

'And you're going to do what?' Mak demanded, sensing she had no intention of following her own advice and going to bed.

'I'll doze here. From the moment I was pregnant I took up dozing. I can doze just about anywhere. And I don't want Albert waking up and finding himself alone.'

'Albert?'

She smiled at Mak and he felt a now familiar stirring deep inside him. Tiredness!

'He's got a noble look about him and I think Albert is a noble name, don't you? I did consider Clarence—Clarence the Camel, you know—but he might think that's a bit sissy when he grows up.'

'And Albert isn't?' Mak muttered, but not loudly enough for Neena to hear because right now he didn't want to get involved in an argument over the naming of a camel calf. Besides, she was talking again.

'When Ned gets up he'll rig up something for him, some way that Albert can feed on demand and some music or something to keep him company, but until then I'll stay here. There's straw and bags, I'll be perfectly comfortable.'

Mak knew he should argue, but with what—the on-demand feeding? What did he know? Her staying there? He doubted he'd budge her.

He walked away, but the image of her, sitting on the floor, dirty and dishevelled, the camel's head on her lap, wouldn't go away.

Might never go away.

And *that* thought made him shiver…

Neena watched him go, her mind churning. A man who'd check out the constitution of camel milk in the early hours of the morning couldn't be all bad. But what if her suspicions were right—what if he'd come to take her baby from her, if not physically, then at least to persuade her to let the child be part of a family of which she had a very poor opinion?

She had to be wary of him—and not be taken in by little acts of kindness. Except that kindness, right now when she was feeling so terribly, terribly tired, seemed particularly important.

She studied the calf's funny face through teary eyes and told herself it was just pregnancy making her weepy, and thinking of the pregnancy—of *her* baby's welfare—she stretched out on the bag-covered straw and settled the calf so its legs were stretched away from her, then she patted Baby Singh, talked softly to him for a few minutes, telling him about the little camel he'd have for a playmate, wondering about family—a concept not all that familiar to her, although deep down she knew that every child deserved to have a family.

But *that* family?

She wouldn't think about it now. Mak Stavrou was here for a month. She'd work it out before he left; right now she needed to sleep.

But every time she closed her eyes an image of her visitor was fixed to the inside of her eyelids and she was forced to study his face and try to work out just why it had so appealed to her.

It couldn't just be the strength of his facial bones, obvious because of the way his tanned skin stretched tautly over them, or the thick black eyebrows above dark hazel eyes, or the long nose kept from perfection by a thickening in the middle, or lips, pale but rimmed with a line of even paler skin so the sensuous fullness of them was emphasized.

'Oh, boy! Talk about trouble,' she told the sleeping Albert. 'Six months pregnant and I'm fantasising about a stranger. And not just any stranger—a Hellenic Enterprises stranger!'

As if one stranger from Hellenic Enterprises wasn't enough!

She patted the baby then curled her hands around the bump.

'It's okay,' she told him. 'We'll work it out. Together we can conquer the world.'

But the promise lacked conviction so she added, 'And if we can't there's always Ned and one thousand, four hundred and forty-two other Wymaralongites. Who needs family when we've got all of them?'

And on that note, she finally slept.

'How could you let her bring that animal home?' Ned demanded, when Mak, refreshed from four hours' solid sleep and now starving, made his way into the kitchen.

'You could have stopped her?' Mak enquired, and the old man shook his head.

'Nah! Never been any different, she hasn't,' Ned admitted, twiddling a knob on the coffee machine and pulling a mug out of a cupboard. 'Kittens, puppies, tortoises she picked up off the road, a duck one time, a galah with a broken wing— you name it, we've nursed it or reared it or sometimes had to bury it. But a camel—that's going too far. What's she going to do when it grows?'

'I imagine there are camel farms somewhere that will take it, or some tourist operator on the coast who uses them for beach rides. A sanctuary perhaps. I've never come across a baby camel before so am not sure about what one does with it when it grows.'

'Tourists riding on her camel? Yeah, I can see her letting that happen! People peering at it in a sanctuary? No, we're stuck with it.'

Ned handed Mak the mug of coffee, and waved his hand to milk and sugar on the table, somehow making the simple act a gesture of acceptance. Although Mak guessed Ned might be looking to him as an ally in some endeavour. Persuading Neena to part with her new pet?

Whatever it was, the man's suspicion of the previous night seemed to have vanished.

'Has she gone to bed?' Mak asked, and Ned nodded.

'Under protest, but I told her if she didn't sleep it would harm the baby—that usually works if ever you need to get her to rest.'

Definitely an ally, Mak realised.

'And the calf?'

'Happy as Larry,' Ned assured him. 'I've rigged up a bag of old clothes and I've got formula in a plastic bottle inside it. The calf nudges and sucks and as long as the milk comes out he doesn't know he hasn't got a mother.'

Mak shook his head, aware this was becoming a habit, but it was obvious from Ned's conversation that he was just as dedicated to Neena's strays as she was. Or perhaps he was just used to being the one who had to work out how to feed them! A strange relationship, the wizened old man and the beautiful young woman—Mak would have liked to ask about it, but he didn't think the alliance between him and Ned was strong enough just yet.

Until Ned spoke again and he realised the alliance was less about the camel than about practical matters.

'Neena usually does a few hours on Saturday mornings at the surgery. Young Paula Gibbons is the nurse-receptionist on duty and I phoned her to say we're running late, but with Neena not long gone to bed I thought you might do it. Meet some people, talk to them about the town. You *are* a doctor?'

So Ned's suspicions were still alive and well, Mak

realised, and the old man had just been manoeuvring him towards this moment.

'I am and I'm happy to do it, but won't Neena—'

'Object? Sure she will. She'll mutter about people taking over her life but if we didn't do that occasionally she'd run herself ragged. Here, eat this before you go.'

Mak had been taking little notice of what Ned was doing as he talked, but now a beautiful omelette appeared in front of him, golden brown on the outside and within its fold melting cheese and fine slices of ham and tomato.

He ate, had a quick wash then followed Ned's instructions to the surgery, where Paula, a bright redhead, guided him through the patients for the morning, every one of whom asked him if he was Neena's locum for maternity leave and every one of whom had only good things to say about their local doctor.

Could someone so obviously not only respected but loved in this community be the devious woman he suspected she was?

Or was he only questioning his opinion of her because he was attracted to her?

Instantly attracted! This was something that had never happened to him in his entire life and therefore something of which he should be extremely wary—maybe even suspicious. Other experiences had taught him that attraction could make you forget common sense and for many years, as far as women were concerned, common sense had ruled his life.

And would continue to rule it. No matter how wonderful the townspeople thought this woman, he had to judge her for himself, and that would be impossible if he let the attraction get in the way.

He saw the last patient for the morning, had a chat to Paula—another Neena admirer—and headed back to the house. He wanted to go out to the geo-thermal site and speak to Bob Watson, head man out there, having ascertained the previous evening that Bob would be on duty today.

Neena woke to bright sunshine flooding through her window, and stared confusedly around her. She was on her bed, wrapped in her lightweight cotton robe, clean and naked, though she couldn't remember showering.

Or could she? Memories of Ned chasing her out of the stables, threatening to turn the hose on her if she didn't go immediately. Somehow she'd made it to her room, stripped, showered—even washed her hair, from the feel of it, still slightly damp—then collapsed on the bed. But when? How long had she been asleep? And what was happening to her house guest? Ned might have turned him out by now.

Which, considering how she kept remembering the feel of his fingers touching hers as he'd taken the calf from her, was probably a good thing.

She'd think about the calf—about Albert!

She smiled and patted Baby Singh, picturing the camel calf's rubbery lips and curly eyelashes, his huge, soft, doe-like eyes.

'Such fun to have a pet again,' she told the baby, then she heaved herself off the bed and began to dress, anxious now to check that all was well in her small world. She hadn't phoned Brisbane to see how the burns victims were, or visited the hospital—though someone would have phoned if she'd been needed. And—

Her eyes fixed on the small digital clock beside her bed.

She'd missed morning surgery!

She shot out of her bedroom and blasted down the hall to the kitchen door.

'Ned, why didn't you wake me? It's lunchtime. My patients—'

'Have been seen. I brought back some notes in case you were concerned about any of them.'

Neena stared at the man who'd answered.

Her house guest, far from having been turfed out by Ned, had achieved the honour of being allowed access to the kitchen. In fact, he was sitting at the kitchen table—in *her* chair—eating lunch and chatting amiably to Ned.

'You saw my patients?' she demanded, anger and disbelief holding her motionless in the doorway.

'It's what I'm here for after all,' he said coolly. 'To gauge your workload, and even after less than twenty-four hours I can see you need another doctor.'

'So now you know that, maybe you can leave,' Neena snapped, then realised just how ungracious that sounded. But her kitchen, now she'd entered it, seemed to have shrunk, making the man seem closer than he was, the atmosphere thick and heavy.

'Not on the strength of one morning's surgery,' he said, so cool in the face of her rudeness she wanted to throw something at him. Something hard!

'Sit down and have your lunch.' This from Ned, and she knew his voice well enough to know he, too, was angry, but with her.

As well he should be!

'I'm sorry, that was terrible of me,' she muttered at Mak from the doorway. 'Yelling at you when I should be thanking you.'

He nodded a gracious acceptance of her apology, but she suspected he was laughing at her inside for his eyes were twinkling with delight, which made her mad again. But she *had* to enter the kitchen! For a start, she was starving. But her legs were heavy and stiff with dread because, for only the second time in her life, Neena was feeling physical responses to a man. Well, maybe not the second time—but only once before had they been as strong as this and that once had ended in heartache, pain and trouble.

'How's Albert?' she asked, directing the question at Ned, trying to ignore the other person in the room.

'Blooming,' the man she was trying to ignore replied. 'I've just been talking to him. He quite likes the Mozart but would prefer a little rock music from time to time.'

Neena frowned at the light-hearted comment. She didn't want to like this man—bad enough to be getting physical reactions from him, but liking him?

'Sit down and eat,' Ned told her, pulling a plate of cold meat and salad from the refrigerator and putting it down at the other end of the table from Mak, setting cutlery beside it and pouring her a glass of cold water.

So here she was, right opposite Mak Stavrou, where every time she looked up she'd see some bit of him, like how the dark hair on his arms curled around his watch. At least the table was long so she wouldn't be accidentally bumping his feet or have her knees knocking his…

Although not thinking about him was hard as once again came the memory of the previous night, of the touch of his hands on hers.

Ridiculous, fantasising about a stranger's touch!

'Lovely salad, Ned. Are these tomatoes from our garden?'

'You'll note she says "our",' Ned growled at Mak, 'though it's years since she dirtied her hands in the vegetable patch. Reckons looking after the roses is enough for her, not that roses take much looking after out here.'

'I noticed the rose gardens on my way to the stables,' Mak replied, smiling at Neena. 'My mother grows roses but I don't think I've ever seen such a wonderful display.'

'The dry climate means you don't get mildew or most of the

bugs you get closer to the coast,' Neena replied, keeping the words crisp and impersonal, the mention of his mother reminding Neena of her doubts about why this man was really here.

Reminding her he could well be the enemy!

An enemy who had helped out this morning, she reminded herself. She asked him about the patients he had seen, and managed to eat most of her lunch while they discussed them.

'I'm going out to the drilling site this afternoon,' the man who was disrupting her life announced as he stood up from the table, rinsed his plate and put it in the dishwasher. 'I need to see some people and explain why I'm here. I want to talk to them about what they see as the impact on the township.'

'You might as well stay out there, then,' Neena told him. 'They're putting on a Christmas party for the town tonight. Every man and his dog will be there.'

Mak turned towards her and leaned against the kitchen bench.

'And every woman and her camel?'

Neena had to smile.

'Maybe not the camel, but as Ned is Father Christmas—yes, I know he's not a normal size Father Christmas but he does a great ho-ho-ho—we have to go.'

'Then I shall certainly stay for it,' Mak said with a smile that made moths flutter in her stomach and caused regret that she'd mentioned it.

He departed soon after and Neena went up to the hospital to check on patients there, then crossed to the retirement home to sit with her old friend Maisie for a while.

But Maisie's common sense, and their shared remembrances, failed to soothe the turbulence in Neena's chest. The arrival of the man from Hellenic Enterprises had thrown her into such a muddle she couldn't begin to think logically about him.

Or why he'd really come!

'Don't think too much,' Maisie said as Neena was leaving, and although Neena hadn't done more than mention Mak in passing, avoiding any discussion of him, she knew Maisie had picked up on her unhappy state of mind and had guessed he was the cause of it. 'Sometimes our instincts are our best guide.'

'Not mine!' Neena muttered, but only after she'd walked out of Maisie's room.

Back home she played with Albert for a while, walking him around the stall, talking to him, fondling his ears and scratching at his coat. But eventually she had to leave this safe retreat and get ready for the Christmas party.

Upstairs, she found a parcel on her bed and knew before she opened it what it would contain. Each year Ned made a trip to the two-dollar shop in Baranock and brought back Christmas shirts for the two of them, the surgery staff, the hospital staff and all the folk in the retirement home. This year his choice for her was a bright red singlet with a very tipsy reindeer on it, the deer's horns festooned with glittering streamers, its front feet holding a foaming mug of beer.

'Great! First time Mak Stavrou sees me dressed up and I'm wearing a tipsy reindeer!'

The words echoed around her bedroom, coming back to hit her with some force. Why on earth did it matter how she looked when Mak Stavrou saw her? her strong, grown-up and independent self demanded, but deep inside, another weak and feeble self knew that it did…

The site, usually three orderly rows of dongas, the de-mountable living huts now common in all mining areas of Australia, had been transformed. The dongas were strung with Christmas decorations, forming an aisle that led visitors down to a large marquee, brightly lit and covered in swathes of greenery the men had found somewhere in the bush. Christmas baubles and tiny fairy lights glittered in the leafy branches, making a magical grotto of a very ordinary large tent.

Was it fate that the first person Neena saw was Mak Stavrou or had she been looking for him? She hoped she hadn't been, but on the other hand she wasn't too keen to think it might be fate.

He was coming towards her with Bob Watson, the head of the geo-thermal exploratory crew.

'I'll go and get changed,' she heard Ned say behind her, and he promptly deserted her.

'Neena!' Bob greeted her, taking her hand and giving her a kiss on the cheek. 'Merry Christmas. You've already met Mak. Thanks on behalf of the company for taking him in. We could put him up out here but what's the point when he needs to see what you do in town and maybe take just a little work off your shoulders?'

Bob had barely said the words when he stepped away, holding up his hands in a mock surrender.

'No, don't rip up at me. I know you can handle *anything*.' He turned to Mak and added, 'And not only does she believe it, but she can! Wonderwoman, I call her.'

Neena knew she was probably as red as her singlet, and far from ripping up at Bob she was struck dumb, for Mak had pulled on a Santa hat and now that Neena looked around, she realised all the Hellenic work crew were wearing them. And whereas most people looked a trifle foolish in red pointy hats with white trim and a white bobble on the end, seeing Mak in his had suddenly evoked not memories of Christmases past but images of future Christmases, though why she should be seeing him beside a tree in her old house and, worse, seeing small children laughing up at him, she had no idea. In fact, the vision made her shiver, *and* miss whatever Bob was telling her.

'He suggested I take you through to the food tent,' Mak said, presumably picking up on her vacant state, but hopefully not on the cause of it.

Don't think too much, Maisie had told her, but when Mak put his hand on the small of her back to guide her through the throng, she ceased to think at all. *Couldn't* think! And didn't then throughout the evening, not when Mak piled ham and turkey on her plate, not when he led her to a blanket-covered bale of hay to sit and eat her dinner, not as she chatted about nothing very much and listened to him talk about cheap energy—about which he seemed particularly keen—and especially not when he led her out of the marquee to where a dance floor had been laid on the desert sands, and suggested she might dance with him.

'Because you're really the only woman I know in town,' Mak told her. 'Apart from Paula, whom I met this morning but who seems to be attached to a very large farmer.'

So she danced with Mak beneath the stars—with a stranger to whom she was attracted—a stranger that the few brain cells still operating in her head warned her to avoid.

At all costs!

Don't think too much, she reminded them, hoping they'd calm down, because dancing with Mak was like dancing on a cloud, high above the real world, the bright light of the stars scattering magic all around them.

Of course it had to end. Sirens approaching from the distance told them not that a disaster was at hand but that Santa had arrived, not in a sled drawn by reindeers, or even leaping kangaroos, but in the local fire engine.

'At least it's red,' Mak remarked as Neena eased out of his arms and turned to watch the arrival.

He didn't sound any happier than she felt, but maybe she

was imagining that. Or maybe he just liked dancing and he didn't know anyone else...

He still had one arm around her shoulder, but as excited children surged forward to grab the sweets Santa was throwing from his perch atop the fire engine, Mak touched the bump—very gently at first then settling his hand on it.

And as they'd been dancing with it pressed against him Neena could hardly object, although when he murmured, 'Next year you'll have someone special with whom to share your Christmas,' she felt a wave of sadness sweep over her. Yes, it would be good to have a baby in the house for Christmas, but right now the two of them as a family, even with Ned and Maisie added, seemed a little meagre.

Neena and Mak were separated by the crush of people moving to see Santa and though she talked and laughed with all those present, the magic had gone out of the evening. Until later when she and Ned—now Ned again—were about to leave and Mak caught up with her, guiding her into a shadowy spot outside the marquee.

His touch had started tremors in her limbs and shivers up her spine—ridiculous, she knew, but how to stop them?

'Bob's offered me a bed in his donga,' Mak began. So that was how to stop tremors and shivers—they disappeared immediately! 'Just for tonight so I can go out with him in the morning to see another site where they are drilling.'

Neena could only stare at him—her brain once again gone AWOL. *Surely* she couldn't have been thinking he'd been going to kiss her!

Shivers, tremors—of course she had been. Or if not thinking it, then hoping...

'That's okay,' she managed, her words cutting across his explanation that he hoped to be back in town by lunchtime. 'The house is never locked so we'll see you when we see you.'

She walked away, her legs feeling ridiculously weak and trembly. Must be all the dancing…

Mak watched her join up with Ned in a group of people, then after kisses and hugs and various other forms of farewell, the pair of them walked into the darkness. Was it because they'd danced that the last thing he'd wanted to do in that shadowy corner was tell her his plans for the following day? What he'd *wanted* to do—so badly he'd barely restrained himself—had been to kiss her. Hold her in his arms and kiss the breath right out of her.

He lifted his arms and raked his hands through his hair, cursing silently in Greek as he tried to make sense of a situation that was fast spiralling out of control. He'd been here less than twenty-four hours and the woman he was supposed to be checking out—a woman of whom he was still suspicious—had woven a spell around him.

Had he forgotten how perfidious women could be? Forgotten his vow never to become involved—emotionally involved—with one of them again? Where was his head, where were his brains?

He strode out into the darkness, thinking a brisk walk might sort things out, knowing the lights were bright enough to guide him back to the camp. But with every stride some memory of Neena intervened. Bob telling him what a great doctor she was, and how she attacked any problem with grit and determination, sorting out not only the townspeople's illnesses but the tangles some of them made of their lives.

Now an image of Neena with Albert's head on her knee popped into Mak's head, and he heard her quiet voice soothing the little orphaned animal to sleep. Would a woman who took in stray animals deliberately get pregnant?

He shook his head and picked up his pace, wondering what on earth he was doing out here in this godforsaken desert land. Then he heard the sound of carols drift through the hot night air and knew.

It was about Christmas, and Christmas was about family.

CHAPTER THREE

MAK returned as Neena was eating her lunch. She'd had a good sleep-in, for once undisturbed by any emergency, but Sunday had brought no relief from the problem that was Mak. He'd visited her dreams, a tall, dark-haired man in a Santa cap, teasing her so her body had heated in her sleep and she'd tossed and turned.

Now he was here in person, chatting on to Ned about the drilling site and geo-thermal plant and totally oblivious of the ructions he'd caused in the night—ructions he was still causing…

She had to escape him!

'I'm off to the hospital,' she told him. 'Nick dropped off a loaner car for me yesterday afternoon. I know you worked yesterday morning, but there's no need for you to hang around with me today. Ned can show you around the town, not that there's much to see, though most tourists are interested in the bore head. Our artesian bore was one of the first sunk in Western Queensland.'

He'd lost her! The seeds of the tentative, if not friendship then working relationship Mak thought they'd achieved, not to mention the rapport he'd sensed as they'd danced last night, had been washed away in the bright light of day.

'I'll come to the hospital with you. If your week doesn't acknowledge Sundays, why should mine?'

Dark eyes studied him—wary? Suspicious? Then she shrugged her shoulders as if he was of no importance whatsoever.

Which in her mind was probably true, so why should it bother *him*? Because they'd danced beneath the stars? Was she regretting that as much as he was? From his side it was because it had thrown him off track—made him forget just why he was here, which was to persuade this woman to let her child be part of his family, and hope that the child could help to reunite and rebuild his family.

'If you like,' she said, pushing aside her half-eaten meal and standing up. 'I'll pop down and visit Albert and meet you at the car in ten minutes. That suit you?'

She wasn't really asking, so he didn't reply, puzzling instead over the change in her manner.

Did it matter?

Not really as far as his official job was concerned, but if he was to persuade her to let Helen and his mother be part of the baby's life, then he had to win her trust.

How he was supposed to persuade her to vote the baby's shares with Helen was a whole different ball game, but he was sure trust had to come into it!

But how did he go about winning trust? He was a doctor, for heaven's sake, people usually trusted him automatically— he didn't have to go out of his way to prove himself.

He carried his plate over to the counter by the sink, where Ned was leaning, a broad smile on his grizzled face.

'Prickly little thing, ain't she?'

Mak glared at him, not needing the snide observation to bring home the fact that Neena Singh had definitely gone off him!

* * *

'The hospital has twenty beds, but they're rarely full.'

Neena passed on this riveting fact as the man settled into the beaten-up loaner four-wheel-drive and did up his seat belt. Determined to keep things on a purely professional basis and to forget—for the moment—why he was here and, more difficult, the way he was affecting her, she continued in the same vein.

'The flying surgeon used to operate here but with the town's decline in population—before the exploratory teams turned up—and the widening of the road between here and Baranock, he now operates there once a month, so any surgical patients from Wymaralong will spend their first twenty-four hours post-op in Baranock then come back to us.'

'And are people obliging enough to save their acute appendicitis until the surgeon's due to visit?'

Neena swung to face him, frowning at the slight smile—smug, surely—on his face. The smile focussed attention on his lips—lips that had already featured in her dreams, lips she'd thought for one fleeting moment last night might actually kiss her!

Professional, she reminded herself, turning into the tree-lined drive that led up to the low-set hospital.

'The flying doctors take the acute appendicitis cases straight to a bigger hospital. The flying surgeon does elective stuff, carpal tunnel, hip replacements, hernias—even in the city I imagine patients have to wait for surgery.'

'Too long,' Mak agreed, so honestly that Neena found herself liking him again.

Well, liking a colleague was okay, wasn't it?

'At St Kit's we try to keep the waiting lists as short as possible, but I doubt we'll ever have the facilities or the staff in any city hospital to reduce them to zero.'

'I've read about the problems,' she said, pulling up in the

shade of one of the spreading pepper trees. 'In fact, the more I read the more I think our services are better in the country—for some things. Having to send people away for operations—and for childbirth—is disappointing, but it's unavoidable these days.'

He was coming around the car towards her, a tall man in lightweight cotton trousers and a dark green polo shirt. Did he wear green to make his eyes seem greener?

Or would a man like him not realise that?

She didn't have a clue what kind of man he was, and probably would never know him well enough to guess, and *that* thought, as he fell in beside her to walk into the hospital, sent a twinge of sadness through her heart.

Stupid heart! This was a man who'd come into her life less than forty-eight hours ago—what could she be thinking?

'We've a terrific bunch of nurses at the moment—in fact, they've always been top class. For a long time, before I came back here, they put up with locums coming and going, and virtually ran the hospital and catered for the townspeople's medical needs themselves.'

She took the two steps in a stride and stopped at the top as a middle-aged woman in dark blue long shorts and a paler blue shirt came out of the front door, a door already festooned with Christmas decorations.

'I know you were out dancing last night so I phoned Ned and told him to tell you we didn't need you,' she scolded, and Neena, feeling about six years old in the face of Lauren's disapproval, hurriedly introduced Mak.

'We do need another doctor—even without the power plant going ahead, the town's population could carry two GPs,' Lauren said, shaking Mak's hand and sizing him up at the same time. 'Come on in, I'll give you the tour. You.'

She turned to Neena.

'You can make the tea. I bought some more of those lemon-flavoured decaffeinated teabags for you so don't think you can sneak a real one because I'll smell it.'

Neena scowled at her. 'Never fall pregnant in a country town where every citizen feels impelled to count your caffeine intake every day,' she grumbled at Mak.

'I'll try not to,' he said, a teasing smile twisting those mesmeric lips. 'Caffeine addict, were you?'

'Was she ever.' Lauren answered for her. 'The worst! Coffee morning noon and night, then she gets pregnant and tries to convince us all that tea has no caffeine in it—as if we'd fall for that!'

Mak was once again struck by the protective attitude towards Neena—a loving protection that he assumed she must have earned. He remembered the conversation as they'd driven up to the hospital—remembered her saying she'd come *back* to town.

'Did she grow up here that you're all so watchful of her?' he asked Lauren as the straight back with the long black plait dangling down it disappeared through a side door.

'She did. Her father came out here from India at a time when it was nearly impossible to get doctors in the country. He was newly married and wanted to build a better life for his family, but sadly his wife died in a car accident when Neena was four, and she was the only family he had.'

'She and the townsfolk,' Mak suggested, and Lauren smiled.

'It took a while. We're not a trusting lot, out here in the bush, but he was so good to everyone, and then his wife dying so, yes, the town took him to their hearts. Then— But you're here to see the hospital, not hear the history of the town. As you can see, we've four four-bed wards straight off the central corridor and one more right at the back, but the back three are permanently closed. Mr Temple here—' she led him into the ward on the right '—is in while Neena gets his medication sorted. He goes back home—he lives out of town—and forgets to take his tablets, then takes too many—'

She broke off as she reached the bed of the ward's only occupant.

'Mr Temple, this is Dr Stavrou. He's here to help out for a while.'

'While Neena has her baby?' the old man asked. 'You know if it's a boy she's going to call it after me?'

'Call it Mr Temple?' Lauren teased, and the patient glared at her.

'You know I've got a name, it's on me chart, I just don't hold with this modern habit of everyone calling everyone by their first names as if they're all best mates.'

'I quite agree,' Mak told him, surreptitiously checking the chart to see what the man's name was, but the scrawl was indecipherable. Surely not Clarence. If Neena wouldn't call a camel Clarence she wouldn't—

'It's Charles, if you're trying to read it upside down,' Mr Temple said. 'That's a perfectly proper name for a baby. It's a real name, not a made-up one like Autumn.'

'Mr Temple's great-granddaughter is called Summer,' Lauren explained. 'And his granddaughter is expecting her second one, but she's only teasing you, Mr Temple, about calling it Autumn. Maybe if she has a boy she'll call him Charles.'

'Can't have a whole class of Charleses in the same class at the school in five years' time!' the patient grumbled.

Mak listened to the conversation while a strange feeling of contentment swept through him. Wasn't this what he'd envisaged when he'd begun to study medicine—spending time with patients, quality time, not the rushed politeness of the ER? Of course, it was impossible to think that this situation could be re-created in a city practice or city hospital.

Or could it?

Lauren was leading him out of the ward and into the one across the passage where two middle-aged women were sitting up in bed knitting, metal walking frames by their beds suggesting they might be post-op hip replacements.

'The terrible twosome,' Lauren introduced them. 'Marnie and Phyllis. Twins, though you wouldn't know it to look at them, and determined that if one experiences something the other must as well. Marnie fell at the clothesline and broke her ankle, had to be airlifted out so it could be pinned and plated and she's back here until we get her weight-bearing on it, and Phyllis, not to be outdone, broke her leg last week. Simple fracture of the tib and fib, Neena set it here. We've only kept Phyllis over the weekend because she's having trouble with crutches and the walking frame will be hard for her to manage at home.'

'And because I'm company for Marnie and with shearing next week I won't get the layette finished for Neena's baby if I have to go home,' Phyllis told him, holding up the tiny garment—in bright purple wool—that she was knitting.

Marnie's wool was green and Mak wondered if politeness would decree Neena's baby had to wear the garments being knitted out of kindness and no doubt love.

'Green and purple?' he said to Lauren as she led him into the big kitchen at the back of the building.

'They're not still knitting, are they?' Neena demanded, picking up on the conversation immediately. 'Honestly, Lauren, can't you tangle the wool in the walking frames?'

'My baby had to wear a bright orange jumpsuit knitted by the twins, and it was midsummer at the time, so live with it. Put the things on when you know the twins'll be in town on mail days, and the rest of the time dress him however you want.'

She waved the teapot at Mak and at his nod poured a mug of tea, pushing a plate of biscuits towards him.

'Does everyone in this town consider you're having a boy?' Mak asked Neena, who was sipping distastefully at her aromatic drink.

'We're kind of assuming it because of the general nuisance value,' Lauren said.

'Boys being more annoying than girls?' Mak guessed, deciding a second biscuit, each bite rich with chocolate pieces, wouldn't go astray.

'When they're younger, definitely,' Lauren said. 'Girls rarely think of taping kites to their backs and jumping off the garage roof to see if they can fly.'

'He only broke one leg,' Neena put in. 'And you have to admit, you worry a lot more about your girls now they're older.'

'All teenagers are a worry,' Lauren decreed. 'You got kids?'

This last was directed at Mak and he knew enough about hospital gossip to realise this was also an 'are you married' question.

'No kids,' he said, deliberately not taking the bait, though again feeling a faint twinge of what couldn't possibly be regret. After Rosalie, his distaste for the marriage experience had been so strong he'd decided it was something he would never repeat. But kids? Back then, he'd been excited about the prospect of a baby, about being a father…

'Lucky you,' Lauren said, and he could feel the next question hovering on her lips, but at that moment there was a loud crash and Neena and Lauren rushed from the room.

'Phyllis, didn't I tell you to buzz me before you tried to use the crutches?' Lauren was saying when Mak arrived at the scene of the accident—a fall on the veranda outside the kitchen.

'Yes, well, Marnie reckoned he looked a bit like The Rat and I had to check.'

Neena and Lauren had her back on her feet and were settling the crutches under her armpits, both of them looking slightly flustered. But Phyllis had no intention of moving, not until she'd studied Mak's face intently enough to make a judgement, finally shaking her head.

'Nah, she's wrong. The Rat had the charm thing going— sparkly eyes whenever he looked at any woman. Smile about to pop out, always there ready on his lips. This bloke looks okay. Solid!'

She nodded at Neena as if her judgement was approving something, though what Mak didn't like to think, then, with Lauren by her side, she started back to bed.

'Pity she didn't break her wrist when she fell,' Neena muttered as he followed her back into the kitchen.

'Nice attitude for a doctor,' he told her, and she turned to frown at him, studying him.

'She couldn't knit with a broken wrist,' she said, but Mak had the strangest sensation that knitting was the last thing on her mind. He'd figured out 'The Rat' was none other than his dead nephew, but from the look of disappointment on Neena's face, she, too, had found no resemblance.

Shouldn't that be good?

'Phyllis thought I looked okay,' he told her, and won a half-smile.

'Phyllis thinks all men look okay—she's a fifty-seven-year-old spinster—she and Marnie run the family property. Marnie was married at one time, but to another Rat, but that doesn't mean they judge all men by his behaviour. In fact, at one time, Phyllis rather hoped she might become my step-mother, but my dad was hung up on my mother even after she died and that was never going to happen.'

Mak shook his head—it was definitely becoming a habit. 'Are all country towns this—with everyone seeming to know everyone else's business? Do you ever get any privacy?'

Neena smiled at him and patted the small neat baby bump protruding under her T-shirt.

'I must have at least once, mustn't I?' she said, and although she spoke lightly, the smile had slid off her face and the sadness in her eyes made him want to hug her.

Hug her? A woman pregnant by his nephew—the nephew commonly known in town as The Rat? A woman who might have deliberately become pregnant? More to the point, a woman who carried a rifle in her car? He'd seen it there when he'd put Albert inside in the early hours of Saturday morning.

Hugging just wasn't on the agenda.

Not now, and not ever.

Though hadn't he held her in his arms when they'd been dancing? Even touched her bump? And she hadn't objected to that!

'Where next?' he asked, taking another biscuit because chocolate was good energy food, and they were the best biscuits he'd ever tasted.

'Retirement units next door—it's not quite a nursing home, but some of the people living there are getting on a bit and Maisie, one of the oldest, has been having breathing problems. It's congestive heart failure but…'

'But?' Mak echoed, when it became clear Neena wasn't going to expand on the subject.

'Come and meet her, but be warned, she's another lifelong spinster with an eye for single men, and although you ducked that question from Lauren earlier, can I assume you *are* single?'

'I am,' Mak replied, and found himself wishing she was

asking for personal reasons, although he knew full well that wasn't the case. He was going to be working with her—it was natural she'd want to know something of his background, and marital status was part of that background.

'Maisie will be delighted,' Neena told him, her smile back again—a more healthy smile this time.

She stood up and led him off the back veranda of the hospital and across a gravelly strip of land where nothing grew towards a newish building, brick with a green tiled roof.

'The local service clubs got together to build it, and having it close to the hospital means we can share the staff. All meals are supplied, although some of the units have small kitchens so the residents can be self-sufficient if they like. Being Sunday, there'll be a barbeque late this afternoon if you want to stay for it.'

She led the way into the cool building, and along a wide corridor towards a big open room. Four women and two men were sitting in there, watching television or reading. Neena spoke to a young man in dark blue shorts and a paler blue shirt, the male version of the uniform Lauren had been wearing.

'Maisie?'

'In the greenhouse,' he said, and though he looked enquiringly at Mak, Neena didn't introduce him, leading him out of the room and further down the hall.

'The building was designed to be eco-efficient. Like most western buildings, it has an evaporative air-cooling unit on the roof, and the greenhouse provides shade from the western sun. It also gives the residents who are interested something to do, looking after the plants.'

She opened a door that led directly into the shade-cloth covered room—no, it was larger than a room, more the size of a village hall. And everywhere were orchids in full bloom, long stems of them bending across the narrow passage between the shelves of plants.

'But they're beautiful,' Mak said, noticing for the first time a woman in a wheelchair down the end of the greenhouse.

'They are, and a lot of them have been propagated from plants Maisie brought from her home when she shifted in, and she's the one who's taught the others how to care for them. Right now I'd guess she's tagging the flowering plants she wants to go on display in the hospital and in the common room here. Hi, Maisie, I've brought you a visitor.'

'Nice-looking man, from what I hear,' the old voice croaked. 'Come closer so I can take a look at you.'

Mak walked obediently closer, hoping shock wasn't registering on his face as he saw how old the orchid cultivator was. Rheumy brown eyes were almost lost in a maze of wrinkles, while toothless gums shone in her wide smile.

'I'm Mak Stavrou,' he said, bending over to take her hand, and without thinking, to lift it to his lips for a gentle kiss.

'Mac like in MacKenzie?' she asked, letting her hand linger in his.

'No, spelled with a K and short for Makarios, a Greek name meaning blessed. My parents had a daughter first and, being traditional Greeks, thought the family needed a boy. It took a while, hence the name, although my sister turned out to be the one who followed in my father's footsteps.'

'I hope you are blessed,' Maisie said, and Mak heard the wheeze in her voice and realised that even this short conversation had tired her.

'Is there anything you need?' Neena asked, and when Maisie shook her head, they stayed a little longer, Neena telling him the names of the various orchids, pointing out which ones were native to Australia, showing off Maisie's work in a way that was obviously pleasing to her but not exhausting her.

'Is she on diuretics? Heart medication?' Mak asked when they'd said their goodbyes and left the greenhouse, taking an outside door and heading across the car park towards the car.

'Not any more,' Neena said, the sadness so evident in her voice Mak had the urge to hug her again.

'Why not?'

He had to ask.

'She doesn't want it. She says it's time to go and she doesn't want her body rattling with pills and potions when she turns up at the Pearly Gates. That's a direct quote, I might add. She's a great believer in the Pearly Gates. She's also quite sound in her mind, so I have to respect her wishes.'

'But she seems to have a lot of life in her yet and she loves the orchids—wouldn't she want to see them flower again?'

Neena turned towards this man who had come so suddenly into her life and was now disrupting it quite enough without arguing over Maisie's medication—a subject that already tormented her.

'She's one hundred and five, Mak,' she said. 'She's seen the orchids bloom enough. And don't think I haven't been trying to persuade her otherwise. She's been part of my life for ever. She's Ned's mother, and she was our housekeeper when my mother died, passing the job on to Ned when she retired.'

'She brought you up?' Mak said softly, and Neena nodded, the sadness she felt almost overwhelming her.

'And right at the end I disappointed her—great, isn't it?' she said bitterly, then she strode away.

Perhaps her pregnancy hadn't been deliberate. The thought struck Mak as he followed her back to the car, his steps slowing as hers speeded up.

But she was a doctor—she'd have a supply of morning-after pills in her surgery, every GP would have them these days. So even if becoming pregnant *had* been accidental, continuing with the pregnancy had been deliberate.

And persuading Theo to include the unborn baby in his will? Had he *not* been careful? Had she worked on that?

Just because everyone in town thought she was the bee's knees, it didn't mean she wasn't as devious as most women. Look at Helen, at his mother, at his ex-wife—all past masters in the art of getting their own way.

'You not ready to move on?' Neena called, and he realised his forward progress had stopped altogether, his mind lost in the past. No, he wasn't married, as he had told Lauren earlier, but he had been once, persuaded into marriage by a woman whom he'd believed was carrying his child.

When the pregnancy hadn't progressed—an apparent miscarriage—they'd struggled on for a while, Mak believing marriage was for keeps, but six months later his wife had announced she was in love with his best man and wanted a divorce.

The fact that his best man had been a corporate raider who had earned more in a month than Mak had earned in a year probably had nothing to do with it, but he'd wished he'd brought the two of them together earlier. It would have saved a lot of emotional torment of the 'where did he go wrong' type, not to mention a lot of fuss and embarrassment.

'Have you ever been married?'

The question from the woman leaning negligently against the car fitted so well into his thoughts he wondered about ESP, then hoped she didn't really have it as he'd been having some unlikely thoughts about her.

'Phyllis not into divorced men?' he asked, and she smiled at him.

'I don't think it's an issue for her. In fact, I don't know why I asked. I suppose because you're older than the young unmarried male schoolteachers and nurses we get out here. Except for them, we don't get a lot of single men coming to town, so it isn't only Phyllis you'll have to watch out for.'

'Surely having the work crews here helped redress the imbalance,' Mak said, then realised he'd probably hurt her as a fiery blush swept into her cheeks and she climbed hurriedly into the car.

CHAPTER FOUR

MAK joined her, glancing sideways, wanting to judge her mood—wanting to apologise, but how?

Her profile could have been carved from stone, so little did it reveal, but as they left the hospital grounds she turned left, off the road they'd driven in on, taking him in a direction he didn't recognise. To his surprise there was a hill in what he'd thought a dead flat landscape—a rough and rocky hill, the road winding up it to a lookout at the top.

Neena parked the car and got out, determined to get things settled with this man. For the good of the town she had to work with him, so best things got sorted out right now.

'This is our local lookout—that's a lake fed by the bore below us, and up here, a few years back, the local council received some arts funding and had a camp of sculptors visit the town, producing the artworks you see along this walk.'

Her house guest looked bemused but she didn't care. This was a favourite place of hers, a place her father had always brought her when she'd been cross or out of sorts, frustrated by the way her world was working. Up here, with the wide red desert sands stretching to the horizon in all directions, she would find peace steal into her soul and her world would return to rights.

She doubted that would happen this afternoon, but at least she felt the presence of her father here—some family support!

She led Mak past the big sculptures, The Working Man, The Rainbow Serpent, The Shearer and The Drover, to the small statue at the end, a very freeform figure of a mother and a child, carved from the red sandstone of the hill and called simply Serenity. Not that she'd tell Mak that!

She waved him down onto the seat beside the statue.

'I was wondering,' she began, her heart hammering against her ribs at the temerity of what she was about to ask. 'Mak Stavrou, Greek name, Hellenic Enterprises, Greek business—is there a connection?'

She watched him as she spoke, and saw the frown that puckered his forehead. Would he lie?

And would she know if he did?

Probably not, but she knew she couldn't go on pretending that she believed his story when she had so many doubts. Doubts she wanted to dispel—just as she wanted him to assure her she was wrong...

Mak considered what to say, sorry he hadn't talked about this earlier—yet what time had there been? As they'd treated burns victims together? As they'd danced beneath the stars?

He remembered that brief interlude with a pang, while he considered how to answer. No way could he lie. Even if she asked him to leave town forthwith, he had to tell the truth. It was better that way—no more deceit, no more discomfort about not being fully honest with her.

'I was Theo's uncle.'

'And his mother sent you?'

'No way! Well, the job came through her and it's a genuine job—the company wants to help the town, and I have the qualifications to look at the medical services. As to the rest, well, the baby will be family, he will be my sister's grand-child, my mother's great-grandchild.'

She turned towards him, but it was only a glance—a frowning glance.

'Is it the family tie or the fact that Theo, for whatever reason, willed the baby shares in the company? Which brings you here?'

Mak hesitated, wondering how to answer, again feeling that it was essential there was honesty between them.

'We're Greek, so family ties are very important, and to be perfectly honest with you, Neena, the family part of it was what prompted me to come. I'd like to think the baby knows his family—that he knows we'll always be there for him—and for you, of course. Personally, I'd like to help you plan for his future—that's probably something to do with the fact that I'm now the senior male in the family. As you might have gathered, family is something I feel strongly about.'

'Is there a but following that very touching admission?' she asked and he glimpsed the steel in this woman who carried such a load of responsibility on her own—steel she must need from time to time.

Truth! he reminded himself, making a helpless gesture with his hands before answering.

'There is now,' he admitted. 'The share situation has become complicated. How much do you know about the shares?'

He saw her frown deepen, then she shrugged.

'I had a letter from a solicitor saying Theo had been killed in an accident and had left his shares in the company to the baby. I was shocked to hear about his death—he was too young to die so senselessly. I filed the letter away somewhere and thought no more about the share thing.'

He was too young to die so senselessly? Not 'I was dev-astated,' which was surely what she'd have said if she'd loved him? Was his suspicion that the pregnancy might have been her idea correct? Why did it keep recurring?

Dragging his mind off that tangent—it was something he could think about later—he asked, 'You've only received one letter?'

She looked at him, still frowning, definitely perturbed.

'No, there might have been more, but I've been busy so I just put them all into a folder to look at some other time—after all, the baby isn't here yet, so the shares can't be of any importance to him.'

How to explain? Mak took a deep breath.

'Not to him, but they are important within the context of the company,' he began, although he doubted she would care about a company of which she knew so little. 'The share situation became complicated when my father died before Theo. Although my father's sisters' sons have always been part of the company, Theo was the designated heir.'

Mak hesitated, wondering how she would take the revelation he was about to impart. If monetary gain had been her aim all along, she would surely be delighted, although probably too smart to show it.

He took a deep breath and told her.

'Your unborn baby is now the majority shareholder of Hellenic Enterprises.'

She stared at him, then shook her head and stood up, her body stiff with tension as she paced around the stone statue nearest to them. 'I can't even begin to consider the implications of that, although now all the strange offers I got from Theo's mother make more sense.'

Neena folded her arms across her chest and glared down at Mak.

'She was trying to buy me—trying to buy my votes—and I thought it was just the baby she wanted!'

He wanted to protest, to tell her Helen wanted the child to be family just as he did, but how could he when the complication of the shares—and Helen's fears they'd lose control of the company—made the situation look so bad?

'The baby *will* be her grandchild,' he reminded Neena. 'He or she will be all she has left of her son. He will be family.'

'He will not necessarily be part of *that* family!' Neena spat the words at him then took another turn around the statue.

'It's no good,' she finally announced. 'I just can't get my head around it at the moment. I'll think about it all some other time.'

She stared out over the lake. The revelation about the number of shares—could the bump beneath her rib cage really be the majority shareholder of the company?—was too startling to take in right now, although she was more suspicious than ever of the man who had come into her life.

The same man she'd thought might kiss her.

She felt the presence of the stone woman and child close beside her, but today the serenity she usually found in this place was missing, not only because of the conversation but because her awareness of Mak's body claimed all her senses, tingling in her skin, prickling at the short hairs on the back of her neck, heating her body, although the sun was sinking towards the horizon and a cooling breeze was whispering across the lake.

Was she mad?

How could she possibly be attracted to this man?

And if it *was* attraction, then surely common sense dictated she send him away—far, far away?

Now she knew who he was and why he was really here, she'd be justified in asking him to leave.

But how could she send him away if the town could gain

from his visit—and the town *would* gain if he was genuine in
his desire to assess the needs.

If…

'That family'. She spoke of his family in the same way Helen
had spoken of her—'that woman'. The conversation, in spite
of the fact that there was now no deceit between them, had
made Mak feel distinctly uneasy. If he had a scrap of common
sense he'd leave town right now, riding off into the sunset—
or maybe it was the sunrise from here—like a defeated
cowboy in the old movies. But the thought of leaving town
held no appeal whatsoever.

And if he was perfectly honest with himself, his reluctance
had less to do with the shares, or Helen and her grandchild—
even his mother's grief—and more to do with a growing fascination with the woman by his side, a woman to whom he
felt an undoubted attraction, but, worse than that, in whom
he felt a deepening interest. She was beautiful, yes, and that
accounted for the attraction, but beyond the beauty he sensed
a strength and determination and commitment that made her
something special.

But hadn't he thought Rosalie special at one time?

If he thought about it deeply enough, he knew he'd
probably have to answer no. She had been beautiful and intelligent and fun to be with, certainly physically attractive to
him, but special?

He let out a long sigh. As if this particular woman, special
or not, would want anything to do with *him* of all people!

'The sun's setting, we have to shift to the other side of the
statues,' the special woman said, standing up and walking
away from him.

He followed, but didn't walk far, for as he passed the
strange carved shape labelled Serenity, he saw the colours of

the sunset, brilliant, vivid stripes of purple and vermillion, of hot orange and a lurid pink, all somehow working together to paint a vision the likes of which he'd never seen.

'That's unbelievable,' he managed to murmur as the colours faded to mauves and dusky rose.

'We do good sunsets,' his companion said, still watching the colours change, her back straight, her body still, as if movement might spoil the magic of the moment.

The following day began predictably enough. After breakfast, bacon, eggs and sausages served by Ned, who had obviously never heard of cholesterol, and a visit to Albert, who had to be the funniest-looking small animal Mak had ever seen—all legs and lips—Neena took him to the surgery.

'As you no doubt discovered on Saturday, we've two consulting rooms,' she'd said, as she introduced him to 'the girls' who ran the practice on weekday mornings, 'so what if you take all the male patients? A number of them will be thrilled to have a male doctor to talk to.'

Mak nodded, still trying to get his head around a medical receptionist who looked at least eighty and a practice nurse who wasn't much younger.

And so they worked through the morning; the three men from the power plant were the first patients he saw, their wounds healing well. After examination, he had them redressed by the septuagenarian nurse.

They broke for lunch, freshly cut sandwiches, platters of fruit, tubs of yoghurt, provided by a cheerful, fresh-faced young woman from the local café.

'If you want something hot, you only have to tell me,' she said to Mak. 'Dr Singh, not Neena but her dad, liked a hot lunch.'

As Mak had by now worked out that the previous Dr Singh

had been dead for at least eighteen years and this young woman looked about that age, he did wonder about this information.

Wondered aloud!

'We've always got our lunch from the café,' Mildred, the receptionist, told him. 'And the same family still run it. Young Keira will take it over from her parents one day. Her brothers aren't interested. They're on the rodeo circuit.'

Mak had to smile.

'Imagine growing up where going on the rodeo circuit was a job opportunity!' he said, as Neena came to join them in the lunchroom.

'Or helicopter mustering,' she said. 'Have you had your lunch?'

She was wrapping a couple of sandwiches in a paper napkin as she asked the question, then she found a cool-bag and popped them in, added a tub of yoghurt and a bottle of water and headed back out the door.

'Come on,' she said from the doorway. 'You can drive while I eat.'

'But the afternoon patients?' Mak queried.

'They'll wait. They know I only go out to emergencies and one day it might be one of them that needs me.'

Mak followed her out of the room.

Helicopter mustering? Had the helicopter crashed?

He asked this as he caught up with her and was handed the car keys.

'It's more a gyrocopter,' she said. 'A small, light one-seater. Often home-made, which makes them, in my opinion, far more likely to come crashing down out of the sky. Unfortunately he's been working behind a herd of bullocks coming into town for the cattle sales so there's no nearby airstrip. The fellows with him don't think he's too badly injured but know not to move him, so we'll go out and if we need the flying doctors we'll contact them from there. We take the road west then the turnoff is exactly twelve kilometres on the right—we should be able to see them from there.'

Neena hoped the explanation and directions covered everything her colleague would need to know, as she'd just as soon not have him asking questions. For some reason the timbre of his voice and the intonation of his phrases had lingered in her head and made sleep difficult all night. Bad enough his image was imprinted on her eyelids so she couldn't avoid checking it out from time to time, but to have his voice whispering in her ears—that was too much!

But no worse than having him sitting beside her in the close confines of the car. He drove smoothly and efficiently—as he did everything, she suspected—but though she tried to concentrate on the delicious sandwiches Keira had supplied, her body was so aware of Mak's she felt embarrassed about it.

It had to be something to do with her hormones being out of kilter with the pregnancy. Maybe they were working overtime, and that was causing the way her skin was thirsting for a touch.

She gulped down some water, unable to believe where her mind had travelled.

Skin thirsting for his touch, indeed!

She must have read that somewhere.

And given the revelations of the previous evening, he was the last man in the world with whom she should get involved.

'We'll see them from here?' her tormentor asked as he turned onto the gravel road as directed.

'Check out that cloud of dust in the distance. They'll keep the mob moving and as they're coming down this road—and along the verges beside it—we'll have to drive through them.'

She paused and studied him for a moment, although she didn't need to look at him to remember just how good-looking he was.

Or why he was really here!

'You have to drive very slowly through the herd, and some will nudge against you, but the men will have dogs and bikes and will help all they can.'

He turned towards her, frowning now.

'We drive through a mob of cattle, nudging some of them? What happens if we kill one?'

She had to laugh.

'If we do happen to have a fatal accident with one, then we could cut it up for meat.'

He glanced her way again.

'You're joking, right?'

'Not necessarily,' she said, still smiling. 'They're good fat bullocks on the way to market—someone would certainly cut it up for meat. See, here they come.'

She pointed ahead and Mak saw the cloud of dust she'd mentioned hazing the blue sky, but in front of it, like a red-brown river in flood, moving inexorably across the land, came the herd of red cattle, the stream as wide as the road and verges, maybe a hundred metres across, moving slowly, slowly, slowly, but gaining on them every second.

'Slow!' Neena reminded him, not that he'd needed reminding. The beasts were looking bigger by the moment and the thought of driving through them was challenging, to say the least.

A dusty cowboy on a motorbike pulled up beside the car and Mak let down the window.

'We left Tom where he fell. He's in shade and got water, about a kilometre behind us now.'

Neena seemed to think this was not unusual information,

thanking the man and telling him she'd be in touch when she'd seen the patient.

'You okay to drive through?' the man asked Mak.

'I reckon so,' he said, then wondered if he'd already been in Wymaralong too long, 'reckon' being one of Ned's favourite words.

The cowboy rode off, taking a wide arc around the cattle, and Mak moved the vehicle forward, surprised at how little fuss the cattle made as he drew closer. Most moved sideways so a pathway was opened up, although every now and then one beast refused to give way and they had to wait for it to move, or try to edge around it.

'They're worked with bikes and vehicles these days so they don't object to them,' Neena said, while Mak looked around in wonder. It seemed to him they'd reached the middle of the herd, for as far as he could see in all directions were slowly moving cattle.

'I should have brought my camera,' he said to Neena, who smiled at him with the warm delight that made things buzz inside him.

'You won't forget it,' she said. 'It's the kind of image that stays in your mind for ever.'

'Like last night's sunset,' Mak said, then regretted it as the smile faded. She was obviously remembering the conversation that had preceded the sunset, and remembering he was—in her opinion—the enemy. But apart from being at least fifty per cent responsible for the pregnancy, what else did she hold against Theo and by extension his family? Had he made promises to her?

Hurt her so badly she couldn't forgive?

But would she have kept the baby, in that case?

Mak knew no matter how much thought he gave these questions, he wouldn't come up with answers. One day, perhaps, he could ask her—after all, she'd been totally blunt with him…

'Ah, nearly through,' she said. 'Now a kilometre or so. Drive fairly slowly—he might be in a paddock off the road. I'll keep an eye out this side, you watch the other.'

'Looking for a man lying in the shade of a tree?'

'Looking for a man and a machine that should retain at least some resemblance to a very small helicopter.'

'Got him!' Mak said, only minutes later, pulling the car off the road and into the meagre shade of a gum tree. The strange machine was in the shade of the single tree in a bare paddock on his side. He looked along the fence-line for a gate.

'We'll climb through, have a look at him, then if we have to drive closer, we'll cut the fence. Nick will have transferred the wire and fence strainers from my car to this one.'

Mak had no idea what fence strainers were but he was reasonably sure no women he had ever known would know, either—let alone be able to use them. More education lay ahead, he could see that.

At least he knew about barbed-wire fences and getting through them. He put his foot on the lowest wire and lifted the next one as high as he could to allow Neena to first throw her bag through then to clamber through herself. She turned to do the same for him, but things were never as easy as they looked and his shirt caught on a barb, and she had to lean over and free it, the faint scent of her body permeating his senses and stirring his libido.

This had to stop!

He picked up the bag and strode towards their patient, who was looking remarkably cheerful.

'Think I've done me knee again,' he said to Neena. 'M'back's okay and m'spine because I can wiggle my toes and move my fingers and my neck doesn't hurt, but the darned thing came down so quickly I put out my foot without thinking and jarred m'whole leg.'

Neena shook her head—what else could you do with an accident-prone cowboy?

'Tom, this is Mak, Mak, Tom. Tom badly damaged his knee about twelve months ago, coming off a quad bike. He went to Brisbane where the surgeons put it back together again far better than any of us expected, but believe me, they're not going to be pleased to see you again, Tom.'

Mak was examining the injured joint, poking and probing, his long fingers pressing against the swelling, his eyes on Tom's face as he looked for any signs of discomfort.

'I think it might be nothing more than a bad sprain,' Mak said. 'But we'll need to X-ray it to be sure. In fact, an ultrasound would be even better. Do you have an ultrasound machine?'

'We do, indeed,' Neena told him. 'Now! In fact, it was a donation from Hellenic Enterprises. Some bloke came out a while back and asked what we needed and came up with the ultrasound.'

Her voice trailed away and Mak guessed she was second-guessing this so timely donation. Seeing it now as a bribe?

Which it could well have been, but it did explain the amount on Con's expense sheet, and it would be invaluable today.

'Then do we get him into the car and take him back to town?' Mak asked, avoiding the subject of the ultrasound.

'After you've checked the rest of him over. Would you do that while I bring the car through? There's a cervical collar in my bag, whack that on him just in case.'

Neena was glad to get away, even if escape from Mak's presence was only temporary. She'd had to touch his body as she'd unhooked his shirt and all the attraction stuff that she'd first felt with Theo had come back—only worse—and if falling for Theo had been a big mistake then falling for his uncle would be even more disastrous.

She looked along the fence-line, hoping to see a gate, but as there was no sign of one and she knew the paddock ran for kilometres, it was going to be a cutting job. Cutting the fence was the easy part—the strands of barbed wire springing away so she didn't have to move them out of the way of the car to drive through without damage to what paintwork it sported.

Mak had bound the wounded knee and splinted it with a stick—instinctive medicine or a bushie in the making?

'We'll lift him between us,' she suggested, moving to Tom's side.

'I don't think so,' Mak said, then he bent and easily lifted the lanky cowboy in his arms. 'You open the back door.'

Unused to being given orders, Neena hesitated, but only for a second—Tom must be getting heavier and heavier in Mak's arms.

He did allow her to help settle their patient so his legs were stretched along the seat.

'We'll drive back to the road then fix the fence,' she told Tom. 'See if you can fit the seat belt around you somehow while we're doing it.'

'We're doing it?' Mak said.

'It's easier with two,' she said, and grinned to herself—back in control. He'd know *nothing* about fixing fences!

She stopped just beyond the fence and got out her small roll of wire, two pairs of thick leather gloves, pliers and the handy fence strainer.

'May I ask why you carry all this gear? I can understand the gun I saw in there—no doubt it's to put injured animals out of their misery—but fence-fixing equipment?'

Neena was already twisting a length of her wire to one side of the severed barbed wire.

'It might take an hour to drive to the homestead and then another hour to get back to where Tom was, if we followed roads and tracks and went through gates. They run to huge paddocks out here, so sometimes it's just much quicker to go through the fences rather than around. But leave a fence down in this country and some other person with a rifle in the back of his or her car might shoot you.'

Mak, gloved and ready, started on the lowest strand of wire, using a second pair of pliers to attach a new piece, but his mind was more on his companion than on twisting wire. The more he saw of this woman, the more impressed he was, and he didn't want to be impressed by her. He didn't want to feel anything for her, or even get to know her better.

Yes you do!

The voice in his head was so loud he looked around, thinking maybe Neena had said the words as part of a con- versation he'd missed. But she had fitted some contraption to the top wire, and was ratcheting the two ends of the fence towards each other, her lips were pressed tightly together while a small frown of concentration furrowed her brow.

'Let me do that,' Mak said, standing up and reaching out to take the handle from her.

'No, you twist the ends,' she told him and he saw that the strainers had pulled the barbed wire close enough for him to twist the end to the new piece Neena had inserted. 'That needs strong hands.'

'Wonderful!' he said, when they'd repeated the process four times and now had the whole fence back together.

'Wonderful indeed,' Neena said, 'and although I'll let the property owner know about the mend so he can do a proper job, I'm betting our makeshift patching will still be here when this kid has grandkids.'

She patted her stomach in a gesture Mak hadn't seen before, and for some reason it moved him immeasurably. In fact, he wanted to give the bump a pat himself.

What *was* he thinking?

'Do you want me to drive?' he asked, wanting to distance himself from the emotion he'd felt.

Neena grinned at him.

'Want to show Tom how good you are at driving through cattle?' she teased, and more emotion roiled inside him. 'Go for it,' she said. 'I'll finish my lunch.'

Fortunately Tom took over the conversation, asking Mak about himself, then talking about his own life, working on the property next to the one where he'd grown up.

'And did you build the gyrocopter?' Mak asked, not quite believing what Neena had been saying earlier.

'Yes, it's my third and all of them have crashed, but you get enough good bits left over to start again.'

'Why would you want to start again?' Mak asked, and Tom laughed.

'You get on a bike behind a mob of cattle and you'll understand,' he said. 'At least up in the air, even if it's only ten feet, you don't get half the dust. Besides, the girls all think it's cool that I'm a helicopter pilot.'

'Without a licence,' Neena reminded him.

'Don't need it for the ones I fly,' Tom retorted, 'but the girls don't know that.'

They'd reached the dust cloud of the slowly moving mob of cattle once again and as Mak realised that driving through them this way was a very different matter, he glanced towards Neena, who was smiling at him with such sheer delight he knew she'd been waiting for the truth to dawn.

'They have their backs to me,' he said, although he'd guessed that was the cause of her amusement.

'So you have to nudge them aside,' she told him.

Fortunately, before he'd worked out how to nudge a four-hundred-kilogram beast with a two-tonne vehicle and not kill the animal, the cowboy on the motorbike appeared again by his window.

'I'll push through them, you follow,' he said, so Mak steered the car through the cattle, keeping close to the bike as it thrust its way through the herd.

'Was that some kind of test?' he asked Neena when they were once again on the main road into town.

She smiled at him.

'No, I really did want to eat my lunch, but if it had been a test then you'd have passed with top marks.' She turned to the patient in the back seat. 'He's done well for a townie, hasn't he, Tom?'

'Not bad. He here to stay?'

'No, just passing through,' Neena replied, and Mak felt a flutter of something that couldn't possibly be disappointment that she'd written off his presence so casually.

I could stay, he wanted to say, but that was ridiculous.

But if the company funded another doctor…

And what about your career? Your dedication to emergency medicine? Your teaching ambitions?

It must be the heat, although the vehicle was air-conditioned, but for some reason he kept having these arguments in his head—or had voices telling him things he really didn't want to know.

'Where to?' he asked as the faded Christmas decorations strung across the streets announced they'd reached town.

'How are you at working an ultrasound machine?' Neena asked, then before he could reply she added, 'Actually, if it's foreign territory for you because you've got radiologists who do it, we've nurses at the hospital trained to use it. I'd like you to drop me back at the surgery, then take Tom up to the hospital. If you drive around the side you'll see the emergency entrance and someone will bring out a wheelchair for him. If it's just a sprain we'll keep him here and do the RICE thing for twenty-four hours, but if it's more badly damaged, get the hospital to contact the flying doctors and we'll get rid of him.'

'Hoy! That's me you're talking about,' Tom complained. 'And what's this RICE thing?'

'I thought you'd have been injured enough times to know it,' Neena told him. 'Rest, ice, compression and elevation. We'll keep you in so the nurses can make sure you are resting and you are keeping it elevated and they'll ice it for twenty minutes every hour.'

'Well, that's okay, and if Mak thinks it's only sprained he's probably right.'

'Because he's a man?' Neena asked, and the warning note in her voice made Mak smile, though he hid it as he waited for Tom's reply.

'Well, he's probably had sprains himself,' Tom said, digging himself a deeper hole.

'Whereas girls never sprain things?' Neena's voice was quiet but Tom must have caught on.

'Oh, sorry—that was a sexist thing to say, wasn't it?' he said, reaching over to pat Neena on the shoulder. 'You know I didn't mean anything. Everyone knows you're as good as any man—Whoops, it's getting worse.'

He gave her shoulder a squeeze with the hand that Mak felt had already lingered too long on her person.

'Friends?' Tom said, and she turned and smiled at him.

'Always friends, Tom,' she said, patting the hand that still rested on her shoulder.

Mak pulled up outside the surgery and before he had the car in park she was out the door. At least that meant she was out of Tom's reach! Now she leaned back in, bending so he could see a hint of a full cleavage in the V-neck of her T-shirt.

'You know how to get to the hospital?' she said to Mak.

'I can show him if he doesn't,' Tom reminded her, which was just as well, as Mak's mouth had gone dry and words were beyond him.

Reacting like that to a hint of cleavage?

She was pregnant—of course she'd have full breasts!

He drove off, thinking he'd drop Tom at the hospital then go and sit with Maisie in the orchid house until he'd got some sense back into his head.

And some control back over his body!

Not that he could. He had to do the ultrasound on Tom's knee then, without a radiologist in town, read the results and work out if it *was* just a sprain. Would Tom's faith in male doctors be completely shattered if the knee turned out to be broken?

And while that shouldn't matter at all, Mak found himself hoping he was right, and not only for Tom's sake…

Neena all but ran into the surgery, so relieved to be out of Mak's presence and away from the curious vibes his body caused in hers that she greeted her afternoon staff with wide smiles.

In contrast to her morning staff, her afternoon staff were practically babies. In fact, both of them had been delivered by the practice nurse who worked mornings, and although both were younger than Neena, they were both married with children, working afternoons while their mothers collected the kids from kindergarten and minded them until dinnertime.

'New man in town, huh, Neena?' Louise, the younger of the pair, greeted her.

'Good-looking one, from all accounts,' Lisa added, smiling knowingly at her boss.

'Okay, you two, I don't need the double act. Who's first?'

'Charlie Weeks,' Lisa told her. 'After you called me from the car, I phoned all the patients who were cancelled earlier and he was the first to come back. Some said it wasn't important and re-booked for tomorrow, so you've only got three to see.'

'Which is a pity,' Louise complained, 'as it means we won't have to call in Dr Wonderful as back-up. Is he really here to see if we need another doctor?'

Neena picked up Charlie's file and nodded in reply.

'And if he decides we do, will he be the one who stays?' Lisa asked.

'Definitely not,' Neena replied. 'He's some hotshot ER doctor from the city, currently doing a master's degree. Can you imagine someone like that wanting to work out here?'

But as she spoke she felt a sadness deep inside her, which was ridiculous as she barely knew the man, and she certainly didn't need another man messing up her life. If she managed to get another doctor, she'd make sure it was a woman!

'Come on in, Charlie,' she said to her patient, and she led him into the examination room, her mind switching from trivia—for that's all it was—to work in an instant.

Or most of her mind! As she opened her emails to check on some blood-test results for Charlie she found the email from Hellenic Enterprises telling her that Mak was on his way…

'These internet messages aren't all they're cracked up to be, Charlie,' she said, while his blood-test results printed out. 'Supposedly it's instant information, but if there's a hitch in the system the information can come too late.'

'Too late for what, Neena?' Charlie asked, sounding extremely puzzled, as well he might have been.

'Too late for me to high-tail it out of town,' she said, then she showed him the test results, explained how his elevated PSI count was an indication of trouble with his prostate, but as it hadn't gone up any higher in the six months since the last test there was no need to worry about it.

'We talked about all this when you first found the trouble,' Charlie reminded her. 'And we decided, at eighty-four, even with the problem, I'd probably get another ten years and doing nothing meant the ten years would be good years, while having an operation and chemo with no guarantee of longer than ten years, I'd be sick and sorry for myself.'

He paused, then added, 'It's okay—it doesn't bother me, so don't you be worrying about it.'

Neena smiled. So many of her patients felt they should be the ones comforting her, not the other way around.

'Hear you got yourself a young camel. I've got some good lucerne hay at the moment and I brought in a half bale for when he's ready to try something solid. I'd drop it at your place, but I've got to get back home and Ned always chats, so can I leave it here?'

'I'll come out and get it,' Neena said, as she finished examining the old man, noting down his pulse and blood pressure, aware as always most patients came in for a chat, but needing to keep records of their health all the same.

She walked out with Charlie, told him in no uncertain terms that she was quite capable of lifting a half bale of hay, and proceeded to do just that, tugging it up by the strings until it was resting on the sides of the utility before lifting it into her arms. She was sorry her car wasn't there so she could transfer the bale of hay straight into it. Charlie's ute was parked at the front of the car park and she'd just lifted the bale free when Mak drove in. Guessing the hay wasn't for the surgery, he pulled up beside her, leapt out and seized the bale from her hands.

'You're pregnant, woman, you shouldn't be lifting things.'

'I told her that,' Charlie chimed in, but Neena ignored both of them, simply opening the back of the big car so Mak could put the bale inside.

'What happened with Tom?' she asked Mak when she'd thanked Charlie and watched him drive off.

'Bad sprain but no sign of any ligament damage or disruption of the joint. I've left him there flirting with the nurses. Phyllis and Marnie are gone and Mr Temple told me you said he could go home today, but one of the nurses said he tries that with everyone and not to believe him. Is that right?'

The dark hazel eyes were fixed on her face and although this was very much a colleague-to-colleague conversation, Neena felt her insides heating up to rival the forty-plus temperature out there in the car park.

'He does,' she agreed, turning away from that steady regard. 'Let's get inside.'

But as he began to follow her into the cool of the surgery she realised her mistake, and turned back to face him.

'Actually, most of the patients have re-booked for tomorrow—I've one post-partum appointment and a triple antigen for a pre-schooler and that's it. You could go home.'

'Home's a long way off,' he reminded her with a smile that made her wish she'd kept walking. 'If it's okay with you, I'll come in and talk to the staff about how they've found having the extra people in town.'

'Louise and Lisa will *love* that,' Neena muttered, again heading for the front door.

So they'd flirt a little with him—so what? she told herself, but the cross feeling in her head and the tightness in her chest didn't go away until she'd finished for the day and driven home—alone, as Louise had driven Mak home—and headed for the stables to see Albert.

CHAPTER FIVE

IT WAS obviously fate that as she struggled through the door to drop the bale of hay in the feed shed, she'd catch sight of the man she was trying to avoid. He was leading Albert around the yard behind the stables, his arm around the small animal's neck, talking quietly to him, as if introducing him to the concept of fences and gates and yards.

'Ned said he hadn't had time to walk him today.'

'Monday—baking day,' Neena confirmed, feeling surprised Mak had taken on the job himself. 'You could as easily make the sun rise in the west as change Ned's housekeeping schedule.'

This is good, she congratulated herself. You're having an easy, normal conversation with the man. This is how it has to be. But as she moved closer to him, wanting to pet Albert and feel his rubbery lips in the palm of her hand, the zinging attraction stuff started up again and she excused herself and walked away, deciding a cold shower was better than the feel of rubbery lips against her palm.

Rubbery legs didn't help her escape…

Mak watched her go, wondering if her hasty departure meant she was upset with him for walking the little camel.

Surely not, although he was glad she was gone. Even with

hay all over her T-shirt and bits clinging to her long plait, she was beautiful, and something about that beauty—the unexpectedness of it, or the sense of strength beneath the perfect features—affected him in a way he didn't want to think about.

But seeing her half an hour later, when Albert was back in his shed and Mak had taken the steps two at a time to reach the veranda to find her sitting on the western corner of it, drying her hair in the dying rays of the sun, made him realise that the attraction he felt for her wasn't something that not thinking about it would vanquish.

She had her back to him, so all he could see of her was the curtain of black hair and her hand as it rose and fell, brushing through the silken strands.

Silken strands—where *was* his mind?

Yet he knew that's how they'd feel—as soft as silk.

'Need a hand?'

The words came out without forethought and too late he wished them unsaid, for she'd spun around and was staring at him with an expression that bordered on fear. Or was he imagining that?

'Did you sneak up those steps?' she demanded. Not fear, maybe anger—but why would she be angry?

'I thundered up them,' he told her, moving closer and taking the brush from her nerveless fingers, in spite of the voices in his head warning him to stay right away from her— voices that made a lot of sense. 'Tip your head forward.'

Why had she let him take the brush?

Why was she tipping her head forward?

Neena had no answer to the questions, or the dozens of others her body was posing. All she knew was that sitting here on the corner of her own veranda, feeling the brush run down through her hair, was the most exciting moment of her life thus far.

And if that wasn't the most ridiculous thought she'd ever had, then she didn't know what was!

'Not good, is it?' the man wielding the brush said quietly in a voice that rasped its way past his lips.

And though she knew, she had to ask.

'What?' she whispered.

'The attraction between us. The attraction we both felt when we danced on Saturday night—remember?'

There, it was said—well, he'd said it but did she have to admit to it?

'You're not going to deny it, are you?' he continued, his voice still husky with the emotion she didn't want to acknowledge.

'At least I've got the excuse of my hormones being in a tangle because I'm pregnant,' Neena told him. 'And speaking of which, I don't see how you can possibly be attracted to a pregnant woman anyway.'

'A very beautiful pregnant woman,' he said, touching her head to tilt it to the other side. 'Although the fact that she's pregnant by my dead nephew does complicate matters somewhat.'

Neena pulled away, but not before a shiver went through her when he mentioned Theo. She reached around her head and caught the shining mass of hair between her hands, then with nimble fingers moving almost too quickly for him to follow she plaited her hair and slipped a band around the bottom of the pigtail, flinging it back over her shoulder.

She'd drawn away from him—not physically but mentally—folding in on herself, bringing up an almost tangible shield.

'You still love him?' Mak probed, taking the chair beside her, allowing her space but not too much.

She turned and stared at him, a frown between her brows.

'Why would you ask that?'

'Because if you do, then this attraction might feel wrong to you. As if you're letting down his memory or something. That would make you feel you have to fight it.'

'You're assuming the attraction,' she said, her voice stronger now, so Mak realised she was ready for a fight.

'I am,' he said. 'But I'm nearly forty years old—I've felt attraction before and I know darned well that one this strong is never one-sided. People talk about pheromones and give all kind of reasons for attraction, but as far as I'm concerned, what strengthens an initial interest and builds it into attraction is the response of the other person. In part, I agree it's probably chemical, but it has to be more than that. Something bred into us to ensure the continuation of the species, I imagine.'

Neena stared at him, then shook her head.

'I can't believe we're having this conversation.'

Mak smiled, which sent her heart into excited palpitations.

'It's not exactly a conversation as I'm doing all the talking, but it would help if you put in a bit now and then. Do you find it as inconvenient as I do? Should we agree to ignore it as much as possible, which seems to me the sensible thing to do, especially as neither of us really trusts the other?'

'Well, you're right about that—about the trust. You're the last man on earth I'd trust. So of course we're going to ignore it—that's if it exists at all. What else can we possibly do? Have an affair? As if I haven't made enough of a mess of my life already!'

Neena stood up and walked away, shaking her head, unable to think straight when Mak was sitting next to her, spouting all kinds of rubbish about attraction. He talked as if it was something you could turn on and off at will. She *wished*!

Although she *could* ignore it! Just pretend it didn't exist—

that would be the best idea. She hadn't admitted she felt it—or had she?

Maybe she had!

She tried to replay the conversation in her head, but all she could remember was the feel of the brush running through her hair, guided by Mak's hands.

Mak's hands…

Don't go there! Her head screamed the warning and she knew she had to listen. Back in the sanctuary of her bedroom she shrugged off the light cotton robe she'd put on after her shower and clambered into shorts and a T-shirt. Even with the air-cooler working, it was hot enough to make her cheeks burn.

Although that could have been the hair-brushing thing…

Mak watched her walk away, the last rays of the sun shining through the light wrap she wore so he could see the slim lines of her body, the neat bulge of the baby, the full breasts…

A gentleman wouldn't be looking.

But a gentleman probably wouldn't have mentioned the attraction, either. Just because she'd been honest with him about her feelings towards his family, it didn't mean she'd want him being honest about *his* feelings.

Not that attraction had anything to do with feelings. As he'd said—it was a chemical thing. And as *she'd* quite rightly pointed out, there wasn't a thing they could do about it. Talk about living in a fishbowl!

And for the first time it occurred to him just how hard her decision to go ahead with this pregnancy must have been, the doctor in a small country town suddenly joining the ranks of unmarried mothers. No matter how much people loved her, there'd have been criticism and snide remarks and quite a lot, he imagined, of disapproval.

Yet she'd gone ahead with it, which brought him back to whether or not it had been a deliberate act, as he'd first suspected!

Although she'd sounded regretful when she'd talked about the mess she'd made of her life…

Was it the heat making it too hard for him to think straight?

Or the attraction?

He'd have a shower.

A cold shower.

And not entirely because the temperature out here was hot enough to melt the fillings in his teeth…

They were sitting down to what, according to Neena, was Ned's Monday night special—home-made meat pies—when the phone call came.

'I'll keep them hot,' Ned said, whisking the plates off the table before Mak could take a mouthful.

'But it mightn't be a callout,' he protested, his taste buds in revolt over the denial of the tantalising meal.

'It will be,' Ned said, shaking his head at Mak's naiveté.

Neena appeared at that moment, sticking her head into the kitchen.

'Come on, Dr First Response, you can tell me what to do with this situation.'

He followed her out of the house and down the front steps.

'Where to?' he asked.

'A property about forty kilometres out of town. The flying doctor's on the way. They'll land on the property, our job is to stabilise the guy.'

'Can't the ambulance attendants do that? Does it always have to be you?'

'It does when the ambulance is out of town the other way, taking a woman in labour to Baranock.'

'Maybe next time someone gives the town money they should get a second ambulance,' Mak grumbled, his mind still on the dinner he was missing.

Or was it being back in the car with Neena that was making

him cranky? In the confines of the car all the chemistry she was able to deny or ignore seemed to be stronger.

'What's the problem?' he asked, thinking work talk would be a good diversion from food and pheromones.

'Guy nailed his foot to the floor.'

'You *have* to be joking!'

She turned towards him and grinned.

'Why ever would you think that? You must get nail-gun accidents at your ER.'

Light dawned and Mak had to admit that they did get regular nail-gain accidents showing up.

'But that's not the point,' he said. 'Think about it. I've been here two days and we're had burns victims—okay, they are fairly common—rescued a baby camel, treated a guy from a gyrocopter crash and now we're heading out to a bloke who's nailed his foot to the floor. I know diversity makes medicine more interesting, but this much?'

Neena laughed. He sounded so put out by it all.

'Isn't variety the spice of life?' she teased.

'Maybe, but there's another cliché that fits—the one about having too much of a good thing,' he muttered, so grumpy she wondered what was really upsetting him.

'Is it missing your dinner making you so tetchy?'

She glanced his way as she asked the question and saw his frown.

'Men don't do tetchy!' he told her, but there was no further elaboration, although his frown stayed firmly in place.

Given the conversation they'd had earlier—or he'd had earlier—perhaps it was better not to ask what was upsetting him. So instead she talked about the country through which they were driving, explaining that originally it had all been sheep grazing land, although now more and more farmers were going into cattle.

'And what do the animals eat?' her non-tetchy companion demanded, looking out at the landscape lit now by a nearly full moon. 'Stones?'

Neena laughed again.

'It does look barren, but the little bushes and dried clumps of grass contain good nutrients for sheep or cattle, and after rain or when flood waters wash through this country, it comes alive again, green and lush.'

'I find that very hard to believe,' Mak said, but his voice sounded more relaxed and he was peering with more interest at the country through which they passed.

Finally she pulled across a grid into the property they were visiting.

'Why would someone have been using a nail-gun at this time of the evening?' Mak asked.

'I didn't ask so I can only guess, but I'd say he finished his real work for the day—the outdoor stuff—then decided to get on with his renovations. The property owner is Wilf Harris. He's only recently married, and his and his wife's families are coming to stay for Christmas so he decided to enclose his veranda to make some more room for the influx.'

'And he just happened to have a nail-gun?'

'He probably borrowed it,' Neena said, as the lights of the homestead appeared in the distance.

'And used it with no proper training in its use,' Mak muttered, and Neena realised he was tetchy again.

She said nothing, hoping he'd get over whatever was up-setting him before they met up with the Harrises.

Megan was waiting on the front veranda and she raced towards the car as Neena pulled up.

'I kept him warm but he said not to touch his foot so I didn't, although I gave him a chair to sit on,' she said, the panicky words tumbling over each other as they came rushing out.

'That's fine,' Neena assured her. 'And this is Dr Stavrou. He's a city doctor so he sees a lot of nail-gun accidents.'

Megan turned to Mak as if he were an angel sent from heaven.

'Oh, thank you so much for coming,' she said, throwing her arms around him and giving him a hug. 'He's round here.'

She led the way around the veranda to the back corner where her husband sat, wrapped in a blanket as she'd said, his face ashen with pain.

'I didn't want to make it bleed more by taking it out,' he said.

'What have you had for the pain?' Neena asked, knowing the flying doctor's medical chest that every property had would contain morphine.

'Only a couple of paracetamol. Megan's new to the bush and I didn't want to pass out from the morphine and leave her on her own.'

Neena heard Mak's grunt of disbelief, but he was already kneeling at Wilf's feet, examining the injury.

'I think a saw—a hacksaw—to detach it from the flooring,' he suggested, standing up and turning to Megan, asking her to show him where Wilf kept his tools.

'On the wall in the shed,' Wilf told her, and she led Mak away.

Neena checked her patient, taking his pulse and blood pressure, but thinking how easily Mak seemed to be fitting into country medicine, although his patients usually came to him with their accidents, so he didn't have to deal with them in situ. She found some local anaesthetic in her bag, and concentrated on her patient.

'I'm going to try to deaden all around the wound so you won't feel it while we cut you free,' she told him. 'Did the flying doctors give you an ETA?'

'Depends on a delivery they're doing,' Wilf told her. 'But the latest will be in two hours.'

What could happen in another two hours? The nail had already been in there for an hour. It would have oil on it but be relatively clean and while it was there, it was plugging any holes it had made in veins or arteries. But was it also stopping blood getting to Wilf's toes?

They wouldn't know until they got his shoe off and to do that they'd have to remove the nail.

Mak was back, although she didn't want to ask him his opinion of the best option as a first response person in front of Wilf and Megan. They might be concerned to hear people they trusted with their lives debating options.

'I've deadened the area around the wound,' she told Mak, who squatted beside her, the hacksaw in his hand.

'You right, mate?' he asked, looking up at Wilf.

'Go for it,' Wilf said, but rather than watch what Mak was doing he turned away, and Megan wrapped her arms around him so his face was hidden against her chest.

The screeching of the hacksaw set Neena's teeth on edge, but she sat on the floor across from Mak and held Wilf's foot as still as she could.

'Okay, you're free,' Mak said, within minutes that had only seemed like hours. 'Stay where you are for the moment. Neena, I'll show you where the hacksaw goes in case you ever need it.'

Neena followed him off the veranda, aware he'd been thinking the same thing she had—wanting to discuss the next move but not in front of Megan and Wilf.

'What's your opinion on leaving it in?' he asked as they reached the bottom of the steps.

'I'm dithering,' Neena told him. 'I can't decide, although I think when you take into consideration the golden rule of "first do no harm" then leaving it in is probably the best option. If we reef it out we could do more damage and cause more bleeding. What worries me is whether leaving it in might compromise the eventual use of his foot in some way.'

'I don't see that it can,' Mak told her. 'When's the flying doctor due?'

'Original ETA was within two hours, so I'd say he's getting close now, and it's three quarters of an hour's flight to their base so they could have him in an operating theatre within a couple of hours.'

'Then we leave it in,' Mak said as they walked into the shed, then suddenly he flung the hacksaw onto the ground, seized Neena in his arms and whipped her off the ground, racing out into the hot night air.

'Put me down!' she shrieked, kicking at him. 'What on earth got into you?'

'Snake,' he said, clinging even more tightly to her, hurrying back towards the house.

'What kind of snake?' Neena demanded, still wriggling, although there was something very exciting about being held in Mak's arms.

'I didn't wait to ask it,' Mak said, fairly breathless now, as Neena was no lightweight for all her slight build.

'It was Stanley,' Wilf said from the veranda, smiling as if he'd enjoyed the little drama that had played out in front of his eyes. 'Harmless old carpet snake that's lived in the shed for years. He keeps the rats and mice down.'

Mak dropped his burden, slightly put out that his heroic act had been for nothing—although holding Neena in his arms had definitely been a bonus.

'You didn't need to tell her that,' he complained to Wilf. 'I might have made some points for saving her life.'

'You'd need to do more than rescue her from a snake to catch our Neena,' Wilf said. 'Especially now!'

'Will you two stop talking about me?' Neena ordered. 'Megan, are the landing strip lights on?'

'No, I'll go and turn them on,' Megan said, and disappeared into the house.

'It's good having the lights.' Mak had walked over to Wilf and had casually picked up his wrist to check his pulse, Wilf explaining a new aspect of country life to Mak while he stood there. 'Before we got them we had to take vehicles out to light the strip and guide the planes in, or light fires, but now the strip is lit all the way down. Got solar panels out there that provide the power for the lights. Been a great thing, the solar, out here in the bush.'

Neena had remained at the top of the steps, carefully out of range of Mak's physical presence, although she was beginning to believe that Mars might be too close...

She watched him talking to Wilf, quietly checking their patient over with a minimum of fuss, and an ache started up in her heart, as if the month was already over and he was gone.

No, this couldn't be. Just because he'd talked about attraction—and because he'd danced with her and held her in his arms...

The plane swooping overheard diverted her.

'Mak and I will carry you down to the car and drive you out to the airstrip,' she said to Wilf. 'Have you talked to Megan about whether she wants to stay here or follow you to town?'

'I don't want her staying here on her own,' Wilf said, 'but there're the chooks and the lamb to be fed tomorrow and my mum and dad are down at the coast for a few weeks' holiday.'

'I'll get someone to come out and feed the animals,' Neena offered. 'Actually, Ned can come out and stay here until you get back.'

The words were no sooner out of her mouth than she realised

what that would mean—that she'd be alone in the house with Mak. Not that being alone with him would matter. She'd already decided that the only way to tackle the attraction was to ignore it, and she could do that just as easily without Ned.

She'd walked across to where Wilf was still seated but hadn't bargained for Mak's obstinacy.

'You drive down to the airstrip and get someone from the plane to help me lift Wilf,' he said.

'But I can take one side,' Neena argued.

'No way!' both men chorused, Mak adding, 'and don't suggest Megan help. Just for once in your life do as you're told and go and get help!'

Neena gave him one of her best glares but she did turn away, only to find a vehicle already driving towards them. Megan had met the plane.

They saw Wilf safely dispatched, then waited while Megan tidied the house and packed a bag, eventually following her into town where she'd arranged to pick up her mother for the three-hour drive to the hospital where Wilf would be treated.

'Will Ned mind you offering his services?' Mak asked when he was once again a passenger in Neena's car, heading back to town.

'No, he loves the chance to get back out into the bush. He lived in the country most of his life, working on properties, droving cattle and sheep, breaking in horses. A man of many talents.'

'Including cooking, and taking care of people's clothes— that doesn't seem to fit.'

Neena turned and smiled at her passenger.

'Most outback men are self-sufficient, and at one stage Ned was cook for a gang of shearers and there's no one more fussy about their food than shearers. He cooked at the hospital, too, for a while.'

'Until you got him,' Mak said, and Neena shook her head.

'No, he got me,' she said softly. 'Without Ned I'd never have made it to where I am today—never have got through high school, let alone through university.'

She sounded so sad Mak longed to ask her for an explanation, but he sensed she'd erected a barrier between them and he didn't know her well enough to break it down. Didn't know her well enough to be feeling all the things he felt, either, if it came to that!

He hid a sigh—he seemed to be forever sighing these days—sighing or shaking his head.

Neena had been doing okay in the 'ignoring the attraction' stakes until he'd lifted her into his arms, and suddenly, from being a woman to whom self-sufficiency was practically a religion, she'd turned into a weak and feeble female who wanted nothing more than to be held and protected and fussed over for the rest of her life.

Preferably in Mak's arms.

Which was a very scary thought.

She turned her mind to medical matters.

'If Wilf had turned up in your ER, would you have removed the nail or sent him to Theatre for surgeons to do it?'

'I'd send him to Theatre every time,' Mak replied. 'In ER we'd have X-rayed the foot to see the exact position of the nail, then, if all the theatres were busy, I might have removed it. By sending him to Theatre, surgeons can do any repair work to nerves, ligaments and bones while they have his foot opened up, whereas removing it would only have been a temporary measure until we could get an orthopaedic surgeon involved.'

'So as first response we did the right thing.'

'There's no real right thing,' Mak told her, 'just what seems best at the time.'

'Then what exactly is your master's thesis about?'

'It's more about how we can teach lay people to react when someone close to them is in trouble. Which advertising proves the most effective? How much information is enough—how much too much? You know the FAST campaign?'

'For stroke victims?' Neena queried. 'Facial weakness, arm weakness, speech difficulty, time to act fast.'

'That's the one,' Mak said. 'Every home in Australia has been given one of the little FAST cards and should have it stuck on their fridge, showing them how to test a person they suspect might be having a stroke. If we can educate the public enough that we get response teams to the patient as soon as possible, we can give the victim drugs which can nullify the effect of the stroke before too much damage has been done.'

'But won't having dozens of little cards stuck on the fridge only confuse people?'

Mak's chuckle slithered beneath her skin and started all the responses she was trying so hard not to feel.

'That's one of the things I'm looking at—just how much do people need to know and how much is too much.'

She pulled into her parking spot at the bottom of the steps and climbed hastily out of the car.

'I'll just check on Albert before I come in. Ned will have heard the car and will be heating your dinner.'

Don't come with me, in other words, Mak thought to himself, but being separated from Neena, if only for a short time, wasn't such a bad idea right now. He could still feel the weight of her body in his arms and was carrying the scent of her in his nostrils.

How could he feel such a strong attraction to a woman he didn't entirely trust? And why the attraction, anyway? Hadn't he learned to avoid that? Learned to enjoy relationships that had no ties beyond the physical?

Although attraction was physical…

The idea that this attraction was more than that startled him so much he stopped on the veranda and looked out at the town, trying to work out what was going on, not only in his body but inside his head. The more he saw of Neena—with patients, with Maisie, with the camel—the more he found himself admiring her—and the harder it was to consider she might be the conniving female of his original suspicions.

He swallowed the sigh that nearly came out and headed for his late dinner.

'She out with that camel?' Ned asked as Mak entered the kitchen.

'Just checking on him, she says,' Mak responded.

'While I have to keep her dinner hot,' Ned complained, but he didn't sound too put out about it.

He got me, Neena had said, but although Mak longed to ask the older man to explain this cryptic comment, he didn't feel he could, so he ate his dinner—delicious—then on Ned's suggestion took his coffee through to the living room, intending to turn on the television. But once there, the photos on the piano drew him closer and he sipped his coffee and studied them.

A little girl with two pigtails and no front teeth was photographed in front of the steps of the old house. She was clutching a hamster in her hands and beaming with the pride of ownership. Another photo showed a very beautiful Indian woman, younger than Neena but not her. Her mother? Yes, there she was again with a short, turbaned man, love shining from both their faces. Photos of the couple with a baby, the baby growing, then no photos for a long time until one of Neena in her graduation robes, a man beside her smiling proudly—and though he was younger, the photo was unmistakably one of Ned.

Looking at it more closely, Mak picked out a crowd of people, not anonymous others at the graduation but Wymaralong locals—there was Maisie, on sticks, not in a wheelchair, and

Lauren from the hospital, and the old receptionist and even older surgery nurse. Mak felt emotion stir inside him. She may have been an orphan but she'd never been alone—neither had she ever been unloved, for all the faces in the background beamed with the same pride as Ned's.

So what must they all be thinking of the pregnancy?

Weren't country people more likely to be shocked by an unmarried mother having a baby?

And did the whole town know the story of it that Marnie and Phyllis had talked of? The Rat—indubitably Theo…

Mak almost shook his head, but as he'd told himself he wasn't going to do that any more, he didn't, simply going back to the early photos of Neena, lifting them and studying them, wondering if the baby would grow into a little girl with two pigtails and no front teeth.

A little girl would be nice, he was thinking, when he caught up with his straying mind and hauled it back under control. Neither Neena nor her baby were any concern of his—except for where the baby's life would have an impact on his family, and his own determination to be involved in all plans for the baby's future.

Family!

Family Neena wanted nothing to do with.

He heard her in the kitchen, talking to Ned, no doubt explaining about the accident and speaking to him about going out to Wilf and Megan's house.

'I hope you can cook,' he heard her say, and turned to see her coming into the living room, a cup of something— probably not coffee or tea—in her hand.

'Hot chocolate, my least favourite drink but it's better than nothing,' she said, catching his quick glance at the cup. 'And don't think just because Ned is leaving, you can take over as the caffeine police—I am very aware I have to limit myself. I have one cup of coffee—weak—a day and that is it!'

'I can cook,' Mak told her, wondering if this conversation was in some way a truce between them. 'But I doubt I can mix camel milk formula.'

Neena smiled at him.

'That I can manage,' she said. 'And you needn't cook every night, we can eat at the hospital or the café or the pub. Breakfast you can help yourself. There's always cereal and yoghurt and bread for toast.'

'You don't do cooked breakfasts?' Mak teased, and won another smile.

'I'm the world's worst cook,' she admitted. 'Maisie felt I should know how and she tried to teach me, but I get distracted and things get burnt. She took to stocking the freezer with bread and the pantry with tins of baked beans and packets of instant soup mix so if she did have to go away I wouldn't starve to death.'

'And if you have a daughter, will you get Ned to teach her?'

Had he broken the moment of rapport that Neena paused before answering? But then she smiled again—three smiles in one evening.

'I'll get Ned to teach him or her, boy or girl—why discriminate? Your mother obviously didn't!'

'No, for all she is a very traditional Greek, she made sure both her children not only learned to cook but knew how to work the washing machine and turn on an iron. She was proud when my sister decided to study engineering. I sometimes wondered if perhaps she'd have liked to have had the chance to take up a career herself.'

'Is is too late now?' Neena asked, and Mak, although he'd sworn he wasn't going to shake his head again, found it moving from side to side.

'Of course it isn't,' he said, smiling at the woman whose simple question had provided a possible solution to something that had been concerning him since his father's death—how to shake his mother out of her unhappiness. 'Anthropology— that's always interested her. She needn't do a whole degree but she can begin some study, maybe go along on some digs.'

He moved towards Neena, removed the cup from her hands, set it down, and swung her into his arms, whirling her around and around.

'You are a genius!'

And then, because she was in his arms, as he set her back on her feet, he kissed her.

CHAPTER SIX

IT WAS a friendly kiss, a thank-you kiss, nothing more, Neena tried to tell herself, but as his lips firmed against hers and her body, bulky stomach and all, pressed tightly against his, the embers of desire she had been sure she could control flared into life, heating her body to meltdown.

This from a kiss?

She had to break away—move—put space between them, yet her body refused to obey her brain's commands, staying clasped against Mak's chest, her lips now responding to the kiss, her tongue tangling with his, her heart beating so erratically she could feel its pounding right through her body.

Or was it his heart pounding?

No, hers, for she could hear the thunder of it in her ears, all senses on alert.

All for a kiss…

Mak broke the spell, which was just as well as Neena doubted she could have moved to save herself. He put his hands on her shoulders and eased away from her, then he moved her back towards a chair, sat her down, and returned her cup of chocolate to her hand.

'Well, that was interesting,' he said, as if he'd successfully completed some kind of experiment. He sat down across from her and put his feet up on a footstool, looking as relaxed and at ease as Neena's father had, when he'd finished dinner and had been relaxing in the living room while she'd played the piano.

She actually glanced towards the piano, wondering if she'd see the ghost of her younger self sitting there.

But the tall man sitting in her living room was a very different proposition from her gentle father. The tall man sitting there wanted control over her child—she had to remember that. Theo had seduced her for one reason—the challenge—and this man was doing it for another—she had to remember that, too.

'I was a thirty-four-year-old virgin, I wasn't that hard to seduce, especially not for someone like Theo.'

She had no idea why she'd felt impelled to pass on that information except, perhaps, in case the kiss had given Mak ideas, she needed to let him know she'd fallen for one Greek recently but wasn't going to do it again.

'A thirty-four-year-old virgin?'

'You don't have to make it sound like an extinct animal!' she grumbled, not at all sure why she was having his conversation but now it had started wanting to get it over and done with.

He smiled at her, which was something she wished he wouldn't do.

'I thought they *were* extinct,' he said.

'I'd put them more in the rare category, and so coming under the protected species act—or protection of some kind, which was my situation.'

'As in?' he prompted, and this time it was Neena who sighed.

'I know you haven't been here long, but you've met some of the people of the town.' She walked across to the piano and picked up the graduation photograph, handing it to him.

'Look at them. They're just the ones who came to Brisbane for the ceremony. The whole town helped send me to uni, they fundraised to pay my higher education fees and boarding costs. But I had to work for spending money, and I wasn't a genius so I had to study in virtually all my spare time. Yes, there were boys there, male students, and some I really liked, but—'

'But no time for an affair?' Mak prompted, still looking at the photo.

'When all those people had faith in me? When all they wanted was for me to graduate and come back to them so the town had a doctor again? What if I'd fallen in love with someone in the city? One of those young men? Someone who wouldn't live in the country? Couldn't live in the country? I'd have been letting all the townspeople down, I couldn't have lived with myself.'

Mak shook his head.

'That was some burden of obligation you took on,' he murmured, but as Neena retrieved the photo, *she* shook her head, smiling as she did so.

'Not really,' she said, her forefinger touching the faces in the photo, her smile serene. 'They all loved me, you see. You talk about your family and what they mean to you—well, these people are my family so it was no sacrifice at all.'

'And Theo?'

That story was too tawdry to tell, so Neena shook her head, already regretting sharing even this small part of her life with this man.

'I'd like to know,' he said, his voice deep and husky as if he really meant the interest he was showing.

The timbre of the words shivered across her skin, reminding her just how dangerous he was, while the unspoken memory of the kiss lingered in the room like a large, unwanted ghost.

'I'm sure you would,' she said, putting on a smile so he wouldn't guess how his voice—and the ghost—was affecting her. How his *presence* was affecting her! 'But a girl can only handle so much true confession in one night. Now I'm off to bed. The last few days have been a bit hectic and a good night's sleep's in order.'

She stood up and though she'd intended leaving the room, she noticed the photos on the piano were out of order and moved across to straighten them.

'Do you play?' he asked, as she hovered by the instrument.

'Yes,' she said, lifting the lid and tapping out a few notes from a tune her father had loved.

'Play for me?'

Mak's voice was husky again but this time instead of slithering over her skin it went straight to her knees, which weakened so she had to sit down on the piano stool, her hands spreading across the keys, the notes of the sad love song filling the room.

'Is it Theo you're remembering?' Mak asked, coming to stand behind her as she sat on the stool, her head bowed over the yellowed keys.

'Never!' she told him, strength returning with the denial, enough strength to shut the lid of the piano and stand up so she could escape Mak's presence. 'Apart from the baby, I have no good memories of Theo.'

'Yet you kept his child? It *is* his child?'

'Would he otherwise have left it something?' she said, looking into the hazel eyes, daring him to repeat the question she'd ignored.

He took the dare.

'Why?'

Was it a night for confession? Was it something to do with the moon and stars being in some celestial conjunction that she felt a need to tell someone why she'd made a decision she knew the whole town wondered about? Although maybe the town didn't wonder? Maybe they assumed it was because she'd loved Theo, rat that he had been!

'The baby wasn't to blame for what had happened and I suppose, if you go right back to the beginning, it was because I *had* been a thirty-four-year-old virgin! My marriage prospects weren't all that bright. All the young men in town had been snapped up while I'd been at university, and I don't know that I'd have fallen in love with any of them if they had been available. The pregnancy was an accident yet when I realised I *was* pregnant, it seemed as if it was meant to be.'

She moved away from Mak's too intense scrutiny because she didn't want him seeing the emotion that was stirred up in her body.

'The baby would be family,' she said quietly. '*My* family! I know that is totally selfish but I haven't had a family for a long time...'

And on that note she escaped, heading for her bedroom, her insides churning so badly she thought she might be sick.

Was it *all* about family? Mak wondered when she'd departed so precipitously. His family—her family!

Shouldn't it be about the baby?

He found he had no answer to that or any of the other questions so he, too, went to bed, where sleep took a long time to come, the memory of Neena's lips on his, her body pressed against him, caused him so much physical discomfort he eventually got up and showered again, telling himself the trip out to the Harrises' property had left him hot and dusty.

Neena heard the water running in the shower and couldn't help but wonder what he looked like naked—imagining him, skin slicked with water, standing under the cooling jets. Her knowledge of anatomy and her experience with naked male patients meant that the masculine body held no secrets for her—she'd seen them all, fat and thin, big and small, but Mak's body would be something else! Taut and trim, the muscles beneath the skin—and she knew they were there from the effortless way he'd lifted and carried her—beautifully defined.

And imagining, her own body grew hot and she felt the fever of desire flooding through her veins.

Damn it all! Hadn't she learned her lesson from Theo—hadn't one lot of fever given her immunity from a recurrence?

Although the Theo fever had been purely physical and, as it had turned out, very transient. Mak fever was different. She'd known that as soon as she'd met the man. Mak wasn't anything like the charming, conceited, spoiled young man his nephew had been.

Or was he?

Who was she to judge?

Hadn't her judgement been proven wrong a couple of times before?

She felt her cheeks heat against the pillow as she remembered the youthful indiscretions that had brought Ned into her life, the night he'd caught her in the back seat of a car with the wildest teenager in town…

Why is it we remember the bad things—the things we feel guilty about? she wondered for the hundredth time. She could remember Ned's voice, his anger, as clearly as if it was yesterday, yet couldn't remember her mother's voice.

Damn it all, she thought again, sitting up this time, readjusting the sheet which was the only covering the hot night allowed. I have to think happy thoughts, not gloomy ones. She settled down again, her hands massaging her tummy, talking to the baby about sunsets, and cup cakes, and birthday candles, and the pets they'd have.

Talking until she fell asleep.

She was playing with Albert in the little yard, encouraging him to walk towards her, tempting him with his bottle, when Mak appeared. Another green shirt so his eyes seemed greener than ever, his shoulders broad enough to carry any burden, though green shirts couldn't make a man's shoulders appear broad, and the 'carry any burden' part of that thought was nothing more than sentimental nonsense.

She was *not* a sentimental person. The loss of both parents before she'd legally become an adult at eighteen had taught her that bad things happened and sentiment didn't come into it, yet here she was thinking sentimental thoughts.

'He seems to be doing really well,' Mak remarked, leaning over the top rail of the fence, looking for all the world as if this hot, dry, far west country was his natural habitat.

'Physically,' Neena agreed, wishing she'd had a shower and dressed in something better than her ancient red shorts and tattered T-shirt before coming out into the yard.

Then wishing she hadn't thought of that at all! She didn't care, she reminded herself. She was ignoring the attraction!

Which was about as easy as ignoring the sun that was now beating down from the eastern sky, or the dust that whirled around Albert's feet as he gambolled around her.

'Physically?' Mak queried.

Actually, he'd queried it some seconds earlier while her mind had been worrying about her clothing. Now, probably because she hadn't answered, he added, 'Don't tell me you're worried he has mental health problems?'

'Well, he might have!' Neena told him, disliking the smile that lurked behind Mak's words, for all he had a carefully sober expression on his face. 'Not so much mental as emotional. Do you think he knows he's an orphan? That he hasn't got a mother?'

'He probably doesn't know mothers exist and as long as he's fed he probably won't worry about anything.'

But even as he said it Mak knew he was wrong. Camels were herd animals, they were used to company. And she caught him out on it, raising her eyebrows to question his assertion.

'Okay, so he'd be better with company, but the hours you work you can hardly bring another animal in here to keep him happy, especially with Ned away.'

Neena nodded but he sensed her agreement was reluctant, while the look of sadness on her face made him wonder if Albert was the only thing on her mind. She walked towards the gate and he held it open for her so she could lead Albert back into the stable, and being close to her—close enough to drop a quick kiss on her lips—he remembered the kiss of the previous night and wondered what on earth had got into him. The very last thing he needed was to get involved with Neena Singh.

He'd brought up the attraction and while not quite admitting to it, she'd shied away, making it plain she'd prefer it if they both ignored it. In fact, she'd pointed out that there wasn't any other option—a brief affair during his time in town being out of the question.

And she was right, but as he watched her bend over the little camel and saw the taut curves of her backside in the battered red shorts she was wearing, heat stirred in him again.

He couldn't keep showering—it didn't work anyway. He'd get back to work on his thesis—spend his spare time in his room, checking references on the internet, contacting specialists in other countries, maybe get a discussion group going on first response best practice.

He made his way back to the house, walking into the kitchen. Ned was already gone but cereal packets and bowls had been left on the kitchen table. Mak could find his way around the kitchen—did Neena have her one cup of coffee for the day at breakfast? He could put on the machine.

Or maybe cut some fresh roses. The ones on the kitchen table were wilting. Had cutting roses been part of Ned's duties or did Neena like to cut them herself? A quick search of the drawers produced a pair of secateurs and he ducked down the back steps and into the rose garden, where the heavy scent filled his nostrils. There—the dark red ones like his mother grew, the ones the colour of Neena's lips…

Neena left Albert in the stable, glad it was school holidays—she'd get the two Winship kids from down the road to come up and check on Albert for her during the day. They were sensible and big enough to be able to handle him, to take him out into the yard and put him back in the stable, making sure he had milk and water. She'd have to check on when young camels started eating solid food. Perhaps if she left a biscuit of the bale of lucerne hay in his stable he'd nose around and eat it if he felt like it.

As long as it didn't make him sick…

Worrying about Albert's diet occupied her mind while she showered and dressed for the day ahead, but when she wandered into the kitchen, the scent of roses wiped all other thoughts from her mind.

'You or Ned?' she demanded of the man who was fiddling with the coffee machine.

'Me,' he said, and she could have sworn he looked embarrassed. 'Actually, I just went out to get three or four to replace the ones that were wilting, but they were so beautiful I just had to take one of those and one of those and before I knew it I had too many.'

He *was* embarrassed, and there was something so—vulnerable?—about this tall, strong, capable man going mushy over flowers that Neena felt a peculiar twinge in the region of her heart. Not attraction this time—definitely not attraction…

'We'll take some into work,' she said. 'The girls will enjoy having them on the front desk.'

'The girls?' Mak queried, and the smile he offered with the words twisted the twinge thing in her heart.

'They worked for my father,' Neena explained, pouring cereal into a bowl to cover her inner agitation. 'But you'd probably guessed that. When he first came to Wymaralong, no one wanted to work with him—this was a town that wasn't used to foreigners, particularly those of a different skin colour. Helen had been a nurse at the hospital and had retired years before to have a family, but they were all grown up by then so she answered my father's ad and she brought Mildred along. Mildred's husband was the head of the town council at the time, and once Mildred came on board that signalled acceptance to the townspeople.'

'Apart from the fact that they obviously needed a doctor,' Mak suggested, and Neena smiled.

'There *was* that,' she admitted, 'but Mildred and Helen made his acceptance so much easier.'

'And is that why you keep them on?'

Neena studied him for a moment. Was he really interested or was he just making conversation?

'I *am* interested,' he said, correctly interpreting her look.

'I kept them on because they know everyone so well. This was especially important when I first came back to work here and had to get to know people I already knew as people as patients. It was probably even harder for them—the patients— particularly the older men who were suddenly stuck with only one option—well, two if they wanted to drive to Baranock to see a doctor. Mildred and Helen made it easier for them and also taught me so much. They knew which people came in because they needed company and which ones, if they came, must have something seriously wrong because doctors weren't at the top of their popularity lists.'

Mak was frowning at her, looking so distracted she had to ask.

'What?'

He added foaming milk to the coffee cups and passed a cup to her.

'I was trying to imagine the situation. I've always worked in hospitals, so I have no experience in general practice to compare your situation to, but in the ER, ninety per cent of the people we see *are* emergencies. We get the odd person who just wants some attention from another human being, and when we're busy the nurses work a triage system, but it hadn't ever occurred to me that patients in private practice could be graded in the same way.'

It was Neena's turn to frown.

'I didn't mean to trivialise any of my patients,' she said. 'The ones who come in for company or for reassurance are just as important as the others, you know. It just helped me to know their backgrounds so I wasn't wasting time and tax-payers' money ordering reams of tests for people who needed a chat more than they needed medicine.'

Mak still looked puzzled, but as it was almost time to leave for work and she had to phone the Winships and introduce the two boys to Albert, she excused herself and took her coffee through to the office. Talking about medicine, especially the kind of medicine she practised, was such a rarity she found herself enjoying it, and she didn't want to get used to discussing things with Mak—it would leave too big a hole when he disappeared back to the city.

Mak watched her go, being careful to keep his eyes above the level of her backside, although the short skirt she was wearing was nearly as enticing as the shorts had been. He put the dishes in the dishwasher, found some silver aluminium in the pantry and wrapped up half the bunch of roses, but his mind was replaying the conversation they'd had and again he found himself wondering about his career choice—not questioning it exactly, but wondering…

And what had happened to his resolve to put all thoughts of Neena out of his head and concentrate on his job out here, and his thesis when he wasn't working? He left the roses on the hall table near the front door and went into the bathroom to freshen up before they left the house. Today if Neena wasn't busy at the surgery he'd talk to Mildred and Helen about the extra medical workload, and maybe check out the ambulance station and talk to the personnel there—Paul and Pete he'd met, and there were two more. Someone would be on duty.

One day at a time, Neena told herself as she came out of her room and saw the roses on the table. That's all she could do, get through one day at a time and before she knew it Mak would be gone and life would return to normal—or as normal as it could be again once a baby arrived.

'How are you going to manage once the baby comes? A nanny?'

Neena turned and frowned at the man who'd come up behind her in the hall while she'd been smelling the roses.

'Can you actually read thoughts?' she asked him.

His smile awakened the attraction, which hadn't been all that dormant but had been suppressed enough for her to ignore.

'Worrying about it, were you?' he teased.

'Not worried. I've had plenty of offers, mostly from

mothers of girls due to leave school this year. One of them, Rachel—the girl, not the mother—wants a gap year before she goes to university but doesn't want to go haring off overseas. She just wants to get some money tucked away before she hits the big city. She's the eldest of five so has plenty of experience looking after children—even babies— so I've been thinking she might live in. Then there are a couple of others who are regular babysitters around town who will fill in on her days off.' She sighed, then, because it was one of the things she worried about in the night and talking about it might help, she added, 'My main problem is Ned. He's quite convinced he'll manage the baby and the house but he's not getting any younger and it's too much responsibility for him, but he's going to be upset—'

'For Pete's sake, woman, do you worry over every single person in this town?'

Mak's demand was so loud Neena was startled, but before she could protest he was speaking again.

'You worry about people who waste your time because they need a chat and you keep on your elderly staff because you're grateful to them, and you worry about Albert's mental health—'

'Emotional health,' Neena corrected, not liking the way the conversation was going. 'And I'm the local doctor, I *should* worry about people.'

'Not to the extent that it might put your baby at risk. You're right about a newborn baby being too much for Ned—how old is he, anyway?'

'I don't know,' Neena admitted. 'We only knew Maisie was as old as she was because five years ago she got a letter from the Queen and one from the prime minister as well. Our local member of parliament had sussed out her birth date and got hold of a birth certificate. He sent the required letters off to the powers that be and she was delighted. So, given Maisie's age, I suppose Ned must be close to eighty.'

Mak heaved a sigh and headed down the front steps, Neena following. So much for talking about her problems! Far from helping her, she'd only made things more complicated somehow.

Although…

'Why are you so interested in my care arrangements for the baby?' she demanded, reaching the vehicle and turning to face the man she'd thought might help. 'Believe me, they will be beyond criticism in case you're thinking some court might give your sister custody.'

Mak looked at her, dark eyes flashing anger at him—as soon take a tiger cub from his mother as take her baby from Neena.

'That was the last thing on my mind,' he told her. 'We'd been talking about your work arrangements and I wondered how easy or difficult it might be to get help out here, that's all.'

But he could see she didn't believe him and as they drove in silence the short distance to the surgery, he knew the precarious links of trust he'd managed to build between the pair of them were broken.

Beyond repair?

He didn't know, though even on such short acquaintance he suspected he wouldn't have to wait long to find out. She was a woman who tended to speak her mind.

CHAPTER SEVEN

'FRIDAY I go to Baranock to see my gynaecologist,' Neena informed him, stopping outside the surgery but not opening the door. 'I usually close the surgery for the morning then work afternoons and some evening appointments, but if you want to be on duty you could work the morning.'

Mak stared at her. He'd spent the journey thinking about broken trust and all she'd been worried about had been her patient schedule.

Had he dithered too long that she was speaking again?

'Of course, you might prefer to go out to the site and talk to the different foremen out there or work on your thesis. You're under no obligation to me.'

None of the options she'd offered so far had any appeal, perhaps because he was more worried about the programme she was suggesting.

'You drive the two hours to Baranock and back then do a full day's work? Aren't you worried about the consequences of getting overtired?'

'And making a bad diagnosis?' she challenged. 'You didn't work twenty-hour days when you were an intern? You didn't get used to going without sleep?'

The dark eyes that he'd seen fired with desire now flared their anger at him.

'I wasn't six months pregnant,' he growled. 'And I wasn't thinking of a wrong diagnosis but of your health.'

'Or the baby's,' she muttered, and now she did open the car door.

He put his hand on her arm to stop her getting out, touching the soft skin, feeling flesh and fine bones beneath it.

'There's another alternative. I'll drive you to Baranock and back. That way you might get to doze on the journey, then we'll share the patients later in the day—or I could do the lot. And I am not thinking *wholly* of the baby, but of your health as well. What good will you be to him or her if you've wrecked your own health before the baby even arrives?'

She studied him for a moment, as if trying to assess the truth or otherwise of his words, then a smile lit up her face and it seemed to Mak that another sun had risen in the sky.

He forgot the embargo on shaking his head and shook it in disbelief at his thoughts.

'Can we go in your swanky car? It's bitumen all the way— no four-wheel-driving. It's years since I've been in a decent car. I checked it out. Real leather seats! After driving this old loaner and even my tank, it would be bliss!'

Mak shook his head again, now unable to believe that this woman could envisage such delight from something as ordinary as his vehicle.

'We'll go in my car,' he promised, and now she did get out, stepping light-heartedly towards the surgery door, practically skipping with delight. Mak watched her go—he seemed to be doing that a lot these days—just watched as Neena walked away from him, Neena in so many moods, so many guises. How long would it take to get to know a woman like her? A lifetime?

The week proceeded relatively smoothly—well, smoothly compared to Mak's introduction to medical practice in

Wymaralong. On Wednesday afternoon, they were called out to another accident on a cattle property where a stockman had been crushed against a fence by a large bullock, but once again it was a matter of stabilising the man before sending him off in a plane to a major hospital.

'With all the callouts like this, wouldn't it be better to always have two doctors in the town?' he asked as they drove back to town.

'Definitely!' Neena's reply was prompt. 'But getting one doctor to stay in a town like this is difficult enough—getting two is virtually impossible. It used to be that the State Health Department employed a doctor full time at the hospital and he had the right to private practice. In those days, he would take in another doctor as a partner so they shared both the hospital workload and the surgery work, and they both made a comfortable living. But with fewer people being treated locally—insurance issues forced the closure of the maternity and surgical wards—the hospital doctor was withdrawn. That happened before my father came.'

'Have you tried to get a partner?'

He was driving, so he could do no more than glance at Neena as he asked the question. She was looking out the side window, her head turned away, so all he saw was the back of her head and the thick plait of hair. The nerves in his fingers reminded him of how that hair had felt.

'I did once,' she said, still not looking at him. Deliberately? 'Unfortunately he seemed to think that he could share everything—my house, my life, my bed. I suppose if I'd been able to fall in love with him it would have been an ideal situation, but that didn't happen. In fact, he wasn't a very nice man, which is something Ned picked up on from the start.'

'Ned got rid of him?'

She turned now, smiling at him, though it wasn't a real smile, more like something she was trying on for size.

'It wasn't the first time Ned removed an undesirable man from my life,' she said, the smile fading completely as she frowned at her memories. 'After my father died—I was fifteen—I went a little wild. Maisie was in her eighties and she couldn't cope—oh, she kept the house going but she, too, was devastated by my father's death—so Ned stepped in. He got rid of the boy I fancied myself in love with—without recourse to a horsewhip, though that was threatened—and dragged and bullied me back on track. He supervised my homework, came up to school to see my teachers. I suppose what he did was show me that someone cared.'

It had fallen to grizzled old Ned to show the grieving young woman someone cared? Mak didn't consider himself a sentimental man, but the situation Neena had conjured up made him swallow hard.

'You lost your father when you were fifteen?' Mak knew there were other bits of the story that were more unbelievable, but the implications of this one were more relevant to Neena's situation today—or so he guessed. 'Lost both parents so young?'

The smile appeared again, but it held little joy.

'One might be a mistake but two looks like carelessness, doesn't it?' she said, trying to make a joke of something that must still bring her pain. And suddenly Mak understood a little better why she'd chosen to keep the baby, why she talked of it as family—*her* family.

The town came into view and when she looked up at the tinsel strung across the road between the street lights and said, 'I must get the Christmas decorations up,' he knew the conversation was over, but every little bit of information he gleaned about the woman in the car beside him made him want to know more. It was as if she hid behind a curtain and every now and then lifted a little corner of it so he could take a peek, yet who she really was remained a mystery.

Neena tried to keep her face as blank as possible, although she knew she was frowning inside. For some reason, she kept revealing bits of herself to this man, and she couldn't work out why. It wasn't that he pushed or probed—far from it. He was just there and every now and then she'd feel compelled to come out with something about her past.

He must think she was a nut case the way she kept offering these true confessions—thirty-four-year-old virgin indeed! He'd been right to be surprised. Or had his surprise just been a mask to cover some other opinion he might have of such a sexually repressed woman.

She sighed then regretted it when he said, 'Is the thought of putting up Christmas decorations so tiring?'

Fortunately he was pulling into the car park at the surgery as he spoke—she could get used to this being chauffeured—so there was no need for her to reply. Getting out of the car instead and hurrying inside, hoping they'd be busy enough to not have to see each other for the rest of the day. At least if she wasn't with him she couldn't tell him any more stuff about her past…

But she could hardly avoid him when they got home—the combination of the 'they' and 'home' even in her thoughts causing queasiness in her stomach.

'So, the Christmas decorations—where do you keep them? And don't bother telling me you'll haul them out yourself, because I know Ned wouldn't let you do that and with him away I'm the man of the house.'

They'd checked on Albert and were walking towards the house when Mak asked the question.

More queasiness over the 'man of the house' phrase, but she wasn't going to let him see that.

'They're in a couple of old steamer trunks in the room under the house, but be careful going down there—a snake could have taken up residence.'

'Great! You'd better come with me.'

'To chase the snakes?' she asked, leading him towards the room under the house.

'No, so I can grab you in my arms again to save you. The last time left an impression I'm unlikely to forget.'

Neena turned to look at him, but it was dusk and very gloomy under the house so she couldn't see if he was teasing her or maybe flirting.

'Are you flirting?'

The question just popped out—the same way other things had just popped out since Mak Stavrou had come into her life.

'I might be,' he said, sounding very serious, not flirtatious at all. 'Would you mind?'

'I think I would,' she said, opening the door of the storeroom, turning on the light then standing back and banging an old walking stick on the corrugated-iron walls hoping to frighten any snakes away. 'It's not something I'm good at and last time I tried it I ended up in trouble, so it's best you don't.'

'You don't sound at all certain,' Mak said, taking the walking stick from her and using it to push the boxes and old steamer trunks and wooden chests about on the concrete floor, hoping any snake not frightened by her banging would object to the movement and vamoose.

'About not wanting to flirt?' Neena asked, her voice sounding as puzzled as the expression on her face was.

'Exactly!' he said. 'You think you would mind. That's not a definite no.'

'And *that's* just semantics,' she retorted. 'You know there's nowhere a flirtation can go—you're here and then you'll be gone—what's the point? I might have fallen for one smooth-talking Greek, but to fall for a second one—well, that would be sheer stupidity. Now, are you going to carry those trunks upstairs—the two that say "Christmas Decorations"? Leave them on the front veranda then we'll have a shower and go up to the pub for tea. So far you've only met the sick people in town, it's time you met some healthy ones.'

Going to the pub for tea was not a good idea, Mak discovered some time later. The meal was fine, a good steak with plenty of chips, a bowl of salad served with it, and the people he met all friendly enough, though he sensed this was polite-ness—it would take along time to become a friend of any of them. A genuine friend, as Neena obviously was, talking to the children who stopped by their table to say hello, asking about their pets, chatting to people at neighbouring tables…

It was after the meal that the fun began.

'You might have told me it was karaoke night,' he complained to Neena as the MC got the music started. 'Do we have to stay?'

'Of course,' she said. 'Not only stay, but as a visitor to town you'll be expected to sing a song. But we needn't stay long. Half an hour at the most. Karaoke not your thing?'

'I can't believe it's anyone's thing,' he growled, 'and there is no way I'm going to sing.'

Unfortunately this statement was drowned out by the MC announcing to everyone present that they were honoured to have the company of the new doctor in town and asking if he'd do the town the honour of singing the first song.

To have refused would have looked churlish so, fighting the flush of either embarrassment or anger that was wanting to surge into his cheeks, Mak stood up, walked to the small stage and took the microphone.

'Do you have a favourite?' the MC, a youth who didn't look old enough to be in a pub, asked him, scrolling the available song titles on the screen.

'How about "Tie me kangaroo down, sport",' Mak asked and saw the look of surprise on the lad's face.

'You know that?'

'Let's say I know a student version of it so I know the tune, and if the words are up on the screen I can sing them rather than the rude ones.'

'Well, okay,' the young fellow said, although he still seemed uncertain that a doctor should be singing such a song.

Presumably the pub patrons felt the same way, for they listened in total silence as Mak launched into the song. He glanced towards Neena and saw she was trying not to laugh, but then the audience joined in the chorus and they were away, everyone shouting out the words of the song. He finished to a roar of approval and loud clapping and, embarrassed by the attention, hurried back to the table, accepting pats on the back and 'good on yous' on the way.

'Well, a man of many talents,' Neena greeted him. 'You've won a lot of hearts with that song—well, you won them over just getting up to sing, a lot of strangers would have refused.'

'The other doctor?' Mak queried, though he wasn't sure why the memory of the man who'd wanted to share Neena's bed lingered like a bruise in his head.

'Oh, he would never have lowered himself to eat at the pub, let alone join in the karaoke.' She answered easily, most of her attention, Mak guessed, on the new singer up on the stage, a young woman with a sweet voice, singing a popular country and western ballad. But as the song finished and Neena stood up to leave, she looked at him and said, 'Why on earth would you be thinking of him?'

Mak wondered the same thing himself, but rather than

admit it, he just shrugged, said goodnight to the people close to them and followed her out of the pub. Outside, the main street was deserted except for an occasional car driving slowly past. They'd walked the couple of blocks from the house to the pub, so set out to walk back, Neena leading him down a side street then along a lane at the back of the houses.

'A lot of outback towns have these lanes,' she told him, as the warm darkness enveloped them. 'In the old days, everyone kept goats for milk and meat and the goats grazed on the town common by day. Every evening the goat boys would go out and herd them back to town and they'd come down the lanes and into their own back yards. Today, of course, there are feral goats—descendants of the originals—throughout the west.'

Mak tried to imagine it, the goats coming in a herd down the lane, two or three dropping off into the back yards of the houses. The big pepper trees under which they walked would have been saplings then, and the streetlights in the main street gas—if indeed there had been streetlights.

'You like it here?' he asked, although he really knew the answer, hearing it her voice when she spoke of the town and its people.

'It's home to me,' she said.

'But you went to the city to study. Weren't you tempted to stay there?'

She stopped and turned towards him, and though they were in shadow and he couldn't see her face, he could guess at the expression of disbelief she'd be wearing.

'Down there with all the noise and pollution and traffic and people?' she queried. 'They were the worst years of my life. I was lost. I hated it. All I wanted was to come home, but I had to stay because the people here had faith in me—they believed in me and had made it possible for me to go away and study.'

'But you admitted you felt under an obligation to them. Surely that coloured your decision to return?'

She shook her head.

'No, it might have had I found I loved the city, but as it turned out, I knew it wasn't right for me. All I ever wanted to do the whole time I was there was to come home.'

He heard the loneliness she'd felt in those years in her voice and couldn't help himself, putting his arms around her and drawing her close.

'Poor little homesick Neena,' he said softly, but the physical contact was reawakening the desire he'd been at pains to keep at bay, and as his body heated he held her more tightly, then dropped a kiss on the top of her head.

She didn't slap his face or move away, so he let his lips roam lower, kissing her forehead, her temple, brushing his lips across her eyelids, learning the feel of her face, the shape of it, through the movement of his mouth across her skin. Right up to her lips…

Move, Neena told herself, but her legs wouldn't obey the instruction and the rest of her body remained locked in Mak's embrace. There was something mesmeric about the feel of his lips on her skin, the taste of him as his tongue probed into her mouth. She let him kiss her and from there it was only a very small step to kissing him back, feeling her body come to life as she explored his lips with hers, her hands also exploring now, pressing against his solid back, sliding down to more slender hips, the curve of his buttocks filling her hands.

'I could make love to you right here and now,' he whispered, adding more fuel to the fire already burning within her.

'Not a good idea,' she murmured, lips to lips, not moving even a fraction of a centimetre.

One of his hands had slid between them and was fondling her breast, sending tremors of delight directly to the nerve centre of her sexuality. Now she was moaning against his mouth and though her head kept yelling at her to stop, to move away, she could no more move than she could deny the attraction she felt towards this man.

Her body yielded to the moment, thoughts banished as she revelled in the delights physical attraction could provide. Heat swelled her tissues, and blood throbbed through her veins, her body pulsating with a need she barely understood and had never felt assuaged. Her lips began their own exploration, moving across his cheek, along a jaw slightly rough with emerging whiskers. The feel of that roughness intensified her excitement, and she slid her hands beneath his shirt and felt the contrast of the smooth skin on his lower back, the hardness of his backbone…

'You are beautiful, and you are driving me to distraction!' Mak growled the words as he eased away from her. 'I know all the reasons this is impossible as well as you do, yet it's equally impossible for me to keep my hands off you.'

Neena felt the coldness of separation—the shock of it—a sense of loss.

He had slung his arm around her shoulders and, holding her close, was meandering on down the lane, chatting away as if this was a perfectly normal conversation.

'And it *is* impossible—what could it be but a brief affair? Then there are the complications of the baby, but what I can't decide is whether kissing you from time to time—I'll try to restrict myself to darkness and odd moments—is going to make things better or worse.'

They walked on in silence for a few minutes, then he spoke again.

'Don't you have anything to add to this conversation?'

The lane had ended at a cross street and her house was just ahead. Mak's arm dropped from around her shoulders, although Neena was reasonably sure there was no one around to see them.

More loss!

'I don't think so,' she said, unable to keep a touch of tartness out of her voice, 'but, then, thirty-four-year-old ex-virgins don't have a lot of experience to draw on in situations like this.'

He halted under a streetlight and looked down at her, lifting his hand to run a finger down her cheek.

'Did it bother you a lot, the virginity thing?'

He was frowning at her, as if really interested in her answer, but with the tension of his presence still firing all her senses, all she could do was shrug it off.

'I never thought about it,' she said. 'Well, not often. Everyone has bad days when they're tired and out of sorts and when I was like that I sometimes wished I had someone I could whinge to.'

His frown disappeared and he laughed out loud.

'That's the best reason for getting married that I've ever heard—to have someone to whinge to!'

'Well, it's true—that's how I felt!' Neena told him crossly. 'And I don't see anything funny about it.'

'We should be back in the lane so I could hug you,' he said. 'I'm not laughing at you but at the simplicity of it. Most people think of marriage as a sharing of joys but you're absolutely right, having someone to complain to when things are going wrong *is* important.'

But for some reason, him agreeing with her didn't make Neena feel any better. In fact, it made her feel worse so she strode away, taking the front steps two at a time, reaching the top before she realised she hadn't checked on Albert. She turned to come back down but Mak halted her with a hand in the air.

'I'll check on him,' he said, and Neena wondered if having someone to check on Albert for her might be nearly as good a reason for marriage as having someone to whinge at.

Not that it could be—at least, not with Mak…

And now she knew Mak, would she be happy with an alternative?

It was such a weird thought that she opened up the steamer trunk to distract herself and began to delve through the Christmas decorations. What colours had she used last year? Red and green, she rather thought. So this year maybe gold and white, garlands with gold bells and white flowers hanging off them along the veranda, and tomorrow she'd sort out the lights and put up the Christmas tree then decorate it with white and gold baubles.

Mak came up the steps, reported Albert was asleep and opened the other trunk.

'Wow, you really do Christmas in a big way. Look at all the decorations.'

He pulled out a bag of scarlet flowers, and another bag of red balls, going through the contents of the trunk with the excitement of a child.

'No, I'm going white and gold so anything that's not white or gold, just put back,' Neena told him as he opened up a huge red paper bell.

'No red?' he queried, waving the bell at her, and once again Neena felt a twinge of loss. Hanging Christmas decorations with someone would be nice as well.

'You can pull out any green garlands,' she told him. 'We can thread them around the veranda and put the white and gold decorations in them.'

They worked amiably together for an hour, decorating the front veranda so people walking by could see they'd made a start.

'We'll leave the rest for tomorrow,' Neena said, when the strain of this unnatural togetherness had become too much for her. 'Do you want a cup of something or a cold drink before you go to bed?'

'I'll fix something for myself in a minute,' Mak said, getting back up on the small stepladder to adjust the tilt on an angel he'd put above the door. He'd climbed down as Neena slid past him—or almost slid past him.

'Hoy!' he said, touching her arm to halt her escape. 'That's mistletoe up there with the angel—you know what that means.'

And before she could object he was kissing her again. Worse still, she was kissing him back! Again! Somehow he shuffled them into the hall so they weren't clearly visible to anyone walking by, but their lips remained joined and their bodies fitted into the contours of each other's as if they already knew the bumps and hollows.

Mak held her close and his mouth consumed hers, stealing her heat and tasting her passion, desire enveloping them both. Neena began to tremble under the spell of it, her body firing, melting, aching, a need for fulfilment she didn't fully understand sending tremors deep into her belly.

He wanted to share my bed!

The stark phrase she'd used so recently echoed in Neena's head and she broke away, muttering it out loud, so Mak looked at her with an expression of shock and distaste. A black frown drew his eyebrows together, growing anger evident in his face and the tension of his body.

Well, she couldn't help that! She escaped to her bedroom and collapsed on her bed, so confused by her emotions she didn't know where to start thinking about them.

'Was I the one who said we couldn't have an affair?' Neena asked, watching the fan lazily stir the air above her. She ran her hands over the bump. 'How foolish was that, huh, Baby Singh?'

But deep in her heart she knew having an affair with this man to whom she was so attracted would only make the parting, when it inevitably came, far harder. Better to put up with a little frustration now than an agony of regret later.

The problem was that it was more than a little and, she suspected, more than frustration. Frustration she could handle, but this aching loneliness that seemed to have permeated every cell in her body, that was something else.

But she was used to loneliness—personal loneliness—so why now was it upsetting her?

Resting her hands on Baby Singh's bump, she considered it—well, not for long, because she really knew. Without any conscious effort on her part—and, to be honest, not much on his—she was falling in love with Mak. For a while she'd put it down to attraction—to some late-developing part of her suddenly becoming aware of her sexuality—but in her heart she knew it was more than that. Talking to the man, working with him, discussing patients and medicine in general, an insidious idea had slid into her mind—not to mention her body—an idea that this was good, better than good, special.

That this *might* be love!

Her sigh reverberated around the room, hanging on the blades of the fan and washing back over her…

Mak was experienced enough to know if he'd kept kissing Neena in the hall the inevitable conclusion would be that they'd have ended up in her bed. And now she'd put a stop to it, he somehow felt ashamed of himself—as if, some time in the future, she might remember him, too, as a man who'd wanted only one thing—to share her bed…

Which he did, of course, but he didn't want her remembering him that way—speaking of him with the same distaste she'd used when speaking of that other man…

He strode along the hallway to his room where he sank down on the bed and rubbed his hands across his face, trying to banish the taste of her from his lips, and all thoughts of her from his mind.

Maybe she *was* a witch!

The thought didn't help—bewitchment wasn't going to go away any more than desire was.

Desire?

Or lust?

Wasn't that all it was?

He pictured her in his mind and knew it wasn't lust—what he felt for her was more complicated than lust.

Much more complicated!

CHAPTER EIGHT

NEENA rose early, mixed up enough formula to see Albert through the day, then took it out to the stables where she filled his bottle and put the rest in the small refrigerator she'd turned on out there. She walked the little camel around the yard, chatting quietly to him, but her head was wondering where things stood between herself and Mak Stavrou while her heart was wondering if it really was love or if it was just an over-heated reaction to romantic kisses in a darkened lane.

Whatever it was, head and heart agreed that seeing him again would be awkward, working with him maybe worse than that, but her morning chores accomplished, she had to return to the house, to shower, dress for work, have breakfast then get about her business. Life went on no matter what was happening in the hidden depths of one's heart.

Was it symptomatic of just how confused she was that she dithered in front of her wardrobe, and instead of pulling on a skirt and cotton knit top—her usual work-wear—she considered a white cotton dress she'd bought on impulse in Baranock one day. It had a lacy insert across the bust and hung in soft folds below the insert, so it was cool, but for all its shapelessness, kind of sexy.

A work dress it was not! No, but she *could* wear it to

Baranock on Friday when they went, and maybe while she was there check out the little boutique where she'd bought it and see what else they had. Maybe a Christmassy kind of dress—or something sleek and slinky.

Sleek and slinky when she was six months pregnant?

Ashamed of her own thoughts, she grabbed a denim skirt and pale blue, sleeveless T-shirt and pulled them on, this fantasising about her wardrobe so bizarre she didn't want to think about what might be causing it.

'Good morning.'

Didn't have to think about what might be causing it—he was sitting in the kitchen!

Mak sounded relaxed and friendly but, then, stopping the kiss probably hadn't caused him the slightest anguish so how else should he sound?

She echoed his greeting, surreptitiously eyeing him in an effort to gauge his mood.

As well try to read the mood of the table, Mak's face gave away as little, his hazel eyes meeting hers momentarily then moving on as he crossed to the bench to start the coffee machine.

Neena helped herself to cereal, added milk and a tub of yoghurt, some slices of mango…

'Did you slice the fruit?' she asked, surveying the platter that held not only mango but rockmelon, orange and peach slices.

And now he smiled, a real smile for it lit his eyes and caused such ructions in Neena's heart and lungs and stomach she wished she hadn't spoken.

'I told you I could cook,' he said.

'So you did,' she managed, then concentrated on her breakfast, refusing to look at him again.

'So what excitement is on the agenda for today?' he asked, and she had to look at him.

'More of the same. I'd like to be able to tell you that Thursdays offer some variety but as you have probably gathered by now, most of our variety comes from emergencies and the fewer I have of those the happier I am.'

He nodded.

'Well, in that case I might take the day off from the surgery and visit the ambulance station, then go out to the powerhouse site again. I can find out how many people they are expecting to employ out there both short term and long term. Is that all right with you?'

It was Neena's turn to nod, which she did, because although she'd been uneasy about getting through the day in Mak's company, the thought of not having him around made her feel even worse. Not that she hadn't asked for it—firstly breaking away from the kiss last night then, to make matters worse, putting Mak in the same category as the horrible doctor she'd employed years ago.

'It's probably a good idea,' she agreed, although she knew the pause between his conversation and her response had been far too long.

No more was said, so Neena finished her breakfast, put her plate and cup in the dishwasher and left the room, going through to her bathroom to clean her teeth and put on lipstick before heading to work.

'Well, I'm off,' she called from the end of the hall. His answering, and supremely casual, 'Bye' slammed into her chest like an arrow.

So it was gone, the rapport they'd built between them. And just like Dr Horrible—to say nothing of Theo—it had all been about getting her into bed. Depression threatened to descend like a thick black cloud, but as she crossed the veranda and saw the decorations there—a lot of them decorations her father had bought for her as a child—she pushed it away. She was a strong, independent woman, for all she'd been tempted to think in terms of togetherness by kisses so subtle, yet so hot, just thinking about them warmed her body.

Or maybe that was just the midsummer sun, already burning on her skin and parching the ground across which she walked. If she hurried she'd have time to go up to the hospital before she started work. If Mr Temple was still stable she'd send him home, but make sure he had his tablets in packs with the days and times to take them clearly marked.

She arrived at the same time as a nurse from the retirement village pushed a wheelchair in through the emergency doors—Maisie.

'I phoned your house and got Dr Stavrou. He said you'd already left and I guessed you'd come here. Maisie's had a really bad night.'

Neena was already bending over her old friend, talking quietly to her as she checked her pulse and listened to the rattling agony of every breath.

'Will you at least let me put you on oxygen?' she asked, and Maisie nodded, so Neena followed the two nurses as they wheeled Maisie into a ward and settled her into bed.

'It's time for me to go, Neena,' Maisie whispered, and Neena bit back the tears she longed to shed, opting instead for briskness.

'Nonsense! You can't go before Christmas, you'd spoil the holiday for too many people. And then there's the baby—you have to wait to see the baby.'

Maisie smiled, but her eyes closed and although her breathing was easier once Neena inserted a nasal cannula, she didn't open them again, drifting off to sleep, or possibly into a light coma.

'I'll phone Ned, he's out at the Harrises',' Neena said, patting Maisie's hand then moving away because duty called, no matter that she longed to sit with the beloved old woman for the final hours of her life.

Ned said he'd be in as soon as he could and Neena was saying goodbye to Lauren when the phone rang again.

'Dr Stavrou for you,' Lauren said, handing Neena the receiver.

'Hello!'

The word was probably as wary as Neena felt. He was supposed to be on his way out to the site, or at the ambulance station, not phoning her.

'Lauren told me about Maisie,' he said, his deep voice coming so clearly over the phone it sent shivers down Neena's spine. 'I'm sure you want to stay with her, so I'll go to the surgery. I've plenty of time to do the other visits. You sit tight and I'll handle the patients.'

What could she say?

'Thank you.'

It didn't seem enough but just saying those two words made a lump form in her throat and she had to swallow determinedly before speaking at all.

'Don't mention it,' he said, all business, so matter-of-fact she had to wonder if his previous plans for the day had been no more than an excuse to avoid her company.

She returned to sit beside Maisie, taking her hand and talking to her about the adventures and joys they'd shared.

'Remember that boy in primary school who was always pulling my plaits,' Neena murmured. 'And you went up to him as he walked home and told him you'd pull something else of his, and hard, if he didn't leave me alone. I never knew what you were going to pull, not until we got into high school and had our sex education talks. Can you imagine a young girl today not knowing what boys looked like until they were thirteen?

'And the time in sixth grade when I had to take something

I'd cooked myself and you said chocolate crackles were the only things I'd be able to manage but it was midsummer and by the time I got them to school they were a mess of chocolate, Copha and rice crisps in the bottom of the cake tin.'

Neena kept talking, holding Maisie's hand, aware she probably couldn't hear the conversation but wanting her dear friend to know she was close by anyway, so the things they'd laughed over together all got another airing, the remember this, remember that of so many shared years.

'You know she wouldn't want you crying.'

Ned had arrived and his chiding voice made Neena aware that tears were sliding down her cheeks, and probably had been for some time.

'Maisie always let me cry—she said crying got the hurt out,' Neena reminded him, although Maisie might not have used the same philosophy on her son.

But Ned just nodded and sat down on the other side of the bed, bending forward to kiss his mother's cheek, gruffly letting her know he was there. And now they both remembered, sharing reminiscences of the woman who had brought both of them up, until Maisie's breathing changed, and finally stopped altogether.

'She was a good woman, the best,' Ned said, then he looked across at Neena. 'You okay?'

She took a deep breath and nodded.

'I will be,' she told him, and knew it was a promise. Her life had gone off track but it was time to get it back in order—Maisie had loved order and had taught her charge to believe in it as a basis for a good life. Neena owed it to Maisie to take control once again.

Though perhaps not right now, a smaller, needy Neena deep inside her whimpered. Do I really have to?

'I'll do the certification and whatever has to be done.'

Mak's voice made her turn, frowning, towards the door.

'What are you doing here?' she demanded, order gone before she'd even begun to get it back.

'I asked Lauren to phone me when it happened so I could do what has to be done. It's lunchtime, I'm not holding up any patients.'

Neena just stared at him, her heart so full of gratitude she couldn't speak, but Ned could.

'Thanks, Mak,' he said. 'Come on, little girl, I'll take you home.'

This time Neena managed a smile.

'It's a long time since you called me that, Ned,' she said, new tears oozing from her eyes and trickling down her cheeks. 'Lately it's been "stupid woman"!'

'Which you were,' he reminded her but he put his arm around her and led her away from Maisie's bed. 'But even Mum agreed that everyone's allowed a bit of stupidity in their life. Come along.'

Neena went home with Ned, where they sat down and discussed Maisie's wishes—no funeral, no service, just a private cremation, 'and if either of you turn up I'll come back to haunt you'—then her ashes to be scattered on the hill where the statues were.

'We'll say goodbye to her there,' Ned said, 'and if friends want to come, that's okay, but as she always said, she'd outlived all her real friends by so much that the only people she knew now were people who really didn't know her at all.'

'You and I did,' Neena protested, but she had always known what Maisie had meant—that the people she'd really loved had gone before her…

So they talked until the shadows spread into the room, when Ned reminded her he had animals to care for and should be going.

'You go, I'm all right,' Neena told him, but Ned still hesitated, showing an uneasiness so rare in Ned Neena guessed it had nothing to do with his mother's death.

'That fellow Mak—he's not bothering you?'

The question made her want to laugh at the absurdity of it. 'Bothering her'? As if the muddle in her mind and the chaos in her body could fit into a mild word like 'bother'!

Oh, he might be tantalising her, tormenting her, frustrating her and generally disrupting her life, but bothering her?

'No, he's not bothering me,' she told Ned.

The man who wasn't bothering her returned to the house as she was putting the finishing touches to the Christmas tree. She'd set it up, as Maisie always had, in the bow window in the living room so the lights of it could be seen from the street.

Why she was putting it up at all, she didn't know, but it had given her something to do, and in doing it she remembered her old friend and carer, for it was a task they'd shared for so many years.

'I picked up a pizza at the café,' Mak announced as he walked in, the smell of cheese wafting from the box he carried. 'They assured me there that you liked anchovies.'

His hazel eyes were studying her—gauging her mood? Her grief?

'Thank you,' Neena said. 'For the food, for thinking of it, for today at the hospital, for today at work.'

'Nonsense, it's what I'm here for, but you really do need two doctors in this town, even without the workers out at the site. What do you do for time off? How do you manage then? Are there locums available? Do the flying doctors provide that kind of cover? What happens?'

He was sounding crosser and crosser as he fired the questions at her, but Neena could only shake her head.

'Can we eat while I answer?'

He looked taken aback for a moment, then he grinned at her.

'Sorry, but although there wasn't one emergency today, it finally sank in how difficult it must be to run the practice on your own. And once the baby arrives it will be impossible.'

Uh-oh! He'd remembered why he was really here—to take over the baby's life. Neena was following him into the kitchen, drawn by the smell of the pizza and the fact that it seemed a long time since she'd eaten, so the realisation did no more than warn her to be wary. She *had* to eat, and an argument now would spoil the food.

'I've got a locum booked while I take maternity leave and I'm hoping he or she might like the place enough to want to stay.'

'You don't know who you're getting as a locum—don't know if it's a he or she?'

Mak was slapping plates on the table, his voice rising in disbelief as he asked the question.

'I've booked one through an agency,' Neena explained, watching the slices of pizza land on her plate and wondering if she could pick one up and start on it before Mak sat down.

He found the roll of paper towels and plonked it in the middle of the table and finally did sit, but before she could start eating he was questioning her again.

'And is that satisfactory for the town? Having a stranger of whom you know nothing coming in to take your place?'

She looked at the pizza and sighed. No chance of eating until she'd sorted out what was really bothering Mak. It couldn't possibly be the locum.

'The town is used to locums. After my father died they went for ages without a doctor at all, then the government stepped in and we had a series of locums, some good and some not so good, and in the years since I've been practis-

ing, I *have* been away at times, mostly to attend conferences
to help update my skills and knowledge. And yes, I know the
town needs another doctor and I have, from time to time, tried
to find one, but it's not that easy.'

She glared at him across the table.

'Satisfied?' she demanded. 'Now can I eat?'

'Go right ahead,' he said, but she knew she hadn't touched
on whatever lay behind his bad mood. Well, too bad, she
hadn't had that great a day herself. She took a bite of pizza
and found it had been seasoned by something wet and salty.
Surely she wasn't crying again.

'Bloody hell!' Mak was on his feet, angrier than ever,
striding around the table, lifting her from the chair then sitting
down on it with her on his knee. 'I'm sorry, I shouldn't be
upsetting you today of all days, and you need to eat. Lauren
said you'd had nothing all day. Here, let me wipe the tears.'

He ripped a paper towel off the roll and dabbed at her cheeks
then lifted a slice of pizza and held it to her lips. 'Eat!' he com-
manded, and she took a bite, chewed and swallowed then took
another, her body stiff with tension, afraid to relax against Mak's
bulky warmth in case all the attraction stuff started up again.

Not that it hadn't already, for he'd rested one hand against
her hip and heat was radiating out from it, sprinting along her
nerves and puddling in her belly.

'I'm sorry I was cross. That's the last thing you needed
today. It's just that spending only one day doing your job on
my own, I got to realise just how hard it must be for you—
how impossible, really. I mean, I read all the time about the
problems of getting doctors in country areas and, worse,
keeping them there, but the realities of the job these country
doctors do just doesn't come through in those news stories. I
mean, who else is there to certify the death of a loved one for
them? It's ridiculous you have no back-up, no support.'

Neena shifted on his knee, sure her weight must be bothering him, wanting to move but enjoying the comfort of his solid body.

Enjoying the heat!

'It's not that bad,' she protested, her mouth still half-full of pizza.

She should move, get off his knee. She'd stopped crying, so why keep sitting there?

Because it felt so good?

No, that was a reason to move!

'We manage—me and all the other doctors running single-practitioner practices out here in the bush.'

'I'm not worried about all the other single practitioners out here in the bush, I'm worried about you.'

He was stroking her back now and the rhythmic touch was so soothing—so hypnotic—Neena wanted to lean back against him and forget everything but the feel of his body and the warmth of his arms around her.

But this was Mak Stavrou. She'd let one of his family get close to her and—

'Worried about me or the baby?'

The words popped out and though she regretted them immediately they couldn't be recalled.

He was cursing, or at least she assumed that's what it was, for the flow of words were presumably in Greek and he'd stopped stroking her back, which made her feel sad.

She should move.

But as when she'd decided that the first time, nothing happened.

'Forget the baby!' He'd finally reverted to English. 'Let's just keep this conversation about us.'

'Oh, Mak,' Neena sighed. 'You must know there can be no us.'

'Because of some presumptuous idiot you once employed, or because of my nephew, who seems to be known around town as The Rat?'

Mak's voice was pure steel, and though now the conversation had turned nasty and her legs might have obeyed an order to move, he'd wound his arms around her, tucking her hard against his body, making escape impossible. His hands rested on the bump and she knew he must feel the baby kicking.

'Because our lives are so far apart.' It was a weak response but she'd had to say *something*.

'So we don't even explore the attraction between us? And don't bother denying the attraction, Neena. We'd have ended up in bed last night if you hadn't inconveniently remembered the other doctor.'

Now she moved, turning on his lap so she could see his face, see his eyes burning with intensity as they fixed on her face.

'Is that all you want? To explore the attraction? To end up in bed?'

He cursed again and drew her close once more.

'Why does everything I say to you end up sounding like that?' he muttered, the words muffled because his lips were pressed against her head. 'No, it isn't all I want. I want to know you, and not just biblically. I want to learn more about you— like the anchovies on pizzas and why you've never cut your hair and what it is about this place and its people that has such a strong hold on your heart. Little things and big things and, yes, sex is part of it, part of getting to know you, but it's not just about sex.'

He paused then added, 'And it's definitely not about the baby. It's about you and me. Maybe we'll discover that there's nothing more than the attraction, but if we don't, if the attraction leads to deeper emotions, then we'll work out the geographical problems and any other problems—together.'

Neena could feel the tears starting again and blinked them back. She answered the least consequential bit of Mak's statement, because that was about all she could cope with right now.

'My father liked my hair long—my mother had long hair, I suppose that's why.'

Mak laughed and she could feel the deep chuckle as a movement in his chest. Feel his ribs, and the muscles that encased them, feel the strength of his legs—feel his desire…

Desire!

'And it *is* about the baby,' she added sadly. 'Though not in the way that you mean. It was my fault, the pregnancy—but in the beginning, it was all about exploring an attraction—'

His fingers found her lips and pressed against them.

'It takes two to make a baby and I don't want to know.'

She sighed, but now she did move. As if she could tell Mak about that night with Theo—tell Mak what his nephew had done…

She stood up on the pretext of getting a glass of water and took the chair across the table from where he now sat.

'I wouldn't have taken you for a coward,' Mak said, as she selected another piece of pizza.

She put it down on a piece of paper towel, the delicious aromas that had tempted her now making her feel nauseous.

'A coward?'

The green eyes were on her face, studying her intently—seeking a lie or evasion, she was sure.

'Isn't that what you are? Aren't you hiding from life behind one bad emotional experience? Aren't you living vicariously through other people's lives because you're afraid to have a life of your own? Oh, I can understand it—you'd lost your mother when you were so young, then to lose your father as a teenager, for a long time you'd have been too wary to get close to anyone, lest you lose them, too. Is that what happened with Theo—did you send him away? Or did you fall in love with him and when he walked away—as Theo surely would—you suffered another loss and decided that was it?'

He was waiting for an answer, the mesmerising eyes demanding one.

'I thought you didn't want to know,' she snapped, angry because a lot of what he'd said was probably true. 'What do you want me to say? Yes, your psychobabble about my avoiding relationships is spot on? It probably is, I've considered it myself, and as for Theo—as for your precious nephew—well, I did explore the attraction and then, at the end, I decided the exploration had gone far enough. I knew he was as shallow as he was clever and charming, I knew his sole aim was to get me into bed, and though I thought I'd be able to go along with it, for the experience if nothing else, at the last minute I decided not to—I said no.'

She took a breath, thinking it might calm the anger, but it was too white hot to stop.

'Theo took it as a tease, we struggled a little, and that's probably when he lost the condom—and I lost the struggle. What's done is done. The baby's mine, not yours or your family's. Goodnight!'

She stormed out of the room before she made a total idiot of herself by bursting into tears.

Again!

Mak sat in the kitchen and swore some more, not that it helped.

Theo had raped her!

The implications of it loomed so large in his head he couldn't think about it, although for the first time he didn't feel sadness over his nephew's death—he felt regret the wretch wasn't alive so Mak could kill him himself.

How had she handled it?

Who would she have turned to? Not Ned or Maisie—she was too protective of them.

No one! He knew that was the answer. She hadn't reported it to the police, or Theo would have been charged and the family would have known.

So she'd kept it all inside her where most of her hurts seemed to be.

His heart ached as he thought of her situation—alone in a way he could never imagine. Then discovering she was pregnant!

How could he not shake his head? So much fell into place now, especially Neena's reluctance to have anything to do with his family.

Feeling totally useless and inadequate, Mak tipped the remnants of the pizza—more than half-uneaten—into the bin and tidied the kitchen. More than anything he wanted to go to Neena, to hold and comfort her.

Comfort she wouldn't accept—not, at least, from him.

He left the house, checked on Albert, then took to the streets, hoping to walk off the tension and—yes, anger in his body. He was in the darkened lane, his anger beating out the rhythm of his strides when his mobile trilled in his pocket. Habit had kept it on him, although he hadn't expected to receive any phone calls.

'Have you talked to her about giving me a proxy for the shares?' Helen's voice demanded, and Mak, who'd been reliving the kiss he'd shared with Neena in the lane, was jolted out of his reverie.

'No!'

Well, what else could he say?

'But it's what you're there for,' Helen bleated, and Mak forbore from reminding her that her original story had been a keen interest in her unborn grandchild. 'The cousins have called an extraordinary general meeting for the third of

January—the woman should have got a notice of it from the solicitors. She'll have a copy of the notice and a proxy form and an agenda for the meeting, including notice of motions. The cousins want to merge with a big power company but first they have to vote on a new board chairman—well, with Dad dead we have to do that anyway—but if one of them wins the vote, they'll take Hellenic in a different direction. This talk of a merger is just an excuse to sell it off! We owe it to Dad, Mak—*you* owe it to Dad!'

And although aware she was dumping a classic guilt trip on him, Mak couldn't help but accept a little of it. His father *would* have loved Mak to follow him into the business, his father *would* have hated seeing the business go out of family hands…

'I'll talk to her,' he promised Helen, though he wasn't sure just how he could follow through on the promise. As if the bloody shares mattered, given the enormity of what Neena had suffered.

And was possibly still suffering if she hadn't had counselling, or sought help of some kind…

CHAPTER NINE

NEENA set the mood for the day as Mak entered the kitchen to find her already there, sipping at her weak coffee.

'Coffee maker's on, and I found some fruit bread in the freezer. I'm having it toasted for breakfast as a change from cereal. I left it on the bench so if you want some, help yourself.'

He studied her for a moment—a slim, small figure huddled in a bathrobe in a kitchen chair, her plait hanging over one shoulder. Her attention remained fixed on her toast, and the magazine she was leafing through. So this was how it was to be. No mention of the revelations of the previous evening, no further discussion of Theo, no further discussion at all!

And in spite of having a thousand questions, Mak decided to play along with it. After all, what *could* he say? I'm sorry my nephew raped you? Hardly!

'What time do we need to leave?' he asked, as he brought his coffee and toast to the table and sat down opposite her.

Now she looked up, dark eyes half-hooded, dark shadows beneath the eyes causing a physical pain in Mak's chest.

'And don't tell me you'll drive yourself,' he added, before she could protest. 'You're exhausted, and driving in that state would not only put you and the baby at risk but could endanger other lives. At least with me driving you might be able to sleep.'

She nodded and returned her attention to the magazine.

'Time?' he prompted.

'Eight-thirty.'

She stood up, put her coffee cup and toast plate into the dishwasher and left the kitchen, the voluminous bathrobe Mak hadn't seen before wrapped tightly around her slight body.

Sadness enveloped him. He'd felt something for this woman that had sneaked past his defences and filled empty spaces in his soul and now, before he'd had time to explore where those feelings might go, he'd lost her.

Although maybe not, he decided a little later. It was eight twenty-five and he was beside his car, opening the door to let in some fresh air before they took off. Neena came tripping down the steps, right on time, and smiled at him. Not a full-blown, isn't-life-wonderful, Neena kind of smile but it wasn't a polite mask of a smile either.

Hope sneaked into his heart, then he remembered the revelations of the previous evening, and despair slammed into hope and left it reeling.

Hope had been foolish anyway, he told himself, holding the car door for his passenger and trying not to see the way the lacy stuff at the top of her dress revealed her full breasts.

They drove out of town in silence, Mak wondering how and when he could raise the issue of the rape, something he suspected she needed to talk about.

'This is bliss—not only being driven but being driven in such luxury!'

The softness of her voice—the genuine delight in it—was the last thing Mak expected. He glanced towards the woman he'd been expecting to stay silent for the two-hour drive and saw a genuine smile.

A wholehearted Neena smile that made his stupid heart skip a beat!

And *that* made him angry.

Well, not angry, but uncomfortable.

'Is that it? You tell me last night that my nephew raped you and this morning all you're concerned about is being driven in a good car. And for your information, it's not *that* good a car!'

She turned to him, and he saw the shock on her face.

'Did you not expect me to talk about it?' he continued, his gruffness evidence of his emotion. 'Is that how you handle all your problems? By ignoring them? If what happened to you had happened to a patient, what would you have done? What would you have suggested?'

Now she frowned.

'You mean reporting it to the police, getting counselling, that kind of thing?'

'Of course I mean that kind of thing. What did you do? How did you get through it? Who did you turn to? Who helped you?'

He knew he was sounding angrier and angrier but he couldn't help it—the thought of her emotional pain and trauma was like a red-hot poker in his gut.

'Well?' he demanded, when the silence had gone on too long.

'I thought it all through myself,' she said, her chin tilted to match the defensiveness in her words and the defiance of her pretty dress. 'I considered all the options, though not the reporting business. That was never one of them, although it did make me understand why other women might opt not to report such things. I had agreed to do it, Mak. I had told Theo yes. I know that sounds stupid and pathetic but I'd decided I didn't want to die a virgin—that I wanted to experience sex at least once in my life. I knew Theo for what he was—I knew there was no future in it—and that was probably why I decided he'd do for the—'

She stopped and Mak took his eyes off the road for long enough to glance her way. Her skin was pale and her hands were twisting tightly in her lap, and although he wasn't a psychologist he suspected this confession, though hard, might be good for her—cathartic.

'Experiment,' she finally said, adding, 'Because that's all it was, an experiment.'

'You still said no,' Mak growled.

She nodded, and turned to look out the window, but not before he saw the tears streaming down her face. He pulled over, got out of the car and walked around to her side, lifting her out and sitting back down with her on his knee, holding her, murmuring to her, mostly in Greek because they were the only words he could use in this situation—words of love she wouldn't understand.

Gradually he felt her tense body relax against him, and she took his hand and held it against the bump.

'You haven't asked,' she whispered, while he marvelled at the feel of the baby kicking against his palm.

'About why you kept it?'

'Yes!'

He held her more tightly.

'That part I think I understand. You had Maisie and Ned for family, both of them getting old, and though the whole town treasures you, you had no one of your own.'

'Selfish, wasn't it?' she muttered with a defiant little sniff that nearly broke his heart.

'No way!' He held her more tightly, then kissed her on the neck. 'You are the least selfish person I have ever met, and you have so much to offer to a child, not least of which is wholehearted, abundant love.'

Her body, which had tensed, relaxed against him once more and Mak felt if they could sit like this for ever he would be happy, but the practical soul he knew lived inside Neena moved them on.

'We have to go—I'll be late for my appointment.'

He kissed her cheek, then stood up and turned to deposit her back in her seat, walking around the car and getting back behind the wheel.

Was she feeling better?

He hoped so, because he wasn't. He was more confused than ever. The only certainty seemed to be that the last person Neena would ever see as a possible lover was the uncle of the man who'd raped her—charming, immature, bloody Theo!

'No wonder he left you the shares—talk about conscience money!'

Rage at his nephew's behaviour had forced the words from his lips, but as soon as they were out he regretted them, for Neena was frowning at him.

'I'm sorry,' he muttered, 'but I get so angry just thinking of it. He was a grown man—he knew the meaning of the word no. And how dared he think that willing the baby some shares would make things up to you in some way! He wasn't expecting to die, which makes it one more empty gesture.'

'We should talk about the shares,' Neena said quietly. 'After all, it's why you're here.'

'Not any more, it isn't,' Mak growled. '*Nothing!* Nothing our family could give you would even begin to make restitution. The shares are the baby's and what you do with them as trustee until he comes of age is entirely up to you.'

'But I need to understand things in order to know what to do,' Neena persisted. Mak flicked a glance at her and saw a little frown on her face. 'I need to talk about it, Mak, and now seems a good time.'

'Did you open the solicitor's letters?'

She shook her head, which was what *he* wanted to do.

He sighed instead.

'Short version—my cousins, who are also shareholders, want to merge the business with a bigger concern. Having the experimental power station coming on line in the not-so-distant future has vastly increased the value of the company and vultures are circling.'

A huge wedge-tailed eagle lifted off the ground as he spoke, some unidentified piece of roadkill dangling from its talons.

'Apt timing,' Neena said, nodding at the bird, then peering upward through the side window to watch its flight. 'But are these companies vultures? Might they not be good for the business?'

A sense of shame washed over Mak as he realised just how far he'd detached himself from the family concern. Early on, he'd always read the annual reports and he'd made sure he kept abreast of new developments—mainly so he could discuss things intelligently with his father—but in recent years medicine had begun to dominate his life more and more, and Hellenic Enterprises had slipped into the background of his life.

And now he had to admit it.

'I truthfully cannot say.'

'Yet you'd like me to give you the baby's proxy?'

He shook his head, dismayed by the impassable rift that had developed between them.

'I have never said that, but if you did you can believe I would look at all the information available about the proposed merger. I would not fail your child by using the proxy irresponsibly.'

'But you'd be drawn to vote with your sister?'

Mak sighed.

'My father built the company from nothing. My sister has worked under him since she was at school, learning from the bottom up. Yes, my sister would like the family to retain ownership and, yes, there is sentiment involved because my mother has taken my father's death very hard, and for her to see us lose the company he lived for would make things worse.'

He paused, glanced towards his passenger, but she was staring straight ahead and her profile told him nothing of her thoughts.

Well, here goes!

'But for all of that, should you offer me the proxies, I hope I would still make a judgement based on sound business principles rather than emotion.'

Now she turned to face him, the little frown he hated seeing furrowing her brow.

'I'm not at all sure that's the answer I wanted to hear,' she said, shaking her head as if perplexed by it. 'My focus for this baby has been about family—it's because of family that I didn't kick you out that first night, because, no matter what, you are the baby's family and as I don't have an extended family then it seems to me your family can give him that. But will you destroy your own family—and it *would* cut you off from them—by voting for sound business principles if that's how it turned out?'

Mak threw his hands up in the air, though only momentarily, re-grasping the steering-wheel almost immediately.

'What do you want of me? What do you want me to say? Is there any way I can win in this ridiculous situation? Read through the information yourself, I'm sure there'll be something in there about the merger. Vote the baby's proxies yourself—leave me out of it!'

I wish I could, Neena whispered, but only in her head. She had been so determined to be happy, to put the previous night behind her, to enjoy this time out in Mak's company, to revel in being driven in his lovely car, and now it had all been spoilt.

It was her own fault—revealing all that anguish stuff last night. Had the sadness of Maisie's death brought it all bubbling to the surface again? Had that one extra loss proved too much for her?

No way! She was stronger than that! And it was probably just tiredness that had tears leaking from her eyes. Again!

She turned towards the window so Mak wouldn't see them and, not wanting to rummage in her handbag for a tissue, lifted her hand to wipe them off her cheeks. Did she sniff that Mak grabbed her hand, felt its dampness, swore, braked and pulled the car onto the shoulder of the road?

Without a word he got out, stalked around the bonnet, opened her door, unsnapped her seat belt and all but hauled her out for the second time.

'Women!' he muttered, shaking his head and producing a perfectly laundered white handkerchief with which he proceeded to mop her tears. 'Honestly, you get a man so tied up in knots he doesn't know which way to turn.'

He peered down at her as if searching for an elusive droplet of water, then, apparently satisfied, he shoved the handkerchief back into his pocket and leaned forward to kiss her lips. A gentle kiss—a don't-cry kiss—that's all it was, although it made the tears start again.

'Stop that right now,' he ordered, taking her into his arms and holding her hard against his chest. 'I know you need to cry, to grieve for Maisie—and to grieve for a lot of things—but I'm equally sure you don't want to arrive for your obstetric appointment with swollen red eyes. What's more, I can't concentrate on driving with you weeping silently beside me. Tonight we'll go up to the hill near the lake and you can cry all you want there, okay?'

He looked so fiercely earnest Neena had to agree, breathing deeply and banishing the tears.

'Good,' he said, and kissed her again, then, as her lips responded, the kiss deepened until the hot, dry, desert landscape disappeared from around them and it seemed to Neena they were afloat on a cloud of joy and softness, fluffy and white, a cloud made just for two. The past with all its sadness was forgotten, and physical sensations so sublimely new and interesting they made her shiver stole through Neena's body. She pressed closer to Mak, her mind lost in the sensations he was generating, sadness burned away in a kiss.

'Sunstroke,' she muttered as she broke away from him, and collapsed on weakened bones back into the car seat.

'Sunstroke?' he echoed, reaching in to wrap the seat belt around her.

'Only thing that could explain the weird flights of fancy in my head,' she mumbled, and though Mak looked puzzled he seemed to accept the explanation.

He took his seat, belted up and started the car back along the road to Baranock.

'We'll sort it all out,' he said, somehow making the words sound like a promise, and although Neena wasn't at all certain what 'all' they could sort out, she decided to believe him and relaxed again, seeking and finding the pleasure just being in the car—with Mak—had given her earlier.

'Still adamant you don't want to know the sex?' her obstetrician asked, when she'd completed her examination and run through all the questions she asked every visit, ticking off the positives and not finding anything negative in Neena's pregnancy.

'Still adamant,' Neena told her. 'I want the surprise.'

'She doesn't even hint at what it is?' Mak asked when

Neena passed the conversation on to him a little later. They were sitting in a small café in the main street of Baranock, Mak drinking coffee while Neena sipped a strawberry milk-shake.

'No, she's very good, although I know she'd love to tell me, but I can't help feeling if I know the sex then I might start getting preconceived ideas about him or her.'

'Yet you talk about it as a him,' Mak probed.

Neena grinned at him, unable to believe they were so relaxed together after the tension that had formed earlier in the car.

Not to mention last night...

'I think him sounds better than it, don't you?'

His answering smile tugged at her heart, but she knew it was like the sunstroke image of the two of them alone on their cloud. Nothing could come of this attraction for so many reasons, but that didn't mean she couldn't just relax and enjoy his company today. One day soon, perhaps even tomorrow, she'd read through all the unopened letters from the solicitors and think about whatever they contained, but for now she was just going to enjoy Mak's company and the drive back to Wymaralong—a little capsule of time alone with him.

Neena had been dozing so the oath woke her, and she looked up to see the trailer on the cattle train ahead of them swaying dangerously.

'He's going far too fast,' she whispered to Mak, her eyes mesmerised by the sway of the trailer, fortunately empty of cattle. 'We need to get past him.'

'We'd never make it. He's taking up all the road. We'll drop right back.'

He braked sharply as he spoke, but it was too little, too late, for the momentum of the swaying trailer had tipped the rig, and with metal screeching and dirt flying everywhere the rig rolled, the trailer coming adrift, skidding back along the road, slamming into the car within a beat of Mak's evasive swerve.

Blackness everywhere, blackness and noise. Noise she couldn't understand—people yelling, men's voices—idiot— too fast, she's pregnant…

Who was pregnant?

She was pregnant. She tried to feel the bump, to find Baby Singh, but the blackness was solid and she couldn't find her hands.

'Neena, can you hear me? I've got your hand—your left hand. I'm squeezing your fingers. Squeeze my hand if you can hear me. Neena, talk to me.'

Someone saying her name—asking her to squeeze her hand. Where was her hand? Left hand, he'd said. How could she tell right from left in the dark like this?

How could she find her hand when she couldn't even find her baby?

She wanted to cry but she'd promised Mak she wouldn't cry until later. Who was Mak? Why couldn't she cry till later?

She squeezed both her hands—or she thought she did. She must have done something for the voice was telling her how clever she was, urging her to talk.

'Where's my baby?'

'Neena, the baby is all right, I'm sure of it. We can't get at you, but I've felt all around and he's still there where he should be. I've felt a kick, so he's okay, now concentrate on you. Are you hurting anywhere?'

Was she?

She didn't seem to be but in the dark it was hard to tell.

'Dark!' she managed, then she was floating on a cloud, all fluffy and white, floating on a cloud with Mak and he was kissing her and it was the most beautiful, delicious, delectable sensation she'd ever experienced.

'We *have* to get her out! She could be haemorrhaging to death under there for all we know. She's pregnant, we need to get to her.'

Mak was squatting low on the road, his arm shoved through an incredibly small space in the crumbled sedan, clinging to Neena's hand. He was yelling his frustration at the fire crew wielding the rescue equipment, although he knew yelling wasn't helping anyone. He'd never seen men move more slowly, cutting here, snipping there, carefully peeling back bits of wrecked trailer and his car as if every piece was a sacred relic. It had taken them for ever to remove the drums of molasses that had been in the trailer when it had swung in an irrational but deadly arc straight into the passenger side of his vehicle.

And all he'd been able to do had been to watch in horror as the woman he'd grown to love had been encapsulated in death and destruction. That she was still alive seemed a miracle—if she *was* still alive!

He squeezed her fingers but her hand lay still and motionless in his. Dark! She'd said it was so dark…

'Okay, that's the last piece of the trailer, now we'll cut through here, attach a wire rope to there…' the fire-crew boss indicated the windshield frame of the car '…and pull the trailer and the top of the car off in one piece, which means we need you out of the way in case the whole shebang comes crashing back down.'

Mak gave the cold fingers one final squeeze and moved reluctantly away, but only far enough to be safe if the load collapsed. He held his breath as the tow-truck winched the wreckage upward then, as it inched forward, tearing the metal with teeth-clenching screeches, finally leaving a clear passage to the front seat of the car, Mak darted forward, ripping away the torn side and front airbags, the lover beating the doctor by seconds as he touched Neena's face with trembling fingers before feeling for a pulse beneath her chin.

She was alive!

Think first response—think pregnancy implications. The foetus is extra-sensitive to changes in blood oxygen levels. Mak clamped an oxygen mask across Neena's face while behind him the ambos and the fire crew all protested.

'You can't start oxygen while we're cutting and shifting metal because of the sparks,' someone said.

'Then stop cutting and shifting for a few minutes while I stabilise her. She's pregnant, the baby needs oxygen—they both do.'

He felt her pulse again, mainly because it had been such a strong beat earlier he thought he might have been mistaken but no, the beat was still strong—and steady!

'Neena, can you hear me?'

An ambulance attendant was wiping the thick dark molasses from her face. She was drenched in it, the beautiful white dress a mess.

Yet her pulse was strong!

Mak grabbed a stethoscope from one of the ambos and pressed its diaphragm against her belly. He heard the foetal heartbeat and felt another kick. The ambo was sliding a backboard in behind Neena's body while another tried to fit a cervical collar.

'I can't get at it,' he said. 'Her head's trapped. Does she have long hair? Is that what's caught somewhere?'

Does she have long hair?

Mak saw the shining curtain of it in his mind's eye, felt the silk of it against his fingers, but knew they had to move her.

'I'll cut it,' he said, his heart racing because he knew what pain the loss of her hair would cause her. But emotional pain was better than death and they had to get her free as quickly as possible. For all her steady pulse she could be bleeding internally—bleeding externally, for that matter. There was still only a small part of Neena and the baby visible.

He talked quietly to her as he cut, using heavy shears someone had handed him, telling her it would grow again, that everyone would still love her just as much—that he'd still love her.

'Stand clear, Doc, we do this part best,' the ambo said when he'd cut the hair.

He stood clear, though he longed to gather her in his arms and lift her out, to hold her close for ever. But these men were the experts at moving injured people, so he bit back his impatience and watched.

'Unbelievable,' one of the ambos said, as they strapped Neena onto the stretcher. 'When I saw the way the trailer had landed on that car I didn't think anyone would have survived, yet there's hardly a mark on her, apart from all the molasses that must have spilled from the drums in the trailer.'

And no indication of internal injuries, although she was slipping in and out of consciousness, which Mak didn't like.

'I'll ride with her,' he told the ambos as they loaded her into their vehicle.

The older of the two men smiled.

'Thought you might want to do that,' he said. 'Looks to me as if Wymaralong might have two doctors again.'

Mak opened his mouth to protest. Of course he couldn't stay in Wymaralong. He was a specialist ER doctor, his life was in the city. But one look at the grey-faced woman on the gurney made him wonder, and as he sat in the back of the ambulance, using wet tissue to clean the muck from her face, the idea of becoming a country doctor instead began to grow on him.

Although wasn't he assuming too much?

What made him think Neena would want him?

A couple of hot kisses?

She'd never said she loved him but, then, he'd never told her how he felt—hadn't known it for sure until he'd seen that trailer careening towards them and had known, no matter what he did, it was going to hit Neena's side of the car.

Then he'd known. He'd felt pain judder through his body and had yelled his futile protest. Oh, yes, then he'd known…

CHAPTER TEN

'I CAN'T stay here in hospital. There's nothing wrong with me. I've got patients to see.'

She was still in the ER at Baranock hospital and already protesting that she wanted to be released. Mak looked at the slight figure beneath the sheet on the ER examination table, at the angry cuts and abrasions the accident had left on parts of her body and the mess thick in her hacked-off hair.

'Your obstetrician is on her way and she's already said she wants to keep you in for a few days' observation. You've had a shock, the baby's had a bad jolt—'

Neena sat up, her hands automatically cradling the tight bump of Baby Singh, panic in her voice.

'Placental abruption! I need an ultrasound. What if my placenta's come adrift and the baby is suffering?'

'The staff here have done an ultrasound and everything's fine,' Mak soothed her. 'But the obstetrician will repeat it just to be sure. Relax, and be thankful you've both come out of it so well, but be sensible as well, and stay here to rest.'

'But my patients!' she wailed, and Mak shook his head.

'I would never have taken you for a wailer,' he chided. 'I'll look after your patients and, believe me, that's a sacrifice. I'd far rather be here looking after you.'

'Looking after me?' Neena frowned up at him, suspicion gathering in her foggy brain. 'Why should you want to be here looking after me?'

Mak smiled at her—a funny kind of smile that made her stomach feel distinctly queasy.

'Don't you know?' he said quietly. 'Don't you really know?'

She shook her head, which was when she realised something else was wrong. Her head felt light—unanchored. More weirdness. She forgot about Mak's puzzling question and lifted her hands, feeling her hair, all knotted and thick.

'I need a shower. My hair's a mess.'

Her hands continued their exploration as she spoke, continued to feel for her plait...

'It's gone—my hair's gone!'

Panic raced through her body, panic and despair, and yes, again a loss—too much loss—too much loss...

Mak was speaking, something about having to cut it off.

'You cut off my hair?' she yelled at him, sitting up so she could see his face more clearly. 'But I told you why I kept it long—I remember telling you. It was *my* hair and, yes, it was a nuisance but I loved it.' She fell back down and closed her eyes, adding in a whisper of grief, 'And you cut it off!'

'It was only hair,' the nurse who stood beside Mak murmured quietly, but Mak wouldn't accept her empathy. He shook his head.

'It was more than that to Neena,' he said. 'It was her link to the past, to her family, to a family she lost when she was far too young.' He began to walk away, then turned back to the nurse. 'After the obstetrician's been, would you help Neena shower and maybe get someone in to neaten the ends of her hair so it doesn't look quite so bad when she sees it?'

The young woman gave him a peculiar look but she nodded her agreement.

Mak was leaving the hospital—he was ninety per cent sure Neena was okay but he'd phone the obstetrician later—when he ran into Lauren.

'I was doing my last-minute Christmas shopping here in Baranock and heard about the accident,' she said. 'Is Neena okay? The baby?'

Mak nodded, then knew Lauren needed more information.

'By some miracle, both are fine,' he said. 'Her specialist is due to check her out any minute but we—well, I—had to cut off her plait to free her from the mess and she's devastated about it.'

'It's hair!' Lauren said, and Mak smiled.

'I know that and you know that, but Neena?'

Lauren nodded.

'She grew it for her father. It's funny because we all rely on Neena to be the sensible one—the rock. When things go wrong in Wymaralong, whether it's a lost dog or a major disaster like a house fire, we turn to her for guidance and support and she's there for everyone, but she's never had anyone to lean on, apart from Maisie and Ned—and she's lost Maisie. Now her hair—it's a bit like Samson in the Bible, isn't it? Maybe she's lost her strength with it.'

Mak found he wasn't as concerned about the hair as he was about the image of Neena Lauren had conjured up—the image of the woman who had no one to lean on. Yet she'd decided to go ahead with a pregnancy that, in the beginning at least, must have caused huge emotional turmoil in her, and she'd held her head high in the small town, though talk would have been rife.

Would she lean if there was someone there to lean on?

Lean on him if he was there?

Lauren was still talking, something about popping in to see Neena then giving him a lift back to Wymaralong.

'You will come back, won't you?' she added anxiously, and Mak smiled.

He'd never find out if Neena would lean unless he was there, now, would he?

'Of course,' he told Lauren. 'I'll find a rest room and clean up a bit then would love a lift back to town. I'll phone the girls at the surgery and tell them to put the afternoon patients back a bit. What time, do you think?'

Lauren did the sums in her head and announced they'd be back by four-thirty, then she dashed away to check on Neena.

Mak moved more slowly, uncertain where this decision was taking him but knowing it was the right one.

Neena lay on her back in the hospital bed in Baranock, the sheet pulled up to her chin, so the bed was neat, apart from the bump of Baby Singh. She had her hands clasped around the bump and one part of her mind was whispering fervent thanks that he was okay.

All the time!

As for herself, she was clean, her hair, what there was of it, washed and gleaming, her head still feeling incredibly light. She had pads on her eyes because spilled molasses had got into them and though it had all been flushed out, her eyes still stung.

Apart from that, she was fine. She'd even slept for a while—or maybe more than a while because it was dark outside now.

So everything was okay.

Except that it wasn't.

She wasn't!

She was edgy and unhappy, and though part of that was because she was doing nothing—you will lie there and do nothing for at least two days, her obstetrician had ordered—

and doing nothing didn't come easily to her, but the major part of it was that Mak wasn't there.

Which was stupid considering she barely knew the man!

He'd been in her life for what—six days? And she was missing him?

Get real!

Get over it!

Be pleased he was good enough to go back to Wymaralong and fill in for her. Most professionals, after the introduction he'd had to bush doctoring, would have seen her safely into hospital and headed back to the city.

Except, of course, there were the shares.

Had they come to some decision about the shares? She remembered talking about them on the drive to Baranock but couldn't remember what, if anything, had been decided.

Though she did remember a kiss—a wonderful kiss—so wonderful she'd felt as if she was floating on a fluffy white cloud—or maybe that had been part of the accident. How could they have been kissing on the road to Baranock with Mak driving?

But something must have happened because when she thought about the drive—or the shares, come to that—she felt hot all over and a softness radiated out from between her thighs and she had to move uncomfortably on the bed for all the specialist had told her to lie still.

The phone interrupted her thoughts, and she heaved herself up until she was sitting against the pillows before answering it. It would be Ned, for sure—checking on her—ready to nag about her not looking after herself, although it hadn't been her fault.

'Hello! Are you there, Neena?'

Not Ned at all—Mak!

Neena smiled at the phone.

'Neena, can you hear me?'

He was sounding anxious, which made her smile some more, but the third time he demanded to know if she was there, she realised she'd better answer him.

'Yes, I'm here,' she said.

'Well, try a hello next time you pick up the phone,' he grumbled. 'I thought you'd passed out or fallen out of bed or something.'

He sounded so cranky she had to laugh, which didn't help his crankiness one bit.

'I was phoning to let you know that everything went well at the surgery, I've seen all the patients—nothing urgent's happening, and the obstetrician said you're okay but you have to rest. You *will* rest, won't you? You won't go wandering around the hospital offering advice and comfort to all the other patients.'

'I *will* rest, Mak,' she promised him, wishing again that he was there so she could see by looking at him if he was as anxious about her as he sounded or if he was just being a fussy doctor.

'Good, I'll come to see you on Sunday—if anyone crashes a helicopter the ambos can look after him—and Lauren said there's an ambulance going to Baranock on Monday to take someone down for surgery, so you can come back with them.'

He was coming to see her on Sunday?

Coming to see her but not to take her home?

Coming to see her to talk about her patients and Saturday surgery, or coming to see *her*?

'Neena, are you there?'

Again the demanding tone.

'Yes, I'm here,' she said, although the smile inside her was so all-encompassing she couldn't think of anything else to say. Fortunately he didn't seem to expect a conversation for he ordered her to keep resting, promised to phone again the next day and said goodbye.

Altogether a very strange conversation, but she was still smiling so it must have been okay.

By Sunday Neena was reconciled to her hair, in fact, she rather liked the way the new short style framed her face and swished around her head when she moved it. And although she'd obeyed the 'rest' orders of both the specialist and Mak, she had persuaded one of the nurses to visit the boutique and get her a couple of pretty nightgowns and a loose floaty dress in fine cream cotton that she could wear back to Wymaralong on Monday.

She was wearing one of the pretty nightgowns now, although she didn't really expect Mak to drive all that way to visit her. Well, she half expected he would, because he'd phoned three times on Saturday and each time he'd said he would.

She actually didn't know what to think about Mak…

Mak felt stupid. He was dressed in his cream chinos and his best green polo shirt, the one Helen had given him for his birthday because, she said, it would make his eyes look greener.

Neena had probably never noticed he had green eyes.

And she'd think the bunch of roses he had gripped in his hands were a silly idea when she was coming home the next day.

And he didn't even know if she liked chocolates, for all the check-out girl in the supermarket had assured him she did.

Though why the girl had assumed they were for Neena was another thing he didn't know.

So he stalked through Baranock hospital, roses and chocolates in hand, mind in total confusion, so although the directions had been simple he lost the way three times. Then there she was—sitting up in a bed at the end of a four-bed ward—

looking so incredibly beautiful for a moment he was sorry he'd come.

Why?

Because he'd driven for two hours practising all the things he wanted to say to her, and now he was here he was tongue-tied.

He couldn't possibly be tongue-tied. He was a well-educated professional—he had words for all occasions.

He was tongue-tied.

She smiled at him, which didn't help one bit.

'Are those for me?' she asked, her smile growing wider, though whether because she liked the roses or was delighted to see him in such a dither, he couldn't tell.

'From the garden,' he managed, although she'd have known that from the moment she saw them. 'And these—I hope you like chocolates.'

She smiled again and thanked him, but the smile and the look of her, the clear olive skin of her chest and shoulders rising out of the gathered neckline of her nightdress, the sharp bones of her face, the shapely red lips—the beauty that stole his breath every time he looked at her—was too much.

He sat down on the bed and took both her hands in one of his, then touched his other palm to her cheek.

'I love you, you know,' he said, and watched her eyes widen in wonder. 'I didn't know until I nearly lost you—well, perhaps I knew, but it was all so awkward, and it happened so suddenly I had to be suspicious of it, but it's love all right, because nothing else could make me feel so totally stupid, so ill at ease, so at a loss as to what to do or say or how to act or anything.'

The words dried up and he stared at her, desperate to find some reaction in her face, her eyes.

Nothing!

He'd made a complete fool of himself and she felt nothing!

The silence lasted a year and a half then he had to break it.

'Have you got nothing to say?' he demanded, as the discomfort of the silence and his own idiocy stirred a kind of anger in his chest.

She smiled again, then whispered, 'No.'

'No? That's it? No you don't love me?'

She reached out and touched a finger to his lips.

'No, I've got nothing to say,' she explained. 'What can I say when you've stolen my breath—the same way you stole my heart?'

And she leaned forward and kissed him, gently at first then with increasing passion, so the very least he could do was kiss her back.

Did 'stole my heart' mean she loved him? the part of his mind not concentrating on the kiss wondered.

The kiss seemed to be telling him she did, so he intensified the exploration of his lips and tongue and held her closer, one hand resting on the bulge of the baby, guarding it as he fitted her body to his in the way he knew was meant to be.

Applause from the other beds eventually made him break away and, though hugely embarrassed, he stood up and took a bow for both of them.

'We've just got engaged,' he explained to the three watching and applauding women.

'Well, given the size of her, I'm glad about that,' one of them said, but most of Mak's attention was on the woman in the bed by the window. He hadn't actually asked her to marry him, had he?

'Did I ask you in the nervous ramble when I came in?' he asked, sitting down on the bed but far enough away from Neena that kissing couldn't start again.

'I don't think so, though love was mentioned,' she told him, taking his hand and holding it tightly. 'And, anyway, Mak, can we really be engaged? Can we really take these feelings further? I can't leave Wymaralong, not only because it's the place of my heart but because of what I owe the people there. Not that they ever expected repayment for their generosity, but it's what I want to give them. And you belong in a city hospital—your skills and training, everything you've worked for, mean that's where you should be.'

It was a problem Mak had been struggling with himself for the past two days, and although he hadn't fully worked out a solution, he knew there were options available that could make his professional life in Wymaralong as fulfilling as he needed it to be.

'I'm sorting that out,' he told her, shifting so he could tuck her close to his body, their backs to the audience in the ward. 'I've been working on my master's because I want to teach, and a lot of teaching these days can be done over internet links. Lectures can be put on the 'net and as long as the students have some face-to-face sessions during the year, that's all they need. I can keep up with the first response research, and if the week I've spent at Wymaralong is anything to go on, I'll still be getting plenty of hands-on experience. On top of that, the town needs two doctors—why shouldn't one of them be me?'

Neena was tempted. It all sounded so wonderful it was hard to believe.

'The baby?' she asked, because he had to get a mention.

'The baby will be mine,' Mak said firmly. 'I will be the only father he or she will ever know. Later we can talk about Theo and explain as much or as little as you want to explain, that's up to you, but the baby will be mine.'

'Really?' Neena asked, unable to believe things could be this simple.

'Really,' Mak said, and he kissed her again, long and hard, so she had no breath left to argue with him over it.

But after he'd gone, with the coming of darkness, doubts grew and although Neena told herself there was no way Mak would be committing himself to her and to Wymaralong for the sake of shares in the family company, the spectre of doubt hovered over her head.

So much so she rummaged through the information stored under 'not needed right now' in her brain and came up with the name of the solicitor who had been in touch with her over Theo's will, and as soon as offices opened in Brisbane next morning, she was on the phone to him.

'No, you cannot give the shares away or sell them. They are to be held in trust for the baby, so really, until he or she reaches his or her majority, you must hold on to them.'

'And vote them in the case of business decisions?' Neena asked.

'You will hold the proxies and you can vote them yourself or give your proxies to someone else should you so wish.'

Mak would be the obvious choice, Neena thought as she hung up the phone, though Mak knows little of the business.

Time to start taking control of her life again. She phoned the surgery and asked to speak to Mak.

'And put the phone down in Reception,' she told Mildred. 'I'll hear if you keep listening.'

Mildred huffed then put her through and Neena heard the click of the disconnection.

'Do you really want to marry me?' she demanded of the man on the other end of the phone.

'I do,' Mak said, so circumspectly Neena knew he had a patient in with him. Well, too bad.

'And do you really love me?'

'I do,' Mak said again, as if already practising for a wedding. 'Didn't I tell you that when I phoned this morning?'

'Yes, several times,' Neena told him. 'I just wanted to be sure.'

'Be very sure,' Mak said, and the conviction in his voice sent shivers down her spine.

She said goodbye and phoned Information, then dialled a number and asked for Mrs Cassimatis.

'And who shall I say is calling?' a snooty receptionist demanded.

'Tell her Dr Singh—Neena Singh from Wymaralong.'

'Helen Cassimatis!'

The voice was brisk and businesslike, but Neena sensed the hesitation in it—hesitation that sounded very like fear.

This was confirmed with Helen's next words.

'Has something happened to Mak?' she asked, her voice faltering with anxiety.

'Oh, dear, I didn't mean to frighten you. Mak's fine,' Neena assured her, then hesitated, uncertain how to proceed. Fortunately Helen spoke again.

'Mak tells me I may have misjudged you. I'm sorry.' The words were quiet but they held real regret and had a ring of sincerity that made Neena swallow hard.

'I may have done the same to you,' she admitted huskily. Then she took a deep breath and began again. 'That's why I'm phoning.'

'Oh, yes?'

Neena smiled to herself. This sounded more like the Helen of the emails—brisk and confident. Another deep breath and Neena plunged ahead.

'I'm phoning to ask you and your mother to come out for Christmas. You can fly to Baranock and I'll have someone meet you there. Mak tells me you usually have a family Christmas and you've been too busy with work to organise it so I wondered if the two of you might like to join us out at Wymaralong.' She hesitated then added, 'Spend Christmas with your family-to-be.'

The silence at the other end stretched to infinity then back before Helen said, 'Do you mean that—about the family-to-be?'

'I do,' Neena told her. 'The baby will need a grandmother and you're the only one available, and a great-grandmother, well, that would be so special. So what do you think? Wymaralong for Christmas?'

More silence then a muffled voice.

'I can't talk now because I'm crying but I'll phone tonight. I've got Mak's mobile number, I'll call him.'

'No, don't do that,' Neena said quickly. 'I want your visit to be a surprise. I'll phone you.'

'Thank you,' Helen said, her voice still thick with tears. 'Thank you so much.'

Pleased with her morning's work, Neena rode up front in the ambulance on the return trip to Wymaralong, and though she wanted to go to the surgery she'd promised Mak she'd go straight home and keep on resting.

'Best for Baby Singh,' he'd said.

'Best for Baby Stavrou,' she'd corrected, and had heard his sigh of pleasure.

For Christmas, Neena slipped the proxy papers in a cylinder and wrapped them like a bon-bon, put Helen's name on them and put them under the tree. For Mrs Stavrou she had some pretty jewellery her mother had brought from India. It had been around long enough to become fashionable again but as Neena never wore jewellery herself, she was happy to give it to the older woman.

Mak raised his eyebrows at the growing number of parcels under the tree but showed no interest in reading names or cards, so her surprise was safe. Mak actually showed little interest in anything other than work and being with her, touching her, holding her, kissing her, and now that he was convinced she was well, even sleeping with her, although the first few nights they shared a bed precious little sleeping went on.

'I do love you, you know that,' he said for about the millionth time. It was Christmas Eve and she was preparing a picnic supper to take up to the hill above the dam.

'I do,' she said, stopping the preparations of a simple salad long enough to give him a kiss. 'Now, go down and check on Albert while I finish here. You know Ned's joining us up on the hill, and the girls from the surgery, and Lauren and her family.'

She didn't tell him Ned had driven into Baranock earlier to collect his mother and his sister—for that was her Christmas present to him, his mother and his sister joining them for the celebrations—a family time for all of them. And though the nerves in her stomach were so tight she worried about Baby Stavrou's comfort, she knew it would be all right because the love that had grown between herself and Mak was strong enough to leap any hurdle.

An hour later they all stood, Helen, Mrs Stavrou, Ned, Mak and her friends, and watched the sun go down over the red desert landscape. They raised their glasses and toasted the sunset, then toasted the future—Mak and Neena's future, Hellenic Enterprises' future, and the future of the little town in the far outback of Australia that now had two doctors.

EPILOGUE

THE baby gave a cry and Mak let go of Neena's hand to turn and take the still wet bundle from the obstetrician.

'A baby girl, for all your conviction,' he teased his wife as he handed her the baby and watched her hug the precious bundle to her breast.

'Well, we've already got a boy with Albert, so a baby girl is good,' she whispered, touching the wrinkled face with a gentle forefinger. 'Don't you think?'

She looked up at Mak with so much love in her eyes he felt his heart move in his chest. This was stupid. They'd been married nearly three months now and he still felt strange tugging movements in his chest when his wife looked at him! Shouldn't he be over that?

He sat down beside Neena and probed a finger at the newborn child, who turned dark blue eyes in his direction. Then one scrawny arm moved and her tiny hand grasped his probing finger and held tight, and his heart bumped around in his chest once again.

'My two girls,' he whispered, not ashamed of the tears that filled his eyes and clogged his voice. 'My two beautiful girls.'

THE CHRISTMAS BABY BUMP

BY
LYNNE MARSHALL

Lynne Marshall has been a Registered Nurse in a large California hospital for twenty-five years. She has now taken the leap to writing full time, but still volunteers at her local community hospital. After writing the book of her heart in 2000, she discovered the wonderful world of Mills & Boon® Medical Romance™, where she feels the freedom to write the stories she loves. She is happily married, has two fantastic grown children, and a socially challenged rescued dog. Besides her passion for writing Medical Romance, she loves to travel and read. Thanks to the family dog, she takes long walks every day! To find out more about Lynne, please visit her website www.lynnemarshallweb.com.

Special thanks to Sally Williamson
for her constant support and
for keeping me on the right path with this story.

CHAPTER ONE

MONDAY morning, Stephanie opened the door of the cream-colored Victorian mansion and headed toward the reception desk. Though the house had been turned into a medical clinic, they'd kept the turn-of-the-century charm. Hardwood floors, tray ceilings, crown molding, wall sconces, even a chandelier made everything feel special. She could get used to showing up for work here.

A man with longish dark blond hair in a suit chatted with not one but two nurses at the receptionist's desk. Nothing short of adoration gleamed from the women's eyes. He looked typical trendy Santa Barbaran—businessman by day in a tailored suit and carefully chosen shirt/tie combo, outdoorsman on the weekends by the tone of his tan. Not bad, if you liked the type.

"Of course I'll help you out, Dr. Hansen," one of the young and attractive nurses gushed.

"Great." He held a clipboard. "I'll pencil you in right here. Anyone else?"

Was he taking advantage of the staff? Unscrupulous.

"Sign me up for Saturday," the middle-aged, magenta-haired receptionist chimed in.

Hmm.

"Got it." As he scribbled in her name his gaze drifted upward. The warm and inviting smile that followed stopped Stephanie in her tracks.

"May I help you?" he said.

Flustered, and not understanding why—okay, she knew exactly why, the guy was gorgeous—she cleared her throat. "I'm Stephanie Bennett. I have an appointment with Dr. Rogers."

"Yes," the older receptionist said, back to all-business. "He's expecting you, Dr. Bennett. I'll let him know you're here."

Before she could take a seat in the waiting room, the man with the bronze-toned suntan (even though it was November!) offered his hand. "I'm Phil Hansen, the pulmonologist of the group. If you'd like, I'll take you up to Jason's office."

"It's nice to meet you," she said, out of habit.

A long-forgotten feeling twined through her center as she shook his hand. She stiffened. Tingles spiraled up her arm, taking her by surprise. No wonder the ladies were signing up on his clipboard. She stifled the need to fiddle with her hair.

"Oh, that's fine," she muttered. Then, finding her voice, said, "I'll wait for him to..." Before she could finish her sentence and drop Phil's hand, another man, a few years older but equally attractive with dark hair, appeared at the top of the stairs. Working with such handsome men, after being celibate for over three years, might prove challenging on the composure front. She'd imagined typical stodgy, bespectacled, aging doctors when she'd signed on as a locum. Not a couple of *Gentleman's Quarterly* models.

"That would be Jason," Dr. Hansen said, his smile narrowing his bright blue eyes into crescents. Instead of letting go of her hand, he switched its position and walked her toward the stairs, as if they were old friends. "Here's Stephanie Bennett reporting for duty."

"Great. Come on up, Stephanie. After we talk, I'll show you around."

Phil brought her to the stairway complete with turned spindle rail, dropped her hand on the baluster, and patted it. "Thanks for stepping in," he said in all sincerity. "You'll like it here."

Considering the odd feeling fizzing through her veins, she was inclined to agree.

Stephanie saw the temporary stint in Santa Barbara as the perfect excuse for missing the holidays with her family in Palm Desert. Thanksgiving and Christmas always brought back memories too painful to bear. Not that those thoughts weren't constantly in her mind anyway, but the holidays emphasized *everything*.

The promise of going through the season surrounded by well-meaning loved ones who only managed to make her feel worse was what had driven her to take the new and temporary job. She'd only been dabbling in medicine since the incident that had ripped the life from her heart, shredded her confidence, and caused her marriage to disintegrate. A huge part of her had died that day three years ago.

The Midcoast Medical Clinic of Santa Barbara needed an OB/Gyn doctor for two months. It was the perfect opportunity and timing to get away and maybe, if she was lucky, start to take back her life.

As she walked up the stairs, she overheard Phil. "Okay, I've got one more slot for Friday night."

"I'll take it," the other nurse said, sounding excited.

Was he full of himself? That fizzy feeling evaporated.

Phil sat at his desk, skimming the latest *Pulmonary Physician's Journal* unable to concentrate, wondering what in the hell he was supposed to do with a kid for ten days. But he couldn't turn Roma or his father down.

His father had recently survived his second bout with Hodgkin's lymphoma. His stepmother, Roma, who was closer to Phil's age than his father's, had called last night. She'd wanted to talk about her plans to take Carl to Maui for some rest and relaxation.

Reasonable enough, right?

No!

Just the two of them, she'd said. Had she lost her powers of reasoning by asking him to care for Robbie? The kid was a dynamo…with special needs.

Robbie, the surprise child for his sixty-five-year-old dad and his fortysomething stepmom, had Down syndrome. The four-year-old, who looked more like a pudgy toddler, always got excited when his "big brother"— make that half brother—came for a visit. Phil didn't mind horsing around with the kid on visits, because he knew he'd go home later on, but taking on his complete care was a whole different thing. Robbie's round face and classic Down syndrome features popped into his mind. The corner of Phil's mouth hitched into a smile. The kid called him Pill. Come on. No fair.

"And it's only for ten days. Your dad needs this trip and if we don't jump on booking it right now we won't

get these amazing resort rates and airfares. Please, please, please!"

Roma knew how to surgically implant the guilt. His father's craggy sun-drenched face, with eyes the color of the ocean, the same eyes Phil had inherited, came to mind. The guy deserved a break.

How could he say no?

Those eyes had lost their sparkle when Phil's mother had left fifteen years ago, the week after he'd first been diagnosed with cancer. How could someone who was supposed to love you do such a thing? Phil had cut his Australian surfing tour short to come home and see his father through the ordeal. It had been a life-changing event for both of them, and he'd never spoken to his mother again. Last he'd heard, she was living in Arizona.

After that, Phil couldn't fathom his dad pulling out of his slump. How could either of them ever trust a woman to stick around?

Carl Hansen had been granted a second chance with Roma, followed by a huge surprise pregnancy. *"Hell, if I wait around for you to settle down and have a grand-child I'll be too old to enjoy it. May as well have my own!"* his father had joked with Phil when he'd first told him the news.

Carl and Roma had had a tough go when Robbie had been diagnosed with Down syndrome after amniocentesis, but they'd wanted him no matter what and hadn't regretted one moment since. Then, after fifteen years of remission, Carl had been hit with cancer again and, on top of being a new parent of a handicapped baby, he'd had to go through chemo. Carl and Roma were nothing less than an inspiration as far as Phil was concerned.

Ten days wasn't a lifetime. Anyone could survive ten days with a kid, right?

"We'll be home in time for Thanksgiving," Roma had said, "and I promise the best meal of your life." Hell, she'd had him at please, please, please.

He'd already started the sign-up sheet for babysitters and backup. Good thing he'd always managed to stay friends with his coworkers and ex-girlfriends—maybe he'd call in a few extra favors.

"You've already met René's replacement, Stephanie Bennett," Jason said, breaking into Phil's thoughts. His partner stood in his office doorway, and beside him the redhead. "She comes with a great endorsement from Eisenhower Medical Center."

All Phil's worries vanished for the time being as he took her in.

Her gaze darted to Jason and back to him, her cheeks flushing pink.

Though noticeably uptight, she had possibilities… Hold it—toddler on board!

"Hi, again. Jason's giving you the official tour, I see." He stood behind his desk. "Let me know if there is ever anything you need, Dr. Bennett."

Her delicate mouth, which sat appealingly beneath an upturned nose, tugged into a tentative smile. "Call me Stephanie," she said, as she tucked the more-red-than-brown, shoulder-length hair behind an ear. "Please."

Though she was saying all the right words, he sensed her standoffishness. He'd never had trouble making friends and acquaintances, especially with women, and sometimes had to remind himself that it didn't come as easy for other people.

"Okay, Stephanie, welcome aboard." He remembered

how cool her hand was when he'd shook it, and an old saying came to mind, *Cold hands, warm heart.* It got him thinking about what kind of person she might be behind that cool exterior.

He engaged her sharp gaze, enjoying the little libido kick it gave him. A spark flashed in her butterscotch-colored eyes. Had she felt it too? "Oh, and call me Phil. My extension is 35, same as my age. If you ever need me, I'm right across the hall and I'll be glad to help out."

She nodded her thanks.

"Now let me show you your office," Jason said to Stephanie, ushering her across the waiting room.

As quickly as she'd appeared, she left without looking back. That didn't keep Phil from staring and giving a mental two-note whistle as she followed Jason.

Phil sat and leaned back in his chair, thinking about Stephanie in her copper-and-black patterned jacket, black slacks and the matching stylish lace-lined scoop-neck top. He liked the way her hair was parted on the side and fell in large, loose waves over her cheek and across her shoulders. He liked the set of her jaw, more square than oval yet with a delicate chin. He liked the ivory color of her skin without a hint of the usual freckles of a redhead, and wondered if he might find a few on her nose if he got up close, really close. Just a sprinkling maybe—enough to wipe away that sleek image, enough to make her seem vulnerable beneath her obvious social armor.

And just as he was about to dream a little deeper, his intercom buzzed. It was his nurse. "Your dad's on the phone," she said.

The trip.

Robbie.

How in the hell was he supposed to impress Dr. Bombshell while babysitting his half brother?

Stephanie spent most of the day getting used to the Midcoast Medical OB/Gyn doctor René Munroe's office, as well as the new setup. She'd held a mini-meeting with her nurse, discussing how she liked to run her clinic and telling her exactly what she expected. She wanted to make this transition as smooth as possible, and stuck around later than she'd planned, logged in to the computer, reading patient charts for the next day's appointments. For this stint, she'd concentrate on the gynecological portion of her license.

There had been one stipulation for her taking this job, and Jason Rogers had agreed to it. Though she'd take care of the pregnant patients, she wouldn't be delivering their babies. Fortunately, after perusing the patient files, none of Dr. Munroe's pregnant patients would be at term during her stay. And Jason had eased her concerns by mentioning that it would have been very hard to get her privileges at their local hospital anyway. She'd been in the process of picking up the pieces of her career, knew she could handle the clinical appointment portion, but no way was she ready to deliver a baby again. The thought of holding a tiny bundle of life in her arms sent her nearly over the edge.

Her stomach rumbled and in need of changing her thoughts, she packed up for the day. As she crossed the reception area, the front clinic door swung open and in rushed Phil Hansen with a little dark-haired boy tagging along beside him. The slant of the boy's eyes with epicanthic folds, and the flattened bridge of his nose, hinted at Down syndrome.

"Hold on, Robbie, I've got to make a call," Phil said, shutting off his beeper and reaching over the receptionist's desk to grab the phone.

Robbie smiled at her as only a child with no fear of strangers could. "Hi," he said.

"Hi, there." Her insides tightened and her lungs seemed to forget how to take in air, knowing her son, Justin, would have been close to Robbie's age…if he were still alive. She looked away. Before her eyes could well up, she diverted her thoughts by eavesdropping on Phil's conversation.

"I'll be right there," he said, then hung up and blew out a breath. "Great. What the hell am I supposed to do now?" he mumbled.

She cringed that he cussed so easily around a child.

Phil's gaze found her. A look of desperation made his smooth, handsome features look strained. He glanced at Robbie and back to her. "I need a huge favor. I just got a call from the E.R. One of my patients inhaled his crown while the dentist was replacing it, and I need to do an emergency bronchoscopy to get it out." He dug his fingers into his hair. "Can you watch Robbie for me? I'll only be gone an hour or so."

What? Her, watch a child? "I can't…"

"I don't know what else to do." His blue eyes darkened, wildly darting around the room.

He was obviously in a bind, but didn't he have a child-care provider?

She glanced at the boy, who was oblivious to Phil's

predicament, happily grinning at a picture of a goldfish on the wall.

"Pish!" he said pointing, as if discovering gold.

"I'm really in a bind here," Phil pleaded. "The E.R. is overflowing and they need to get my patient taken care of and discharged. I can't very well plop Robbie down in the E.R. waiting room."

Oh, God, there it was, that lump of maternal instinct she'd pushed out of her mind for the past three years. It planted itself smack in the middle of her chest like an ice pick. She studied Phil, his blue eyes tinted with worry and desperation. She'd give the wrong impression if she refused to help out, and she'd come to Midcoast Medical to help. He'd seemed so sincere earlier when he'd offered his assistance anytime she needed it. A swirl of anxiety twisted her in its clutch as she said, "Okay."

"You'll do it?" He looked stunned, as if he'd just witnessed a miracle.

Well, he had. Never in a million years would she have volunteered to do this, but as he was in such a bind…

She nodded, and her throat closed up.

"Thank you!" He grabbed her arms and kissed her cheek, releasing her before she had a chance to react. "You're the best."

"What am I supposed to do?"

"Just watch him. I'll be back as soon as I can. Be a good boy for Stephanie, Robbie," he said before he disappeared out the door.

Why couldn't she have left earlier, like everyone else in the clinic? Dread trickled from the crown of her head all the way down to her toes. Her heart knocked against her ribs. She'd made a knee-jerk decision without thinking it through. She couldn't handle this. There went that swirl of panic again, making her knees weak and her hands tremble.

The boy looked at her with innocent eyes, licking his lips. "I'm hungwee."

She couldn't very well ignore the poor kid. "So am I, but I don't have a car seat for you, so we can't go anywhere."

She'd spoken too fast. Obviously, the boy didn't get her point.

He held his tummy and rocked back and forth. "Hungweeeeee."

Oh, God, what should she do now? She scratched her head, aware that a fine line of perspiration had formed above her lip. He was hungry and she was petrified.

Think, Stephanie, think.

She snapped her fingers. The tour. Jason had taken her on a tour of the clinic that morning, and it had included the employee lounge. "Come on, let's check out the refrigerator."

Robbie reached up for her hand. Avoiding his gesture, she quickened her step and started for the hallway. "It's down here," she said, as he toddled behind, bouncing off his toes, trying to catch up.

She switched on lights as they made their way to the kitchen in the mansion-turned-clinic. "Let's see what we can dig up," she said, heading for the refrigerator, avoiding his eyes at all cost and focusing on the task. She had every intention of writing IOU notes for each and everything she found to share with Robbie.

Some impression she'd make on her first day, stealing food.

Heck, the fridge was nearly bare. Someone had

trained the employees well about leaving food around to spoil and stink up the place. Fortunately there was a jar of peanut butter. She pulled out drawer after drawer, hoping to find some leftover restaurant-packaged crackers. If the kid got impatient and cried, she'd freak out. Drawer three produced two packs of crackers and a third that was broken into fine pieces. Hopefully, Robbie wouldn't mind crumbs.

"You like peanut butter?"

"Yup," he said, already climbing up on the bench by the table. "I wike milk, too."

Stephanie lifted her brows. "Sorry, can't help you there." But, as all clinics must, they did keep small cartons of juice on hand for their diabetic patients. "Hey, how about some cranberry or orange juice?"

"'Kay."

"Which kind?"

"Boaff."

"Okay. Whatever." Anything to keep the boy busy and happy. Anything to keep him from crying. She glanced at her watch. How long had Phil been gone? Ten minutes? She blew air through her lips. How would she survive an hour?

After their snack, she led him back to the waiting room, careful not to make physical contact, where a small flat-screen TV was wedged in the corner near the ceiling. She didn't have a clue what channels were available in this part of the state, but she needed to keep the boy distracted.

"What do you like to watch?"

"Cartoons!" he said, spinning in a circle of excitement.

She scrolled through the channels and found a cartoon that was nowhere near appropriate for a child.

"That! That!" Robbie called out.

"Uh, that one isn't funny. Let's look for another one." She prayed she could find something that wouldn't shock the boy or teach him bad words. Her hand shook as she continued to flip through the channels. Ah, there it was, just what she'd hoped for, a show with brightly colored puppets with smiling faces and silly voices. Maybe the fist-size knot in her gut would let up now.

She sat on one of the waiting-room chairs, and Robbie invited himself onto her lap. Every muscle in her body stiffened. She couldn't do this. Where was Phil?

His warm little back snuggled against her and when he laughed she could feel it rumble through his chest. She inhaled and smelled the familiar fragrance of children's shampoo, almost bringing her to tears. Someone took good care of this little one. Was it Phil?

She couldn't handle this. Before she jumped out of her skin, she lifted him with outstretched arms and carried him to another chair, closer to the TV.

"Here. This seat is better. You sit here."

Fortunately, engrossed in the show, he didn't pick up on her tension and sat contentedly staring at the TV.

It had been a long day. She was exhausted, and didn't dare let her guard down. Robbie rubbed his eyes, yawning and soon falling asleep. She paced the waiting room, checked her watch every few seconds, and glanced at the boy as if he were a ticking time bomb. Her throat was so tight, she could barely swallow.

Several minutes passed in this manner. Robbie rested his head on the arm of the chair, sound asleep. Stephanie hoped he'd stay that way until Phil returned.

A few minutes later, one of the puppets on the TV howled, and another joined in. It jolted her.

Robbie stirred. His face screwed up. The noise had scared him.

Oh, God, what should she do now?

After a protracted silence, he let out a wail, the kind that used up his breath and left him quiet only long enough to inhale again. Then he let out an even louder wail.

"It's okay, Robbie. It was just the TV," she said from across the room, trying to console him without getting too close. She patted the air. "It was the show. That's all." She couldn't dare hold him. The thought of holding a child sent lightning bolts of fear through her. She never wanted to do it again.

Flashes of her baby crying, screaming, while she paced the floor, rooted her to the spot. Robbie cried until mucus ran from his nose, and he coughed and sputtered for air, but still she couldn't move.

It took every ounce of strength she had not to bolt out of the clinic.

Phil's patient had been set up and ready for him when he'd arrived in the nearby E.R. The dental crown had been easy to locate in the trachea at the opening of the right bronchus. He'd dislodged it using a rigid scope and forceps, and done a quick check to make sure it hadn't damaged any lung tissue. He'd finished the procedure within ten minutes, leaving the patient to recover with the E.R. nurse.

He barreled through the clinic door, then came to an abrupt stop at the sight of Robbie screaming and Stephanie wild-eyed and pale across the room.

"What's going on?" he said.

She blinked and inhaled, as if coming to life

from her statue state. "Thank God, you're back," she whispered.

"What happened?" He rushed to Robbie, picked him up and wiped his nose.

"I was 'cared," Robbie said, starting to cry again.

"Hey, it's okay, buddy, I'm here." Phil hugged his brother as anger overtook him. "What'd you do to him?" he asked, turning as Stephanie ran out the door. What the hell had happened? Confused, he glanced at Robbie. "Did she hurt you?"

"The cartoon monster 'cared me," he whimpered, before crying again.

Phil hugged him, relieved. "Are you hungry, buddy? You want to eat?"

The little guy nodded through his tears. "'Kay," he said with a quiver.

What kind of woman would stand by and let a little kid cry like that? Had she been born without a heart? Phil didn't know what was up with the new doc, but he sure as hell planned to find out first thing tomorrow.

CHAPTER TWO

STEPHANIE snuck in early the next day and lost herself in her patients all morning. She gave a routine physical gynecological examination and ordered labs on the first patient. With her first pregnant client, she measured fundal height and listened to fetal heart tones, discussed nutrition and recommended birthing classes. According to the chart measurements, the third patient's fibroid tumors had actually shrunk in size since her last visit. Stephanie received a high five when she gave the news.

Maybe, if she kept extra-busy, she wouldn't have to confront Phil.

Later, as she performed an initial obstetric examination, she noticed something unusual on the patient's cervix. A plush red and granular-looking area bled easily at her touch. "Have you been having any spotting?"

"No. Is something wrong?" the patient asked.

To be safe, and with concern for the pregnancy, she prepared to take a sample of cells for cytology. "There's a little area on your cervix I want to follow up on. It may be what we call an ectropion, which is an erosion of sorts and is perfectly benign." She left out the part about not wanting to take any chances. "The lab should get results for us within a week."

"What then?"

"If it's negative, which it will most likely be, nothing, unless you have bleeding after sex or if you get frequent infections. Then we'd do something similar to cauterizing it. On the other hand, if the specimen shows abnormal cells, I'll do a biopsy and follow up from there."

"Will it hurt my baby?"

"An ectropion is nothing more than extra vascular tissue. You may have had it a long time, and the pregnancy has changed the shape of your cervix, making it visible."

"But what if you have to do a biopsy?"

How must it feel to have a total stranger deliver such worrisome news? Stephanie inhaled and willed the expertise, professionalism and composure she'd need to help get her through the rest of the appointment. Maybe she shouldn't have said a thing, but what if the test result came back abnormal and she had to drop a bomb? That wouldn't be fair to the patient without a warning. She second-guessed herself and didn't like the repercussions. All the excitement of being pregnant might become overshadowed with fear if she didn't end the appointment on a positive note.

"This small area will most likely just be an irritation. It's quite common. I'm being extra-careful because you're pregnant, and a simple cervical sampling is safe during pregnancy. I'll call with the results as soon as I get them. I promise." She maintained steady eye contact and smiled, then chose a few pamphlets from the wall rack on what to expect when pregnant. "These are filled with great information about your pregnancy.

Read them carefully, and afterward, if you have any questions, please feel free to ask me."

The woman's furrowed brow eased just enough for Stephanie to notice. She wanted to hug her and promise everything would be all right, but that was out of her realm as a professional.

"Oh, I almost forgot to tell you your expected due date." She gave the woman the date and saw a huge shift on her face from concern to sheer joy. Her smile felt like a hug, and Stephanie beamed back at her.

"This is a very exciting time, Mrs. Conroy. Enjoy each day," she said, patting the patient's hand.

The young woman accepted the pamphlets, nodded, and prepared to get down from the exam table, her face once again a mixture of expressions. "You'll call as soon as you know anything, right?"

"I promise. You're in great shape, and this pregnancy should go smoothly. A positive attitude is also important."

Stephanie felt like a hypocrite reciting the words. Her spirits had plunged so low over the past three years she could barely remember what a positive attitude was. If she was going to expect this first-time mother to be upbeat, she should at least try it, too.

After the patient left, she gave herself a little pep talk as she washed her hands. *Just try to have a good time. Do something out of the ordinary. Start living again.*

A figure blocked the exam-room doorway, casting a shadow over the mirror. "You mind telling me what happened last night?" Phil's words were brusque without a hint of yesterday's charm.

Adrenaline surged through her, and she went on the defensive. "I don't do kids." She turned slowly to hide her nerves, and grabbed a paper towel. "You didn't give me a chance to tell you."

"How hard is it to console a crying kid?"

Stephanie held up her hand and looked at Phil's chin rather than into his eyes. "Harder than you could ever understand." She tossed the paper towel into the trash bin and walked around him toward her office. "I'm sorry," she whispered before she closed the door.

Phil scraped his jaw as he walked to his office. What in the hell was her problem? Last night, he'd found her practically huddled in the corner as if in a cage with a lion. It had taken half an hour to console Robbie. A bowl of vanilla ice cream with rainbow sprinkles had finally done the trick. Colorful sprinkles, as Robbie called them. For some dumb reason, Phil got a kick out of that.

What was up with Stephanie Bennett?

He didn't have time to figure out the new doctor when he had more pressing things to do. Like make a schedule! He'd put so much energy into distracting Robbie last night, horsing around with him and watching TV, that he'd lost track of time, forgotten to bathe him and missed his usual bedtime medicine. A kid could survive a day without a bath, right?

His beeper went off. He checked the number. It was the preschool. Hell, what had he forgotten now?

Stephanie arrived at work extra-early again the next morning, surprised to see someone had already made coffee in the clinic kitchen. She was about to pour herself a cup and sneak back to her office when Phil swept into the room. Her shoulders tensed as she hoped he didn't hold a grudge. Wishing she could disappear, she stayed on task.

"Good morning," he said, looking as if he'd just rolled out of bed, hair left however it had dried after his shower.

"Hi," she said. She didn't want to spend the next two months avoiding one of the clinic partners. Phil had been very nice at first, it seemed to come naturally to him, and, well, she needed him to forgive her. "Look, I'm sorry about the other night."

"Forget about it. Like you said, I didn't leave you much choice." He scrubbed his face as if trying to wake up. "Didn't realize you had a problem with kids." He glanced at her, curiosity in his eyes, but he left all his questions unspoken.

She had no intention of opening up to him, and hoped he'd let things lie. Maybe if she changed the topic?

She lifted the pot. "Can I pour you a cup, too?"

"Definitely. Robbie kept me up half the night with his coughing."

"Anything wrong?" She leaned against the counter.

"No virus. Just an annoying cough. He's had it since he was a baby." He accepted the proffered mug and took a quick swig. "Ahh."

"So what do you think it is, then?" Discussing medicine was always easy…and safe.

"I've been wondering if he might have tracheobronchomalacia, but Roma, his mom, doesn't want him put through a bunch of tests to find out."

"Is that your wife?"

He laughed. "No, my stepmother. Robbie's my half brother."

"Ahh." She'd heard the scuttlebutt about him being

quite the playboy, and she couldn't tolerate a married guy flirting with the help.

A smile crossed his face. "Did you think he was my kid?"

She shrugged. What else was she supposed to think?

"I'm just watching Robbie while my dad and Roma are in Maui." He stared at his coffee mug and ran his hand over his hair, deep in thought. "Yeah, so I want to do a bronchoscopy, but Roma is taking some persuading."

"You think like a typical pulmonologist," she said, spooning some sugar into her coffee. "Always the worst-case scenario."

"And you don't assume the worst for your patients?"

She shook her head. "I'm an obstetrician, remember? Good stuff." *Except in her personal life.*

"You've got a point. But I'm not imagining this. He gets recurrent chest infections, he's got a single-note wheeze, and at night he has this constant stridorous cough. I've just never had to sleep with him before."

"You're sleeping with him?" The thought of the gorgeous guy with the sexy reputation sleeping with his little brother almost brought a smile to her lips.

"Yeah, well…" Did Phil look sheepish? "He was in a new house and a strange bed. You know the drill."

She couldn't hide her smile any longer. "That's very sweet."

He cleared his throat and stood a little straighter, a more macho pose. "More like survival. The kid cried until I promised to sleep with him."

Heat worked up her neck. "That was probably my fault."

He looked at her, and their eyes met for the briefest of moments. There was a real human being behind that ruggedly handsome face. Perhaps someone worth knowing.

"Let's drop it. As far as I'm concerned, it never happened," he said.

Maybe she shouldn't try so hard to avoid him. Maybe he was a great guy she could enjoy. But insecurity, like well-worn shoes you just couldn't part with, kept her from giving him a second thought.

"It's not asthma," he said, breaking her concentration. "If I knew for sure what it was, I could treat it. He may grow out of it, but he's suffering right now. You think I look tired, you should see him. The thing is, he might only need something as simple as extra oxygen or, if necessary, CPAP." He rubbed his chin.

All the talk about Robbie's respiratory condition made her worry about him. Especially after she'd made the poor little guy cry until he was hoarse the other night. She sipped her coffee. "Is there any less invasive procedure that can give the same diagnosis?" Keeping things technical made it easier to talk about the boy.

"Bronchography, but he's allergic to iodine, and I wouldn't want to expose him to the radiation at this age. And all I'd have to do is sedate him and slip a scope in his lungs to check things out. Five minutes, tops. I'll see how things go."

"So where is he?"

"He's in day care with his new best friend, Claire's daughter. Thankfully she took pity on me and chauffeured him today."

No sooner had he said it than Claire breezed through the door. The tall, slender, honey blonde had a mischievous glint in her eyes. "It's called carpooling."

"Ah, right." Phil said, then glanced at Stephanie. "Learning curve."

"Morning," Claire said.

Stephanie nodded. She'd met the clinic nurse practitioner the other day in a bright, welcoming office that came complete with aromatherapy and candles. She was Jason's wife, and seemed nice enough, but Stephanie hadn't let herself warm to anyone yet.

"So, Robbie didn't want to go with his group after driving to the preschool with Gina talking his ear off," Claire said. "Gina's my daughter," she said for Stephanie's benefit. "He looks so cute in his glasses. When did he get them?"

Phil grinned. "Beats me, but I found them in his things, so I talked him into wearing them."

"See, you're a natural."

He refilled half of his mug. "That'll be the day. Two nights, and I'm already planning to scope him for that cough of his. How does Roma manage?"

"Like all mothers. We follow our instincts. Give it a try." Claire winked at Stephanie, as if they belonged to the same secret sorority. If Claire only knew how wrong she was.

Stephanie took another swallow of coffee, wishing she could fade into the woodwork.

"Do you have any kids?" Claire asked.

"No." Stephanie couldn't say it fast enough. She stared deeply into her coffee, trying her best to compose herself. Phil watched her. "Well, I'd better prepare for my first patient. I have a lot to live up to, filling René's shoes." She reheated her coffee and started for the door, needing to get far away from all the talk of children. Maybe it had been a mistake coming here, but she'd committed herself for the next two months, and she'd live up to her promise.

"You'll do fine," Phil said with a reassuring smile. "I've got to take off, too. Need to make a run to the hospital this morning."

She peeked over her shoulder. He stopped and poured the rest of his coffee into the sink, then glanced at Stephanie. Eye contact with Phil was the last thing she wanted, so she flicked her gaze toward her shoes. What must he think of her and her crazy behavior? But, more importantly, why did she care?

On her way out the door she passed the cardiologist, Jon Becker, and nodded. He gave a stately nod then headed for the counter and the nearly empty coffee pot.

"Hey," he said. "I made the coffee and now all I get is half a cup?"

Hunching her shoulders, Stephanie took a surreptitious sip from her mug and slunk down the hall. How many more bad first impressions was she going to make?

"Make a full pot next time," she heard Claire say. "Quit being so task oriented," she chided, more as if to a family member than a business colleague. "If you're going to be a stay-at-home dad, you need to think like a nurturer."

"Claire, all I wanted was a cup of coffee, not a feminist lecture on thinking for the group."

Stephanie couldn't resist it. A smile stretched across

her lips, the first one in two days. Jon looked at least forty, and he was going to be a stay-at-home dad?

She'd been so isolated over the past three years, and had no idea how to have a simple conversation with coworkers. Maybe it was time to make an effort to be friendly, like every other normal human being.

A familiar negative tidal wave moved swiftly and blanketed her with doubt.

You don't deserve to be alive. She could practically hear her ex-husband's voice repeating the cutting words.

On her way back to the extended-stay hotel that night, Stephanie realized how famished she was. On a whim, she stopped at a decent-looking Japanese restaurant for some takeout.

After placing her order, she sat primly on the edge of one of the sushi bar stools. She sipped green tea, and glanced around. Down the aisle, there was Robbie, grains of rice stuck to his beaming face like 3-D freckles. Across from the boy, with his back to her, sat Phil. A jolt of nerves cut through her as she hoped Robbie wouldn't recognize her. He might start crying again. How soon could she get her order and sneak out? Just as she thought it, as if sending a mental tap to his shoulder, Phil turned and saw her, flashed a look of surprise, then waved her over.

She couldn't very well pretend she hadn't seen him. She waved tentatively back then shook her head as Phil's ever-broadening gesture to join them was accompanied by a desperate look.

Be strong. He's the one babysitting. It's not your responsibility.

He stood, made an even more pronounced gesture with pleading eyes.

The guy begged, but she couldn't budge. She shook her head and mouthed, "Sorry." He might think she was the most unfriendly woman he'd ever met, but no way was she ready to sit down with them, as if they were some little happy family. No. She couldn't. It would be unbearable.

She avoided Phil's disappointed gaze by finishing her tea.

Fortunately, the sushi chef handed her the order. After she paid for the food, she grabbed the package, tossed Phil one last regretful look, and left.

Strike two.

Stephanie walked her last patient of the morning to the door. The lady hugged her as if they were old friends. One of the things she loved about her job was telling people they were pregnant.

"Have you got all the information you need?"

The young woman's head bobbed.

"Any more questions?"

"I'm sure I've got a million of them, but I can't think of anything right now except…I'm pregnant!" She clapped her hands.

Stephanie laughed. "Well, be sure to write all those questions down and we'll go through them next time."

"I will, Doctor. Thanks again." The woman gave her a second hug.

Stephanie waved goodbye, and with a smile on her face watched as her patient floated on air when she left the clinic.

"I was about to accuse you of being heartless, but I've changed my mind now," Phil chided.

Stephanie blushed. She knew exactly what he referred to.

"How are things going with Robbie?" her nurse asked Phil in passing.

"Just dandy," he said, with a wry smile. "I finally figured out it's a lot less messy to take him into the shower with me instead of bathing him in the tub by himself."

The nurse giggled. "I can only imagine."

Stephanie fought the image his description implanted in her mind, obviously the same one Amy had. He seemed to be a nice guy. Everyone liked him. Adored him. The fact that he was billboard gorgeous, even with ever-darkening circles under his eyes, should be a plus, but it intimidated her. And after the way she'd treated him and Robbie, she didn't have a clue why he kept coming around.

"You doing anything for lunch today?" he asked.

Could she handle an entire lunch with this guy? "Why would you want to take me to lunch?"

"Why not? You're new in town, probably don't know your way around…"

His cell phone went off, saving her from answering him.

"Cripes!" he said. "Hold on a sec." He held up one finger and answered his phone.

After a brief conversation, he hung up with a dejected look. "Evidently Robbie got pushed by another kid and skinned his knees." He scratched his head, a look of bewilderment in his eyes. "He's crying and asking for me, so…"

"It's a big job being a stand-in dad, isn't it?"

"You're telling me. Hey, I have an idea, why don't we have lunch tomorrow?"

Swept up by the whole package that was Phil, including the part of fumbling stand-in dad, she answered without thinking. "Sure."

The next day, at noon, Stephanie found Phil standing at her door wearing another expression of chagrin. "I completely forgot we have a staff meeting today."

"Yeah, I just got the memo," she said.

"You should come. We've got some big decisions to make."

"I don't have any authority here."

"Oh, trust me, on this topic your input is equally as important as any of ours."

"What are you talking about?"

"We have to decide how we're going to decorate the yacht for the annual Christmas parade."

"It's not even Thanksgiving yet!"

"Big ideas take big planning. Besides, have you been by the Paseo? They've already put up a Christmas tree. Huge thing, too. I took Robbie to see it last night."

His deadpan expression and quirky news made her blurt a laugh. When was the last time she'd done that? "Well, seeing I've never been on a yacht, not to mention the fact that I suck at decorating, I can't see how I'll bring a lot to the table."

"Come anyway. You might enjoy it."

I might enjoy it. Wasn't that the pep talk she'd given herself the other day? Be open to new things? Start acting alive again?

"It's a free lunch," he enticed with lowered sun-bleached brows.

"I'll think about it."

"If you change your mind, we'll be in the lounge in ten minutes."

"Okay."

His smile started at those shocking blue eyes, traveled down to his enticing mouth and wound up looking suspiciously like victory. The guy was one smooth operator.

After he left, Stephanie surprised herself further when she brushed her hair, plumped and puffed it into submission, then put on a new coat of lip gloss before heading to the back of the building for the meeting. She stopped at the double doors, fighting back the nervous wave waiting to pounce. The place was abuzz with activity. Claire called out various types of sandwiches she had stored in a huge shopping bag, and when someone claimed one, she tossed the securely wrapped package at them. One of the nurses passed out canned sodas or bottled water. Another gave a choice of fruit or cookie.

"I'll take both," she heard Phil say just before he noticed her at the door. "Hey, I saved you a seat." He patted the chair next to him. "What kind of sandwich do you want?"

"Turkey?"

"We need a turkey over here," he called to Claire.

Stephanie ducked as the lunch missile almost hit her head before she could sit. A smile worked its way from one side of her mouth to the other. These people might be crazy, but they were fun.

"Sorry!" Claire called out.

"No problem." She had to admit that she kind of

liked this friendly chaos. It was distracting, and that was always a good thing. When her gaze settled on Phil, he was already watching her, a smile very similar to the one she'd seen in her office lingering on his lips.

"I'm glad you decided to come."

If he was a player, she got the distinct impression he was circling her. How in the world should she feel about that? Lunch was one thing, but what if he asked her out? Hearing how he struggled with Robbie had shown her another side of him. This guy had a heart beneath all that puffed-up male plumage, she'd bet her first paycheck on it. She wasn't sure she could make the same claim for herself.

"Okay, everybody, let's get going on this." Jason stood at the head of the long table, his mere presence commanding attention. Dark hair, pewter eyes, suntanned face, she could see why Claire watched him so adoringly. "Last year we came in third in the Santa Barbara Chamber of Commerce Christmas Ocean Parade, and this year I think we have a fighting chance of taking first if we put our heads together and come up with a theme."

"You mean like Christmas at Christmastime?" Jon looked perplexed by the obvious.

"He means like Santa and his helpers, or Christmas shopping mania, or the North Pole," Claire shot back.

"How about trains?" Jon said. "Boys love trains at Christmas."

"What about trains and dolls?" Jon's nurse added, with a wayward glance.

"How about Christmas around the world?" Stephanie's nurse, Amy, spoke up. "We could cover the yacht with small Christmas trees decorated the way other countries do, and the mast could be a huge Christmas tree all made from lights."

The conversation buzzed and hummed in response to the first ideas. It seemed everyone had a suggestion. Everyone but Stephanie. She particularly liked what Amy had suggested.

What did she remember most from Christmas besides the beautifully decorated trees? Santa, that's what. "Could we have a Santa by the big tree?" She said her thought out loud by mistake.

"Yeah, we need a Santa up there," Phil backed her up.

"And I nominate you to be Santa," Claire said, pointing to Phil with an impish smile. "You'd be adorable."

"Me! You've got to be kidding! I scare kids."

"Oh, right, and Robbie doesn't adore you. Yeah, I think you should be Santa and Gina and Robbie can sit on your lap." Claire wouldn't back down.

"No way," he said, with an *are-you-crazy* glare in his eyes. Out of the corner of his mouth he said, "Thanks a lot," to Stephanie.

"Great idea," one of the nurses blurted across the table, before a few others chimed in. "Yeah."

"But I am the *un*-Santa." He glanced at Stephanie again, this time with a back-me-up-here plea in his eyes.

Not about to get involved in the debate, she lifted her brows, shrugged and took a bite of her sandwich.

"Look," Jason said. "We need to get more people involved on the yacht, and you haven't been much help the last couple of years." There was a sparkle in Jason's eyes, as if he enjoyed putting Phil on the spot. "Should everyone be elves?" he asked, his mouth half-full of sandwich.

"What if one person stood by each decorated country's tree dressed in the traditional outfit?" Amy seemed to be on a roll. "You know, lederhosen, kilt, cowboy hat…oh, and what's that Russian fur thing called? Ushanka? And what about a dashiki or caftan, oh, wait, and a kimono, or a sari or…"

"That's a fantastic idea," Claire said.

Revved up, Amy grinned, and Stephanie nodded with approval at her. Phil squeezed her forearm. Okay, everything was a great idea except for Santa.

General agreement hummed through the room, and several people soon chimed in. *Wow. I like that. Good idea.*

The receptionist, Gaby, wearing glasses that covered half of her face, took notes like a court reporter.

"Did you get that?" Jason asked her.

Gaby nodded, never looking up, not breaking her bound-for-writer's-cramp speed.

"Ah, then we shouldn't need a Santa anymore," Phil said, sounding relieved.

"Of course we will," Claire said. "One Santa unites them all, and Phil will be it."

Stephanie's eyes widened and from the side, she noticed his narrow betrayed-looking gaze directed at Claire.

"I say we take a vote on who should be Santa, the captain of the boat or me," he said, just before his beeper went off. "Damn. It's day care. I've got to take this." He strode out of the room, the doors swinging in his wake.

Jason snagged the opportunity. "Okay, everyone agree Phil's Santa?"

Everyone laughed and nodded. Poor guy didn't stand a chance. Stephanie had to admit she sort of felt sorry for him.

Phil stepped back into the room, half of his mouth hitched but not in a smile. "I've got to make a quick run over to day care. Robbie's refusing to cooperate with nap time."

Jason nodded. "Let us know if you need to reschedule some appointments."

"It shouldn't take long. I've just got to make the kid understand he has to follow the rules—" Phil snapped his fingers as if the greatest idea in the universe had just occurred to him "—or he won't get afternoon snack!"

Stephanie laughed. The guy was barely coping with this new responsibility, but he wasn't griping. He seemed to catch on quickly, and, she had to admit, it made her like him even more. She glanced around the table at all the adoring female gazes on him. Okay, so she'd finally joined the club.

"So who's Santa this year?" Phil asked, one hand on the door.

Jason grinned. "You!"

He flashed a glance at Stephanie, pointed, and mouthed, "You owe me."

CHAPTER THREE

PHIL finished entering the list of orders in the computer
for his last patient of the afternoon. His mind had been
wandering between the appointments, and Stephanie
Bennett was the reason. She was as guarded as a locked
box. Then out of nowhere today this fun-loving Santa-
of-the-world fan had emerged, and it had backfired and
landed him on a date with a red suit.

Something held her back from enjoying life, and he'd
probably never find out in two months what it was, but
romantic that he was, he still wanted to get to know her
better. The time restraint was a perfect excuse to keep
things casual and uninvolved. Just his style.

But there was Robbie—a full-time job. No way could
he squeeze in a romantic fling until his father and Roma
came home.

He pushed Enter on the computer program and shut
it down.

Good thing he'd lined up Gaby for child care on
Saturday morning.

Jason had asked him to stop by his office on his way
out today, so he trotted up the back stairs to the second
floor. Aw, damn, he'd caught Jason and Claire kissing.
He stepped back from the doorway. They seemed to do

that a lot and hadn't even heard him. Yeah, they were newlyweds but, still, they were married, with children! He marveled at the phenomenon. Come to think of it, his dad and Roma did a lot of smooching, too.

Maybe players like him didn't corner the market on romance.

He decided to talk to Jason later, then padded down the stairs and veered toward Stephanie's office, a place he'd been drawn to like a magnet lately. Just as he passed Jon's door he heard his name.

"Hey, Phil, come take a look at the latest pictures."

Oh, man, he knew exactly what those pictures would be. Evan, his newborn son, seemed to be the center of Jon's universe these days. Being just outside Jon's office, Phil couldn't very well avoid the invitation.

What was with his partners? They'd all settled down, leaving him the lone bachelor. The thing that really perplexed him was that they all seemed so damn blissful. Well, he wasn't into matrimonial bliss. No way. No how. He liked his freedom. Liked being alone. He glanced at Stephanie's office. At least now he knew someone else who liked being single.

Except for Robbie staying with him, he hadn't lived with anyone since his med-school roommates. And he really didn't miss their stinky socks and dirty underwear tossed around the cramped apartment. Come to think of it, Robbie's socks ran a close second, and the kid knew nothing about putting things away. He smiled at the image of his little half brother strutting around in his underwear with pictures of superheroes pasted all over. Even his nighttime diapers had cartoon characters decorating them. What in the world had his life turned into?

An odd sensation tugged somewhere so buried inside he couldn't locate it, but the feeling still managed to get his attention. *Heads up, dude. Take note. Maybe there's something to be said for a good relationship and a family.*

No. Way. Maybe it worked for other people, but he wasn't capable of sustaining a long-term love affair. Wasn't interested. He knew just as many people whose marriages didn't work out. Hell, his own mother had walked out on them.

Nope. He liked the here and now, and when things got too deep or involved, he was out of there. Maybe he was more like his mom than he wanted to admit. His list of ex-girlfriends kept growing; many of them had since married and he was glad for them. It just wasn't his thing.

Phil greeted Jon and fulfilled his obligation as a good coworker to ooh and aah over Jon and René's new son. Then he patted him on the back, told him he was a lucky dog, and excused himself with a perfectly valid reason. "I've got to pick up Robbie."

On his way out of the clinic, he glanced at Stephanie's closed office door. What were the odds of him running into her at dinner again tonight?

Nope. If he wanted to spend some more time with her, he couldn't depend on something as flimsy as fate. He'd need a plan.

Gaby had signed up to watch Robbie on Saturday morning. Maybe he'd make plans with Stephanie then. As for dinner tonight, he had a date with his kid brother for a grilled cheese sandwich and tomato soup.

Just seven more days.

* * *

Stephanie was aware that René mentored nurse practitioner students from the local university once a week, but hadn't realized she'd be taking on this aspect of René's job along with everything else. Thursday morning she was shadowed by a bright and pregnant-as-she-was-tall young woman filled with questions. Maria Avila had thick black hair and wore it piled on top of her head, and if she was trying to look taller, the extra hair didn't help. Her shining dark eyes oozed intelligence and curiosity and her pleasant personality suited Stephanie just fine. After a full morning together, they prepared for the last appointment.

"If my next patient consents, I'll guide you through bimanual pelvic examination."

Stephanie fought back a laugh at the student's excitement when she pumped the air with her fist.

"Have you done one before?"

"I've done them in class with a human-looking model," Maria said.

Stephanie raised her brows. "That's not nearly the same thing. I'll do my best to get this opportunity for you. Now, here's the woman's story." Stephanie recited the medical history from the computer for Maria. "What would you do for her today?"

Maria sat pensively for a few minutes then ran down a list of questions she'd ask and labs she'd recommend. Her instincts were right-on, and Stephanie thought she'd make a good care provider one day.

The examination went well, Stephanie stepped in to collect the Pap smear, and Maria was ecstatic she got hands-on experience. Fortunately the patient was fine with the extra medical care as long as Stephanie followed up with her own examination.

One of the ovaries was larger than normal, and tender to the touch. It could be something as simple as a cyst, but she wanted to make sure. She also wanted Maria to feel the small, subtle mass that she'd overlooked when she'd first performed the exam.

From the woman's history she knew there wasn't any ovarian cancer in her immediate family. She met some of the other risk factors, though. She had never been pregnant, was over fifty-five, and postmenopausal.

"Have you had any pain or pressure in your abdomen lately?"

The woman shook her head.

"Bloating or indigestion?"

"Doesn't every woman get that?" the patient said, with a wry smile.

"You've got a point there." Stephanie grinned back.

When she finished the exam, as she removed the gloves and washed her hands, she mentioned her plan of action. "I'm ordering a pelvic ultrasound to rule out a small cyst." She didn't want to alarm the woman about the potential for cancer due to her age, but finding any pathology early was the name of the game when it came to that disease. "I'll request the study ASAP."

The grateful woman thanked both of them and on her way out she hugged the student RNP, Maria. "Good luck with your pregnancy, and keep up your training. We need more people in the field."

Her comment drove Stephanie to ask, "Are you in medicine?"

"I'm a nurse."

Stephanie figured, being a nurse, the patient was already in a panic about what her slightly enlarged ovary might be.

"Don't drive yourself crazy worrying about the worst-case scenario, Ms. Winkler, okay? The nodule didn't feel hard or immovable. It's most likely a cyst."

The extra reassurance helped smooth the woman's wrinkled brow, but nervous tension was still evident in her eyes when she left.

Stephanie briefed Maria on possible reasons why she'd missed the subtle change in the ovary and offered suggestions on hand placement while performing future examinations for best results.

They walked back to her office as Stephanie explained further for Maria.

"The worst thing we can do is leave a patient waiting for results, but sometimes our job is like a guessing game. We have to go through each step to rule out the problem. Fortunately, modern medicine usually gives us great results in a timely manner."

"Waxing philosophical, Doc?" Phil's distinct voice sent a quick chill down her spine.

How long had it been since that had happened with a man? Not since the first morning when she'd seen him, to be exact. "Can I do something for you, Phil?"

With a slow smile, he glanced first at Stephanie then at Maria, whose cheeks blushed almost immediately. What was with his power over women?

"Yeah. You can meet me at Stearn's Wharf Saturday morning around nine."

Was this his idea of asking her out? In front of the student nurse practitioner?

"Uh. You sort of caught me off guard."

"Hmm. Like how you bamboozled me into being Santa?"

Okay, now she got it. It was payback time. She grimaced. "If it matters at all, I abstained from voting."

"Warms my heart, Doc." He patted his chest over his white doctor's coat.

But meeting at the beach for what was predicted to be yet another gorgeous Santa Barbara day sounded more like reward than payback.

Maria cleared her throat. "I should be going and let you two work this out."

"Oh, right." Stephanie felt a blush begin. What kind of impression would she make with her student, making plans for a date right in front of her?

"Thanks so much, Dr. Bennett. You've been fantastic and I've learned a lot today," Maria said.

"You're welcome, and I guess I'll see you next week?"

"Actually, that's Thanksgiving. But I'll be here the week after, that is if I don't go into premature labor first!" The otherwise elfin woman beamed a smile, looked at Dr. Hansen again, subtly turned so only Stephanie could see her face, and mouthed, "Wow!" with crossed eyes to emphasize his affect on her, then left.

Stephanie didn't even try to hide her grin. *Yeah, he's hunky.*

Stephanie couldn't have asked for a more beautiful day on Saturday morning. There wasn't a cloud in the cornflower-blue sky, and the sun spread its warmth on the top of her head and shoulders, making the brisk temperature refreshing. The ocean, like glittering blue glass along the horizon, tossed and rolled against the pier pilings, as raucous seagulls circled overhead. At home, the clean desert air was dry and gritty, but here on the wharf the ocean breeze with its briny scent energized her.

She hadn't exactly said yes or no to Phil's proposition on Thursday. She'd said she'd think about it, and he'd said he was planning to surf that morning anyway, so come if she felt like it. Well, she'd felt like it, and by virtue of the glorious view, she was already glad about her decision.

A group of surfers was a few hundred yards to the left of the pier, and though the odds were stacked against her, she tried to pick out Phil. With everyone wearing wet suits, it proved to be an impossible task.

"Here's some coffee."

Jumping, Stephanie pivoted to find Phil decked out in a wet suit, holding his surfboard under one arm and a take-out cup of coffee in another. He handed it to her as she worked at closing her mouth.

He was a vision in black neoprene. The suit left nothing of his sculpted body to her imagination—from neck to shoulders to thighs to calves, every part of him was pure perfection.

"Thanks," she said, taking the coffee, unable to think of a single thing to say.

"I'm glad you showed up."

"Me, too."

"If you're still around later, I'll meet you on the beach in…" he glanced at a waterproof watch "…say an hour or so," he said, throwing his board over the forty-foot-high rail.

She watched in horror as he hopped onto the wood post and dived into the ocean. Was he crazy?

"Hey, no jumping from the pier!" a gruff voice yelled from behind. The white-haired security guard didn't stand a chance of catching him.

Stephanie gulped and looked over the rail just as Phil surfaced. He swam to his board, straddled it like a horse, looked up and waved. *Yee haw!*

She shook her head, waiting for the surge of adrenaline to wane. "You almost gave me a heart attack," she yelled.

He laughed. "This is the lazy man's way of getting past the breakers," he shouted with a huge grin. "Enjoy your coffee. I'll see you on the beach later."

He paddled off, and like an expert he caught the first wave, dipping through the curl, zigzagging, riding it until it lost its momentum.

As she sipped her coffee, she watched Phil surf wave after wave, never faltering. He looked like Adonis in a wet suit playing among the mere humans. Today the ocean was only moderately roiled up, offering him little challenge and nothing he couldn't handle standing on one leg. But it was still exciting to see him in action. She remembered several pictures on his office wall with his surfboard planted in the sand like a fat and oddly shaped palm tree, and him receiving a trophy from someone, or a kiss from an equally gorgeous girl. What a charmed life he must lead. Doctor by day, surfer by weekend.

She checked her watch after an hour or so and began walking back to the mouth of the pier. After removing her shoes, she strolled along the wet, gritty sand as she watched Phil ride the curl of a strong, high wave almost all the way to the shore.

He stepped off his board as if off a magic carpet, bent to tuck it under his arm, and waded the remaining distance to where she stood.

"You make it look so easy," she said, waving and smiling.

"I've been surfing since I was twelve."

All man—hair slicked back from his face curling just below his ears, sea water dripping down his temples, broad shoulders and narrow hips—the last thing she could envision was Phil as a prepubescent boy.

"Second nature, huh?"

"Something like that. Hey, I know a great little stand that sells the best hot dogs in Santa Barbara. If you like chili dogs, I'll get out of this suit and we can walk over there."

She nodded as he pointed to the street and the amazingly lucky parking place he'd managed to snag. They walked in friendly conversation toward his car, a classic 1950s Woodie, the signature surfer wagon, complete with side wood paneling.

"Oh, my gosh, this is fantastic!" she said.

"My dad gave me this for my sixteenth birthday, when he realized surfing was my passion."

"It's gorgeous." *So are you.*

For the first time that day, Phil made an obvious head-to-toe assessment of Stephanie. She'd worn shorts, a tank top and zipped hoodie sweatshirt. "You're looking pretty damn great yourself."

A self-conscious thought about her pale legs, compared to his golden-bronze skin, made her wish she'd worn her tried-and-trusted jeans, but seeing the pleased look on his face as he stared at her changed her mind.

He unzipped his wet suit and peeled it off his arms

and down to his waist, revealing a flat stomach, cut torso, and defined chest. Just as Stephanie began to worry about what a guy wore under a wet suit, he tugged down the garment to reveal black trunks.

Oh, my. Seeing so much of Phil Hansen was making her mouth water.

He threw a pair of cargo shorts over the trunks, ducked his head into a T-shirt, and in record time slid into some well-worn leather flip-flops.

"You ready?" he said, shaking out his hair.

"Sure," she said, completely under his wet-and-wild spell.

"Oh, hey, wait," he said, closing and locking the hatch. "I forgot something." He took a step toward her, pulled her close, and kissed her.

His mouth was warm and soft as it covered her lips ever so gently. They were nearly strangers, and this wasn't how she did things, but she couldn't manage to tear herself away. Shock made her edgy…at first. The kiss, like a calming tide, swept over her head to toe, smoothing and relaxing her resistance. She wanted more and pressed into his welcoming lips.

When his hands went to her waist, she tensed again. Their heat started a mini-implosion over her hips, sending pleasant waves throughout her body. She wasn't ready to touch him back, except for right there on those inviting lips. She inhaled the scent of ocean on his skin, and breathed deeper, tasting sea salt as she flicked the smooth lining of his mouth with her tongue.

Their connection seemed to stop time. Her hands dangled at her sides, more out of concern about where it might lead if she touched his broad shoulders. Though she wanted to. She wanted to explore every part of Phil

Hansen, but they were in public on a busy street. This was no time or place for a first kiss of this magnitude.

Still, she didn't move, kept kissing him, savored the sweet, tender, first kiss. A basic, female reaction flowed through her core, warming everything in its path from the tips of her breasts down to the ends of her toes. She hadn't felt this kind of heady response since she'd first fallen in love with her husband.

Her ex-husband.

Okay, that put the hex on this kiss. Aside from the fact that Phil was a good kisser—restrained, not mauling; gentle, not immediately going for the touchdown—and aside from the fact that she liked how he felt—really liked how he kissed—the thought of her condemning and unforgiving ex ruined the moment.

She broke contact and pulled back. He studied her up close as if reading her mind. He wasn't rude or persistent. He knew they'd had their moment and now it was over, yet his probing stare let her know he understood something was up, and that he'd respect whatever the barrier was…for now.

What she saw in the depths of his eyes unsettled her. Besides everything his kiss had done, from heating her up inside to sending chills over her skin, she could read in his look that it was only a matter of time before they'd be doing this kissing business again.

The unspoken promise both thrilled and scared her.

CHAPTER FOUR

PHIL had promised a world-class hot dog and he hadn't let Stephanie down. They sat at a little metal table on the cement walk in front of a red-and-white striped awning on Cabrillo Boulevard. Still trying her best to recover from Phil's kiss, she concentrated on eating the dog slathered in heart-clogging chili topped with cheese, and not the imposingly appealing man across the table… staring at her.

"You said you started surfing at twelve?" she said.

She could handle lunch with Phil. If she repeated it enough times maybe she'd believe it. Tell that to her pulse, which quickened every time she noticed new things about him, like how his sideburns were perfectly matched and at least three shades darker than his hair, with a tinge of red. Just before she took her first bite of hot dog, she wondered what his beard stubble might feel like first thing in the morning, and almost missed her mouth.

"Yeah. I had a knack." He smiled at her and her heart stepped out of rhythm. He had a "knack" for world-class kisses, too. "I was spoiled and my parents let me do just about everything. By the time I was fourteen, I got recruited for the Corona Pro surf circuit, and the rest…" he delivered another one of his knockout smiles "…as they say, is history."

"Growing up in the desert, surfing wasn't exactly on my list of things to do. I'm more of a volleyball girl myself."

He raised one brow with interest. "Ever played beach volleyball?"

She shook her head and reached for her soda. "Looks too grueling with all that sand."

"They play beach volleyball every weekend right down the street." He pointed behind him with his thumb.

"Oh, yeah, I remember I saw the nets the day I drove into town."

"So what do you say? Want to check out the game tomorrow?"

"What about Robbie?"

He sat straighter. "I'll bring him along."

She gave him a hesitant glance; her throat tightened, making it hard to swallow the tastiest chili she'd ever eaten.

"You see right through me, don't you?" he said. "Truth is, I need some help keeping the kid entertained, and I've already run out of ideas."

"Well, don't look at me," she said, swallowing and taking another bite.

His playful gaze grew serious. "What's the deal? I mean, I've never seen…"

Should she tell him? By all accounts, he was still a stranger…who'd kissed her senseless. Did he deserve to know her deepest secret just because he was curious?

"The thing is …" Two years ago she'd had her tubes

tied to cement the point. "I don't do kids." No. Better to keep it vague. Keep the distance.

"But you deliver babies for a living," Phil said, arms crossed over his black T-shirt, brows furrowed, obviously confused.

"I deliver *other people's* babies." She took another bite of her hot dog and did her best to pretend there wasn't anything contradictory about the statement.

Phil finished his first hot dog, washed it down with cola and wiped his mouth. Stephanie intrigued him with this inconsistency—an OB doc who didn't do babies. And she was quickly becoming his dream date. When a woman didn't want kids, marriage didn't seem to be a priority. And since marriage was the last thing on his to-do list, maybe they could have a good time together, for however long this attraction lasted.

Beneath her defiant remark "I don't do babies" he noticed one telling sign—hurt. He could see it in her gaze. Those inviting butterscotch-with-flecks-of-gold eyes went dull at the mention of kids. Something had caused her great pain and the result made her avoid children. He flashed to the moment he'd walked into the clinic the first night, how he'd seen terror in her expression, how she hadn't been able to get away fast enough. He needed to play this cool, or she'd bolt again.

"No wonder you looked so uncomfortable when I left Robbie with you." He wiped mustard from the corner of his mouth.

She gave a wry laugh as a quick blush pinkened her cheeks. "Uncomfortable is a generous description."

"Yeah, okay, more like you freaked out."

She nodded. "Sorry."

"It's all right."

She made a half-hearted attempt at a smile, and his heart went out to her. He needed to lighten the mood. Maybe he could tease her into submission.

"So there's no chance I can change your mind?" He put his hand on top of hers, immediately aware of how fragile she felt.

"Maybe some other time."

"Translation being—get lost, Phil?"

"Not at all." She met his gaze, sending a subtle message, then quickly looked away.

So maybe she was interested in him, just not the whole Phil-and-Robbie package. Once he sent Robbie back to his stepmom and dad, he'd have time to enjoy her company up close and, hopefully, very personal. Especially after that kiss confirmed what he'd suspected since the first day he'd seen her—they had chemistry. And knowing she didn't want to get involved with anyone any more than he did sounded like the perfect setup.

"Okay. I get it. But when my parents get back from Hawaii, and Robbie goes home, I'd like to make an official date with you."

He hadn't removed his hand, and hers turned beneath his. Now palm to palm, a stimulating image formed in his mind. He wished he could take her home and ravish her right on the spot, but she was skittish and he needed to take things slowly.

"Fine." She flicked her lashes and glanced quickly into his eyes, then slid her hand away.

Still high from their kiss, new desire stirred in him. From the jolt he felt, she could have been throwing lightning bolts instead of batting her lashes. They definitely had chemistry.

"Fine?" he said. "Well, then, let's make that date right now, so I'll have something to look forward to."

On Saturday night, Phil watched Robbie sleep. The little guy flipped and flopped and in between he coughed. His eyes popped open for the briefest of moments, fluttered, then clamped shut as if trying desperately to stay asleep, but the constant irritation of that cough gave him a good battle. The restless spectacle put a hard lump smack in the middle of Phil's throat.

Robbie's world would become difficult enough as he got older and realized that other kids looked at him differently, and maybe they wouldn't play with him because of him having Down syndrome.

"Sweet kid," he mumbled against an alien yet firm tugging in his chest. What was happening to him?

He adjusted the covers for the umpteenth time beneath his little brother's chin before taking a stroll to the kitchen for a glass of water. It had taken a few days, but they were starting to get into a routine at night. Robbie had filled him in on the rule about reading a picture book before bed. Phil had complied. Heck, he even enjoyed some of them. After a couple of nights, Phil was even able to sneak back to his own bed.

Robbie drifted in a sweet oblivious tide of ignorance and bliss hanging out with other toddlers. How much longer would it last? And as long as it did last, Phil wanted nothing more than for him to be well rested and on his best play-pal game at preschool.

When Robbie didn't sleep, Phil didn't either. How in hell had Roma and his dad managed the last four years?

And when Phil couldn't sleep, his mind drifted to

Stephanie—the last person he needed to think about if he had any hope of getting rest. Maybe he'd taken advantage of the situation by kissing her at the beach, even though she'd done her share of participation with that kiss. It had been a whim. She'd looked so damn sweet and vulnerable, completely different from work. Well, he'd wanted to kiss her, and he had. And he was glad.

He hadn't given a no-strings-attached kiss like that since high school. Stephanie's wounded and fragile air made him extra-cautious. It also drew him to her. Ironically, he only had two months, but he vowed to take things slowly, to give her plenty of leeway. Even if it killed him.

He scratched his chest and paced back and forth across the kitchen. Stephanie was sleek, not flashy; intelligent, but not street-smart. Her hair changed colors in the sun from brown with a hint of red to full-out copper. Her eyes often looked like honey. And she was sweet, in a withdrawn sort of way.

He scraped his jaw. Did any of the description make sense? All he knew for sure was a deep gut reaction happened each and every time he saw her. That was not normal. For him.

What he'd give for a little affectionate nuzzling with her right about now, especially if it quickly evolved into hot and panting sex. But he was going to take it slow. *Remember?* He sloshed back a quick gulp of cold water.

Robbie coughed again.

Phil had already ruled out enlarged adenoids on the kid. He'd played the old airplane spoon of ice cream flying straight for Robbie's mouth, but only if his brother promised to open wide. He'd flashed his penlight across the back of his throat, in the guise of making sure the runway was clear, and all had looked normal in the tonsil and adenoid department, even though Phil must have looked a fool in order to find out. To be honest, it was kind of fun. He was getting a taste of parenting, and realized some of it wasn't so bad.

More muffled coughing drew him back to the guest room. Robbie's butt was up in the air and his thumb had found its way back to his mouth. Some picture. The nasal cannula delivering a small amount of oxygen he'd tried as an experiment had been removed, giving the boy's forehead the concentrated air instead of Robbie's lungs. Phil smiled and shook his head. The stinker really was something. He thought about taking a picture, but he didn't want to risk waking Robbie up so instead he closed the door all but four inches. Besides, taking a picture would be acting like Jon, and he definitely didn't want to go down that path.

Robbie coughed again. Phil ran his hand through his hair, frustrated. He needed to do a bronchoscopy on him, document his condition, and get him started on either CPAP or negative pressure ventilation. Right now the bigger question was, when in his busy clinic schedule would he have time to do one?

An idea popped into his mind and wouldn't let go. Weren't people supposed to face their demons in order to move on? Maybe one small step at a time. Yeah, that might work. If things went as planned, he'd have a co-erced but hopefully willing helper on Tuesday evening. How bad could a sedated kid be to be around?

Maybe he'd finally have proof his brother had

tracheobronchomalacia. And if he played his cards right, he'd finagle some extra time with the lovely doctor from the desert.

On Tuesday afternoon, Stephanie sat in her office with a mug of coffee. Staring out the window through the gorgeous lace curtains to the bright blue sky, she contemplated her schedule for the next week—except her mind kept drifting to a certain moment at the beach on Saturday. Okay, so she was out of practice, but was she such a bad kisser that she'd completely turned Phil off?

She'd only caught glimpses of him at the clinic since then, and even though she shouldn't care what he thought about her or her kissing, it made her feel as insecure as if she were still in high school. As if she'd made a mistake by letting him kiss her. But she'd wanted him to.

She took another sip of coffee, loathing the teenaged insecurity, just as Phil appeared at her door, bringing with him a sudden tingle-fest.

"Got any plans for tonight?" he asked.

Why did her mood brighten instantaneously? She had no intention of telling him she'd planned on a little shopping at the Paseo before she took in a movie, alone.

"A few. Nothing major," she said, playing it coy.

One look at his great smile and she wanted to get angry for his turning her world sideways. She wanted to hate him for being so damn charming! But all she could muster was a mental, *Wow, I'd forgotten how gorgeous you are*.

"Would you consider doing me a huge favor?" he asked.

She had nothing better planned, so why not? "Depends." Heck, he'd been the one avoiding her. Why make it easy?

He scratched his chin. "As in what's in it for me, depends?"

"It depends on what you want me to do."

"How about I start by telling you how I'll repay you?" A single dimple appeared.

Oh, he thought he was a smooth operator, but she wasn't that easy. No way. "I don't do bribes, Hansen. No babies, no bribes. Sorry."

He nodded, the second dimple making itself annoyingly visible. "Okay, I'll come clean."

He moved closer and sat on the edge of her desk. She immediately picked up the scent of his crisp and expensive cologne. An impeccable dresser, his pinstriped shirt and flashy patterned tie was the perfect complement to the dark gray slacks. And, *sheesh*, without even trying, his hair looked great, waving in all the right places, with an unintentional clump falling across his brow.

"It does involve a kid," he said. "My kid brother, to be exact." He raised a finger before she could protest. "But here's the deal. I need to scope his lungs and I need to do it tonight, and I need some extra hands and credentials to make it legal. You in?"

She stared at him.

"It's not like you'd be babysitting. Think of it as a technical procedure, and I need your help. That's all."

"That tracheobronchomalacia business?"

He nodded. "I want to get it documented and refer him for CPAP immediately."

"What about your dad and stepmom?"

"I finally got their verbal consent over the phone, and while Robbie's with me, I have medical consent."

"I know nothing about pediatric conscious sedation," she said.

"I'll take care of everything. I just need you to monitor Robbie and inject the drugs while I scope him. I'll recover him and you can leave as soon as I'm through."

She considered his request, but made the stupid mistake of glancing into his eyes, which watched and waited and reminded her of the ocean last Saturday at high noon. He ramped up the pressure by tilting his head and giving a puppy-dog can-we-take-a-walk expression. If Phil handled everything, and all she had to do was administer drugs and do the technical monitoring, maybe she could help him out.

"What time?"

"I've got to pick him up from day care in ten minutes. Mmm, how about in half an hour?"

That didn't give her much time to think it over, or change her mind. She pulled out her drawer and, having learned from her snack expedition the other night with Robbie, found a pack of peanut butter with cheese crackers, tore it open with her teeth, and tossed the first one into her mouth.

"You're on," she said, sounding muffled.

As naturally as old friends, he kissed her cheek. "You're the best," he said, and took off, leaving her chomping on her snack, blowing cracker flakes from her mouth when she sighed. And there was that damn feeling he brought along with him every time they talked—flustered.

The new and state-of-the-art procedure suite at Midcoast Medical provided the perfect setting for Robbie's examination. Jason had had the equipment installed after a successful second-quarter report. Every penny they made beyond salaries went right back into their clinic with upgrades and added services. Phil no longer had to rent space at the local hospital to perform his bronchoscopies, taking him away from the clinic, and making his nurse able to increase her hours to full-time as a result.

But this examination was after hours, and he'd lined up a great replacement for his regular nurse—Stephanie.

She hadn't bargained on Robbie being awake when she arrived, and Phil had to do some quick talking to make her stick around.

"I can't do this on my own, Stephanie. Please. Five minutes. It will only take five minutes. I promise."

She looked pale and hesitated at the procedure-room door, but something, maybe it was Robbie looking so vulnerable and unsuspecting, made her change her mind.

Robbie fought like the devil when Phil tried to insert an intravenous line, and he thought she'd bolt right then and there. Surprisingly, she held the boy's arm steady, and with her help they got the IV in and the keep-open solution running. She'd been an unexpected decoy with her medley of wacky kids' songs. Robbie even giggled a few times. If she didn't do kids, how did she know all those children's songs?

Gowned, gloved and masked, Phil watched Stephanie draw up the quick-acting, deeply sedating medication. He knew there was a fine line between true anesthesia and conscious sedation, and though he wanted to make Robbie comfortable, he didn't want him too sedated, just out of it long enough to get a minitour inside his lungs. After she had set up Robbie with pulse oximetry, heart and blood-pressure monitor, and supplemental oxygen, he directed her to give the standard pediatric dose for fentanyl and benzodiapine instead of a newer, short-acting drug.

"No offense, but I only use Propofol when I have an anesthesiologist working with me." He smiled at her through his mask.

She tossed him a sassy look. "Believe me, no offense taken, I already feel out of my element here." With skilled and efficient hands she titrated the drugs into the IV as he applied the topical numbing spray to Robbie's throat, and within seconds Robbie drifted into twilight sleep.

"I called ahead to the preschool to hold his lunch, but Robbie loves to eat so much he almost snuck a snack around three today. Fortunately, they caught him, so we shouldn't have a problem with emesis." He flipped on the suction machine, using his elbow to protect his sterile gloves. This would be his backup contingency plan in case Robbie did vomit.

"I'm going to use a pediatric laryngeal mask airway instead of an endotracheal tube." He showed her the small spoon-shaped device. "As Robbie has the typical shortened Down syndrome neck, an endotracheal tube would have been tricky anyway," he said as he lubricated the tablespoon-size silicone mask and slipped the tube inside Robbie's slack mouth. The boy didn't flinch. "See? I don't even need a laryngoscope with this gizmo."

Once the LMA was in place, Phil immediately reached for his bronchoscope and slipped the flexible tube down Robbie's trachea for a quick look-see.

"See that?" he said to Stephanie, who took turns intently watching the procedure on the digital TV screen, keeping track of the heart and BP monitor readings, and watching Robbie in the flesh. Sure enough, due to softened cartilage, his trachea showed signs of floppiness and collapsed while he breathed under the sedation. The same thing happened while he slept each night. "This is classic TBM." Keeping things short and sweet, and already having digitally recorded his findings, Phil removed the scope and quickly followed suit with the laryngeal mask airway. Even though sedated, Robbie coughed and sputtered. "All the kid needs is continuous positive airway pressure while he sleeps, so he won't have to cough every time his trachea collapses."

"That's great news," Stephanie said, watching Robbie like an anxious mother hen.

True to the short-life drug effect, Robbie started to come out of his stupor. "There you go, buddy, we're all done," Phil said. He bent over and looked into his blinking eyes. "Are you in there somewhere?"

The bleary-eyed Robbie tried to look in the vicinity of his voice. Phil set the scope on the counter and prepared to wipe it clean before putting it in the sterilization solution overnight.

"Can you watch him a few minutes while I clean up?" he asked.

She nodded, undoing her mask and letting it hang around her neck, though keeping a safe distance from Robbie.

As with many recently sedated children, Robbie woke up confused, fussing and crying. Phil worked as quickly as he could. "You're okay, Rob. I'm right here, buddy," he said. The boy seemed to calm down immediately.

Phil smiled, assuming the sound of his voice had done the trick, but when he glanced over his shoulder, he saw a sight that made him smile even wider.

The I-don't-do-kids doctor was holding Robbie's hand and patting it.

"You at all interested in getting takeout and keeping me company tonight while I help my kid brother recover from major surgery?" He'd lay it on thick, and hope for the best.

She remained quiet for a few seconds, then let go of Robbie's hand.

"I can't, Phil. I'm sorry."

On Wednesday morning, Stephanie hung up the phone after a long conversation with her mother. She'd used the excuse of being on call—which wasn't completely untrue—for not showing for Thanksgiving. If things followed the usual routine, her sister would be on the phone within the next ten minutes, and Mary was ruthless when it came to arm-twisting. All the more reason to get started with her appointments.

Phil had surprised her last night with both his technical skill and tender banter with his brother. The more she got to know him, the more she suspected his playboy reputation was just a cover. Helping out with Robbie's exam hadn't been nearly as bad as she'd thought it would be, another surprise. Maybe she was getting used to him. She'd watched the boy sleep, and yearning had clutched her heart. If only her son could be alive.

She closed her eyes and bit her lip. Someone tapped on the door.

"Your next patient is ready."

Thank heavens for work.

By midmorning, Amy delivered the latest batch of lab reports and special tests.

Stephanie shuffled through the stack with an eye out for two in particular. The first was great news—it was just an ovarian cyst for Ms. Winkler. The next report wasn't nearly as welcome. Celeste Conroy's Pap smear showed abnormal cells. She picked up the phone.

After she'd calmed the woman down, she suggested her plan. "I'd like to perform a colposcopy, which is a fancy way of looking at your cervix up close with a bright light and magnifying glass."

The proactive next step went over better than the bombshell dysplasia news.

"And while I'm examining your cervix, I'll take a tiny biopsy of that questionable area. This will give us a better idea of exactly what we're dealing with."

After a brief silence, several questions flew from the young pregnant woman's mouth. Stephanie answered each as she was able.

"The exam is not threatening to your pregnancy, though after I do the biopsy, there may be some mild cramping and light bleeding. We'd have to monitor you carefully to make sure the bleeding was from the biopsy and not from the pregnancy, but the risk is extremely low that your baby will be in jeopardy."

After a few more minutes of convincing the patient to arrange an appointment on Friday, the day after Thanksgiving, she hung up.

And now she had a good reason to stay in Santa Barbara for Thanksgiving. She needed to be well rested and in top form on Friday. Mary could twist her arm all she wanted, but she wouldn't give in to Thanksgiving dinner in the desert.

Her next call was pure pleasure. "Ms. Winkler? This is Dr. Bennett from Midcoast Medical. I've got your ultrasound results back, and you can rest assured that your enlarged ovary is nothing more than a pesky cyst."

She smiled when her patient sang out a loud "Hallelujah!"

By lunchtime it occurred to Stephanie that she hadn't seen Phil in the clinic all morning. She nibbled at her microwaved plate of food, and half-heartedly chatted with a couple of coworkers. It also occurred to her that Thanksgiving was going to be one lonely day. She'd hole up in her hotel room and watch a stack of old DVDs and pretend it was just another day. Maybe she'd eat an open-faced turkey sandwich with dressing and gravy, with a side of cranberries from the deli around the corner, too. Oh, and she'd watch the famous New York Thanksgiving Day parade on TV, she mused with a jumble of faraway thoughts.

"I bet you're wondering where I've been," Phil said, standing beside her.

"What makes you think I've even noticed?" she said, glancing over her shoulder, going along with his playful tone.

"*We* noticed you weren't around," one of the two nurses sharing the community lounge table chimed in. As far as Stephanie could tell, Phil had all the ladies in the clinic wrapped around his finger.

His quirked brow and goofy expression of "see what I'm saying?" made her laugh. It felt good.

"Thank you, Tamara and Stacy," he said. "I'm glad someone noticed."

He sat next to Stephanie, edging out Jon's nurse, though there was plenty of room on the other side of the table, then unpacked a couple of shrimp tacos from his brown bag. "You know, that's what I like about you. You're not under my spell."

She almost spat out her soda. "You have a spell?" She was walking on thin ice because she knew without a doubt he did have a special something that very well could be called a spell, and that she was most likely already under it…especially since their kiss.

"So I've been told."

"He's got a spell," the nurses said together.

She laughed and shook her head. "Well, I don't know about a spell, but I do know you've got a jelly stain on your shirt."

He pulled in his chin and glanced downward. "Oh, that. It's probably from when I made Robbie's sandwich this morning."

With each day, and all the little details she noticed about him, Phil became more irresistible.

Not that she was interested or anything. "So where were you?"

"Where else? The preschool. Seems like it's my second home. How does Roma do it?"

"Don't let this go to your head, Phil, but I think you're doing a pretty good job of pinch-hitting for your parents."

"They're due back tonight, and I'm counting the hours."

The nurses finished their lunch, and announced they were just about to take a walk before the afternoon clinic opened when René Munroe appeared, complete with swaddled baby in her arms and Jon at her side.

"Hi, Dr. Munroe!" one of the nurses said, rushing

over to look at the newborn. "Oh, he's adorable. May I hold him?"

"Sure," the dark-haired René said, glowing with new-mom pride.

Phil popped up and took a peek under the blanket. "Hey, he looks just like those pictures."

René rolled her eyes. "Oh, gosh, has Jon been boring everyone with pictures?"

Phil nodded, but the nurses quickly protested, "No! We love baby pictures."

"Oh, hey, René, this is Stephanie Bennett, the doc we hired to cover your patients," Jon said, looking a bit abashed and obviously wanting to change the subject.

They greeted each other and Stephanie already felt as though she knew René from working in her office. While Jon passed the baby around, Stephanie discussed Celeste Conroy's abnormal Pap smear with René and her plans for following up. When René agreed with the next step, Stephanie felt much more confident.

"Would you like me to call and reassure her that I'm in total agreement?" René said.

"That would be wonderful."

"Okay, last chance to hold Evan before I take René out to lunch," Jon said, having taken back his son but seeming ready to share him with anyone who wanted. "Stephanie?"

He offered the teddy-bear-patterned bundle of blanket to her and she froze. Oh, no, what should she do? Would it be completely awkward to refuse? Her pulse sputtered in her chest, and her ears rang. She liked these people and didn't want to insult them.

"Okay," she said, feigning a smile. She held Evan with stiff arms, away from her chest. "Aren't you something?" Memories of her son gurgling and cooing hit so fast and hard she found it impossible to breathe. She blinked back the images as her heart stumbled, and she handed the baby back to René, trying her best to disguise her quivery voice. "You must be so proud."

The huge, beaming smile on René's face gave the answer. She cuddled the baby to her heart and kissed his cheek. "I wuv this wittle guy."

Jon laughed and scratched his nose. "Anyone know a cure for a highly educated woman who suddenly starts talking baby talk?"

The nurses giggled. "It's a requirement of motherhood, Doc," one of them said.

Flushed and edgy, Stephanie willed her hands to stop shaking. She'd looked into those beautiful baby gray eyes and had seen Justin. She'd glanced up to find Phil intently watching her as her lungs clutched at each breath.

Somehow she made it through the goodbyes, but as soon as the couple left she headed for the back door and the tranquil promise of the yard. She needed to breathe, to get hold of herself.

She was staring at the small bubbling fountain and listening to chattering birds in the tree when a hand grasped her arm. It was Phil. He'd picked up on what had just happened. Hell, she'd been so obvious, anyone would have noticed her fumbling attempt at acting normal…if they hadn't been so distracted with the baby.

"I was wondering what you're doing tomorrow," he said.

She welcomed the change in subject, even if it was another sticky topic. How should she best phrase the fact she had no plans for Thanksgiving and not come off as pitiful? Sure, she could go to Palm Desert, but it wasn't going to happen.

She swallowed and said, "I'm having a quiet day."

He glanced thoughtfully at her. "My stepmother is a fantastic cook, and she promised me a Thanksgiving dinner to die for as I've been taking care of Robbie and all, and I thought you might like to be my plus one."

"Plus one?"

"My guest. What do you say? Great food. Even better company. You'll like my dad." He tilted his head, and his crescent-shaped eyes looked very inviting. "Robbie will be so happy to see them that he'll leave you alone. I promise." Phil was the distraction she needed—a guy completely unaware of her past, who didn't ask questions, and with one not-so-subtle thing on his mind.

Did she really need to think about it? Hotel room. DVDs. Deli sandwich. Or plus one.

"You know what? I'd really like that."

The full-out smile he delivered assured her she'd not only made the right decision but she'd also made his afternoon. When in the past three years had she been able to make that claim about a man? And it felt pretty darn good.

He looked as if he wanted to kiss her again, and maybe that's exactly what she needed right now, a kiss to make her forget, but his beeper went off and after a quick glance, a forlorn look replaced the charm. He sighed. "It's the preschool, again."

Late that afternoon, Phil appeared at Stephanie's office door, looking agitated.

"What's up?" she asked.

"The damn weather."

She glanced out her window at another perfectly clear blue autumn sky then back at Phil. "Looks pretty good to me."

"I'm talking about Maui. They're having a terrible storm and the return flight has been canceled until Friday. Looks like Thanksgiving dinner is off."

She couldn't deny the disappointment. Ever since he'd invited her, she'd felt a buzz of expectation, a curiosity about his family, and mouthwatering anticipation of great food. Now a storm on a tropical island had changed everything. "How disappointing…for them. I'm sure they're eager to get home to Robbie and all."

He snapped his fingers. "I've got an idea. Come to my house and I'll order a turkey dinner." His eyes lit up. "It'll be fun, and you can help me warm things up. What do you say?

She'd swung from one end of the emotional pendulum to the opposite over this Thanksgiving, and here was yet a new twist. Hotel. DVDs. Deli sandwich. Or spend an afternoon with a gorgeous guy…and Robbie?

It all came down to one desire. Did she want to have a life again? Or go on living in a vacuum. Hotel. DVDs. Deli sandwich…or…

There really wasn't a decision to make. "What time?"

CHAPTER FIVE

ON THANKSGIVING morning, Stephanie put extra effort into getting dressed. She wanted to look good, but not overdo it. She opted for casual with jeans and boots, a pumpkin-colored top with a flashy hip belt, and a multi-fall-colored knit scarf to ward off the cooler weather.

She'd stopped last night at the bakery she'd recently discovered and got one of the last two pumpkin pies baked that afternoon, the kind of whipped cream you sprayed from a can, and a bottle of deep red wine to go with the turkey. She had no intention of impressing Phil with her culinary skills. Heck, she was living in a hotel, how could she? And wasn't he the one who'd invited her to dinner?

She arrived at his house just before noon, impressed with the rolling brown hills and secluded homes scattered across them. The sprawling country farmhouse was the last type of home she'd expect to see Phil living in. In the distance, and far behind her, the ocean sparkled as if the bold sun had scattered glitter over it. She took a deep breath of fresh air, savoring the special view, suddenly aware that her insides were letting go of that usual tight knot.

Santa Barbara had a completely different kind of

beauty from the tall purple mountains that encased her desert home, and the flat breadth between them. Both were special, but the ocean added that extra touch with which, in her opinion, no amount of saguaro cactus or Joshua trees could compete.

With an odd sense of contentment folding in around her, she tapped lightly on his door before ringing the bell. After a short time the door swung open, with Phil grinning and with Robbie riding piggyback.

"Hey," he said, a little breathless. "Come in."

The spacious living room, with a stone fireplace and wall-long French doors and windows, was bright and open. The light-colored hardwood floors were offset by high, dark beamed and arched ceilings. The family room opened into a modern kitchen complete with cooking island and expensive-looking Italian tile floors.

Toys were everywhere. Pillows and books were scattered around the family room, and furniture was obviously askew.

Phil looked happy, and for a confirmed bachelor he was doing a fine job at playing stand-in father. "We were just horsing around, weren't we, shorty?"

Robbie giggled and nodded, and once Phil released him, he ran off toward a beach ball, blissfully unaware of Stephanie invading his territory.

Maybe she was getting used to being around Robbie, because he hadn't set off any internal alarms today. Or maybe she was distracted by the attractive guy right in front of her. He wore jeans and a white tailored Western-styled shirt with the collar open, revealing a hint of light brown chest hair. And he kept smiling at her, his white straight teeth like something out of a magazine ad.

"You look great," he said. "As always."

The compliment stopped her. At the end of her marriage her husband had thought she was despicable. Couldn't stand to look at her and hadn't minded telling her so. Knowing that, on top of every horrible thought she'd already had about herself, had almost made her lose the will to live. She shook her head, refusing to go there again. She wanted to move forward and she couldn't very well do that by constantly looking over her shoulder, remembering the bad times.

Phil had just told her she looked great. Did he tell all his dates that? "Thank you." She felt her cheeks heat up.

"I mean it." He pinned her with a no-nonsense gaze.

"I believe you." Did she? Did she have the nerve to tell him how fantastic he looked, too?

"Good."

The antsy feeling made her need to change the subject. "This house is amazing," she said.

"Thanks. I've only been here a couple of years, but I like to call it home."

"Oh, here's the pie and some other stuff," she said.

He took her few items into the kitchen, reading the wine label on the way. Instead of sitting, she followed him, sliding her hand over the cool granite countertops and marveling at the state-of-the-art stainless-steel appliances. This was the kind of home a person dreamed about but never intended to actually live in. And what was a bachelor like Phil doing here?

"This seems so unlike you," she said.

"Tell that to my Realtor. I spent a year looking for it. This is the place I intend to stay in."

"A guy like you?"

"Hey, give me a break. I may not be interested in settling down, but a house, well, I have no qualms about where I want to live for the rest of my life."

"We really don't know a thing about each other, do we?" she said, smiling.

His eyes brightened to daylight blue. "Here's something else to surprise you." He washed his hands and opened a cupboard. "I'm cooking today."

The undeniable aroma of turkey hit her nostrils. "I thought you were ordering in?"

"I got to thinking, how hard could cooking a turkey be? My butcher gave me instructions, and they didn't sound difficult."

How many more surprises did he have up his sleeve? "Well, it smells great."

"Hey, you're gonna love the dressing. I made Roma fax the recipe to me last night."

She laughed. For the first time in ages, she felt excited about Thanksgiving.

He washed a few vegetables in the sink. "What would you like to drink?"

"Water is fine." Heaven forbid she should have a glass of wine, relax, and let her guard down.

He delivered her a glass as she sat on one of the stools by the island. "You've got to admit this beats eating in your hotel room, right?"

She gazed across the comfortable and stylish home and nodded. "You win. Hands down, this beats my hotel. I feel like I'm in a *House Beautiful* commercial."

He smiled, obviously liking her description of his home.

"These are from my garden." He held up a handful of new carrots, and medium-size tomatoes.

"You're kidding me," she said. "You garden, too?"

"What can I say? I like being in the sun. I like digging in the dirt and pulling weeds. Don't tell anyone at work, they'd never let me live it down."

"Your secret's safe with me," she said, taking a sip of water and fighting off an ever-growing crush on her surprising host.

"How are you at mashing potatoes?" he asked, just as something hit the back of her butt with a plunk. She jerked around, it was the beach ball, and Robbie had a guilty expression on his face.

"Hey, remember what I said about throwing that thing around in here," Phil chided Robbie.

"Outside, Pill," the boy said. "Go. Peez?"

"I'm busy right now."

"Now!" Robbie said, throwing the ball at Stephanie and hitting her stomach this time.

"Okay, mister, you're in big trouble." Phil headed for Robbie, who didn't take him seriously in the least. The boy must have thought they were playing catch-me-if-you-can, as he ran off on short, squat legs, no chance of escaping Phil's reach.

Phil grabbed him by the collar then held him over his hip. Robbie kicked and griped. Phil glanced at Stephanie, his embarrassment obvious. "Sometimes I just can't control this kid."

"Tell you what," she said, trying not to smile as Robbie continued to squeal with delight. She had half an urge to toss the ball back to him, even though it was against the rules, but Phil was setting limits and she didn't want to confuse the boy. "I'll peel the potatoes while you two work off some extra energy."

"Sounds like a plan." He nodded with a grateful

glance. "Okay, buster, you're gonna get what for," he said with mock seriousness.

"No!" Robbie said. "*You're* gonna get what for!"

Stephanie couldn't help but smile. She watched momentarily as they headed outside, an odd sensation taking hold. Ignoring the nudge toward a change of heart, she headed for the kitchen.

Phil's house was laid out so that the kitchen flowed directly into the family room, and the family room opened to a patio, and beyond that the huge expanse of verdant yard was accented by flowering hibiscus in white and red and assorted leafy bushes. From the large ranch-style kitchen windows she could see their wild game of catch or dodge-the-beach-ball or whatever their version of "what for" was called. Seemed as if all Phil's griping about being stuck with his kid brother for ten days was nothing more than a cover. And Robbie was having the time of his life, laughing, throwing, and running all over the place. Looked like kid's heaven to her. And Phil played the role of a benevolent uncle wanting nothing more than to make the kid happy.

Happy.

That was a word that had slipped from her vocabulary these past three years. As she peeled the potatoes, sliced and dropped them into a bowl of cold water, she pondered how inviting the old and nearly forgotten feeling was. Her lips stretched into a broad smile that reached like a warm glove into her chest and squeezed her heart. Welcome back to the living. Happy felt great.

It hit her before the next breath. She'd admitted being happy and she was in the company of a little boy. Wow. Maybe things were finally breaking through that guilt logjam.

Robbie was a sweet kid. Justin was a memory she'd always hold deep in her heart and never forget, but Robbie wasn't Justin. She wasn't Robbie's mother. She wasn't responsible for him. Why be afraid of him? Did she want to spend the rest of her life cowering around *all* children, or was it finally time to face her fear?

She wiped her hands on the dish towel and walked toward the French doors. As she opened them and walked onto the patio, she swallowed and took a steadying breath. "Um…" Her gaze darted around the yard as she picked at her nails.

Phil quit jogging and gave her an odd look. "Is everything okay?"

Her hand flew to her hair. "Yeah. Um…I was just wondering…"

He took a few steps toward her, a concerned expression clouding his good looks. At the moment, passing the medical boards seemed easier than what she wanted to say. Another deep breath.

"Do you have room for one more in that game?"

By the time the potatoes had boiled, Phil had followed Stephanie back to the kitchen. Robbie looked sufficiently pooped out and sat in front of a children's DVD in his little corner of the family room. On a separate large-screen TV the annual Thanksgiving Texas football game was going on.

"I'd better put the yams in the oven," Phil said. "I got this dish from my caterer."

She glanced over her shoulder at the gorgeous-looking casserole complete with pecans on top. Phil opened a top oven, slid the dish inside then checked on the turkey in the lower oven, basting it as if he'd done this before.

"You're making my mouth water," she said, savoring the smell. She'd worked up quite an appetite running around with Robbie and Phil. And it hadn't wiped her out emotionally either. If anything, it had invigorated her.

"It'll be done in another half hour. In the meantime, I'm having a beer. Can I get you anything?"

Could she even remember the last time she'd had a glass of wine? "I'll try that wine I brought."

"You're on."

By the time they'd set the table, made the gravy, and laid out all the food, the few sips of wine she'd managed to find time to take had already gone to her head. The pleasant buzz filtered throughout her body, heating her insides and causing her to smile. A lot. How could a few sips of wine make her feel that giddy? Maybe this great feeling had a lot more to do with Phil, Robbie, and Thanksgiving than the liquid spirits. She took another sip, loving the way the simply laid-out table looked, and before he signaled for her to sit, she grabbed her purse.

"Wait," she said. "I want to take a picture of this. It's so beautiful." She dug out her cell phone and snapped first a picture of the turkey in the center of the table, then had Robbie and Phil pose for one, heads close to the bird. Then she snapped one of herself at arm's length with the two of them beside her and the turkey in the background. In her opinion, all three were keepers, even if the third one, taken at such close range, looked as if they all had oversize noses and heads.

Things had been so busy all afternoon she hadn't

allowed herself to examine Phil's proximity to her until now as they studied her photographs. She felt his warmth and it called to her. Reacting before thinking, she turned and reached for him, gave him a hug, and kissed his cheek.

"Thank you so much for inviting me," she said, a little bit of her heart going out of her. Though frightening at first, his welcoming reception gave her courage not to pull back inside. Maybe Phil was someone she could let her hair down around.

"I'm really glad you're here," he said with a sincere glint in his eyes, as if on the verge of kissing her.

"Pill! Eat!"

He rolled his eyes. "Can you imagine how hard it would have been to keep him entertained all afternoon by myself?"

She laughed. He'd given her a compliment then quickly yanked it back.

"Eat now!" Robbie chanted.

"Right," he said. "First order of business."

Once everyone was seated at the table, and their plates were filled, Phil surprised her even more. "Robbie? Will you say grace for us?" He looked at her and winked. "I got a note from preschool saying they've been practicing."

The boy's big brown eyes grew serious. He licked his lips a couple of times, obviously considering what to say, then he clamped his lids together. "Thank you for da peshell food. For my fambly. For Pill. And for Theff-oh-nee."

With her head bowed, big fat tears brimmed as Stephanie blinked and whispered, "Amen."

* * *

Thanksgiving dinner had gone better than Phil could possibly have dreamed. After they'd worn him out playing ball, Robbie was on his best behavior. And Phil had almost fallen over when Stephanie had asked if she could join in. She'd chased Robbie around the yard as if she were a kid again, as if it didn't bother her anymore to be around him. After the panic he'd caused her that first night, this was an amazing improvement.

Dinner was exceptional, if he did say so himself. Not one thing got burned, except for the crescent rolls, and that was only a little on the bottoms. They were still edible, especially if you loaded them up with sweetened cranberry sauce straight from the caterer.

Stephanie was more animated than he'd ever seen her. It brightened those gorgeous eyes and made her prettier than he'd previously thought, dazzling him with her easy charm. Too bad his eyelids were at half-mast and his stomach so full that he didn't have the energy to get up and walk across the room to plant a kiss on her. If he didn't move in the next few seconds he'd fall asleep. Some impression that would make.

"You sit, and I'll clean up," she said. "It's the least I can do."

He thought about protesting, but the couch felt great and it was the third quarter in the game and Dallas was only ahead by a field goal. Robbie crawled up and snuggled beside him. That did it. "Thanks!"

By the time Stephanie had finished the dishes, Phil and Robbie had fallen asleep. The sight of the two of them on the couch sent a chill through her heart. A memory flashed of her holding her baby, exhausted, eyelids heavy, the couch inviting her to settle down and rest, just for a moment…

Didn't Phil know how dangerous that was? A pop of adrenaline drove her to rush to the sofa. She delicately lifted Robbie so as not to wake him or disturb Phil. She couldn't very well hold him as if he had a dirty diaper and expect him to stay asleep, so she brought him to her chest. On automatic pilot, Robbie wrapped his legs around her waist, and hung his arms over her shoulders. She anchored him beneath his bottom and across his back, and he nuzzled his head against her neck. A rush of motherly feelings made her feel dizzy. He was so much heavier and bigger than Justin, her four-month-old baby.

She hugged Robbie tight and, determined not to succumb to her woozy feeling, walked carefully down the hall to his room. She could do this. It was time to prove she could.

As she prepared him for his nap, his sublime expression sent her thoughts to Justin. He'd always looked like an angel when he'd slept. *Sweetheart, Mommy will always love you. Please forgive me.*

She bit her lip and fought the pinpricks behind her lids as she wondered how different her life would have been if she'd put her baby to bed that night. Today, through Robbie, she'd pretend she had…

At some point Phil had drifted off to sleep, and the next thing he remembered was a cool hand on his cheek. Her hand. The faint feel of her fingers reminded him of butterfly wings, delicate and beautiful, and easily harmed. Strangely, it made him want to look out for her in the same odd way he wanted to protect Robbie.

He must have stretched out on the couch because she sat on the edge, facing him.

"Are you ready for dessert?" she asked, sending a thought through his brain completely different from what she'd probably intended. "I've made some coffee."

Ah, that dessert.

Through his bleary eyes, her familiar butterscotch-and-cream features came into focus. Without thinking, he took her hand and kissed her slender fingers. "I'd love some," he said, thinking more about what he'd really like right then.

Heat radiated from his gaze, and half of her mouth hitched into a knowing smile as she edged away. "Don't move. I'll bring it to you."

As he woke up a little more, he got suddenly curious. "Where's Robbie?" He sat bolt upright, a sudden knot of concern lodged in his chest.

"He fell asleep, too. I hope you don't mind, but I put him to bed."

"You put him to bed? How long have I been out?"

"An hour, give or take a few minutes."

He scrubbed his face. "Man, some host I am."

"You've been a perfect host," she said, on her way to the kitchen, practically skipping. This was a side of Stephanie he'd never seen, and definitely liked. She'd come outside and played with him and Robbie, though it had felt like pulling teeth to get her to ask. She'd shared Thanksgiving with them, as if they were a small and happy family—this from the woman who hadn't been able to go near them in the Japanese restaurant. And now she'd put Robbie to bed.

While she was busy preparing coffee and dessert in the kitchen, he wandered down the hall to Robbie's room. The door had been left a few inches open, like

Roma had instructed Phil the first night she'd left him. Robbie slept peacefully…in his blanket sleeper.

What kind of a woman would think to put him in his pajamas and leave the door ajar? He thought about some of the women he'd dated over the past year. He'd bet his house that none of them would have thought of it. Hell, they'd probably have left him right on the couch where they'd found him, but not Stephanie.

Phil scratched his head as he exited the bedroom, leaving the door as he'd found it. Who would be that considerate?

A mother, that was who.

Was Stephanie a mother? Then why would she freak out around kids? And if she was a mother, where was her child? Maybe she'd been through a bad divorce, and her husband had gotten custody. Nah, that seemed too outrageous. The woman was a doctor and a great person. Sometimes disgruntled husbands kidnapped their kids. He shook his head, unable to go there, but something tormented her and he intended to find out what it was.

He glanced into the kitchen, at Stephanie pottering around, whistling under her breath. She'd come out of her shell today. He'd just begun to glimpse a different side of Stephanie Bennett, and he liked what he'd discovered. Even with all of his questions, Thanksgiving wasn't a day to dig up her past. He didn't want to spoil her upbeat mood; the lady deserved a break.

A subtle smoothness to her brow made him think she'd made peace with herself today, that maybe she'd conquered a demon or two, and he was glad to witness it.

She looked great, too. Those straight-leg jeans hugged her hips in all the right places, and the silky top revealed the hint of a soft, sweet cleavage. And her hair. What could he say about that gorgeous head of hair, other than he'd love to get his fingers tangled up in it?

By the time he sat down, she showed up with two cups of coffee, handing him one and sitting on the edge of the sofa again. "As I said, you're a fantastic host. I haven't felt this relaxed in ages. Besides, that's the beauty of a huge turkey dinner in the afternoon. You get to nap and wake up in time for a sandwich later." There was that bright smile again. "Oh, and Dallas won."

"Go, Cowboys!" What was it about her smile that drove him over the edge? From this closer range the fine sprinkling of freckles he'd discovered across her nose looked the exact color of her hair. She was a vision he thought he'd never get tired of, and he wanted to hold her, to feel her hair on his face, to kiss those freckles, but he was holding a hot cup of coffee instead.

They'd had a great afternoon together, really gotten to know each other better, and he liked every single thing he'd discovered.

She sat next to him with her leg curled under her. She'd slipped off her shoes, and he noticed polished toenails that matched her top. A fleeting image of her in a bath towel, painting her nails, sent a quick thrill through his veins. He wanted her, pure and simple. He wanted to make love to her, to make her come alive.

No risk, no gain.

He set the cup down, and reached for her. "Come here," he said.

Surprise flickered in her eyes. She put her cup on the table and with no sign of resistance snuggled into his arms. He kissed her cheek then brushed her mouth with his thumb. "You have no idea how much I want to kiss you," he said.

She tasted his thumb. He saw a flash of fire in those butterscotch depths. There wasn't any question what her answer was. She tilted her chin to make better contact as their mouths came together.

He picked up where he'd left off at the beach, slipping his tongue between her soft lips, and found her velvet-slick mouth.

She cupped his face and kissed him hard. He delved deeper, ravenous for her taste, then mated his tongue with hers. They made love with their mouths as time ceased to exist. He had no idea how long they'd necked, all he knew was that she matched his heated response, pressing her body against his, smothering him with her lips. He knew where needy kisses like that led, and there was no going back.

The fine skin of her neck tasted like vanilla. She moaned as if he'd uncovered the most sensual spot on her body. He wanted to explore more, discover every area that drove her mad with desire, but she was fully clothed. He'd have to fix that. Immediately. He cupped her breast, and felt the tightened nipple under the thin fabric of her top. His ears were so hot he thought they might spontaneously combust, and his now-full erection pulsed and strained to be set free.

As difficult as it was, he broke away from her fired-up kisses, stood, and took her hand. "Follow me."

With flushed cheeks and hooded eyes, eyes that confirmed she wanted him as much as he wanted her, she followed him down the long hall.

Stephanie watched Phil throw back the covers of his bed and step toward her. He took her by the neck and kissed her so hard she thought her knees would go wobbly.

This was no time to change her mind. Her mind? Hell, she'd misplaced that right around the time he'd kissed her. If she was going to change her mind it had to be now, but desire shivered through her and the only thing in the world she wanted at this moment was to make love with him. She was on fire. A feeling she hadn't experienced in three years pulsed between her legs, and one thing was very clear. Phil wanted her as much as she wanted him.

Hadn't she been telling herself to start living again? Every sensation coursing over her skin and through her veins shouted, *Do it! Give yourself permission.* Phil's mouth clamped down on hers again, and the no-brainer decision was made.

Completely giving in to the moment, she found a way under his shirt and skimmed the taut muscles on his chest, her hands skating across his substantial shoulders. It had been so long since she'd touched a man this way. She savored the feel of naked flesh. His skin was smooth with a fine sprinkling of hair on his chest, and she wanted to see him. See all of him.

"Let me help you," he said, pulling his shirt over his head, buttons untouched.

She only had time to glimpse his flat stomach and defined arms before he did the disappearing act with her top. A hot rhythm between her thighs drove her to undo his jeans. He yanked them down and stepped out, his erection outlined through his black briefs. With a rush of desire she cupped the full length of him, restless to see him, to feel him inside her.

To feel. Him. She'd been living on anxiety and tension for so long, this surge of lust intoxicated her. Every cell in her body came to life, heightening his touch and sweetening his taste. It empowered her, made her think she could do anything. With Phil. She pulled his briefs down and watched as he stepped out of them. She'd seen his physique in the wet suit the other day, but it couldn't compare to him in the flesh. His powerful legs and full erection was a picture she'd hold in her memory for the rest of her life.

With a dark, hooded stare, Phil studied her. "Your turn," he said. He brushed his warm hands over her breasts, cupping and lifting them as he dropped feathery kisses on her shoulder, and expertly unlatched her bra. "You're beautiful. So beautiful," he said in a hushed, reverent tone, kissing each breast.

Their mouths came together again, his lips full and smooth, as they dropped onto the bed. He unzipped and removed her jeans and lacy thong that matched her bra. "Cute," he said, eyebrows lifted in approval as he tossed it across the room. It landed on a lampshade.

Phil's natural banter and easygoing manner helped her relax when she briefly felt out of her depth. What the hell was she doing, having sex with a coworker, with a man known for being a playboy? But she looked into Phil's eyes, saw unadulterated desire, and lost her train of thought. Again.

Today she needed to be desired. It was a truth she could face, a gift he offered, and she had every intention of accepting and savoring it.

They rolled together into the center of his huge bed, finally feeling every part of each other. The exquisite feel of his muscles and skin fanned the flames licking in her belly. They kissed and tasted, touched and kneaded each other until she was frantic. "Please," she said, taking him in her hand and placing him between her thighs. She touched her tongue to his, and nibbled his kiss-swollen lower lip. "I need you," she said.

From the flashing depths of his eyes there was no doubt he needed her, too.

"Let me get some protection," he said with a bedroom-husky voice.

"Not necessary. My tubes are tied," she said, pulling him closer.

He cocked his head as if momentarily surprised, but it didn't stop Phil from seizing the moment and making her needful wishes his complete command.

CHAPTER SIX

STEPHANIE crawled out of her postsex haze and glanced at the surfing god beside her. She couldn't believe what she'd just done—she'd slept with a man after only knowing him for a couple of weeks. Was she out of her mind?

She'd let him tug her down the hall to his bedroom and have his way with her. Now nestled in the crook of his arm, she blinked. Come to think of it, she'd pretty much had her way with him, too. Maybe that was the freedom that having her tubes tied had finally given her. She'd never forget this night, no matter what happened next, and that realization felt great.

He definitely knew how to satisfy a woman, yet he was anything but mechanical or practiced. What they'd shared had been nothing short of fan-bleeping-tastic. When he'd filled her, she'd let herself go with basic instincts and savored each and every sensation coiling tighter and tighter until release had torpedoed through her. Now feeling like a huge mound of jelly, she admitted how much she'd needed this. How glad she was he'd taken her there.

They snuggled warmly in the center of his king-sized bed, lights dimmed, breathing roughly, completely satisfied. Now that he'd had her, he still hadn't lost interest. No. He folded her into his chest—his muscular chest brushed with light brown swirls and curls—and stroked her hair. She loved the soap-and-sex smell of his skin and marveled at how smooth it was and how substantial he felt. She smiled against his chest, her hand on his upper thigh. Phil was definitely substantial.

His fingers lightly played with her matted hair, sending chills over her shoulders. She'd thought she was tingled out, but his touch settled that debate. When she looked up at him, a grin was on his flushed face. He'd had a workout, too.

It had been so long since she'd been with anyone, wasn't this the point where the first-time lovers were supposed to feel awkward and clumsy? She felt anything but as she shared a completely contented smile with him. There wasn't a hint of regret in his clear-as-the-sky eyes.

"I've been fascinated with your hair since the moment I met you," he said, honey-voiced, giving her shivers all over again.

Truth was she'd been fascinated with his hair, too. She'd loved digging her fingers into it and kissing him hard and rough as they'd rolled around his bed. She liked the thickness, and how there was so much to tug and hold on to. She'd even tasted it when he'd covered her with his compact, muscular body and brought her to orgasm.

"Same here," she said.

He laughed. "You like my hair?"

She nodded, digging her fingers into his scalp, further mussing the dark blond cloud of hair. He grinned before sudden concern changed his expression. His crescent-shaped eyes grew wide.

"Damn. Robbie! I'd better go check on him."

He jumped out of bed and pulled on his jeans but not before she enjoyed the view of his sinewy back and handsome behind. He had an obvious tan line left over from summer from surfer-styled trunks.

While he was gone, she stared at the high, beamed ceiling and thought how romantic his French country-style bedroom was. The man had had impeccable taste when it had come to choosing this house. There had to be more to him than met the thoroughly satisfied eye.

He'd also made her feel like a complete woman again. Wow. She stretched and arched in the comfy bed, senses still heightened, enjoying the finely woven sheets against her back. She could get used to this kind of escape. And wasn't that what this two-month job was? An escape from all things?

Phil returned, his smile wide, sexy. "He's still asleep." He stripped and jumped back under the covers with her. "Now, where did we leave off?" He nuzzled her neck and ran a cool hand across her breast. Even if she tried, she couldn't stop her response.

The deliciously warm current he'd started with his fingertips rolled right to her center and, as quickly as that, she was ready for him again.

Robbie's nap ended much too soon, if you asked Phil. He'd have liked to spend the rest of the night making sexy memories with Stephanie on the best Thanksgiving of his life. But Robbie was awake and protesting by banging on his bedroom door.

"Pill! Whar you?"

"Hang on, Robbie, I'll be right there."

"Don't let him see me in here," Stephanie whispered.

"Okay." He took one last glance at her creamy skin and, yep, her nipples were the same color as her freckles, except, thanks to his attentions, everything about her was much rosier now. He'd have to make a mental snapshot because he had a kid banging on the door.

He hopped into his jeans and strode toward the door, then opened it just enough to squeeze through. "What's up, little dude?"

"I'm hungwee."

"Again?" Phil ruffled Robbie's already messy hair and led him to the kitchen. He smiled at how the boy had put his glasses on lopsided, and how his round belly pushed against the sleeper. The kid was a total wreck, but still managed to look cute.

Did I just use cute *in a sentence?*

He cut up a piece of pumpkin pie, poured him a glass of milk, and sat him at the kid-size plastic table Roma had left. When he was sure Robbie was preoccupied enough with eating, he slipped back down the hall to check on Stephanie's progress.

She'd put her underwear back on, and the sight of her long torso and shapely legs gave him another pang of pure desire. He couldn't wait to unload Robbie back on Roma and his father. If all went well, they'd arrive home tomorrow, and his bachelor life would finally be back to normal.

"Here you go," he said, handing her the clothes he'd found across the room.

"Thanks."

There was still fire in those dilated pupils, and it

took a lot of restraint to keep from grabbing her and throwing her on the bed again. If he was lucky, he'd have six more weeks of great sex with Stephanie—a gift he hadn't expected when they'd hired the locum.

He liked her pumpkin-colored top just fine, but it looked so much better discarded on the floor. And would he ever take those great legs for granted? Not in six weeks, he wouldn't.

Usually, once he'd been with a woman, he was fine with sending her home, preferring his alone time. But he wasn't anywhere near ready to say goodnight to Stephanie. And he still had Robbie to deal with.

"Can you stick around for another glass of wine or some coffee?"

"You know, I've scheduled that colposcopy for early tomorrow morning," she said, clasping the belt over her hips.

He was fascinated watching her, as if he'd never seen a woman dress before. "Then on Saturday night I want to take you to dinner."

She finished zipping her ankle boots, rushed him, and brushed his lips with a moist kiss. "I'd like that."

The simple gesture set off another distracting wave of desire. O-*kay*. They had a great thing going, with no strings attached, and as far as he could tell, they were on the same page.

Stephanie willed all the crazy thoughts about the huge mistake she'd made out of her head. By the time her sex-with-Phil high had subsided this morning, she'd realized her blunder. She'd given herself a pep talk on the drive in to the clinic on Friday. Last night had been a one-time thing. She'd gotten carried away, that's all.

Phil probably felt obligated to take her out to dinner. For her part, she'd blame it on that evil sweet-tasting red wine she'd imbibed and the sexy wonders of Phil. Heck, she'd already accepted his invitation for dinner on the weekend and, considering his allure, it would be extra-hard to tell him there wouldn't be a repeat bedroom performance.

Old habits were hard to break, and there was comfort in safety. Why couldn't she figure out what to do?

Celeste Conroy lay on the examination table, prepared for the special procedure. As she'd done countless times before, Stephanie used the colposcope to examine the area of cervix in question and to take a small biopsy.

It only took five minutes.

"You may feel some cramping today. Take it easy. No lifting or straining for a couple of days, and no sex for a week."

The mention of sex sent her mind back to last night with Phil, making her ears burn. She shook her head, hoping to stop the X-rated visions on the verge of materializing in her mind as she made her last few notations on the patient chart.

Celeste, as always, had a slew of questions, and Stephanie was grateful for the distraction.

"I'll need a week to get the results," Stephanie answered, "and I'll call the minute I get them."

The busy morning postponed her curiosity, but by lunchtime, when she still hadn't seen Phil, she asked Gaby.

"He's at the airport, picking up his parents."

He'd made it clear he wanted to take their acquaintance to a whole new level once his parents took Robbie off his hands. The thought made her insides scramble up with anxiety yet excited her at the same time. Soon an unsettled feeling had her finding the nearest mirror and taking a good long look.

Make up your mind, Bennett. Either go for a fling or keep your distance. Don't leave it up to Phil to decide.

Hadn't she given herself permission to let go last night? And hadn't the results been beyond any fantasy she could have dreamed up? After a long inhalation, a tiny smile curved her lips. She had six more weeks in Santa Barbara before she'd be back in her world—why not totally escape from all things Stephanie? And, besides, she'd had her tubes tied—there was nothing to worry about.

The thought of pursuing a carefree romance with Phil launched a wave of flittering wings in her stomach. Did she have the guts to carry it out?

Well, if this didn't take the prize. If Phil hadn't been so worried about his dad he'd be frustrated by having to hold on to Robbie for a couple more days. The layover at the airport had made Carl sick and Roma had taken him directly to the hospital once they'd landed. He'd picked up a nasty bug and was already showing signs of dehydration. The big iron man Phil had grown up admiring looked far too human in the hospital bed, and it sent a weary wave of dread down his spine.

"I'll keep Robbie for the weekend or until you feel ready to take over," Phil said to Roma.

She sat at her husband's bedside, her dark hair heavily streaked with silver, holding his hand. "If you could bring Robbie by later today, I'd really appreciate it. I miss him so much."

"Go, Roma. You don't have to sit here watching me sleep," Carl said. "Go and see Robbie."

She gave Phil a questioning gaze. How different Roma was from his mother, who'd left when things got tough. His mother's action had jaded Phil and had planted a lifelong mistrust of women. They couldn't be counted on to stick around, so why get serious? Roma broke the mold, but she was the exception.

"Come with me," he said. "Robbie can't wait to see you. I'll drop you back here on my way home."

It dawned on Phil that his fabulous weekend plans, with the hottest lady he'd met in forever, would get put on hold. Again.

Once he sorted things out with Roma and Robbie, he'd give Stephanie a call to give her a heads-up. Either she'd be willing to let Robbie tag along for dinner or they'd take a rain check, but there was no way he'd leave Robbie with a babysitter. The kid would be disappointed enough knowing his mom was back in town yet he still couldn't go home.

How did you explain such a thing to a kid? He'd step back and let Roma do the chore, see how a pro handled it, and maybe learn something.

Later, after he'd heard the latest doctor's report on his father and Robbie was preoccupied with building blocks and making his version of the world's tallest building, or so he'd announced with extra esses and saliva, Phil thought about Stephanie. He thought about how much he'd enjoyed spending Thanksgiving with her, and especially how great it had been to make love to her. And he thought how he'd like to do it again. Soon. But he had to look after the squirt.

So why was there a smile on his face? Because the kid really was a great source of entertainment.

After several attempts, Robbie had made it to ten blocks high, but he'd jumped up and down, knocking the top block off again. Phil stifled a laugh when he glimpsed the expression of frustration cross the boy's face. Phil had to hand it to him, the kid didn't quit. He picked up the same block and balanced it on top of the others, then went hunting for several more.

Phil took the opportunity to call Stephanie. Hearing her soft voice on the phone, it occurred to him how much he'd missed seeing her today, and just how disappointed he was about canceling their plans.

"Looks like I'll be keeping the kid brother for the weekend," he said on a resigned sigh. Though she'd made real progress being around Robbie on Thanksgiving, he wanted her all to himself the first time he took her out to dinner.

Phil felt compelled to give her the whole story about his father's illness, flight home, and current status. Once he'd filled her in they'd settled into an easy conversation, and as Robbie was still erecting the west-coast version of the Empire State building, he kept talking.

Hell, he'd had sex with the woman. They knew each other intimately now. And though completely out of character, he wanted to take the opportunity to get to know her even better.

"Do you have a minute to talk?" he asked. How busy could a person be in a hotel room?

"Sure," she said.

The problem was that, if he wanted to learn more

about her, he'd have to talk about himself. Should he take the risk?

He glanced at Robbie, who'd now moved on to scribbling with crayons in his newest coloring book from Hawaii, and decided what the heck.

"It's been bugging me. I mean, how does a doctor with an aversion to kids wind up being an obstetrician?"

To her credit, she blurted out a laugh instead of taking offense. Though maybe she sounded a little nervous? "I guess it does seem odd, and please don't get me wrong, I love delivering babies. It's just…well, pregnancy and delivery is one thing, and child rearing is another."

"See, now, that's where I get tripped up," Phil said, trying hard to understand her elusive explanation. "It's been my experience that people usually go into a specialty profession because it's their passion. For instance, I chose medicine because of my mother."

Maybe it was the fact that his dad was sick and in a hospital, looking all too frail. Maybe it was because, even after professing to hate his mother all these years, he still missed her, but she'd been on his mind today.

"Your mother wanted you to become a pulmonologist?"

"Actually, she never knew, because I stopped talking to her."

Phil wasn't ready to tell Stephanie the whole story, that he'd been in Australia at a surfing championship when his father had been diagnosed with lymphoma the first time—and that his mother's leaving turned his life upside down. It had made him quit the surfing circuit at twenty to care for his dad and, eventually, head back to school.

"I'm so sorry to hear that, Phil."

He'd confused her. He sensed honest compassion in Stephanie's voice and it felt like a forgiving breath; made him want to be honest with her. Maybe he did owe her an explanation.

"My dad had lymphoma, and when he first got diagnosed, my mother walked out on us. She couldn't deal with his disease. Evidently she didn't give a damn about me either because I never got to say goodbye."

"Oh, God, how awful."

Phil hadn't meant to turn their conversation in this maudlin direction, he'd just wanted to keep her on the phone a little longer, but here he was stripping down barriers and letting the new girl on the block know about the secret of his mother. He could count back ten girlfriends and know for sure they'd never had a clue about his family or whether either of his parents was alive or dead. So why had he opened up to Stephanie?

"Yeah, I haven't talked to her since. I don't have a clue if she knows I'm a doctor or not."

"I see." She sounded suddenly distant.

As he'd gone completely out of character, he decided to get something else off his chest.

"Stephanie, this is a really weird question, but something I noticed yesterday made me wonder if you have a child." The way she'd put Robbie into his pajamas and had left the bedroom door ajar. A novice like himself wouldn't know to do that without being told. But not Stephanie.

She inhaled sharply.

He kicked himself for bringing up the subject. "Are you okay?"

"Yes. Sorry. You caught me off guard, that's all."

He sighed. "Didn't mean to," he said, regretting having mentioned it.

She swallowed. "You and I have something in common."

"How so?"

"You never got to say goodbye to your mother, and I never got to say goodbye to my son."

"Stephanie…" In that moment, he wanted to put down the phone, to crawl inside, and come out the other end. He wanted nothing more than to console her. She had lost a child. "I'm sorry if I—"

"That's okay, Phil. I need to get off the phone now anyway. I'll see you at work," she said, not giving him a chance to say another word.

Confused, he scrubbed his face. All he wanted was an uncomplicated romance, but having lived thirty-five years and dated for twenty of them, he knew there was no such thing.

When Stephanie arrived at work on Monday morning, all the nurses were abuzz with news about the yacht decorations. Gaby had used the office petty cash to purchase six small fake Christmas trees. "They all came complete with lights!" she said animatedly. "Now all we have to do is anchor them on the yacht."

"Great!" Amy said. "And I found my grandmother's decorations from the old country, and my lederhosen still fit!"

Another nurse chimed in. "I've got a bunch of Philippine Christmas lanterns we can use for one of the trees, too."

Stephanie did her usual fading into the woodwork rather than join in.

Claire appeared, honey-blonde hair pulled back into a long swishy ponytail and green eyes bright with excitement. "Sounds great, guys. Bring everything this Saturday for the decorating party." She saw Stephanie and waved her over. "You're coming, right?"

Stephanie had been keeping a safe distance from the clinic employees. Why get too involved when she was only going to be around for a couple of months? What was the point? Up until this moment she'd planned to blow off the Christmas yacht party, but how could she say no and not appear to be antisocial?

"Um, sure." And, besides, it would give her a chance to see Phil in a perfectly safe environment, one where she couldn't get swept off her resolve to keep a distance.

"Great! I'll send the directions to your email." Claire glanced at her watch and strode for the stairs to her second-floor office. "Talk later."

Well, hell, she'd already had sex with Phil, why not get to know everyone else a little better, too?

The nurses continued to rabbit on about decorating the yacht and what fun it always was as Stephanie smiled and made her way toward her office. After spending an ultra-quiet weekend, she had to admit that she enjoyed the hustle and bustle of the clinic, and with the official invitation now she looked forward to the plans for the coming weekend.

When later that morning Phil loomed in her doorway, her gut clenched. It was the first time she'd seen him since they'd made love. Her heart stumbled over the next couple of beats. He looked amazing with his hair freshly washed and combed straight back. She'd come to notice that however it fell, it stayed, and it always looked great. He'd probably expect further explanation about her weird reaction on the phone on Friday night. She wasn't ready to give it.

"Hey," he said, obviously waiting to be invited in.

"Hi. What's up?" Did her face give her hopeful thoughts away? Was he here to invite her out to lunch or, better yet, a quiet dinner with just the two of them—like the one she'd so looked forward to last weekend? If he did, she hoped he'd keep all conversation superficial.

He carried a large specialty coffee drink in each hand and placed one on her desk. "It's a pumpkin latte. Thought you might like it."

"Thanks." Why did the thoughtful gesture touch her so? Why did it feel so intimate? Before she'd gotten strange on the phone the other night, they'd embarked on a new line of communication. The man had opened up about his mother and because she'd been thinking about Justin after being around Robbie, she'd gone overboard with her response. It must have seemed so strange and out of the blue that she wouldn't have been surprised if he'd avoided her, yet here he was bringing her a drink.

He sat on the edge of her desk and studied her. If the morning sun was brighter than she'd ever seen it, and there wasn't a cloud on the horizon, that's what she imagined the color would be, and it was right there in his eyes.

"So Robbie's going to stay with me the rest of this week, until my dad gets discharged from the hospital." He sounded worn out, like he'd had a super-hard weekend.

As she gazed at him, grateful he hadn't probed more about her son, she caught the telltale signs of sleep deprivation. It looked as if ashes had been faintly smudged beneath his eyes, and his voice sounded huskier than usual. Watching his brother had taken its toll, but Phil wasn't complaining. For a guy who professed to keep things easy and uncomplicated, he'd proved to be deeper than that. And though she wasn't in the market for anything permanent with Phil, this side of his character helped her trust him.

Before he left, he bent over and dropped a sweet kiss on her lips. The simple gesture invited chills. He tasted like pumpkin latte, and after he'd left, she enjoyed sipping her drink and thinking of Phil's kisses for the rest of the afternoon.

Phil had finally gotten Robbie down for the night. All he wanted to do was talk to Stephanie. She'd lost a child and was trying to put her life together. She could use a friend at a time like this, yet she'd chosen to leave the desert during the holidays and spend Christmas with strangers in Santa Barbara.

The last thing he could call himself was a stranger to her, not after their intense lovemaking session the other night. The crazy thing was, it wasn't just about sex with Stephanie. He genuinely liked her. So why not call her, just to talk? The thought made him smile. It reminded him of how in high school he used to have to work up an excuse to call a girl when he liked her. But that had been back in a time of innocence, back when his heart had been eager to fall in love, back when he'd still trusted the opposite sex…back before his mother had walked out.

Yikes, he'd put himself into a lousy mood, and now he needed to call Stephanie to cheer himself up. So that made two reasons, more than enough to make the call.

Robbie came running down the hall in his pajamas. Before Phil had put him to bed, Robbie had talked to his mother and had cried a little. It almost broke Phil's heart. The kid had to settle for second best with him when all he wanted was to sleep in his own bed and get a good-night kiss from his parents. Carl was still in recovery mode, and Roma had her hands full. If Robbie went home too soon, he might feel neglected, and get his feelings hurt.

"I thought I already put you to bed," he said.

"Furgot sumtin'." Robbie used his short, pudgy arms to pull Phil close and tell him, "Wuv you."

Without thinking, Phil kissed him on the forehead. "Back at ya, little dude. Now, skedaddle back to bed."

Robbie giggled and ran off.

A scary feeling crept over Phil. It had felt nice to kiss his kid brother and, yep, he'd miss him when he was gone.

He stroked his jaw. Maybe he should get a dog.

All the cozy feelings and thoughts about having another warm, living, breathing body share his house boggled his mind. It gave him a third excuse for calling Stephanie—distraction!

"Hey, what's up?" he said, when she answered after the second ring.

"Hi!" Her welcoming tone pushed all his worries aside. All he wanted to do was talk about her day.

After chatting superficially for a while, he realized the real point of his call. He wanted more one-on-one time with Stephanie. Just before hanging up, he said, "And tomorrow lunch is on me."

She answered without hesitation. "Okay. If the weather's nice, maybe we can eat outside."

If he could conjure up warm weather and sunshine for tomorrow he would, but he already felt the equivalent of a sunny day right there—he rubbed the spot—in his chest. "Sounds like a plan."

The next day, though the sky was blue, temperatures were low. Phil and Stephanie wore jackets and set off for the shore anyway. He'd ordered a hearty fish chowder and sourdough rolls from the best deli in town, and carried it in a warming bag with one hand. He longed to place his other arm around her waist but, not wanting to put any pressure on her, he withstood the urge.

He hadn't figured out yet where they stood. The other night he'd been positive she was interested in a no-strings fling for the duration of her stay in Santa Barbara. Since that night—the hottest night he could remember—Stephanie had partially rebuilt that invisible barrier. He knew it had something to do with that weird comment she'd made about not getting to say goodbye to her baby.

He shook his head. The day was too beautiful to try to figure things out. And since when did he get all caught up in really "knowing" a woman? All he knew was that right now the sun danced off the golden highlights in Stephanie's hair, making it look like a shiny copper penny. She smiled whenever she looked at him, and if he didn't get pushy about it, he might just get another kiss before they headed back to the clinic.

They found a bench along the bike path with a shoreline view and sat. She squinted from the bright sun and had to slip on her sunglasses, covering those gorgeous caramel-candy eyes. He was glad to see the smile never left her face.

The simple fact they had time alone together had sparks flying and itchy messages flowing through the circuit board of his body. He'd much rather strip her naked than hand her a cup of soup, but he kept his true desire at bay, and when she took the first taste he received a smile of orgasmic proportions, and that smile was definitely worth his efforts.

Stephanie wasn't very talkative today, but that was okay. He was happy to be with her. Just before he finished dunking the edge of his roll into the last of his soup, his cell phone rang. It was Roma.

"They're going to discharge your dad this afternoon, so I won't be able to pick up Robbie."

"I'll make arrangements," Phil said, realizing he'd gotten pretty blasé about carpools and favors and paybacks with the other mothers from the preschool. They all seemed to really get a kick out of the "cool" surrogate dad on campus. Normally, he would have played the distinction to the hilt. He'd flirt, use them for all the favors they could offer, and maybe even find out if any of the moms were single. But out of respect for his kid brother, he'd done the right thing by taking care of him and hadn't abused the special circumstances.

And, besides, he'd been completely preoccupied with Stephanie.

"Do you want me to keep him tonight, so you and Dad can get settled?"

"That would be wonderful," she said, after an obvious sigh of relief.

Stephanie looked at him as if he were a superhero or

something. In that moment he admitted it: he might just miss the kid once he went home. Maybe…just a little.

He flipped through his contacts on the phone and made a quick call. "Hey, Claire, can you do me a huge favor and pick up Robbie today when you get Gina?" After almost two weeks, he finally understood the bartering side of child care. "Thanks, and I'll drop her off at your house from day care after I get off work."

Stephanie's arms flew around his neck and she planted a cold kiss on his cheek. It wasn't the sexy kind of kiss he'd been hoping for, but he wouldn't complain. He turned the angle of his face so their lips could meet, and dropped a peck on her mouth. This was all way too affectionate for his taste. He preferred sexy and hot, but the weirdest thing was, he kind of liked it.

"I guess we better be getting back to the clinic," he said. "Looks like Robbie and I are roommates for one more night."

CHAPTER SEVEN

Thursday morning lab results planted a rock-size knot firmly into Stephanie's stomach. Celeste Conroy's biopsy showed squamous cell carcinoma. After last Thursday and Thanksgiving, Maria was back today, sitting on the other side of Stephanie's desk, waiting expectantly for the day's assignment.

"Well," Stephanie said, handing the printed pathology report to the RNP student. "This is a perfect example of what makes this job a challenge."

"Wow," Maria said. "She's pregnant, right? How do you handle something like this?"

"I tell her the truth. We need to find out how extensive the cancer is and I'll need to do a conization of her cervix."

She'd remove a thick cone-shaped wedge of tissue from the area in question of the cervix, extending high into the cervical canal. Her goal would be to leave a wide margin of normal cells around the area of cancer.

"Risks?" Maria queried.

"Yes, but we must always balance them against the benefits. I'll do everything in my power to keep both the mother and the baby healthy." Stephanie glanced over her calendar for the earliest possible appointment.

"I want to do the biopsy on Monday so I can get this mother-to-be some good news before Christmas." She shuddered, thinking of all the potential possibilities, and willed a positive attitude.

"Would it be okay if I came in to observe?" Maria patted her protruding pregnancy as worry lines etched her brow.

"Of course."

Stephanie's pulse had worked its way into her mouth. She punched in the phone number, willing her quivery hand to settle down, then cleared her throat. She needed to sound confident when she gave the diagnosis, for the patient's sake.

Stephanie couldn't believe the choreographed chaos on Saturday morning at the harbor. Even halfway down the harbor she could hear lively Christmas music over the loudspeaker. The pungent sea air seemed to heighten her senses, making her feel alive and excited. She stopped in midstep, having never seen a more gorgeous boat. As promised, everyone from the clinic had showed up with their contribution. She'd even made an extra effort to buy several strings of Christmas lights for the yacht.

Jason greeted her with a captain's smile and waved her aboard. Before she boarded, she noticed the name on the bow—*For Claire*. Something about that special touch pinched at her heart. She'd heard bits and pieces about Claire and Jason's love affair. It hadn't been easy for either of them to admit they'd fallen in love, yet now they made a perfect couple. She shook her head. Why were people so slow to figure things like that out?

"This is my latest indulgence," Jason said, grinning and patting the rail. "I wanted to upgrade, anyway."

Claire, wearing a teal-colored windbreaker and matching ball cap, with her long ponytail sticking out the hole in the back, stood at his side, smiling up at him. "He made sure there were plenty of shady spots when he designed this boat, because of my lupus. Come on, I'll show you around."

Amy and Gaby worked diligently on placing the small Christmas trees at key positions on the bow, stern, port, and starboard. Other nurses and aides helped stabilize and decorate them. They waved hello, and the simple greeting made Stephanie feel like part of the clinic family. Maybe it would have happened sooner if she'd reached out to them. Well, better late than never.

Just when Claire was about to take Stephanie below deck, she saw Phil rushing down the dock with a huge pink box in his arms. He waved at her and smiled, and her insides got jumbled up. Jason met him dockside and shook his hand.

"I brought doughnuts," Phil said.

"Yay," Amy said, as Gaby applauded.

"I'm making cocoa," Claire called over her shoulder, leading Stephanie by the arm down to the galley. Stephanie was grateful for the distraction to buy time to straighten out her suddenly fuzzy thoughts.

Wow. Stephanie had never seen a more modern galley on a boat. Granted, her experience with boats was woefully limited, but still. Stainless-steel appliances, perfectly stained woodwork and cupboards; the compact galley oozed class.

As Claire stirred a huge pot of milk, adding cocoa liberally, she seemed her usual self from work, but more relaxed and completely carefree. "I'd never been on a sailboat until I met Jason. Now I'm ready to give up my practice, homeschool Gina, and sail around the world with him." A soft laugh gently bubbled out. "Don't worry, we won't quit our day jobs. Too many people need us at that clinic, and I love it there. But maybe someday…"

"You must take some great weekend getaways," Stephanie said, gathering the red paper cups decorated with wreaths and garland trim and placing them on a large tray.

"Not as often as we'd like, but we have plans for a longer trip this summer. Thought we'd sail up to San Francisco and back."

"Wow," Stephanie said. "That's impressive." She held the tray close so Claire could ladle out the cocoa into the cups then she shook the whipped cream can and sprayed a dollop on top of each.

"If all goes well, maybe the year after we'll set sail for Hawaii."

"Sounds like a dream come true."

Before she could say more, a familiar bedroom-sexy voice vibrated from the doorway into the main saloon. "You ladies need a hand?" Phil hung in the doorway, opening up his broad chest, cutting a V down to a trim waist. Her throat went dry, so strong was her reaction, and she suddenly needed a sip of cocoa. "I think we've got this covered."

She did her best to act casual, as if the mere presence of the man didn't scatter her nerves.

He jabbed a thumb over his shoulder. "The folks have already eaten most of the doughnuts, but I saved you ladies a couple."

"Thanks. We'll be right up," Claire said, oblivious to the caveman-sexy gaze streaming from Phil's sea-blue eyes and directed at Stephanie.

How in the world would she make it through the day without mauling the man?

She'd been losing sleep, having hot and restless dreams of tussling in bedsheets with a strange man. The dreams had been so realistic; she could practically feel the man's weight on her body, driving himself into her. Hell, she knew exactly who the guy was. Phil. One time she'd woken up with the covers on the floor, throbbing thighs, sheets wadded in her fists, panting, and *very* frustrated. How in the world should she handle her desire where Phil was concerned?

They were both adults—why not enjoy each other?

Later, as she and Phil put the finishing touches on the mainsail Christmas lights, she jumped at his touch.

"Sorry," she said, as electricity powered through her veins.

"You seem a bit flinchy," he said, drilling her with a stare.

"I'm just a little uptight with all the new patients and work and all."

Phil lowered his voice and lifted her hair, hooking it behind one ear. "It's Christmastime, pretty baby, loosen up." The raucous version of *Rockin' Around the Christmas Tree* nearly drowned out his words. "You know, a little TLC might be just the thing you need."

A vision of tender loving care, compliments of Phil, whirled through her mind. She couldn't breathe for a second. He'd spoken the words she'd been afraid to acknowledge. He seemed to know exactly what she'd been thinking, and now her cheeks were probably betraying her by blushing hot pink. She glanced around the busy deck. Fortunately, everyone seemed oblivious to them.

Why not? Why the hell not have a fling? Was she such a wretched person that she didn't deserve a little pleasure in life? Phil had already proved what a fantastic lover he was. He hadn't pushed her into doing anything she hadn't wanted to. Hell, she'd come up with all kinds of ideas in her dreams lately. It could be fun to try them out…with Phil.

Did she really want to balance on the precipice of sexual frustration for another month, or slide back into that incredible place he'd taken her before?

How many times did she need to give herself permission to live?

Her cheeks flamed and her palms tingled, thinking about it. Slowly, she glanced into his darkening and decidedly sexy stare.

"Robbie went home last night," he said, eyes never wavering from hers. "And I owe you that dinner out. What about tonight?"

What about tonight? She knew what he meant, what he wanted.

He'd sounded the same when he'd made love to her. Phil's voice, full of intimate intention, massaged her rising senses, snapping to life key areas and a powerful drive to scratch the itch with him.

So strong was her physical reaction that if everything else could just disappear, she'd be on him, knocking him down and ripping off his clothes right this instant.

Nearly trembling with desire, she found her voice, if only a whisper. "Yes. Tonight."

* * *

That evening, Stephanie had talked herself down from the frantic sexual cliff, but excitement still washed over every cell in her body. She couldn't wait to see Phil again, to be alone with him. The permission she'd given herself to be with him had been so incredibly freeing.

He picked her up at her hotel looking impeccable. He wore a perfectly tailored sport coat, dark slacks, and a pale blue shirt open at the collar. Did he realize how the color brought out his eyes? His hair, brushed back from his forehead, curled beneath his earlobes. And that smile—did she stand a chance resisting it? She didn't want to!

She'd rushed to the Paseo after they'd finished decorating the boat that afternoon and bought a little black dress. Now, standing before his scrutinizing eyes, she tugged at the skirt with shaky hands. Maybe tonight's seduction wouldn't be as easy as she'd fantasized. She didn't want her nerves to ruin things.

"Wow," he said. "You look spectacular."

His reaction nearly knocked her off her spiky heels. It was exactly what she'd wanted to hear. He liked what he saw, and that made her ecstatic. In her fantasy, she was a vamp, but here, in front of Phil, all she could say was, "Thanks."

His gaze lingered several moments then he scanned from her hair to her brightly polished toes. As if his head was a glass globe, she could practically see his thoughts. He liked what he saw and wanted to indulge. Just as quickly, he snapped out of the spell.

"I hope you've got a warm coat," he said, brushing a light kiss across her cheek. Man, he smelled as good as he looked. "We'll be eating outside."

What did she care? It would give her an excuse to cuddle up close to him.

They entered the restaurant, called Bouchon, through a shrubbery-hidden portal, and the first thing Stephanie noticed was shiny light wood floors. The decor was understated yet classy, utilizing matching light wood tables and chairs, and cream-colored tablecloths. Huge modern art canvases supplied needed color on the walls. Her first impression was that the total dining effect was as warm and welcoming as Phil's hand pressing against hers.

Phil seemed to know the proprietor of the restaurant and had gotten them a perfectly placed table on the patio. He guided her with his palm at her waist, the barely there pressure at her back already setting off chill rockets. Even though every seat was taken, their cozy corner felt as intimate as Phil's eyes. The brisk evening air mingled with radiant restaurant heat lamps to create the best of both outdoor and indoor worlds.

Stephanie inhaled and rolled her shoulders, inviting the long-overdue relaxation to settle in.

Phil's taste was flawless. The wine crisp from nearby vineyards, appetizers made from local farmers' market ingredients, and the main course free range from Santa Barbara microranches.

Stephanie savored the exquisite taste of plump sea scallops, sharing the appetizer with Phil and with a perfect glass of Chardonnay. He'd insisted she try the seared duck as her main course, the signature dish of the great chef. Who was she to argue?

He took her hand in his and gazed appreciatively into her eyes. "I'm really glad we finally got our date."

So this was what it had all come down to. She hadn't

planned on sleeping with him on Thanksgiving, but hadn't regretted it for a second. She'd backtracked a bit from her permission, but seeing Phil as a whole person, committed to his job and connected to his family, drove her to know him more. The decision to take the moment by the horns and ride it for all it was worth, or walk away a frustrated and closed-off woman, remained in her hands.

She glanced at Phil, latticed moonlight shadows making him all the more intriguing. The decision seemed obvious.

She couldn't help but smile as warm tingles worked their way through her insides. She could blame it on the wine and great food, but she knew better. Only Phil could set that kind of reaction twisting through her. Her decision final, she'd skip dessert at the restaurant, instead saving up for the special delights that Phil Hansen had to offer.

Three hours later, flat on her back, Stephanie lay panting, staring at the ceiling, flushed and tingling…everywhere! Phil should have a doctorate in making love.

Never in her life had she given in to her desires, completely exempt of expectations, and gone with her mood. Until now. With Phil. He had a way of drawing that out of her. She didn't feel tawdry about it, either. With him, making love came as naturally as breathing, and, boy, was she out of breath.

He nuzzled her neck, sending yet another wave of chills across her skin. "That was perfect," he said, husky and still revved up.

She slipped her arm across his torso and curled into his shoulder. Secure in his embrace, and content beyond words, she sighed. "We'll have to do this again sometime."

His devilish laugh vibrated through his chest. "Why not right now?" He got up on his elbows and looked deep into her eyes. "You're incredible, you know that?"

Did she know that? Had her husband ever told her she was incredible? They'd been in love once upon a time—she'd known that much for sure. When she'd become pregnant, she'd been happier than she'd ever been, but months later things had changed.

Her hand brushed over her abdomen, imagining the fallopian tubes she'd had tied off. She was safe. She'd never get pregnant again.

Phil's mouth pressed gently against her jaw. He glanced into her eyes again, as if he'd seen her secret fleeting thoughts. The next kiss he delivered was warm and caring. The tender gesture nearly split her heart.

She kissed him back, ragged and hard, her fingers digging into that glorious hair. If she was having a fling with Phil, she couldn't allow emotions or any feelings beyond passion and excitement to get in the way.

Sunday, after making her breakfast in bed—Phil had *been* breakfast—he talked her into hitting the beach for a game of volleyball.

She couldn't help but grin at the invitation. Surfing may be his turf, but volleyball was definitely hers. After a few warm-up shots, they *thwopped* the ball back and forth across the net. Her toes dug into the sand, the fresh sea breeze making her skin feel as vibrant and warm as Phil's touch had the night before, as warm as the sun heating her scalp and shoulders. Phil popped a ball off his fingertips, and out of reflex she spiked it over the net, hitting him smack between the eyes. Shock quaked through her body as she rushed to him.

He rubbed his nose, looking dazed. "Great shot, Bennett!"

After she made sure he was okay, the surprised look on his face set her off laughing. She crumpled to her knees, overcome with the giggles.

He swooped her up into his arms and ran toward the water. Weak with laughter, she didn't protest, until he ran knee-deep into a wave and tossed her into the chilly ocean. Her scream was cut short by salt water. Once she regained her bearings, she chased Phil toward the beach and made a poor excuse for a tackle, only managing to grab his ankles and falling flat.

This carefree feeling felt as foreign as having that ocean, crashing and constant, in Palm Desert. She welcomed the new sensation, breathing deeper and feeling more vital than she had in years.

He broke away from her grasp and sat back on his ankles, grinning. His high-pitched laugh and corny smile egged her on. She crawled toward him and threw her arms around his neck then planted a wet and salty kiss on his mouth. Though clumsy at first, the kiss soon turned passionate, his hands wandering, holding her as if he never wanted to let go. With their lips smashing and tongues mingling, she thought how close to heaven it felt being here on the beach with Phil. How he managed to wipe away her worries with a single heart-stopping kiss.

As they rolled around, their kisses became invaded by sand, and soon her sexy moment turned to awareness that every crease and crevice of her body was sticky with beach grit. And after he'd made the same discovery, they lay side by side, flat on their backs, laughing together.

It seemed the playboy of Santa Barbara had resuscitated her life. Yeah, to use his own words, their fling *was* just what the doctor had ordered.

After he'd taken her to the hotel to shower and clean up, they went to lunch at the yacht club. During a long walk along the seashore, Phil invited her to his house again. The memory of being lost in his body, oblivious to her thoughts, lured her back to his bed.

Though anything but rehearsed, their lovemaking became more familiar. They'd explored each other's bodies with abandon, and she'd delighted in discovering his sensitive spots. She loved the texture of his skin, so many shades darker than her own. The ease with which he responded to her touch made her smile. She felt as though she could weave magic with him, especially when he was deep inside her, expertly guiding her to her final release.

Sex with Phil was nothing short of enchanting, and she hoped to stay under the spell for as long as she stayed in Santa Barbara.

Once completely sated, she flopped limply on top of him, and lifted her hair from her hot and sticky shoulders.

He blew lightly on her neck. "Stay with me tonight."

Reality checked back in. "I can't. I've got to be well rested for the conization tomorrow morning."

"Come back tomorrow night, then," he murmured, his hand playing with tendrils of her hair.

"I thought you were a love-'em-and leave-'em kind of

guy?" Her true thought about his reputation had tumbled out before she could censure it.

In one quick move, he grabbed her and flopped her onto her back. Settling himself between her thighs, he gazed confidently into her face. "I'm just getting started with you."

It wasn't the most romantic thing she'd ever heard, yet, as he nibbled her earlobe, it thrilled her just the same. He hadn't grown tired of her yet, and, heaven knew, she wasn't even close to getting bored with him. Couldn't imagine it. Yet she wasn't as easily lured into his spell this time. Her mind wandered.

As life and her job wedged into her thoughts, she switched to the practical side of her life, and pragmatic words followed. "How does it work with you? How do you know when it's time to move on?"

The leftover fairy dust from their heated sex vanished.

He rolled onto his back and stared at the ceiling. "Where'd that come from?"

"I'm curious. That's all."

He rose up onto one elbow. "I'm not nearly as callous as my reputation."

"I didn't call you callous. All I did was ask how you know when a 'fling' is over."

He took her hand and kissed her fingers, cleverly diverting her attention. "Let's just say I'm nowhere near that with you."

The perfect answer from a master. He was a playboy after all, and she couldn't forget it.

Stephanie saw so much potential with Phil, yet he seemed a man of contradictions. Regardless of his stereotypical-playboy dating pattern, he lived in a house perfect for a family. He liked to dawdle in the kitchen, and garden! And when push came to shove about looking after his kid brother, he'd proved himself worthy. Phil was full of potential. Not that she was looking for anyone. No. Not that he'd ever consider her for more than a few nights of great sex.

She glanced at him, as if seeing for the first time the truth of their bond. They had nowhere to go but here, his bed. She was thankful for him forcing her out of her shell, but reality had a mean spirit and it had just smacked her in the face.

Phil took her hand and kissed her fingertips.

How long would she be able to overlook his playboy ways? Would it tear her heart out when he lost interest and moved on? Would he have the courtesy to wait until she'd moved back to Palm Desert? He'd been evasive when she'd questioned him.

She glanced into his unwavering eyes. He smiled at her, but she couldn't return it, wondering instead if anyone would ever be able to tame him. These were not the thoughts of a woman having a fling. She shouldn't be concerned with them. Yet she was.

She fought off a wave of regret, refusing to let it blemish their fantastic weekend. Then with a sudden need to retreat back to her protective shell, to hide behind the medical profession, she kissed his forehead.

"I've got a big day tomorrow." With nothing further to say, she slipped out from under the sheets, gathered her clothes strewn across the floor and bedroom love seat, and padded toward the bathroom.

"I'll let myself out," she said.

CHAPTER EIGHT

PHIL rubbed his temples and squinted. What in the hell had just happened? He and Stephanie had had great sex over the weekend, he'd enjoyed every minute he'd spent with her, then whammo! She'd slipped back into stranger mode.

He sat at the bedside and gulped down a glass of water. His head pounded behind his temples. Sex was supposed to release endorphins, and they were supposed to make a guy feel great. And they had…until she'd withdrawn.

He thought of Stephanie wrapped in his arms one minute and gone the next. He wasn't sure what he wanted with her beyond what they already had—great fun, great sex, good times—but then what? She'd leave for the desert.

Buck naked, he paced the length of his bedroom. Give her a day to herself. Bring her lunch. Invite her for Chinese food after work another night. No pressure. He'd do what he did best—charm the hell out of a woman.

And though it would be hard, he'd keep his hands to himself, because he didn't want to lose what little ground he'd gained with her.

The Christmas lights parade was on Saturday, and he hoped she'd be there. If the magic of Christmas couldn't break down the last of her barriers, nothing would.

He stopped in midpace and stared at his feet. Stephanie had given him the perfect opportunity to let another relationship slip away. Letting a woman loose had never bothered him. Over the years he'd learned new and creative ways to let his lady friends down gently. He'd buy them an expensive bracelet or necklace, tell them they deserved so much better than him. Yeah, he'd even stooped so low as to use his "busy career" as an excuse. And if he saw that special twinkle in the lady's eyes, he'd announce that he never wanted to be a father, even though in reality his own father meant the world to him.

There were always other women out there. But this time around he wanted Stephanie. Hell, he liked her. A lot. He thought about her lilting laugh when they playfully wrestled on his bed. Up close and personal, those tiny freckles bridging her nose turned him on more than he cared to admit. And her skin. Damn, she felt like velvet under his gardener's calluses. And she was a fantastic doctor. Everyone at the clinic had commented, now that she'd started mixing with them, on how well she fit in. Truth was, he liked the whole Stephanie Bennett package.

Complete silence echoed off the walls and drowned out his thoughts. He had to admit that at times like this he missed the thudding of Robbie's pudgy feet, and he definitely missed Stephanie Bennett in his bed.

Was this foreign feeling loneliness?

Maybe it was time to get a dog. In the meantime, he'd see if a football game was on TV.

* * *

On Monday morning, Christmas music streamed through the office speakers, grabbing Stephanie's attention. Gaby had obviously been busy decorating over the weekend. Maybe the boat-decorating party had put her in the mood. She'd set up a miniature Christmas village behind the reception window, complete with mock snow and twinkling lights. Wreaths hung at each doctor's door, and a banner wishing everyone a happy holiday was draped across the entryway to the waiting room.

The cheery atmosphere seemed contrary to what Stephanie had scheduled first thing that morning in the clinic. She got settled in her office and did a quick mental rundown of how the procedure would be carried out then noticed Maria standing expectantly in her doorway. She welcomed her in—having Maria as moral support was nice.

"I'm planning on doing a cold-knife conization. It may produce more bleeding than other procedures, but it doesn't obscure the surgical margins as much as the two other techniques, which is very important."

Stephanie drew a diagram for Maria. "While were there, I'm going to go ahead and perform a cerclage to minimize the bleeding and to protect from premature labor down the road." She sketched as Maria looked on, outlining how she planned to remove the wedge of tissue then stitch the cervix together to keep it tight until delivery.

"Amy is having Celeste sign the consent in the procedure room. Are you ready?"

Maria nodded, her espresso-brown eyes wide and intelligent. She tottered beside her as Stephanie made her way to the special-procedure room. Even though it seemed impossible for Maria's pregnant belly to look any bigger, it did, and Stephanie wondered how she could possibly hold out until her due date.

Stephanie greeted Celeste Conroy with a firm hand-shake as the patient reclined on the table with a paper shield across her lap and her feet in place in the stir-rups. Amy had already set her up for the cervical cone biopsy.

"You remember Maria Avila, the nurse practitioner student?"

Celeste gave permission for Maria to observe, and Stephanie was glad of the extra pair of hands.

Amy had given Celeste a mild sedative on her ar-rival and Stephanie administered a local cervical block. As they waited for it to take effect, Celeste had more questions.

"The consent said a lot of scary things," Celeste said. "Can they all happen?"

"The consents have to list every single possibility. Will they all happen? No. Will any of them happen? Not likely. Please don't let it scare you. The main thing I want to make sure about is the bleeding. Pregnancy increases blood flow to the uterus and cervix, so it might get tricky, but I'll be extra-careful."

"What if we don't get all of the cancer out with this procedure?"

"There is a very low risk that your lesion will prog-ress during the course of your pregnancy. My job is to remove it all today, and I'm confident I can. Let's take this one step at a time."

Reluctantly, Celeste agreed, and as the sedative wove its spell, she plopped her head back on the exam table and stared off into the distance. Stephanie could only imagine the thoughts she must be having.

Once the wedge of tissue was excised and placed in a specimen container, Stephanie used electrocautery to control the rapid local bleeding, then, as planned, performed the cervical cerclage.

"Maria, I'm going to assign you to Recovery. I want to watch Mrs. Conroy for the next four hours. Amy, will her husband be on hand to drive her home later?"

Amy nodded.

Stephanie ran down a long list of things Celeste needed to avoid for the next week, and wrote everything down. Knowing her patient had been sedated, she planned to go over everything again later when her husband was present and ready to take her home.

"Let me know if there's any unusual bleeding," Stephanie said to Maria on her way out.

"Will do."

Stephanie went about the rest of her morning clinic, only occasionally allowing Phil to slip into her thoughts. She wasn't looking for a husband or a future father. She'd gone that route and failed miserably, and had ensured she'd never be a mother again. All she wanted to do was put the pieces of her life back together, and maybe, while she was here, have a little fun. So if he was only a guy to have fun with, why was she thinking about him so much? Maybe it was because he'd turned out to be so great with Robbie. She'd seen him go from clueless to expert in less than two weeks. The guy had father potential written all over him. In a twisted sort of way, after she left, she hoped he'd find a woman who could give him a family one day.

"Dr. Bennett?" Amy interrupted her confusing

thoughts. "Maria sent me to tell you that Mrs. Conroy has soaked through several pads already."

Alarm had Stephanie picking up her phone and dialing Jason Rogers's office. He met her at the patient's gurney, as she finished her examination.

"I need to cauterize more extensively, and then I'd like to admit the patient for overnight observation," she said.

"I'll call the hospital and tell them we're sending her," Jason said.

"I don't have privileges there, so I'll need you to admit her."

"No problem," he said. "Whatever you need."

Having such support and backup from her boss meant the world to her. And after the second round of cauterizing the wedge margins, the cervical bleeding already showed signs of slowing. Still, she couldn't be too careful with her patient, and, more importantly, with the pregnancy.

The transporters arrived, and Maria volunteered to ride over with Celeste so Stephanie could finish her clinic appointments. She'd head over to the hospital as soon as she was finished.

By the end of the day, Stephanie hadn't seen even a glimpse of Phil, and she figured if he was avoiding her she deserved it for pulling back and leaving without a proper goodbye. What did he expect? They really were nothing more than bed partners so she had no obligation to him. Then why did him avoiding her bother her so much? She bit her lip and sighed.

Because she cared about him.

* * *

"Is Dr. Bennett in?" Phil asked Gaby on his way into the clinic on Tuesday morning.

"She's at the hospital, discharging one of her patients."

He'd decided to ask her to lunch today, and was eager to see her again. When he got to his office and booted up his computer, a calendar alert popped up at the moment Jon strode through his door.

"You ready?" Jon asked.

Damn, he'd forgotten the symposium in Ventura he and Jon had signed up for months ago to attend together today.

So much for lunch with Stephanie.

On Wednesday, Phil got called into the E.R. for an emergency thoracentesis in the morning, and by the time he'd caught up with his patient load that evening, Stephanie had already left for the day.

He could give her a call and ask her out for dinner, but he knew how easy it was to blow someone off over the phone, so he decided to wait until Thursday morning when he could see her face-to-face.

On Thursday, when there was no sign of Stephanie at the clinic, Phil discovered through Jason that she'd been invited to the local university to speak to Maria's fellow nurse-practitioner students.

Things weren't looking good, and, though contrary to his natural desire to see her as soon as possible, he decided to wait until Saturday evening at the postholiday-parade party at Jason's house. He'd missed her all week, and wanted to iron out that wrinkle in their relationship, the unspoken knowledge about his dating history. He understood how it must look to a woman like Stephanie. He couldn't make any guarantees, of course, but she seemed worth delving deeper into—dared he use the word?—a relationship. He scraped his jaw. It wasn't just any girl he'd ask to help with the task he had planned.

This is nuts, Stephanie thought as she drove back to her hotel from the university. Maybe the move to Santa Barbara and starting to practice medicine again had been more stressful than she'd expected. Each night this week she'd been dead tired, and the springboard of emotions that getting to know Phil had created couldn't be denied. Maybe she was premenstrual? She rubbed her forehead and mentally did some math. It was December 9 and she was supposed to have started her period on December 2. She'd been like clockwork ever since she'd had her tubes tied. Today she felt a little foggy headed and maybe a little tender in her breasts. She'd probably get her period any day now.

But she was a week late, and hadn't so much as spotted.

She shook her head as she pulled into her parking space at the hotel. It had to be stress.

California had a reputation for perfect weather, and on this Saturday in mid-December, while the rest of the country dealt with snowstorms and arctic cold snaps, the sky was clear and the temperature was in the high sixties. Rain was predicted for early tomorrow morning, but you couldn't prove it by the sky overhead.

Stephanie shaded her eyes with her palm and enjoyed the sight of the setting sun over the glistening blue ocean, then took a deep breath of salty air as she walked down the docks to Jason's berth.

An hour earlier she'd come off the phone from a

conversation with Celeste Conroy, who continued to improve since the bleeding scare earlier in the week. The best part of all was being able to tell her they'd successfully removed the small cancerous area on her cervix, and the tissue margins were all clear. If all continued to go well, the cerclage would keep her from going into premature labor later on.

Stephanie decided to compartmentalize her professional and personal life. With her duties as a physician completed today, she removed the mental stethoscope and…oh, hell…prepared to be Santa's helper. Nerves tangled in her stomach at the thought of confronting Phil after walking out on him the other night.

A memo had gone out at work, "Wear your most outrageous Christmas sweater," and she'd made a quick run to the Paseo to find something to fit the theme, but was too embarrassed to put it on until she got there.

Jason's yacht was decked out with the Midcoast Medical employees' handy Christmas decorations, and from this vantage point the boat promised, when lit up later, to thrill the spectators.

She smiled, even as her stomach fought off another wave of nervous flitters. She hadn't seen Phil all week except for fleeting moments coming and going at the clinic. She'd avoided his gaze once, and another time he made an abrupt turn and entered Jon's office. She'd failed miserably as fling material.

Claire waved and greeted her from the deck. An adorable curly-headed child with huge blue eyes stood by her side, and another baby, getting pushed back and forth in a stroller, sat plump and contentedly swaddled in extra blankets.

"This is my daughter, Gina," Claire said, then nodded toward the stroller. "And this is Jason Junior."

Looking more petulant than shy, Gina hugged her mother's thigh and buried her face rather than say hello. Claire smoothed the girl's hair with her free hand.

Stephanie gave herself a quick pep talk about not letting the children make her nervous. They were Claire's children, not hers, and from the look of it, Claire handled the job with aplomb. It was Christmas, a child's favorite time of year, and there was no way Stephanie could avoid missing her son, but just for today she vowed to not let it get her down. Just for today she'd let Christmas joy rub off on her and she'd smile along with everyone else on this festive occasion. Then, on Christmas Day, she would withdraw into her shell with her constant companion of grief.

She boarded the boat, her sweater in the original shopping bag, and almost immediately lost her balance when someone grabbed her knees. She reached for the boat rail and glanced down in time to hear a familiar squeal of hello. "Robbie, what are you doing here?"

"I get to thit on Thanta's knee," he said, pride beaming from his eyes.

"Me, too!" Gina had found her voice and chose to use it to stake her rightful claim.

Robbie made his version of a mean face at Gina—the silly scrunched-up look almost made Stephanie laugh—and crossed his arms. "He my brother."

"This was my bright idea," Claire said, looking apologetic. "Maybe I should have thought this through a little more."

Phil seemed to materialize from thin air. A sudden pop of adrenaline quickened her pulse. She'd pretend, for Claire's sake, that everything was normal.

Phil hadn't noticed her yet, but Jason and Gaby had obviously noticed him, and laughed. He'd gone for Surfer Dude Santa with belly pad beneath a reindeer-patterned Hawaiian shirt and red velvet pants with suspenders. And good sport that he was, he'd stuck an all-in-one Santa hair and beard combo on his head like a helmet. A huge grin made his eyes crinkle at the edges as he modeled his ridiculous outfit. His California version of Santa might raise brows, but it would fit right in with Santa Barbara and was the perfect touch for their Christmas-themed yacht.

He made a slow turn, hands out to allow Jason and Gaby to see the entire costume, including the surfboard-toting reindeer on the shirt. They blurted out a laugh. He'd been hoodwinked into the job and, instead of griping, he'd good-naturedly put his signature on it. The thought tugged at Stephanie's heart, and a bizarre notion catapulted through her brain. She could fall in love with a guy like Phil...if she didn't watch out.

Phil finally noticed her, and she saw a subtle change in his self-mocking. When their eyes met for a brief second, he nodded and her legs turned to water. She nodded back, unsure if she'd be able to talk coherently to him. Gina and Robbie, rushing to greet Santa, put a quick stop to her fears.

"Santa, Santa," the children chanted.

Suddenly distracted, Phil hugged both of them. An irrational sense of hurt made her fear she'd blown everything by leaving on Sunday night.

"Claire, I tell you, Roma and Dad will do anything for a cheap babysitter and a night out." He gave a good-hearted shrug, as if he was putting on a carefree performance for her sake. "It's a good thing I've got two knees," he said. "Ho, ho, ho."

Though sounding more resigned and not even close to a real Santa impersonator's laugh, he still delighted the kids. And Stephanie thought he might feel as much at a loss as she did about how to handle things between them.

"He's coming to my house first," Gina chided Robbie.

"Nah-uh," Robbie was quick to reply, arms tightly folded over his chest. "Mine."

"Go get dressed," Gaby said from over Stephanie's shoulder. She wore a gaudy red Christmas sweater that clashed with her magenta hair, and nudged Stephanie toward the stairs. "I want to take group pictures before it gets too crowded."

Whisked away to change, Stephanie barely had a moment to think about anything but putting on the Christmas sweater complete with a string of flashing Christmas lights on the appliquéd quilted tree. Aside from her mixed-up feelings about Phil, it actually felt good walking among the living again.

When she went up on deck, Jason had already turned on the lights. Everything twinkled and shone and the sight took her breath away. They really had created a winter wonderland. A dozen colorful strings of lights had been extended from the tip of the mainsail, from where they fanned out and were attached to the deck in a Christmas tree shape. At the top was a huge white lighted star. The half-size internationally decorated trees blinked and blinged, and with the added touch of a Scotsman, a Russian, a cowboy, a Dane and a Filipino standing next to them, they painted an impressive picture. Several lighted wreaths were hung strategically along the boat railing, and pine garland loaded heavily with glittery balls and blinking lights outlined the rails.

To top things off, two huge flashing neon Merry Christmas signs adorned both the bow and the stern. The remaining clinic employees sat on deck, wearing knitted caps and mufflers, assorted loud holiday sweaters and singing Christmas carols. If they didn't win first place in the Santa Barbara Chamber of Commerce Christmas lights parade, they should at least win the gaudiest-boat award!

Swept up with the holiday spirit, Stephanie couldn't help but laugh to herself. She hadn't felt this excited about celebrating Christmas in years, and it felt pretty darn great…until she came face-to-face with Santa.

He looked as uncomfortable as she felt. If only she could think of something witty to say. Something that would break this awkward trance they seemed stuck in.

"Nice sweater," he said, with the hint of teasing in his eyes.

It was the perfect excuse to lighten things up between them, to call a truce, and she grabbed it. "I like your suspenders, too."

They smiled cautiously at each other. His solid bedroom stare cut through her facade and flustered her. She focused on his white cloud of hair and beard for distraction, realizing she'd never think of Santa the same way again.

"Hey, let me get a picture," Jon said, camera in place, ready for his shot.

"Me, too," Gaby chimed in, at his side.

René stood smiling behind Jon, holding a bundle of baby wrapped in half a dozen blankets. "You may as well let them," she said. "They'll just keep pestering you until you pose."

Phil took Stephanie by the arm, pulled her closer, and whispered, "Smile pretty for the camera."

His unflappable charm disarmed her, all the apprehension she'd clung to vanishing. Maybe she was in over her head, but she couldn't deny her attraction to him.

"Great," Jon said. "Now let's go for a group shot."

Jason appeared, decked out in a captain's cap with minilights that blinked on and off. Everyone else lined up around him.

Almost as if being transported back in time, the magic and mystery of Christmas overcame Stephanie. Her skin became covered with goose bumps and her eyes prickled. It felt too good. She didn't deserve to feel this happy…during the holidays.

"Okay, that's enough," Phil said, clutching her arm and nudging her toward his appointed chair as if sensing her mood change. "We have work to do. How did I get talked into this again?" He stared into her eyes, where tears were threatening. "Oh, right—you!"

"I abstained, remember?" she said, grateful that everything seemed back to normal between them. It helped snap her out of the weepiness.

Deeply grateful for this night and all the distractions, she took her place and waved toward Jon on the docks as he snapped several more group shots. Then Jason backed the vessel out of the berth, laying on the air horn for a long and attention-getting blast.

Claire lifted first Gina and then Robbie onto Phil's

lap. He pulled his chin in, as if aliens from planet Xenon had just been dropped from a spacecraft.

"Listen up, you two." Claire held each of their chins in a hand. "Do not get down from Santa's lap. Do you understand?"

Mesmerized by her firm clutch, they gave her their undivided attention and both nodded.

Though more relaxed with Robbie, Phil looked completely out of his element, with Gina bouncing excitedly on his knee. Stephanie hid her smirk. At least he wasn't complaining.

It seemed as if it took forever to line up the participating boats and set sail in Santa Barbara bay. They'd head toward Stearns Wharf, sail around the end and along the other side, then down the coast for a few miles before starting back toward the harbor.

The magnificent sight of a fleet of decorated boats reflecting off the blackening sea made Stephanie's eyes prickle again. When she looked back toward shore and saw the rolling hillsides and houses heavily covered with holiday lights, and the palm tree silhouettes dotting the beach, she couldn't hold back her feelings. For the first time since Justin's death she'd explore the goodness of the season. She couldn't bring him back, but she could celebrate his short existence by refusing to let the sadness dictate her life. Even if it was only for tonight.

Overwhelmed, she let her tears brim and dribble down her cheeks. They weren't the usual tears that burned with guilt. Not today. They were tears of joy and goodwill…and letting go. Today she'd extend that goodwill to herself. A huge weight the size of Santa's gift sack seemed to lift from her shoulders. Suddenly feeling as buoyant as the ocean, she anchored herself to the rail and waved to the passing judges' motorboat, her smile genuine and filled with the spirit of the season.

Jason released the cork from the champagne bottle in his living room, sending it flying through the air as everyone ducked. While he splashed the bubbling liquid into several outreaching glasses, he beamed with satisfaction.

"Here's to a well-deserved win," he said. "We finally did it!"

Everyone cheered.

Phil saw Stephanie standing beside Claire and René, applauding along with everyone else.

The sight of her earlier on the boat had knocked him off balance. He'd felt compelled to make things right, but wasn't sure if she wanted anything to do with him, and he wanted to respect her feelings. He hadn't felt that lacking in confidence and confused over a woman since high school. All he knew for sure was that she'd left abruptly a week ago, and he hadn't been the same since. And that damn ticking clock counting down the days until she left for home didn't help either.

Under the bright lights of the Rogerses' family room, Stephanie's hair was decidedly red. The royal-purple satin blouse she wore accented the color even more. She'd taken off her ridiculous sweater, and he definitely liked what he saw.

He'd miss her when she was gone. Hell, he'd missed her all week. She'd stay here until the first of the year, and if he played his hand right, he'd get things back on track and hopefully have her back in his bed before the night was over.

He snagged an extra glass of bubbly and delivered it to her. "Here's to our win."

Her bright eyes widened and her generous smile let him know she was happy to see him. "And kudos to you for juggling two squirming kids all evening."

He shook his head. "Man, since Robbie has been sleeping with CPAP he has even more energy. I was ready to throw him overboard a couple of times, but I kept thinking Roma would be really mad at me."

She laughed. "You'd never do that."

"Figure of speech." He enjoyed the little patches of red on her cheeks and neck. He'd spent enough time around her to know that meant she was nervous. He still made her nervous. Was that a good thing? Hell, she made him nervous, too, and he liked it.

"Admit it, you love that kid," she said.

"He is my brother." Talking about kids wasn't exactly what he had in mind. He'd had a whole week to devise his plan. "Can I talk to you for a minute?" With his hand on her lower back, he guided her to a quiet corner of the room.

"What's up?" She gazed at him with suspicion.

"We're friends, right? And we're supposed to be honest with each other," he said, noticing her eyes soften at the edges and her lusciously alluring lips pout ever so slightly. He wanted to kiss her, but they were in a room full of fellow employees. Even though whispers and suspicions traveled the watercooler circuit at the clinic, he wasn't about to flaunt their private relationship. "That's why I want you to know that I'm ready to take the next step."

Wide-eyed disbelief had returned. She took a quick

sip of champagne and nearly choked on it. He tapped
her back as her eyes watered.

"Sorry, didn't mean to shock you."

She coughed and sputtered. "What are you talking
about—take the next step?"

"Listen," Phil said. "I know it's kind of hard to take a
man dressed in a surfin' Santa suit seriously, but I want
you to know I've really been doing a lot of thinking over
the last week."

The suspicious glint returned to her eyes.

"Yeah, and the thing is I've decided to try commitment out."

"What?" She blurted a laugh. "Just like that? You're
putting me on."

"Well, maybe one step at a time. Seriously, don't you
think that's progress for a guy like me?"

"Hey, that's great. Really, I think it's great," she said,
but the subtle slope of her shoulders and that naggingly
suspicious gaze wasn't very encouraging. She obviously
didn't believe he'd changed a bit.

"So you have any plans tomorrow?" he said.

The champagne flute was halfway to her mouth when
she tossed him a surprised glance.

"I thought I'd hit the local shelter. Maybe you can
help me pick out a dog?"

Bad timing. She'd taken another sip, and along with
her wry laugh she blew champagne out of her mouth.

"What? You don't think I can handle a committed
relationship with a dog?"

All she could do was shake her head and point her
finger at him with a one-day-I'll-get-you-back-for-this
glower.

He knew he was pushing the limit, but he couldn't

help playing with her, especially when her reaction was so satisfying. "What do you say, are you in?"

Having wiped her mouth, and found her voice again, she said, "I wouldn't miss that for the world."

What had gotten into Phil? He'd brought her a glass of champagne and strung her along with his newfound wisdom about relationships, then got her good. She shook her head and laughed to herself. The guy was completely spontaneous, and she thoroughly enjoyed him. She pushed aside the quick thought about love she'd had earlier.

He was ready to commit…to a dog.

She couldn't very well leave him to his own resources over such a big decision. The guy—the charming and sexiest Santa she'd ever laid her eyes on—needed help choosing a dog. How could she refuse?

Phil had hoped to bring Stephanie home with him tonight, but he didn't want to blow any progress he'd made by imposing his desires. He'd have to wait another day, get her all worked up over some canine's big brown eyes, have her help him make the dog at home then ask her to stay for dinner. If things worked out the way they usually did when the two of them were alone together, he'd put Fido in the yard and bring Stephanie back to his bed.

Not that he was using a dog simply to impress Stephanie. Once he'd thought about it and made the decision, he really wanted one. Loyal. Dependable. Warm. Loving. A dog would never leave him, and was exactly what he needed for companionship.

Phil turned the final corner to his street, rubbed his

jaw, and smiled. Being Santa had been a blast. Who could have guessed? If Stephanie hadn't pushed him into the job, he never would have known. And the constant smile on her face on the boat made all the humiliation worthwhile.

Something seemed different about her, he thought as he parked in his garage. He'd never been known for being intuitive, but he could have sworn she'd left half of her usual baggage behind tonight.

He'd picked up on her playful spirit and tested out the limits. He shook his head and grinned as he unlocked his house door. He'd imagined Stephanie Bennett doing all kinds of sexy things, but he'd never expected to see her spit champagne across the room. A hearty laugh tumbled from his throat as he stepped inside. It echoed off the empty house walls, and once again he was reminded how big and lonely his bachelor pad was.

The rows of metal cages, with every size, breed, and shape of dog filling every single one, almost broke Stephanie's heart. She could hardly bear to look into any of the dogs' eyes. The cages lined the walls of the cement-floored warehouse/shelter, where the smell of urine and dog breath permeated the air.

"I wish I could buy all of them," Phil said, echoing her sentiments.

His sincerity had her reaching for his hand.

He squeezed her fingers and gave her a tender glance. "This is going to be harder than I thought."

On the drive over, on a gorgeous sunny day, they'd discussed the kind of dog he was looking for—big, sleek and muscular. To Stephanie's ears his "kind of dog" sounded a bit like him. If she had her choice, she'd go for something petite and furry. Hmm, was that like her?

Loud barking and yipping made it almost impossible to carry on a conversation as they walked the length of the shelter. Some jumped and yipped incessantly, others hovered in the corners of their cages, and still others paced restlessly back and forth with anxious eyes taking everything in.

"Lots of these dogs got left behind when home owners walked away from their mortgages. With the lousy economy, other people couldn't afford to have a dog anymore," the shelter worker said. "We're hoping the Christmas season will help find some of these dogs homes."

Stephanie spotted a little bundle of cream-colored wavy fur with round brown eyes getting overrun by two other small dogs. It looked like a puppy.

The shelter worker must have picked up on her interest. "That one is a terrier mix. She's a bit older than most of the others."

"Hey, look at this one!" Phil called her attention away, but she glanced over her shoulder one last time at the so-called older dog, before moving on.

Amidst several cages of Labrador retrievers and German shepherds was a medium-size dark-furred dog.

"That one's a collie-Lab mix. One year old. Owner had to move out of state."

Phil petted the dog on his head, and the dog licked his hand.

"Both breeds are smart and they generally have good dispositions. Mixed breeds are often healthier than purebreds, too. They love their owners. Very loyal."

As if it was the easiest decision in the world, Phil nodded and smiled. "What's his name?"

"Daisy."

"It's a her, huh?"

"And she's been spayed."

"Good to know. Hey, Daisy, you like big yards and sunset walks along the beach?" The dog whimpered and licked his hand again.

Stephanie laughed at Phil's ability to charm females of all species.

"What do you think, Steph? Would Daisy and I make a good pair?"

His willingness to open his home to a forgotten pound dog warmed her insides. The change in his attitude since taking care of Robbie was astounding. She had the urge to give him a big kiss and hug, but touched his face instead. He hadn't shaved that morning, and the stubble made a scraping sound as she ran her fingers down his jaw.

"I think you and Daisy will make a great couple, and I promise I won't get jealous about your new female friend."

He smiled and nodded. "Then I'll take her."

As he filled out the paperwork and paid the fees, Stephanie kept going back to the little terrier mix up front. "Hey, sweetie," she whispered. The dog timidly explored the front of the cage, trying to sniff her fingers but not letting her touch his head. There seemed to be a world of sadness in his eyes. "You need a home, huh?"

"We'll take this one, too," Phil said from over her shoulder.

"What are you doing?" she said, rounding on him.

"I know love at first sight when I see it." He gave a magnanimous grin. "Consider him a Christmas present."

"I can't have a dog—I'm living in a hotel."

"The dog can stay with me until you go home. You have a town house in the desert, right?"

"Yes, but I…"

"Hey, don't analyze everything. Let's save two dogs today." Before she could respond, he looked for the shelter worker again. "What's this one's name?"

"Sherwood."

He laughed. "Sherwood. There you go. Stephanie and Sherwood. Sounds like a match made in heaven."

"How old is he?" she asked.

"He's older. Seven. His owner passed away."

That cinched it. The dog was grieving, something she understood completely. Though she felt inept, the shelter worker opened the cage and handed the dog to her. The trembling, compact dog fit perfectly in her arms. Fur partially covered soulful eyes, and a little pink tongue licked her knuckles. He was so trusting, and obviously missed his owner. The thought tied a string around her heart and squeezed. Phil was on to something. Maybe caring for a dog was the perfect stepping-stone for her lagging confidence. She could do this. She could take care of one small dog.

"You'll keep her until I move home?"

"I've got enough room for six dogs in my yard. Let's do it. Come on."

With more warm feelings washing over her, she hugged him and the dog yipped.

"Okay, Sherwood. Looks like you've got yourself

a new mommy," she said, holding the dog to her face and enjoying the tickly fur.

The warm feeling that had started at the animal shelter continued to grow as Stephanie spent the afternoon with Phil. They'd shopped for leashes and beds and the proper food for each breed and, most importantly, travel cages.

Now that they'd unloaded everything at Phil's house, Sherwood had timidly gone into his cage, almost as if it was a security blanket, and Stephanie tried to coax him out.

"Come on, sweetie. I won't bite," she said, down on her knees, head halfway into the cage. She reached for him and he let her hold him then licked her face again.

"Maybe you should carry him like that for a while, until he gets used to the new house," Phil said, his dog dancing around his feet.

She nodded, stirring that warm bowl of feelings brewing stronger and stronger for Phil. He'd been a prince today. For a guy who didn't know the first thing about committing to a woman, he sure had no problem bringing a dog home.

"I can't figure out why I never did this before," he said, petting Daisy's silky black-and-white fur.

"I guess you just needed a nudge."

As if they'd known each other all their lives, he kissed her while each of them held their new dogs. His warm and familiar mouth covering hers felt so right she hoped the day would never end.

And later, when he asked her to spend the night

with him, and she followed him down the hall to his bedroom, she realized the best part of the day was only getting started.

CHAPTER NINE

THE next week went by in a whirlwind. Stephanie and Phil were inseparable. She'd go to his house every day after work: they'd walk the dogs; catch up on any left-over paperwork from the clinic; cook dinner; make passionate love; have breakfast together; and head back to work. By Thursday, Phil suggested they carpool.

A red flag waved in Stephanie's mind. Wasn't car-pooling a thinly disguised assumption that she'd return to his house again that night? Why couldn't he come right out and ask her to move in with him? Was this how all of his "flings" progressed, him keeping a subtle bar-rier until he tired of the woman and quit finding ways to spend time with her?

She only had two more weeks in Santa Barbara—did she really need to complicate her stay by thinking in such a manner? If she'd mentally agreed to "a fling," why were her emotions lagging so far behind?

Giving herself a silent pep talk, she agreed to drive to work with him then mentally ran down the pros and cons of her decision. This was a fling—an unbelievably wonderful fling with a guy who made her happy in all respects, a guy who never asked questions or made demands.

"You think this carpool business is a good idea?" she asked.

"It's good for the environment." He grinned.

She shook her head and rolled her eyes.

"You're already staying here every night. Sherwood wants you around." He glanced across the front seat at her then quickly back to the road. "I kind of like having you around."

This from a guy who supposedly didn't like to get involved or commit to relationships. She really needed to get her mind straight over this fling business.

"What are you really asking me, Phil?"

He pulled into his assigned parking place at the clinic and parked then turned toward her with an earnest expression. "Since our time together is limited, I'm asking you to spend as much of it as possible with me." He reached for her hand and rubbed his thumb across her knuckles, igniting warm tingling up her wrist to the inside of her elbow. "We should explore this thing we've got going on."

So that was it. They had a "thing." Well, heck, she'd known they had a *thing* since the first time they'd kissed.

That red flag waved again. *He wants to have you in his bed every night, not have you move in or get involved or anything. He knows your time is limited. It gives him freedom to do whatever he wants with you... knowing you'll leave after Christmas.*

"Talk to me," he said. "I can see a million thoughts flying around your mind. Share one of them with me." His voice was husky and sincere. "Please."

She took a deep breath. "This is all so new to me. I guess I just need to know the rules."

"I'm the king of no strings, Steph. I think you know that."

She hesitated with a long inhalation. "No strings. Right."

Their eyes met and fused. For long silent moments they searched each other's souls for the truth. She wasn't positive what she read in his stare other than it made her feel dizzy and fuzzy-headed. She wasn't ready to tell him that it was too late, she'd probably fallen a little in love with him. How silly of her to think that. Love wasn't something you could do a little of. Love was like being pregnant—you either were or you weren't. Was she in love?

Hell, she'd really messed up with this fling thing. Next time, if there ever was a next time, she'd sit on the sidelines and leave it to the experts. Like Phil. He knew how to keep a sexy and satisfying relationship in its place. Just do it. Have a good time. Don't make any promises. Maybe it was a surfer's creed: ride the wave for all it's worth then move on to the next.

Apparently, Stephanie didn't have the no-strings gene.

Phil put his hand on the back of her head and pulled her toward him. His kiss was tender and meltingly warm. He kissed her as if he loved her, but that was her interpretation, her head was mixing everything up again. She'd blame it on being hormonal and still waiting for her period.

What he offered and what she felt were two different things. She needed to remember that. He only wanted her for two more weeks.

His lips kept nudging her, asking her to give back, to kiss him as if she meant it. She couldn't resist another second. Whatever words he'd just avoided saying, he communicated beautifully with his lips. I. Want. You. With. Me.

Did she need to know anything more than that?

As predicted on the previous night's news, the storm front moving down from Alaska had worked its way along the coast, first bringing gray skies, clouds, and cold temperatures on Thursday night, and by Friday morning, a week before Christmas Eve, full-out rain.

As the morning wore on, Stephanie became aware of something worse than stormy weather—nausea. Realizing exactly where she stood with Phil— nowhere!—had affected her more than she'd thought.

She sat with a new patient in her office. As she calculated the pregnant woman's expected due date, it hit her. Her hand trembled to the point of being unable to write.

She cleared her throat and verbally gave the due date, then used her best acting skills to hide the anguish brewing in her heart. "Congratulations. You'll have a late-summer baby. August, to be precise."

The young woman clapped her hands and beamed with joy. The complete opposite of how Stephanie felt. A late-summer baby?

The instant she'd ushered the ecstatic woman from her office, she got out the lab kit and drew a vial of blood from her arm, labeled it with a bogus name, and hand carried it to the laboratory for a STAT test.

After lunch, spent sitting in the darkness of her office, Stephanie frantically flipped through her reports, looking for the single most important lab of her life. She knew it was preposterous. She'd had her tubes tied! What were the odds? They certainly weren't in her favor—she'd looked it up—three different times. But defying the odds, she'd missed her period and showed early signs of pregnancy with fatigue, tender breasts, and mild nausea. It simply couldn't be!

With dread and a trembling hand, she continued to skim through the reports, and after a few more, there it was—her pregnancy blood test—and it was positive.

Her stomach protested as if she'd taken a five-hundred-foot free fall. Her pulse surged. She couldn't breathe. Her body switched to fight-or-flight mode.

She surged from the chair and strode toward the door on unsteady legs, her footsteps soon turning to a jog. She reached the clinic entry in a full sprint and just as she saw Phil on the periphery of her vision, she sprang outside and down the street, through the icy, pouring rain.

With all systems on automatic panic, she ran without a destination, unaware of the weather. She ran from her breaking point, she ran in a futile attempt to keep her sanity, her only goal to prolong the inevitable, to avoid the truth—she was pregnant.

"Stephanie, come back here!"

What in hell was she doing running down the street? Didn't she know it was practically hailing?

Phil raced down the sidewalk, slipped in a puddle, and nearly crashed into a bush. He recovered his balance, knocked a rolling trashcan out of his way then hurdled another, all while keeping Stephanie in his sight.

Not waiting for the streetlight, she crossed Cabrillo

Boulevard, recklessly dodging a car, and headed for Stearns Wharf.

He didn't have a clue what had made her snap and take off for the pier in a storm like this, but he sure as hell planned to catch up and find out, if she didn't get herself killed first!

She'd reached the beach, and headed for the pier. It may not have been such a great move, clearly not well thought out, but he had no choice. If he wanted to catch her, he'd have to tackle her, and finally he got close enough. He lunged and brought her down with a mild thud onto the wet sand.

She rolled onto her back, squealing. "What are you doing? Are you crazy?"

"I'm not the one sprinting between cars in the rain, darlin'," he panted. "Now, are you going to tell me what's going on?"

"Let go of me." She squirmed to break free.

"Not gonna happen. Calm down and talk to me." He pinned her arms above her head.

She sighed like an outsmarted teenager, wagging her head back and forth. Her tears blended with the rain. "I'm pregnant."

A rocket left his chest, headed straight toward his head, and exploded. The shock waves zapped every ounce of strength left in his hands. "What? You're what?"

"I'm pregnant!"

"But your tubes are tied!"

She glanced up at him. "See? There's a reason I was running."

He sat back on his knees, raking his hands through

his soaked hair. His vision blurred from the combination of rain and disbelief.

"I'm kicking myself for tackling you." He hopped up, pulling her up with him, before he spit out some sand. He couldn't leave her floundering on the beach. "Come here." He drew her into his rain-drenched arms, into a gritty, sand-wrapped hug. "What do we do now?" He felt her trembling and wondered, coupled with his jarring reaction, how much he was contributing to it.

"I can't have this baby." She wouldn't look him in the eyes. She kept shaking her head.

"I know you don't do kids, but maybe this is a good thing. Maybe you can get beyond that hang-up now."

"No!"

"Okay. Maybe just give yourself time to think this over."

"You don't understand." She sounded tormented.

Maybe he'd been too wrapped up in his own reaction. Sure, he was shocked, but the craziest thing followed—he wasn't upset about it. She obviously had an issue about the pregnancy, hence the jogging on the beach in the pouring rain. This was all new territory for him, too. He needed to handle her delicately, find out what she was thinking—because he cared. He gave a big fat damn about her and her feelings, and, most importantly, about the baby they'd made. "Try me. Tell me why you can't have this kid."

She tried to pull away, but his strength had returned and he didn't let her.

"Let me go!"

"No!" He clenched his teeth and fought to keep her near. "Tell me why you don't want the baby."

"I killed my baby." She spit out the words as if they were poison.

"What?" His pulse paused; a distant rumble of thunder helped jump-start it. "I don't believe that."

"I killed him. I let him fall." Her head drooped so low, he could barely hear her.

Lightning snapped and forked into branches over the ocean. Her confession deserved wisdom that he didn't have, but he wanted more that anything to do right by her. He'd never experienced anything close to this new-found desire in his life.

"Let's sit down. Get out of this rain." He led her to the covered bus stop a few feet away by the porpoise fountain. "Tell me what happened. I want to know everything." He took her by the shoulders and forced her to look at him. "You've got to tell me."

"You'll hate me when you find out."

"No. I won't." And he meant it. By God, he meant it.

She paced within the small confines of the bus stop as if she was a panicked animal, gulping her tears, gasping her words.

"Justin was a super-colicky baby. He never grew out of it. He was four months old and this time he'd cried three nights in a row. You have no idea how terrible it feels not to be able to console your child." She shuddered, and he fought the urge to wrap her in his arms for fear she'd quit talking.

"No matter what I did, he wouldn't calm down. I paced and sang. I rubbed his back. I gently bounced him. I walked and walked…all night long."

She hiccuped for air, hugged herself, hysteria emanating from her eyes. He wanted to console her, but couldn't fathom how. No wonder she'd freaked out with Robbie that first night.

"My arms ached. My back throbbed. I was exhausted. No matter how long I walked, no matter how I held him, sang to him, kissed him, he kept crying. Then finally the crying stopped. Justin had calmed down and gone to sleep in my arms. I didn't know what to do. If I moved he might start up again."

She spoke as if reliving the moment—locked in another time and place. Phil knew she couldn't have killed her baby. He knew there was a logical explanation, one she couldn't accept.

"If I put him in his crib I knew for certain he'd wake up. I eased onto the couch and he kept sleeping on my chest. So peaceful. So beautiful. For the first time in hours I found comfort. Comfort in the feel of my precious baby in my arms, and comfort for my aching back, my burning, sleepy eyes. I laid my head against the cushions and my son's gentle breathing lulled me to sleep."

A feral flash in her eyes alerted him that the hysteria was back. "I fell asleep!" she said, pain contorting her face. She continued her story as if he wasn't there. "I fell asleep," she sobbed. "And the next thing I knew… Oh, God, my baby!"

She dissolved into tears, crumpled to the bench. Phil rushed to lift her, to hold her up, to embrace her. After she settled down a bit he cupped her shoulders and stared into her eyes. "Tell me, sweetheart. Tell me everything."

She hiccuped another sob. "Justin fell off my chest, he fell off the couch, and…" She cried so hard she heaved, fluids pouring from every orifice on her face. She wiped her eyes with her palms, even as she cried more. "He hit his head on the table…"

Phil had never heard a woman cry like this in his life. He'd never seen such primal torture. He'd never imagined the depth of pain ripping at her.

"It damaged his brain." Then, as if finally giving in to the nightmare, her shoulders slumped in total defeat. "He died the next day."

Phil held her so tight he worried she might not be able to breathe, but she held him back, all trembles and shivers. "I never got to say goodbye, Phil," she whimpered, collapsing against his chest.

"Baby. Oh, honey. No. No, it wasn't your fault. Who let you believe it was your fault?" He pulled back to look at her. She avoided his eyes. "You weren't a single mother. Your man should have helped. You shouldn't have had to do it all yourself. Don't you see, he should have been there for you." Feeling anger at the bastard who'd let her down, Phil kissed her cheek.

They held each other tight for several minutes. What the hell should he do now? A maelstrom of emotions, fears, and doubts knocked him off balance. He could only imagine how Stephanie felt. She thought she'd killed her baby, didn't deserve to ever be a mother again, had had her tubes tied to make sure she never would be, and still wound up pregnant.

And he was the father.

He didn't know what else to do, so he put his sopping wet jacket over their heads, and escorted Stephanie back to the clinic. When they got close, he flipped open his cell phone and called Jason as he steered Stephanie away from the clinic and toward his car.

"Jase, I'm taking Stephanie home. She's not feeling well."

Phil undressed Stephanie. She'd slipped into a stupor, trembling from the cold. He was in near shock, too, but one of them needed to function. He turned on the shower and waited for it to heat up then thrust her inside. She gasped, but didn't fight him.

He ripped off his wet and gritty clothes and climbed in with her, easing her head under the water, making sure her body warmed up.

"Come on, honey, turn around. Let the water hit your back." The steamy shower felt good. He dipped his head under the stream and shook it.

What in the hell were they supposed to do now?

Sherwood and Daisy came sniffing around the bathroom, obviously aware that something wasn't right.

With Stephanie still out of it, Phil tried to gather his thoughts. He'd never been in this position before. He watched her through the water. She stared blankly at the tile. His heart ached for her. He could only imagine the torture she'd lived through, the guilt, the self-hatred, and now her hibernating nightmare had been reawakened.

He washed her hair and lathered his own. The excess sand and mud gathered around the drain.

"Are you warmer now?"

She didn't respond.

"Let's get you dried off then I'll put you to bed."

Her worst fear may have materialized, except there was one thing different this time around.

He was the father.

CHAPTER TEN

PHIL bundled a second blanket over Stephanie, but she still trembled. He made a snap decision to share his body warmth, and climbed under the covers then spooned up against her. She snuggled into his hold. Heavy rain sounded like Ping-Pong balls on the roof, and crackles of thunder in the distance made the cuddling even more intimate.

After the shower, he'd blow-dried and brushed her hair, and now it splayed across the pillow, tickling his face. It seemed odd to smell his standard guy shampoo in her hair instead of the usual flowers-and-dew-scent shampoo she used. Up on one elbow, he pushed the waves away from her shoulder and dropped a kiss on her neck.

"We'll get through this, Steph," he whispered.

They'd leaped a thousand steps ahead in their relationship with today's news. What should they do? He'd just finished a crash course on parenting with Robbie and had barely made the grade, but this was different. They'd made a baby. Together. Was he ready for this?

And what about Stephanie? The last thing in the world she wanted was a child. He'd never been in this position before. One thing was certain; he didn't want to run away from the challenge. A part of him was excited about being a father.

A swell of tender feelings made Phil pull her closer. He pressed another kiss to that special spot on her shoulder.

Stephanie needed oblivion. She needed to find one tiny corner of her mind and hide there. She didn't want to think. Couldn't bear the truth.

A vague memory of Phil bathing and drying her then brushing her hair filled her heart with gratitude. Even in her haze, she could sense the delicate way he'd treated her. Now his warm hands surrounded her and pulled her close. His breath caressed her neck. He kissed her... there. Chills fanned across her breasts and she suddenly knew how to keep from thinking about anything but Phil.

She turned into his arms and eager mouth. His kiss was different. The passion was still there, but this one felt warmer than all the others had. Phil handled her gently, lovingly, taking their kisses slowly, yet building each on the next until she longed for more of him. She needed his hands touching her everywhere, and guided one to her breast. He didn't require schooling on the rest. She cupped his head at her chest as he kissed and taunted her. Desire burrowed through her, down to her belly.

As his arms explored and caressed every part of her, her legs entwined with his locking him tight. With his passion obvious, she moved against him, placing him at her entrance. His hand moved between them, touching and teasing her, making her squirm for more. She needed to forget everything, and Phil's deep kisses and sex would soothe all the aching in her soul.

His tongue delved into her mouth as he simultaneously entered her with a slow, determined thrust. She gasped as she stretched and gloved him. He kissed her harder and quickened his rhythm, the building heat pulsing through her center. Her inner muscles throbbed as he edged farther inside. His breathing went rough and ragged and he cupped and tilted her hips for deeper access. She gulped for air and ground against his powerful penetration, her muscles and nerves winding tighter and tighter with every lunge.

He held her at the peak of pleasure with the steady pace, and she thrived on every sensation swirling through her body. She never wanted the exquisite feeling to end and, languishing there with her, it seemed his only desire was to please her. Feeding on the suspended moments of bliss, her hunger grew. He'd made her frantic and dependent on him to take her all the way. As if reading her thoughts, he doubled his rhythm, pushing and nudging her to the brink, holding her there until she begged for release and he erupted.

Tears streamed down her cheeks as she quivered and gave in to the pulsations pounding through her body, floating her outside of time and mind and, like a heavy sedative, numbing her to harsh reality.

Phil had taken her there—to oblivion.

Stephanie cracked open an eye. The room was still dark. She'd been sleeping, one glance at the bedside clock told her, for hours. Phil breathed peacefully beside her, his warmth like a snug cocoon. Sherwood had curled into a ball at the foot of the bed, and Daisy sprawled out on a nearby rug.

The snapshot of domestic tranquility shocked her back into the moment.

An odd fragment of thought repeated itself in her mind. *Who let you believe it was your fault? You weren't a single mother. Your man should have helped. You shouldn't have had to do it all yourself. Don't you see, he should have been there for you.*

She blinked and sat up as the course of the afternoon came roaring back through her mind. Phil rustled and turned. She studied him. Had he said those words merely to console her or did he really believe them?

Was a guy like Phil capable of committing to one woman? Would it matter if he could? She shook her head—she couldn't handle this pregnancy. She never deserved to be a mother again.

She lay back on the pillow and stared through the shadows at the ceiling, desperately in need of sorting through her problems.

She studied Phil's mop of dark blond hair, his straight and strong profile. She ran her finger along the length of his red-tinged sideburn. In other circumstances, she could see herself waking up next to a guy like Phil for the rest of her life. If things were different.

It was a fool's dream.

You don't deserve to be happy. You're a murderer.

Out of reflex, she curled into a ball and covered her eyes. The negative thoughts her husband had charged her with day after day until they'd divorced became so strong she couldn't ward them off. A queasy feeling took hold in her stomach, and self-hatred pulled her deeper inward. She definitely couldn't keep the baby.

"Are you all right?" Phil took her by the shoulders and shook her. "Hey, what's going on? Are you having a nightmare?" He pulled her to him and kissed the top of her head.

"Yes," was all she could whisper. "A nightmare."

"Come here," he said, rubbing her back and kissing her again.

He wanted to protect her. Had her ex-husband ever offered to protect her at the worst moment of her life? No. He'd blamed her. He'd called her out as the monster she was.

What kind of person would do that? he'd accused.

Along with the vivid memory, Stephanie whimpered, and Phil drew her closer to him. His warm chest and strong arms gave little solace. She didn't deserve solace.

"Let me take care of you," he said. 'I don't want anything bad to happen to you."

What happened to two weeks of good times? No strings attached? Now, only because she was pregnant, he wanted to take care of her? If she weren't pregnant, would he still want her? Could she trust a man like Phil to be there if she needed him?

He was practically a stranger, and she needed to think things through.

Confused and unable to respond to his caring words, she bolted from the bed.

He looked like a man about out of patience.

"Phil…" She paced the length of the rug. "This wasn't supposed to happen with us."

"You're right. But it did, and now we have to figure out what to do."

Why did he sound so reasonable?

The jumble of feelings and fears caused that queasy sensation to double into a fist of nausea. Before she could think another thought, she sprinted for the bathroom.

Phil sat outside the washroom door, listening to Stephanie heave as if exorcising a demon. He scrubbed his face. What in hell was he supposed to do now? Was he anywhere near ready to be a father? At the moment it seemed the bigger problem was that Stephanie felt determined *not* to be a mother again.

What kind of mind game had her ex-husband played on her to make her feel so unworthy of a second chance?

Behind the door, the toilet flushed and the faucet was turned on. For Stephanie's fragile sake, no matter how much he wanted to, he wouldn't dare broach the subject that *they* were having a baby until she brought it up.

Maybe he could distract her. Why not pretend things were the same as they were two days ago? What normal activity would they have done this weekend before everything had changed?

"I was thinking that maybe today we could shop for a Christmas tree," he called through the door, feeling completely at a loss for what to say or do. All he knew was that he wanted to make things easier for her. Maybe he could distract her with something fun and frivolous like buying a Christmas tree. It was the season.

She didn't answer.

Lame idea. Okay, he'd think of something else. He'd help her get through the shock of it by keeping her busy, and maybe in the process he'd manage to work out his own feelings. "Or we could take the dogs to the beach."

Still no answer.

A few minutes later, she emerged from the bathroom fully dressed.

He went on alert.

"I'm going away," she said. "I need to be alone."

He jumped to his feet. "What? Don't I figure into this?"

With eyes as flat as stone, she looked at him. "Ultimately, it all comes down to me and what I decide to do."

He words were like a slap to the face. Just like that, she'd shut him out. He needed to buy time, to keep her there. "At least let me fix you something to eat."

"I don't want anything."

"You can't just think about yourself anymore." Ah, damn, that had been the wrong thing to say. Why was he such an idiot?

She gave him a measured look. He wished he could see inside her mind, to figure out what was going on. He was at a loss and she wasn't having a thing to do with his fumbling attempts to keep her there.

Stunned silent, he watched her gather up her purse and leave.

Phil couldn't stand staying in his house alone, so he herded the dogs into his Woodie and drove to the beach. Sherwood stayed close to his side as Daisy romped through the waves, chasing the Frisbee he threw again and again.

Never in his life had he been more confused about

a woman. He'd covered for his true feelings when he'd insisted they carpool to work together. He hadn't wanted to scare her off by asking her to move in with him for the rest of her time in Santa Barbara, though that was exactly what he'd wanted. Hell, these new feelings scared him enough for both of them. The problem was, for the first time in his adult life he was open to exploring where this "thing" between him and Stephanie might lead. And she'd have nothing to do with him.

He'd never cherished a woman in his life, yet last night, after she'd told him her darkest secret and they'd made love, he'd felt the subtle shift of his heart. She'd transformed from hot girlfriend to the woman he loved…and she was carrying their child. Had he just admitted he loved her?

He swallowed, wanting nothing more than to prove he could be the kind of man she deserved. A man who believed in her, who'd never let her down. Was he capable of such a thing?

He'd learned an important fact about himself when Robbie had been thrust on him. When he set his mind to something, he could do it. No matter how foreign or hard, he could make it work. He and his little brother were closer than ever before, and Phil was quite sure he could do even better by his own kid. The thought excited him, and he wanted to make things work out with Stephanie. He'd never wanted anything so much in his life.

Yet, just like his mother, when life had gotten tough, she'd split.

Daisy scampered toward him, soaking wet, and dropped the slobbery Frisbee at his feet. Deep in thought, he hardly noticed he'd thrown the toy back to sea. Sherwood snuggled on his lap. Without thinking, he rubbed the dog's ears.

"Don't worry, boy, she'll be back for you. I'm the one she left."

Phil couldn't sleep all weekend. He felt like hell on Monday, and with a million lectures planned for Stephanie, he was surprised to find out she'd called in sick. As hard as it was, he'd given her the weekend to sort things through, but she still wasn't ready to face him. Or their baby.

Frustrated, he scraped the stubble on his jaw. Damn, he'd forgotten to shave, but it didn't matter. He was far more concerned whether Stephanie had made a rash decision or not. Damn it, he deserved to be in on *any* decisions she made about their baby, but she wouldn't answer her phone. He'd called by the extended-stay hotel, only to be told she'd checked out.

He dialed her cell number again and it went directly to messages, then he shoved it back into his pocket. Gaby give him a strange look.

"What?" he said.

"Nothing." She went back to her task as if it was the most important thing on the planet.

Jason buzzed him on the intercom. "Hey, just wanted to tell you that Claire is going to pick up as many of Stephanie's patients as she can. I'll see a few myself."

"I'm a pulmonologist." Phil censured the expletive he wanted to utter. "I don't know squat about gynecology. Can't help." He clicked off without giving Jason a chance to respond.

* * *

Stephanie cried about everything. What to eat. What to wear. Whether to get out of bed. Whether to run away to the desert. Every single thing about life set her off.

She'd changed hotels, and gave strict instructions that no one was to know which room she was in. Yet deep inside she wished Phil would find her. And that made her cry, too.

With each passing day, she grew more aware of the life forming inside her, and with that knowledge she forged a private bond with the baby. The thought of giving it up…made her cry.

She couldn't fight her desire to be in Phil's arms any more than she could resist his easy charm, so she'd opted to stay away. When she'd bared her soul to him, he'd acted more like a prince than a playboy. He'd gathered her close to his chest and stroked her cheek with his thumb, and she'd almost believed that things could work out for them. Almost.

She'd seen all the evidence over the past month. He'd professed to be a confirmed and happy bachelor, yet he owned a house fit for a family. He loved to putter around in the yard and garden just as much as he liked to surf. And he was a great cook, better than she was.

When she saw how he was with Robbie, she knew he'd make a great father for some lucky child some day. And when he'd suggested they each buy a dog, it had almost been as if he'd wanted to test the waters on commitment.

But that was her side of the story. What he really thought or felt would remain a mystery, because she couldn't face him. Not with what she had planned.

She sighed and pulled the comforter closer. Besides,

he deserved a lady who wanted kids, and she'd finally
made up her mind what she was going to do. And the
decision…made her cry.

CHAPTER ELEVEN

STEPHANIE'S sense of duty drove her back to work on Wednesday. That and the fact she couldn't bear to be alone with her tortured thoughts another day.

She entered the MidCoast Medical clinic cautiously, peeked around the door and edged her way inside.

The first voice she heard was Phil's and she almost ran the other way. A fist-size knot clenched her stomach, forcing her to stand still.

"Gaby," he said, "I asked you to bring Mr. Leventhal in this morning. Why is he still on the schedule for this afternoon?" He sounded irritated.

"It didn't work with his schedule, Dr. Hansen." Smooth professional that she was, Gaby didn't let his snit bother her. "Welcome back, Dr. Bennett."

Stephanie had never seen Phil look so horrible. He had dark circles under his eyes similar to football players' black antiglare paint, and when was the last time the man had shaved? His hair was in need of a good combing, too, and…did he actually have on two different-colored socks?

He stopped in his tracks when he noticed her. She didn't look any better than he did. His consuming stare made her forget how to breathe. All she could do was nod and make a straight line for her office. She felt his glare on her back the entire way, and prayed he wouldn't follow her.

With a trembling hand, she reached for the doorknob. How would she make it through the day?

Feeling emotionally and physically drained, she wondered how much longer she could keep going like this. After the New Year, she'd move back to Palm Desert, but first she had to get through Christmas, and she owed the medical clinic the time she'd signed on for. After she put on her doctor's coat, she wrapped her hands around her waist and realized she'd been doing that a lot lately. The baby was quickly becoming a part of her every thought.

Maria Avila came waddling into the clinic. "My back is killing me," she said.

"Why don't you go home, take a load off your feet? You don't have to do this today," Stephanie said.

"Are you kidding? This is what I live for. If I go home, I'll have two kids under the age of five to chase around. Heck, I know where I'm better off." She gave a wry laugh, and her face lit up with her usual infectious grin. "Besides, I need to make up for that clinical day I missed on Thanksgiving."

Stephanie couldn't help but smile back as she shook her head. "Here's our first patient. Why don't you do the honors?" At least one of them wanted to be there.

Maria snatched the chart. "Great!"

All morning Maria shadowed Stephanie. Occasionally, she rubbed her back and sighed, but never complained about the highly charged pace Stephanie insisted on keeping. It was the only way to keep her mind off Phil and their baby.

At lunchtime, Stephanie holed up in her office with a sack lunch, and Maria waddled off to the nurses' lounge.

"I'm gonna go put my feet up," Maria said, on her way out of the office.

No less than five minutes later, just as Stephanie finished a small sandwich, a rapid knock alerted her to someone at the door. Her heart stammered, and she prayed it wasn't Phil.

The door swung inward as it became evident her prayer hadn't been answered. He closed it and strode toward her desk, his intense gaze knocking the wind out of her.

"Have you made up your mind yet about what you plan to do?"

She stared at her desk. There wasn't the slightest tone of compassion in his voice. He hadn't wasted one second on preliminaries. If he wanted to be direct, she'd join him. "I'm going to give the baby up for adoption."

Her decision hit Phil as if a boulder had dropped on his chest—it crushed him and made it hard to breathe. Give their baby up? He'd been on the verge of telling her he loved her the other morning, the day she'd left. She'd put him through hell this week while he impatiently waited for her to make her decision. Now she'd made the second-worst decision he could have imagined. Give up their baby?

Could he honestly love a woman who would walk away from her child? She wasn't an unwed teenager— she was a well-established adult who could easily care for a child. Yet she wanted to give the baby away. It didn't make any sense, but he'd never been in her shoes.

He couldn't imagine how it must feel to bear the brunt of a child's accidental death.

He wanted more than anything to be angry at her for resisting this special gift, but he couldn't. The fact was he loved her. He wasn't sure if she felt anything for him, though. Her careless disregard for his feelings proved otherwise.

"The baby is mine, too. Remember?" he said. "We made it together."

She glanced at him, as if it had never occurred to her that he might want to be involved in the decisions.

He stood before her, hands at his sides, opening and closing his fists. "How selfish of you. You haven't even asked me what I'd do."

Surprise colored her eyes. She sat straighter. Had it really never occurred to her that he'd want to be involved with any decision she made about their baby? Things were more screwed up than he'd imagined.

"I'm sorry if that's what you think. Doesn't it always fall on the woman?" She stood and met him eye to eye. He fought the urge to grab her arms and shake her. "You've got your carefree life. You've never given me a hint that you were interested in anything more than sex and a good time, and suddenly I'm supposed to consult you because I got pregnant? Is that it?"

She'd challenged him, and he needed to tell her the truth. If nothing else, she deserved the truth.

"The day I met you," he said, "I was really turned on by your looks, but the more I got to know you, the more I knew you'd been hurt in life. I just wanted to be your friend and, if I was lucky, maybe be your lover. I never would have dreamed what followed."

"That I'd screw things up and get pregnant?"

He ignored her defiant tone. "That I would fall in love with you."

Stephanie needed to sit down.

Tingles burst free in her chest and rained over her body. She squeezed her eyes closed, and soon large tears dripped over her cheeks. She clenched her jaw to keep from blubbering. If only she weren't pregnant, she'd be free to love him, too. "Phil…"

"I want you to know where I stand." He knelt in front of her and looked into her face. She bowed her head to hide her tears.

At a loss for one single word, Stephanie withdrew into her thoughts. She loved him; *he* loved her, so why couldn't they have a happy ending? Because she couldn't bear to lose another child—she still didn't trust herself.

"If you're giving up the baby," he said, "give it to me."

"Give it to you?" Oh, God, how could she do that? She loved Phil, and he wanted to keep their baby. Remembering the special love she'd felt from him last Friday night, and how he'd taken care of her like a mother hen, she believed he loved her, but would he want her if she wasn't pregnant? Now she'd lose both the baby and Phil. Could she remove herself so easily from the equation? If she changed her mind and wanted to keep the baby, would he want her, too? Or would he hate her?

"I'll do the best I can as a father."

She couldn't believe what he was telling her.

By putting him in this situation, not by choice, she'd never know if he stayed with her out of love or obligation, and not knowing for sure would kill her and eventually ruin their relationship. Oh, God, her mind was so mixed up, she couldn't think straight.

"Please don't hate me, Phil. You can't under-stand…"

He shook his head and paced the floor. "Yes, losing your baby was a tragedy. I can't imagine how it must feel, but, Stephanie, you're alive, not dead, and you've got to let it go. That was three years ago. It's time to move on."

He was right, she knew he was right, but she was so damn stuck in her self-loathing rut…

Amy came rushing through the door. "Maria's water broke, and she's having contractions!"

Stephanie jumped to her feet, her legs having turned to rubber bands. Maria had gone into labor, as she'd been threatening for six weeks since Stephanie had first met her.

Words, as dry as the desert, crawled out of her mouth. "Have you called the paramedics?"

"She wants you, Doctor," Amy said, eyes huge from adrenaline.

She hadn't signed on for this. It said so in her con-tract—no delivering babies.

"Where is she?" Stephanie asked in a wobbling voice, following Amy to the procedure room.

Phil remained at her side, supporting her elbow and walking briskly with her. "You know what to do, and I'll be here, right here. We'll get through this together."

His words of encouragement meant more than she could say.

Stephanie rushed into the procedure room, where Amy had left Maria between contractions. Phil was right on her heels.

"Maria, do you think you can make it to the hospital?" Stephanie said.

"Feels like the kid's head is between my knees!"

Claire appeared. "I'm here if you need me." Word had traveled fast through the clinic.

Surrounded by her clinic family and Phil, Stephanie felt confidence spring back to life. She'd delivered more babies than she could count. She could do this. She went to the sink and splashed water on her face and washed her hands, then gowned up and gloved. "Let's have a look," she said.

This was Maria's third baby, the woman knew the drill.

She'd check for effacement, dilatation and station. "One hundred percent, ten centimeters, plus three. I guess your baby doesn't plan to wait for an ambulance," Stephanie said, her heart kicking up a couple notches on the beat scale.

Amy rushed around the room gathering everything they might possibly need.

Stephanie glanced over her shoulder at Phil, who was looking a little pale, but was still there.

He touched her arm and nodded. "You'll do fine. Now I'm going to step out of your way, but holler if you need me."

As if on cue, Maria let out a guttural sound.

Stephanie saw Maria's abdomen tighten into a hard ball. Now was the time to click into the moment and do what she'd been trained for. All other thoughts left her mind. Half an hour later, she positioned herself at the birth canal before giving a terse command. "Push!"

A tiny head with dark hair matted with vernix crowned.

"Keep pushing!" She slowly guided the baby's face-down head through the birth canal. "Okay, now stop pushing." She made a quick check to make sure the umbilical cord wasn't wrapped around the baby's neck. It wasn't. "Push. Push."

Soon the entire body flopped into her waiting hands, and the baby let out a wail.

Stephanie held the newborn as if he was made of porcelain. The squirming bundle of perfection mewed and tried to open his eyes. A booster shot of adrenaline made her hands shake. *What if I drop him?* Her arms felt as if they carried the weight of the world.

Phil appeared at her side, and put his gloved hands around the child for added support. His eyes met hers and she saw all the confidence she lacked right there. He believed in her. That look told her he knew she could do it. He'd never doubted her. He knew she could handle her own baby, too.

She bit her bottom lip to stop herself crying. Hadn't she done enough of that lately? "It's a boy!" Emotionally wrung out, she held the baby close enough for Maria to see. "He's gorgeous."

Maria grinned and nodded in agreement as Stephanie laid the newborn on her stomach.

"May I?" Phil asked, snipping the umbilical scissors in the air.

"Be my guest," Maria said, cuddling her baby to her breast.

Phil glanced at Stephanie. "I wanted to get a little practice in before our baby arrives," he whispered into her ear, before severing the cord.

His words meant more than anything in the world just then.

After the placenta was delivered, and the ambulance arrived to transport Maria, Stephanie cleaned up and went back to her office. Phil was right at her side. His eyes were bright with the buzz from Maria's delivery as he closed the door.

"You were fantastic. You can handle anything you set your mind to," he said.

The high from the delivery had boosted her confidence, and Phil's support meant everything to her. He stepped closer and touched her shoulder.

"We're going to have a baby. Steph. Look at me. In case you're wondering, I want you and I want our kid."

She gave him a questioning glance, her heart thumping so hard she thought it might crack a rib.

"I'm ready to make the leap," he said. "And it's all because of you, sweetheart."

If she'd ever doubted that he loved her, that doubt vanished. Even though he knew her tragic secret, he still loved her. He was the best man she'd ever met.

"Nothing will sway me. Now that I've discovered you, I can't let you go," he said. "I've fallen crazy in love with you." He took her into his arms. "I'm here to tell you I'm ready. I want you. You're the woman I love. But there's one thing that will hold us back, that is if you don't love me, too."

Why hadn't she told him? He'd opened his soul and she'd been wallowing in self-pity. He hadn't cursed her and run off when he'd found out she'd dropped her baby. He'd forced her to open her heart with small steps and a dog named Sherwood. He'd made love to her as if she were a goddess. He'd forced his way inside her fortress and conquered her heart. The guy deserved to know how she felt.

"I do. I love you, Phil. More than I can ever express."

A relieved grin stretched across his face and he covered her mouth with his, whispering over her lips, "It's about time you admitted it."

After he'd kissed her thoroughly, leaving her breathless and weak-kneed, he held her at arm's length.

"You need to forgive yourself. *Really* forgive yourself. Your ex-husband let you down. He was a jerk. These horrible things happen in life, and somehow we have to dig deeper and keep going.

"I love you and I promise to never let you down. And if I do, you have my permission to call me on it. I won't run. I won't hate you. I'll love and respect you. I'll always love you, Stephanie."

She crumpled into his embrace on another wave of tears, and he welcomed her with open arms. With the deepest feeling of connection to another human being she'd ever felt, she hugged him back.

They belonged together, both broken and jagged along the edges but a perfect fit. Filled with hope, she knew without a doubt that his unconditional love would finally help her heal.

"So what do we do now?" he said, against her ear.

She pulled back and gazed into his sea-blue eyes. As he'd said everything she needed to hear, and she had admitted exactly how she felt, there really wasn't much left to say or do. Except one silly thought popped into her mind. "Let's go and buy that Christmas tree."

His full-out laugh was the second-best sound she'd heard all day, the first having been the newborn baby's cry.

On Christmas Eve, Stephanie had come down with a mild cold. Phil insisted she stay in bed, but she didn't want to miss such a special holiday, her first Christmas with the man she loved.

Their decorated tree blinked and twinkled in the corner of the family room. A few gifts, mostly for the dogs, were wrapped and tucked beneath. Christmas carols played quietly in the background. The incredible aroma of roast beef filled the air as it cooked in the oven, along with Yorkshire pudding, making her mouth water.

Carl and Roma arrived with hyperactive Robbie. What was it about Christmas that got kids so wound up?

She grinned at the boy, and stooped to his level before he had a chance to tackle her. Her legs were still sore from Phil's tricky maneuver at the beach the week before, and Robbie's version of hugging was to throw his body against hers.

"Pill," Robbie said, quickly losing interest in Stephanie when he noticed his big brother.

"Dude!" Phil hugged him, and Stephanie had to blink when he kissed his brother on the cheek. "Merry Christmas."

Robbie's gaze darted everywhere. "Wow, did Santa come to your house already?" He saw the gifts and ran for the tree.

Daisy and Sherwood intercepted him, hopping in circles and demanding their fair share of attention.

Easily distracted, Robbie giggled and jumped around with them.

Stephanie grinned, thinking the dogs were protecting their doggy cookies and leather chews but knowing they loved any and all attention they could get. She watched Robbie roll around on the floor with them, and soon felt a hand on her shoulder.

It was Carl.

"Thank you," he said.

She looked into the same blue eyes she'd woken up to that morning, and imagined how Phil would look thirty years down the road. She liked what she saw.

"For what?" she said.

"For making my son happy. For helping him finally grow up."

She shook her head and hugged Carl. "He's done the same for me."

Christmas evening, one year later...

Stephanie sat bundled in a blanket and snuggling with Phil on the couch. She stared at the Christmas tree in the dimmed living room. It really was the most beautiful tree she'd ever seen. The decorations reflected the colorful blinking lights across the family-room ceiling, and the effect was nothing short of magical.

Their family and friends had come and gone and they were finally alone. She looked up at her husband, who bore a mischievous grin.

"I've got an idea how to make an already perfect day even better," he said. He dipped his head and kissed her neck, sending feathery tickles over her chest. She reached for him and kissed his jaw, enjoying the evening stubble and waning spice of his aftershave.

"That sounds wonderful," she whispered.

He stood, held her hands, and pulled her to her feet.

Baby gurgles and coos came through the nursery intercom. From their brand-new Santa-delivered dog beds, Daisy's and Sherwood's ears perked up.

Stephanie smiled at Phil. "Shall we wait to see how long before she realizes she's hungry?"

They looked at each other briefly and said in unison, "Nah."

Phil led her down the hall and together they peeked in on the center of their universe—their four-month-old daughter, Emma.

The contented baby lay on her back in her crib, reaching for the tiny stuffed animals dangling from the mobile over her bed. Her foot made contact with a teddy bear and she squealed with delight.

Stephanie and Phil laughed quietly. They loved watching her, and wanted to steal a few more moments enjoying the show before she noticed them. But it was too late. The baby glanced at the doorway and squealed even louder when she saw them. She flapped her arms and legs as if she might fly to them.

Stephanie rushed to her and lifted her into her arms, smothering her with kisses. Emma cooed and gurgled, and laughed. She'd reached a euphoric stage in her life, and everything seemed to make her happy.

Phil wrapped his arms around both Stephanie and Emma and hugged them tight. "How're my girls doing this Christmas night?"

Stephanie pressed her cheek to Emma's and glanced up at Phil as if she was posing for a picture. "Just fine, Daddy. We couldn't be happier."

MILLS & BOON®

Want to get more from Mills & Boon?

Here's what's available to you if you join the exclusive **Mills & Boon eBook Club** today:

✦ *Convenience – choose your books each month*
✦ *Exclusive – receive your books a month before anywhere else*
✦ *Flexibility – change your subscription at any time*
✦ *Variety – gain access to eBook-only series*
✦ *Value – subscriptions from just £1.99 a month*

So visit **www.millsandboon.co.uk/esubs** today to be a part of this exclusive eBook Club!